C0-FTF-461

I hope you enjoy the book!

POISONED AT THE PARTY

Warm Wishes,
Joe Redden

JOSEPH REDDEN

Copyright © 2014 Joseph Redden
All rights reserved.

ISBN: 149921832X
ISBN 13: 9781499218329
Library of Congress Control Number: 2014907740
CreateSpace Independent Publishing Platform
North Charleston, South Carolina

To Mom and Dad,

Thank you for all your help with all of my writing projects.
I would never be able to do this without your support.

CHAPTER 1

"Flat as pancakes," muttered Patricia Talbot as she eyed herself in the full-length mirror. For exactly eight months, twenty-six days, thirty-six hours, and one week, her mother had been telling her to give it time. Well, at fifteen, time was not on Tricia's side, and she was growing increasingly unhappy with her lackluster breasts. Girls her age, were practically top heavy and had boyfriends, for crying out loud!

She slipped on her school uniform. The green plaid skirt did not help her appearance.

She rushed out her bedroom door. Her mother was standing at the foot of the steps. Veronica Talbot was a force to be reckoned with. She was tall and lean with a regal face and a long, delicate neck. Her lips always seemed to be set in permanent disapproval of everything anybody did. Veronica was always elegantly dressed for every occasion. Tricia knew that she could never look as classy as her mother.

Veronica was looking at her wristwatch. "Come on, Tricia! We have to be going soon!"

"All right, all right," Tricia said practically out of breath. She rushed into the kitchen and scoffed down a bowl of Cheerios. She was finished eating in ten minutes. That was all the time her mother allowed her to eat so they would not be late.

"Come on, Tricia. We've got to get moving!"

"Okay, okay," she said with a wave of the hand.

"Let's go!" barked Veronica.

Tricia grabbed her book bag from the hall credenza. They marched down the front steps and approached their burgundy SUV. Every week day it was the same ritual. They could never leave without a major hassle.

Veronica's put-upon husband, Charles, was standing with his hands to his hips on the driveway. He tried to keep in good shape. At fifty-six, he found a good, hard workout at the gym helped release the tension of living with a powder keg like Veronica. It was a good escape. He had done this for close to twenty years of their often stormy, roller-coaster-ride of a marriage.

Otherwise, he was sure that the stress would have eaten him alive, and he would have dropped dead of a heart attack or a stroke at an early age. Either that, or he would have just divorced her.

Friends and close colleagues wondered why he stuck with her. Was he a masochist? He heard the whispers behind his back. But deep down, despite her faults, Veronica was still the complicated, enticing, exciting and sexy woman that he fell for more than two decades ago.

He was tall and lean, with a sturdy chin, square jaw, and painstakingly coiffed salt-and-pepper hair. He wore horn-rimmed glasses over sharp blue eyes and had on a button-down shirt under a navy blue suit.

Their feet crunched on the fallen leaves as they approached him.

"You look nice, Tricia," he said.

She groused and climbed in the back of the SUV. Charles got in the front passenger seat, as usual, while Veronica gripped the keys and hopped behind the wheel. He gripped the hand rail as she sped out of the driveway. Stones and dust scattered behind them.

Veronica glanced at her watch, out of breath. The veins in her neck protruded. She craned her neck back at her daughter and said, "Why do you do this to me? Why can't you ever be ready when we have to leave?"

"I'm sorry." Tricia wasn't really. She didn't know why her mother had to act like she had three heads.

They said nothing. Veronica cranked up the volume on the radio. An opera was the perfect choice. A bunch of people singing in a foreign tongue, basically arguing to music. When the Talbots argued, though, it was never set to music.

They hadn't made it five miles before the cursing started. Not from Charles or Tricia, of course.

Charles grimaced as Veronica practically rear-ended the poor slow poke in front of her. There was a solid yellow line, so she could not pass the man.

"Dammit!" Veronica screamed. "Where did this bozo learn to drive? Did your grandmother teach you?"

"Can't you ever just leave it alone?" Charles asked in bewilderment.

"Why don't you just be quiet and let me do the driving?"

He said nothing else. The rest of the trip to Tricia's school was a repeat of that ugly incident. It was always the same thing on days when Veronica did the driving.

Tricia gazed out the window and watched one farm blend into another, wishing she could have a normal mother. She wondered what it would be like to live on one of the Amish farms. Then she regarded her father with disgust. Why couldn't he ever stand up to the almighty Veronica Talbot?

And then it started to rain, which made matters even worse. Tricia eyed her mother as they got to within three miles of the school. There was a traffic pile up down the narrow country road. Her mother screamed and it looked like spit actually spewed out of her mouth.

Veronica pounded the steering wheel and shouted, "Dammit!"

"Calm down," Charles said. "We're almost there."

"I don't care a fig about whether or not we're going to get to the school on time! We're almost there. Tricia has plenty of time to get to home room!"

"What is your problem?" Charles asked in the calmest tone he could muster.

"You know very well what's wrong! I'll be late to the meeting."

"Oh, good God!" Charles exclaimed in exasperation. "Can't you give it a rest?"

Veronica was fuming. Tricia wondered if she could actually see steam coming out of her ears.

"You're the one who wanted to move out to the country," Charles reminded her.

The driving rain only made it worse. The windshield wipers drowned out the sounds of the screeching opera singers.

Veronica said nothing. She sat there silently cursing out all the drivers on the road. When traffic eased up, she sped down the hill. The wheels screeched as she rounded the bend.

Charles and Tricia held on for dear life. The vehicle jerked violently as Veronica slowed to twenty-five mph. She pulled into William Penn High School and let Tricia off at the circle in front of the building.

Tricia scrambled out and glared at her mother.

Veronica stuck her head out of the window and smiled. "Have a good day, honey."

"Yeah, yeah," Tricia growled.

The wheels squealed as her mother sped out of the parking lot. Tricia merged with her classmates and entered the building.

* * *

The mood on the rest of the trip to Philadelphia was icy. Charles stared blankly out the window, wondering why in the hell he didn't drive on his own.

He cringed when the traffic started building up on the interstate the closer they got to the city. Veronica pounded the steering wheel at another holdup. She cursed and did her best impression of a monster from a horror movie.

She cut somebody off who was trying to change lanes. She tailgated. Two or three times she came within inches of sideswiping motorists. In essence, Veronica was a menace on the roads. Road rage books were probably written about her, thought Charles.

She pulled into the parking garage and sped up the ramp. He glanced at his watch and said, "There, we got here. It's not so bad. We're only about ten minutes late."

"But I wanted to get here ten minutes early!" she shrieked. "I can't believe all the damn traffic!"

"It's perfectly simple. Sell the house and move back here. I swear, Veronica, the rate you are going, you'll have a coronary! Or give me one."

She did not respond. Instead, she gathered her portfolio and hurried out of the vehicle. He had to jog to catch up to her.

* * *

Dana Phillips did not know how much longer she could put up with Veronica Talbot. It was no secret that the two women had locked horns on more than one occasion. They were both dynamos at the Creative Concepts advertising firm in Philadelphia. Unfortunately, neither listened to each other. They always had their own ideas about how to proceed with any given project. Mass confusion often resulted. No one knew who to listen to, and everybody was angry and frustrated. It was Veronica's fault, thought Dana. She purposely tried to wreak havoc so everybody would cave in and do it her way.

Dana was not about to cave in to Veronica's unreasonable demands. She was born stubborn and insisted on doing things her way. She gave as good as she got. She had worked too damn hard to let Veronica get away with it this time! One of them would end up in the ER by the end of the work day, and Dana knew that it was not going to be her.

Dana had dedicated about ten years to Creative Concepts and decided life was too short to deal with a prima donna like Veronica Talbot. Maybe it was time to move on. She had thought about it for quite a while now. She was not getting any younger. If she wanted to make her mark and be noticed and appreciated for her achievements, she needed to disembark now before it was too late. Before Veronica tarnished her reputation to potential employers. Dana knew she possessed the self-discipline and leadership abilities to shine somewhere else. Maybe she should try for bigger fish in New York City. Why should she waste her time working with the devil incarnate running the company into the ground?

She couldn't figure out why James Dobson hadn't fired Veronica years ago. He was a nice man–too nice to be president of the company. He might as well let Veronica make all the decisions. Her husband, Charles, sure as hell wouldn't do anything.

For the last ten years she had watched Veronica demasculinize him for all to see. And he just stood there and took it. Oh, how Dana wished, that just for once Charles would stand up to her. But he never did.

At thirty-eight, Dana had the looks. She was five eight with hour-glass curves and finely toned calf and thigh muscles. She had a round, firm chin, sensual lips, and high cheek-bones. Her long, sandy hair matched her rosy complexion.

Veronica Talbot clutched her head and groaned. She was getting another migraine. Having to deal with incompetent colleagues was enough to bring one on, big time. She glared at Dana with an intense feeling of hatred for the woman. Veronica's piercing blue eyes were as cold as ice.

"Oh come on, Veronica, you do this every time and I'm getting sick of it!" Dana snapped. "You cause a problem. And then everybody does what you want. But not this time."

"I need a Tylenol or something. I'll be right back." Veronica started for the door, but Dana stood in the way.

"Not this time, Veronica. Don't you dare go to James because things aren't going your way. How petty do you have to be?"

Veronica folded her arms and glared at her nemesis.

"Come on, you guys, surely there must be a compromise," Michelle Delancey suggested.

She was the level-headed one every office worker around the world needed to prevent fisticuffs from occurring. It was her ability to remain calm in a highly stressful work environment that earned her Brownie points with James Dobson. She was also a savvy businesswoman who did not put up with crap from anyone, especially someone with the initials V.T.

At forty-five, Michelle knew what she wanted and how to get it, without sacrificing her soul in the process. She was not as bloodthirsty as Veronica. She knew how to handle situations and people in a calm, systematic manner. She was no push over, either. In a kind way, she often got what she wanted, while Veronica chose a different tact.

All it took was for people to look into Michelle's sweetly expressive face to calm themselves down. Her voice was soft and velvety one moment, and strong and assertive the next. She had long red hair that she brushed back. Her lips were full and ripe. She had a statuesque figure and was always smartly dressed.

Michelle looked from Dana to Veronica, who glared at each other.

"I think we need a breather," Michelle said after a long silence. "Go outside and clear your heads for a few minutes. We don't have to decide anything right away."

Tom Daniels nodded his agreement. He was a beefy man in his early sixties, who often provided the voice of reason. He had a wizened face and a ruddy complexion. Though he was not working on this particular project for personal reasons, they had called him in to help quell the current situation.

"Michelle is right," he said. "You ladies are hot under the collar right now. Could you just take a break and come back in a little while? Maybe then you'll be able to calm yourselves down."

"I will not let her take a few minutes to waltz into James's office and bad-mouth me!" Dana exclaimed. "Not this time!"

Veronica sneered at her. "Oh get over yourself!"

"I don't think either of you are capable of handling Mr. Adkinson's account," Michelle blurted. "Maybe I should take care of it. I'd be glad to work with you on it, Dana."

"Gladly," Dana said in an exasperated tone. "As long as Veronica and I don't have to work together."

Tom leaned back in his seat and put his hands on his thinning hair. "I don't know why James doesn't take a long look at the dynamics of this office. You're usually the cause of a lot of tension around here, Veronica."

Veronica slapped her forehead and said, "I don't need this right now!"

A twinkle sparkled in Tom's eyes. "I've got a great idea. Go get Craig or Bart and film her right now. We don't need to hire actors to play stressed-out people for Randy Fisherman's antidepressant ad."

Veronica gave him a sideways glance. Then she stormed out and marched down the long corridor to her office.

Dana drew a deep breath and shook her head. "We can't keep going on this way. Somebody has to go. And it's not going to be me."

Tom looked incredulously at her and said, "You really don't think James would can her, do you?"

"She's costing the company a lot of wasted productive time," Michelle was quick to point out.

"It's just her way," Tom said. "She's high-strung. She usually gets perturbed about something and calms down five or ten minutes later. I'm sure when she's had time to think that she'll see your side of things, Dana. There's got to be a way that you two can compromise on it."

Dana rolled her eyes and said, "You think?"

* * *

Forty plus years of quick meals and drinking after stressful days had taken their toll on James Dobson's health. He suffered from indigestion and occasional chest pains which he did not take time from his busy schedule to have checked out by his physician. He also did not listen to his doctor's warning for him to eat healthier and drink less alcohol. The only exercise he got was walking from the parking garage and into the building, or back and forth from the hall to his office. On the plus side, James had quit smoking eight and a half years ago. Sometimes he got an overpowering urge to light up every time he got around the Dragon Lady.

At sixty-five, he had worked his way up in the advertising business and was not about to retire any time soon. In the past few years, he had seen a lot of changes in the industry–some good and some bad. He knew he did not have to worry about losing his job to youngsters who were practically attached to their electronic gadgets. He was the owner and the boss. He could call it quits when he wanted, on his terms. For decades, he had seen many bright stars crash and burn in the fast-paced and highly competitive advertising game. He had seen a lot of colleagues he'd started out with lose their jobs left and right when the digital age was thrust upon them. Most of them could not compete with twenty-something computer whiz kids fresh from colleges of art and design. While they were crapping in their diapers, James and his peers had done things the hard way and produced spectacular, thought-provoking ads that people still remembered decades later. Sometimes he heard fifty-somethings humming tunes to jingles while in line at the grocery store. They did not always remember the words, but they remembered the tune and fudged the rest.

James had drooping shoulders and an overflowing belt line. What used to be a muscular frame was now flabby and dumpy-looking. Remnants of his once wispy chestnut brown hair stuck up in unattractive clumps on an otherwise bald scalp, and sagging jowls surrounded tobacco-stained teeth. The time for working out and trying to look good had sailed away a long time ago.

He tried his best to ignore the shouting from down the hall. He knew eventually Veronica Talbot would be paying him a visit. Maybe he should pick this moment to get a snack in the break room. He didn't act quickly enough. The knock at his door was loud and menacing.

"Come in."

Veronica Talbot entered and closed the door. She sat across from him, her eyes wild with rage. He removed his horn-rimmed glasses and pretended to clean them as a stall tactic. He put them back on and stared at her in bewilderment.

"What's wrong?"

"You won't believe what Dana did this time!" Her voice shook.

"What did she do?"

Veronica ran her fingers through her hair and said, "She refuses to do the abortion ad."

James looked incredulously at her and said, "She what?"

"She apparently has some issues with it. The most lucrative ad we've had in months and she refuses to do it."

"It would be nice to hear her side of the story."

"Warren Adkinson is livid! He threatened to take his business to another company. Do you know how much money she's cost us just because she's taking a political stand? Good God! You should fire her!"

James listened patiently and said, "I don't want to fire anyone. I'm always hearing your one-sided view-point. Maybe. . .maybe I should listen to what she has to say." He dialed Dana's cell phone number and said, "Could you please come in here right away, Ms. Phillips. Thank you." He hung up and stared in disbelief at the raving woman as he dialed Creative Director Ben Goldstein's private line and asked for him to come in too.

"There is no excuse for it!" Veronica said when he hung up. "You should fire her!"

"I'm getting sick of all the turmoil, Veronica. I'm sick of it."

"So am I, James. It's no way to operate a company."

"Are you implying that it's my fault?"

She gasped and said, "Of course not! It's not your fault!"

Dana popped her head in the door. "You wanted to see me, Mr. Dobson?"

He waved her in, and she sat as far from Veronica as she could.

Ben Goldstein came in behind her and grimaced when he saw Veronica. He was a harried-looking man who was in desperate need of a vacation that he never took advantage of. His face was worn and thin. He looked like he was on his last rope. One more incident like this might just send him over the edge. He took a seat across the room and sat in silence, waiting in white-knuckled horror for the fireworks that were about to start.

"What's wrong?" Dana asked.

"Veronica told me that you refused to do the Adkinson ad. Is that true?"

Dana shot Veronica a predatory look. "Is that what she said?"

He nodded reluctantly. "Why don't you tell me what happened?"

"I am dead set against abortion, James."

"I understand that," he replied coolly. "But you just managed to foul up a mega deal, Ms. Phillips. When someone is willing to pay that much money, you put aside your personal feelings and damn well do it!"

"As usual, Veronica isn't telling you the whole story. I intended to do the ad, but I suggested that we offer an alternative viewpoint. That's all. I thought maybe we could mention that there are other options besides abortions. Unfortunately, Warren Adkinson didn't go along with my idea. He refused to go along with it."

Dobson looked from Dana to Veronica and tapped his pen on the desk calendar.

"And that's when he decided to have our competitors do it," Veronica put in.

"That is totally unacceptable," James said after a long, uncomfortable silence. "Ms. Phillips, if you felt uncomfortable about doing the project, you should have come to me right away. I would have made someone else project manager. There is no excuse. What do you have to say for yourself?"

"I'm sorry, Mr. Dobson," Dana said. Her voice quavered. "You're right. I should have come to you first thing. I didn't think it would snowball like this. It's blown up in my face! Warren Adkinson was unyielding. He wouldn't compromise."

"She just cost us mega bucks! Fire her!" Veronica demanded.

James leaned back in his seat and folded his hands. He stared intently at Dana, who was trying to hold it together but was starting to lose it under the scrutiny. He looked across the room at Ben Goldstein, who had been quiet throughout the whole ugly ordeal.

"What do you think I should do, Ben?"

"I was hoping you wouldn't include me in this," he replied sheepishly. "Dana is a hard worker. She has done excellent work since she's been with us. I think she meant well. She was trying to work around her problems with the project."

Veronica glowered at him. He cowered and avoided eye contact with her.

"She should have damn well come to you or Ben about her problems with it! It is inexcusable! You should fire her!"

"It isn't your authority to decide!" Ben shot back.

Dana forced a smile and said, "I'll stand by whatever decision you make. I am truly sorry that I didn't discuss all of this with you before, Mr. Dobson."

"Thank you for your honesty," James said. He waved her on.

Dana rose unsteadily to her feet and stumbled as she went out the door.

James looked at Ben Goldstein and said, "What should we do?"

"It was an unfortunate incident, James. We'll get another client with lots of money. I say we give her another chance."

"That's what I think too."

Veronica's eyes widened with rage. "I can't believe you two!" she screeched. "You're too nice, James. That's your problem!"

"And why don't you think I shouldn't just get rid of you? You seem to be the cause of a lot of the trouble around here. We go around in circles every week because you're having a problem with one of your colleagues." He pointed to a stack of paperwork on his desk. "I never have time to get my work done because I have to deal with the latest drama coming out of your mouth!"

"If you don't fire her, I'll have to take actions into my own hands."

"And what precisely is that supposed to mean?"

She gave him a look that was as cold as ice. "I think we both know why you won't fire me."

James understood her meaning and backed off. Ben eyed them suspiciously but said nothing.

"And you're going to do nothing about it, Ben?"

"Give the woman a break!" he cried in exasperation.

Veronica erupted into another loud outburst. Ben gathered his papers into his briefcase and stood. He marched toward the door and said, "Life is too short to deal with this crap!"

"Ben, what do you mean?" James asked in alarm.

"I quit!" he shouted back, waving his hands. "I quit! You deal with her. I don't care what you do! Good luck!"

"Ben, you can't just leave!" James shouted back. "I need you!"

"Just let him go!" Veronica cried.

James gave her a dirty look and drummed his fingers on the desk. What in the hell was he going to do now?

* * *

After taking time for the smoke to clear, James called everyone together in the large meeting room to fill them in on what had happened. Some of them had seen it coming. Others were already hoping to fill the spot. They looked at Veronica, knowing full well that she was the reason for Ben Goldstein's swift departure.

James waited for everyone to calm down and said, "I know this might come as a complete shock to some of you, but Ben leaves with no hard feelings against anyone in particular. He was having chest pains, and...and his wife urged him to work in a less stressful environment. I wished him all the best and thanked him for his many years of dedicated service." He looked around the room and stopped on Veronica. She was practically salivating. She could not contain her excitement.

"His position is open," James continued after thoughtful consideration. "As you all know, the job comes with creative control of advertising campaigns. I will talk to each candidate one on one and will make my decision within the month. Thank you all for coming."

A cold, calculating look flashed across Veronica's face. Dana glowered at her on the way out. Michelle and Tom exchanged knowing glances as they followed Dana. Everybody else muttered their disbelief under their breath and filed out behind them.

Veronica grinned like a Cheshire cat. "I would very much like to take the job, James."

He shoved paperwork into his folder and avoided eye contact. "As I said, I will make my decision next month." He got up and walked hurriedly out of the room.

An evil glint shot across her eyes. She was already thinking of a plan to screw over the competition...

* * *

Nicholas Bradshaw had worked with Veronica Talbot for seven years too long. It seemed like it had been twice as long. The gray hairs he spotted in his abundant dark locks were in fact his. Six to be exact. The stress of dealing with Veronica had taken its toll on both his physical health and his outward appearance. It was definitely not a good sign for someone so young and vital.

At twenty-seven, Nicholas exuded confidence. He was blessed with matinee idol good looks, with a mole on his left cheek and a cleft in his chin. He had a rather regal, almost aristocratic face. He wore trendy glasses with large black frames. He was dressed for success in tan khakis and a dark blue button-down shirt. His paisley tie with the purple swirls screamed creativity. He was the best graphics design artist in the tri-state area, and he knew it. He did not need a pat on the back for a job well done. This cocky attitude of his often rubbed people the wrong way. He did not apologize for his vanity. And he was not shy about expressing criticism whenever Veronica Talbot did something to tick him off.

He had many reasons to be angry with her at the moment. Everyone had their eye on Goldstein's spot after he left for greener pastures. Nicholas shook his head and silently watched as his coworkers sucked up to boss man, James Dobson. Nicholas thought he had seen it all–but then he found out that he was still a tad naive.

It wasn't long before nasty rumors were circulating about Veronica and James behind closed office doors. Nicholas knew that Veronica was capable of a lot of truly nasty acts–but was she really sleeping with the boss to get the promotion?

Nicholas wasn't the only one at the firm who feared the wrath of Veronica Talbot now that she had gained power. They all worried about what she would do. Who was she pissed off with the most? Everybody assumed that Dana would be the first to go. Hell, it could be anybody. She had made some whispers here and there that she was going to shake the place up like Shake'N Bake.

Nicholas knew he had worked too damn hard to be bounced out by that vengeful bitch.

He resented Veronica even more now. He should have damn well gotten the promotion, not her. He needed a change of scenery at Creative Concepts. He wanted more to do.

Veronica's image grinned back at him on the laptop screen. He cringed as he read the copy in the background. He could not believe that Veronica had been promoted to Ben Goldstein's position. She was the one who had forced him to quit. James may have claimed it was for medical reasons, but everybody knew that Veronica had driven Ben nuts.

With his mouse, he drew horns on her head. A few clicks later, he made it look like she was holding a pitch fork.

Anna McWilliams was working on another ad at the cubicle across from him. She was Plain Jane personified, easily forgettable. She was as thin as a broomstick with a long neck. She had owl-like glasses and frizzy long brown hair. There was a dour look about her, mostly because she had a mouth that turned down at the corners.

What Anna lacked in the looks department, she made up for in the business department. At thirty-four, she had an abundance of energy and had proven to be quite versatile in everything she did at the company. She was a gifted graphics artist who had garnered much acclaim from Mr. Dobson. She knew in the back of her mind that James and Veronica had spent many long hours behind closed doors discussing possible changes. Anna knew that

Veronica disliked her with a passion. Veronica thought she was a queer duck. An oddball.

Anna had been called much worse names over the years. She blocked out the negative comments by concentrating on her art. She had made some blunders lately and wondered if she would be first on the chopping block when Veronica took over creative control. Would James's admiration for all the hard work she'd done be enough to save her from the wrath of Veronica Talbot? Veronica had been talking to her coworkers individually all week. Anna was petrified about losing her job.

Anna got up and leaned over Nicholas's cubicle wall. She looked at his masterpiece and smiled wryly.

"Be nice," she said.

"You should talk. She treats you like garbage, and you can say that?"

"I am a forgiving person. You should try it sometime, Nick."

He was about to say something when Veronica stalked past them on her way back down the hall. Nicholas minimized the image and feigned a polite smile as she hurried past. A foreboding breeze rustled papers on his desk as she marched down the hall.

"What's her problem today?"

"What do you think?" Anna said.

"The usual."

The arguing drifted to their cubicles. Everybody in Philadelphia and surrounding areas could probably hear them. They got up and eavesdropped from the hall. Nicholas put his ear to the door and snickered like a small child.

"You shouldn't have to do that," Anna said. "You can hear them loud and clear."

Dana's voice was so loud it could probably shatter glass. "You took my jingle idea to James, didn't you?"

"I don't know what you mean."

"Good God, Veronica! Don't you have a conscience? You're a soulless witch!"

Nicholas frowned. "She did it again."

"Come on. We shouldn't be doing this." Anna pulled him down the hall.

"Ow! You've got a grip on you, McWilliams!"

"Are you going to her party on Saturday?"

"Do I really have a choice?" he asked in a sarcastic tone.

They sat back down in their chairs and tried to get some work done. It was difficult because of all the shouting. Nick put ear-phones on and cranked up the music as he worked on a new logo design for Thomas Jefferson University Hospital.

CHAPTER 2

Tricia Talbot grimaced as she checked herself out in the full-length mirror. Willing herself to have more going on upstairs was not going to work but it was worth a try to look again.

She had blocked herself up in her bedroom all afternoon so she wouldn't have to deal with her mother's constant raving while she got ready for the party.

There was a knock at the door. Tricia turned and said, "Come in."

The family's housekeeper, Kelly McDougal, popped her head in and beamed. She was a robust woman with a warm and inviting smile and large brown eyes. She had a shock of black hair that she kept tied up while she was cleaning. Otherwise, she let it fall just above her shoulders.

"You look fine," she told Tricia for the umpteenth time.

Tricia rolled her eyes and glanced at her reflection in the mirror. She seemed to be memorizing what she looked like with that expression for future reference.

"Your mother is having a fit. You'd better hurry up and get dressed. The party is about to start."

Another eye roll and Tricia marched over to her bed. She picked up a dark blue dress and a pastel pink one. She held them up and asked, "Which do you like the best?"

"Definitely the pink one."

"Fine. Tell her I'll be down in ten."

Kelly McDougal smiled and closed the door behind herself.

Tricia went over to the window and gazed out at the pond across the road, then at the woods in the distance. The leaves were emblazoned with fiery reds and oranges that made the pond look like liquid flames. There was a slight nip in the air, and her attic bedroom was much colder now. She felt like a prisoner in the old house that was in the middle of nowhere.

She jammed the earbuds of her iPhone in her ears and plopped on her bed. She did not hear the banging on her door and her mother's voice booming from the hall. Everyone in California could have heard her, she was so loud–except Patricia Jean Talbot.

All of a sudden, she looked up to see the tall, slender figure of her mother throwing herself into the room. Veronica's blonde hair was meticulously coiffed. She looked stunning in a snug-fitting white cocktail dress accentuated with a pearl necklace. A spasm of irritation shot across her face. She stomped over to the bed and yanked the earplugs out and tossed them on the bedside table.

"How many times have I told you not to put those damn things in your ears! You'll probably go deaf by the time you are thirty! Come on! Get dressed. The party is about to start any minute! Come on! Get moving!"

Tricia folded her arms and groused. "What's the big deal? I don't see why you're going to all this trouble. You've been acting like a dictator all day!"

The veins in Veronica's long, swan-like neck stood out in livid ridges. She clutched her temples and took a deep breath. "I don't need your attitude right now, young lady. This party is very important to me. I've worked hard to get here."

"Whatever." Tricia ripped off her sweatshirt and stared at herself in the mirror once again. "I look awful!"

"You're fine. With a little makeup–you'll be fine. Not beauty-queen fine, but passable."

"Gee, thanks. What I really need to boost my ego!"

"You'll be a beautiful swan soon enough."

"That's what you said a year ago." Tricia pointed to her lack-luster chest and said, "I don't see any action going on here in that department."

"If nothing happens, you can always be a ballerina. You want to dance anyway, right?"

Tricia glared back at her mother with her smoldering blue eyes. "Sometimes I can't believe you."

"I don't have time for this right now!" shrieked Veronica.

"Sometimes I don't think you're really my mother!"

"Come on, baby, we've been through this too many times before."

"I wish Kelly was my mother."

Veronica stood stone-faced as she looked down at her daughter. Ignoring the slight, she clapped and said, "Just get dressed. I want you downstairs in ten minutes."

"Fine!" she whined.

Veronica stormed out. Tricia wiped tears as she gazed out the hazy window. She saw a black BMW speeding down the road and pulling up to their house. She saw a tall, slender man wearing sunglasses get out, but couldn't make out who he was. She could tell he had good taste. A beautiful blonde pulled herself clumsily out of the front seat and stumbled over to him. He wrapped his arm around her, and they paraded toward the house. Boy, did she have it all together in the boobs department!

"Maybe she could lend me some of her boobs," Tricia muttered.

As they got closer to the house, Tricia got a better look at the man. He was ruggedly good looking with thick dirty-blonde stubble. His hair was tied neatly into a pony-tail. He had an air of confidence about him as he swaggered up the steps with his babe wrapped around his arm.

Tricia started to get dressed, wishing she could have an outfit like that woman.

* * *

Mindy Sawyer gushed the moment she stepped foot inside the foyer. She pulled her arm free of Craig Holloway's grip, waving her hands in disbelief. She glanced up the staircase at the magnificently crafted woodwork on the walls leading upstairs. The rails were a dark mahogany. A large crystal chandelier reached above the balcony on the second floor landing. An antique cabinet was at the right with faded oil paintings of hunting scenes hanging over it. A silver ice chest and glasses were on top with bottles of wine and champagne behind them. There was a note informing guests that there was more liquor to choose from in a bar in the basement. Ladder-back chairs were on either side of it. A musket and horns hung in between a large mirror at the left.

"Oh my goodness gracious!" exclaimed Mindy. "Can you believe it? This place is like a palace! My God!" She whipped out her cell phone and snapped pictures from the door toward the staircase. Then she took pictures of the furniture.

Craig Holloway looked around, unfazed. He was more interested in dazzling her with his charismatic charm. He automatically reached for the champagne on the buffet and poured himself a drink. Then he reached for a bottle of white wine and poured some into a glass. He handed it to her and led her through double doors to the right.

It was as if they had stepped back into another time–a hundred years or more ago–as they entered the living room. A faded Persian rug stretched across the room. The antique furniture looked old and expensive and uncomfortable. More oil paintings of nature scenes hung on the walls. An upright piano was to the left of the double doors.

Mindy's excitement intensified as she took pictures of the room from many different angles. Craig gave a cursory look around the room and let Mindy finish taking pictures. He saw Dana Phillips and Michelle Delancey across the room and waved at them. Dana had on a tight-fitting navy blue outfit that accentuated her figure. A satin scarf was draped around her neck. Michelle looked stunning in a kelly green dress.

He led Mindy over to them and introduced her. Michelle beamed and shook her hand. "It's so nice to meet you. Craig hasn't told us anything about you yet."

"That's because he's so busy," Craig said with a bit of bite in his comment. "Excuse me. I need another drink." He went back out to the foyer, leaving Mindy to fend for herself. They engaged in small talk.

"Where did you meet?" asked Dana, knowing Craig's track record with women had a limited shelf life. She fought the urge to mention it.

"At the Foxfire Club in Center City. I'm a waitress there."

"I understand that that's the hot new singles club these days," Dana said.

"It's great! You've gotta try it out."

"If my ex would take the kids off my hand for the night. Like that'll happen."

Mindy was struggling for the proper response when Craig came back in.

"What did I miss?"

"I was just telling them about the Foxfire."

"We'll have to go there some time," Michelle said. "It sounds like fun! We could make it a girl's night out."

Dana nodded her head enthusiastically. "Boy, do I need a night out like that right about now." She nudged Michelle and said, "Come on, you've got to see their master bedroom!"

Michelle smiled politely at Mindy and said, "Well, it was really nice meeting you, Mindy. Maybe we can talk later?"

Mindy smiled brightly and said, "Sure."

Dana and Michelle walked hurriedly through the double doors.

* * *

Tricia heard another car door slam. She went over and looked out to see an enormous African American man in a leather jacket walking hand in hand with that blond guy that she had seen around her parents' office a few times. His name was on the tip of her tongue. Whatever it was, they looked extremely happy as they marched up the driveway. A couple of other people had arrived as she was getting dressed. A fire-engine red Mazda and Ferrari were by the oak tree.

Muffled voices drifted from downstairs. Tricia dabbed her face with a damp cloth and hoped that no one would notice that she had been crying. She gave herself the once-over in the mirror one last time and slipped across the rickety wooden floor and closed the door behind her.

On her way down the hall, she saw Dana and Michelle coming out of her parents' bedroom. They were so excited that they were talking over each other.

"Are you having a good time?" Tricia asked them.

Michelle gushed. "It's such a beautiful house!"

"Your mother has excellent taste," Dana observed.

Tricia smiled flatly at her and said, "If you like living in a museum."

They hurriedly descended the steps after her.

* * *

Anna McWilliams scowled as Veronica flitted about the room, chatting with her colleagues. She had endured the wrath of Veronica for far too long. For several years, Anna had quietly watched Veronica berate coworkers, and had done nothing. Veronica played Mrs. Nice at the party. Anna knew. And so did her colleagues. Veronica was not the saint she pretended to be that afternoon.

Anna felt sorry for Nicholas Bradshaw. He should have gotten the promotion. She knew how hard he worked.

He looked extremely uncomfortable as he sat on a ladder-back chair, his long legs stretched out too far. He was nursing a beer, engaging in meaningless small talk with Craig's latest girlfriend, Mindy. He feigned a toothy grin as Veronica walked by. Then he turned his attention back to the beautiful blonde.

Anna wondered how Veronica had wormed her way into Ben Goldstein's slot, and so did everyone else. She did not know how much more she could take of Veronica's tirades.

Sometimes she felt like shoving Veronica off the twenty-first floor. Surely, it would be considered an accident. No one could prove that she had anything to do with it. Her morbid thoughts were interrupted by the shrill voice of Craig Holloway who paraded across the room with his latest trophy girlfriend.

Anna sneered as Craig made an ass of himself with the buxom blonde. Anna sipped her soda and tried to remember how many women he had had his arm around since she knew him. He seemed to have a new woman for every season. She knew the type. Big boobs, not so big brains.

Anna watched everyone come and go. She listened to partial conversations and made nice to people that came over to say hello. There was nothing Anna despised more than office parties, especially ones that Veronica Talbot had anything to do with. She usually only went to bars at her friends' insistence. Her demeanor came off as cold and aloof, and men were often scared off by her. If they showed any interest at all. Sometimes she thought she was a man repellant.

Dana Phillips came up to her and said, "Are you having a good time, Anna?"

"If you call going to a party Veronica is throwing fun, I would say that you are out of your mind."

Dana forced a smile. "We just have to make the best of it."

"It would be nice if everyone could share your optimism, Dana. Maybe we could solve all of the world's problems with it."

Dana smiled, excused herself, and walked back over to chat with Michelle. They laughed at something Michelle said. Anna couldn't make it out, because one of the caterers had asked her if she wanted another cheese puff.

Across the room, Edna Dobson sat on a three-corner chair and drank like a fish. She was a crab of a woman. Her husband, James, did his best to ignore her all evening.

Nicholas finished off his drink and laid the glass on an end table. He whipped out his cell phone and video taped the party. He panned around the room, making sure to get pictures of all the fancy furniture to show his friends. Unfortunately, Veronica wandered in and out of the shot. Her chilling voice could be heard in the background as she greeted guests in the foyer. He would have to edit that part out. He didn't want to frighten away friends and family.

He closed in on Mindy Sawyer's long legs and slowly moved up to her bosom. She was so busy talking to Dana and Michelle that she didn't notice. But Dana did. She stomped toward Nicholas with her hands waving.

"Really, Nicholas?"

"It was an honest mistake."

"Grow up!" Dana stomped back over to Mindy and Michelle.

Nicholas panned across the room and stopped on Edna Dobson, who waved and smiled.

"Say hello for the camera!"

"Hello."

He turned around and videotaped Anna on the love seat. She waved and smiled coyly.

"Say hi!" Nicholas cried.

"Hi!"

"Are you having a good time?"

"It's really fun."

"Maybe later on we could go downstairs and see if there are any skeletons buried down there."

"Maybe you could explore on your own and report back to me."

He moved around the room and videotaped other guests.

Bart Sullivan sat on the love seat with his partner, Daryl Forster, the most sought-after African American model of recent years. Bart was a mild-mannered twenty-six year-old who had a pleasant air about him. He was clean shaven, with spiky blond hair and bright blue eyes. He had on an argyle sweater with pink diamonds and a wool scarf. Bart seemed dwarfed by his boyfriend's presence.

Daryl was a hulking figure. He wore a tight-fitting black muscle shirt. Large dangling rings hung from his ears. His hands and biceps were gigantic.

Tricia plunked herself in front of them and pumped them with a million questions about the modeling industry. Then she began talking about personal matters that most people wouldn't discuss with complete strangers. Tricia prided herself on not being shy.

"It doesn't make you a lesbian if you look at girls that way," Bart said with a laugh. "Everybody subconsciously checks each other out."

Craig looked sharply at him. "Well, you'd better not be doing that to me in the men's room, if you know what I mean, dude."

Bart erupted into fitful laughter. "Oh, Craig, there is nothing you've got that I am at all interested in seeing."

"Let's keep it that way." Craig looked suspiciously as everyone around him laughed.

He wasn't sure if it was an insult or a compliment.

Bart looked back at the troubled young woman. "Some girls are slow bloomers, sweetie."

"That's what my mom says all the time!"

Bart winked and said, "Just give it time."

"Thanks."

Veronica stomped over to them and glared at her daughter. "What on earth are you two talking about? Give it a rest, Tricia!"

"Oh lighten up for once, Veronica," replied an exasperated Bart. "If you would actually take time to listen to your daughter, you might find out that she is upset that other girls have boobs and she doesn't. They're making her life hell!"

Veronica's face hardened. "This conversation is entirely inappropriate!" She waved her left hand in a theatrical manner, pausing to think of her next comment, then she walked hurriedly away from them.

"Are you two going to tie the knot?" Tricia asked out of the blue.

Daryl looked dreamily at his partner and said, "We're thinking about it."

"We just haven't set a date."

Daryl squeezed Bart's hand and said, "We've both been so busy."

"Isn't that romantic?" Tricia said with a gleam in her eyes.

Charles cringed at his daughter from across the room. If he didn't have to put up with Veronica's moods on a daily basis, he had to worry that Tricia would say the wrong thing or offend someone. He went over to them and said, "Are you giving them the third-degree, Tricia?"

She rolled her eyes and said, "No, Dad."

"Well, it sounds that way to me from over there. Why don't you give them a break?"

Bart smiled sheepishly and said, "She's a treat, Charles. We don't mind."

"Don't embarrass your mother, please," Charles implored.

"Fine," Tricia whined.

"Why don't you go downstairs and watch television or something?" Charles suggested.

"Fine!" Tricia leapt up and looked back at Daryl and Bart. "Wanna see something really neat?"

"Sure, I'm game," Bart volunteered.

They followed her over to the upright piano. To the right, there was a wall with paintings hung on it. Tricia pulled up a latch that would have probably gone unnoticed to guests. She pushed the wall, and it turned.

"Wow, a hidden door!" Bart exclaimed.

She turned it around, and another set of pictures was revealed.

"Wow, you've got seasonal paintings!"

"Talk about a great way to put up pictures you don't know what to do with!" Daryl cried. "We gotta try that."

"But that's nothing!" Tricia shrieked with glee. She leaned on the wall, and a small door appeared on the left. She led them down rickety wooden steps that led to a combination family room and bar. "This is our family room."

Bart and Daryl looked around, their mouths agape as they took in the surroundings. A sofa and chairs were arranged across from a bar. A large HDTV was mounted on the wall opposite the steps. Tom Daniels sat at a bar across the room, drinking scotch.

Tricia thought Mr. Daniels was ancient.

Bart sat next to Tom. Daryl took the empty seat at the end.

"What would you like?" asked the bartender, who had been hired for the party.

Bart asked for vodka, and Daryl wanted bourbon. After a few moments, the bartender gave them their drinks. Then he handed Tricia a Coke. She plopped on the sofa, propped her feet on the coffee table, and watched TV.

"I bet you couldn't wait to get away from Broom-Hilda," Bart remarked smartly. He glanced back at Tricia and said, "Sorry."

"That's okay. I've called her much worse things."

Tom groaned and said, "Please, don't mention her! It's enough that I dragged myself here–just give me a little escapism, please."

"She'll eventually figure out that we came down here," Bart said.

"Don't remind me!" Tom implored.

"I don't know how you can work with her," Tricia said.

Bart craned his neck to look at her. "She treats you the same way?"

"I've learned to tolerate her. At least you're with her for only a few hours. I have to live with her all of the time–when she isn't at work. She's usually at work more than she's at home, though."

Bart frowned and said, "That's too bad." He reached in his pants pocket and pulled out his cell phone. He patted Daryl's shoulder and scooted upstairs.

* * *

A little while later, Tom Daniels sat alone at the bar. He finished off his scotch and glanced at his wristwatch. Fifteen minutes. The bartender hadn't gotten back from his break yet. Tom slipped behind the bar and found a half-empty bottle of scotch and helped himself. He sat back on the stool and drank heartily.

He gazed at the mirror on the shelf and wondered who the old man in the reflection was. For close to thirty years Murray Abrams, MD, had badgered him not to drink so much. Abrams would always say, "'You have to stop drinking and smoking. It's ruining your health.'"

After nearly four decades, Tom had finally quit smoking. But he was not about to give up his only other vice. About a year ago, Abrams had passed away, and Tom had to find another doctor.

Alone with his thoughts, Tom wondered and worried just what changes Veronica had in mind. Could one of those changes include getting rid of tried and true employees like him? He wasn't all that caught up with the modern-era gadgets and technological wonders. He was lousy at it. Kids half his age could do wonders with computer graphics and what-not. His pitch ideas were old school. He didn't understand what the clients wanted a lot of the time.

He and Veronica had some heated discussions over his lackluster computer savvy. He could do things those young kids couldn't do, but she didn't care. He was slowing up the process. It was the "old time and money" speech.

As he sat there, he worried and drank. The bartender wasn't there, and he was all alone. Maybe he'd put a mickey in Veronica's drink to get even. Sure, it would be a little harmless prank. A little pepper in her drink. Maybe he'd do a little rummaging in the bathroom. People usually kept Ex-lax in the medicine cabinet. He had seen rat poison on the kitchen counter under the microwave. He could swipe it when no one was looking. The place was crazy with people all afternoon. Nobody would even notice.

He hadn't seen Michelle in quite a while and wondered where she had wandered off to. He went upstairs and stood on the front porch, gazing at the beautiful scenery. The trees by the pond across the road were breathtaking in all their autumnal brilliance. The weeping willow tree looked so graceful next to the little dock.

He saw Bart leaning against the oak tree, jabbering on his cell phone and smoking a cigarette.

"Have you seen Michelle?"

"No, sorry, friend," Bart said.

The leaves crackled under Tom's feet as he walked toward the back of the house.

"Michelle!" he yelled.

She was nowhere to be seen. He went back inside and saw her coming down the steps.

"There you are, dear," he said. "I was wondering where you were."

"I was curious, so I did some exploring. Sorry, babe." They went back to join the others in the living room.

* * *

Veronica's voice was loud and piercing. Tom cringed as the frightened-looking caterer helplessly clung to the tray of crab puffs while Veronica chewed her out in the foyer.

"These taste terrible!"

The woman stared in astonishment at her and said, "I'm so sorry to hear that, Ms. Talbot."

"Do something about it!"

"I'll take care of it right away. I'm so sorry." She rushed into the kitchen.

Veronica wiped perspiration from her forehead and saw Tricia standing wide-eyed at the living room door.

"You shouldn't have been so mean to that lady, Mother."

"Maybe someday you'll understand. You pay people enough money, and you get bad service. Now that I think of it, the shrimp has a tart taste too." She marched toward the kitchen and Tricia braced herself for another blow up. She slipped into the living room and closed the double doors so nobody could hear her mother's loud and unpleasant screaming. They probably got enough of it at work and didn't need to hear it when they were supposed to be having a good time. Tricia's face turned beet red, but she kept her thoughts to herself.

* * *

"Is there something wrong with your refrigerator at your restaurant? My God! It tastes awful!"

"We took a bite of them and they taste okay to us, Ms. Talbot," the woman assured her.

"I can't believe it! You have to be lying."

"We aren't lying!"

An assistant was quick to defend her. They went on to explain how they ensured quality in their food preparation process.

"Well, I'll have to take the matter up with your manager later. This is unacceptable."

She walked hurriedly out of the kitchen and went into the living room. She chattered as if nothing had happened.

* * *

Bart blew a deep stream of smoke into the air as he talked on his cell phone. He waved at the bartender, who was taking a smoking break himself. Bart just needed a break from Veronica Talbot.

His feet made a crunching sound as he stepped on fallen leaves. A red and orange path covered the grass. At this hour, the sun was setting. It was getting cooler outside now. He leaned against the sprawling oak tree in the driveway and inhaled deeply as he talked. Wind blew the smoke back in his face, and he coughed.

He stubbed out his cigarette and went to his BMW. He reached down for his laptop, slammed the door and walked hurriedly back into the house. The bartender was still on his break.

James Dobson was standing by the staircase with a bewildered look on his face.

Bart eyed him suspiciously and asked, "What's wrong?"

"You missed the fireworks. Veronica was just chewing out the poor caterers."

Bart's face was drawn. "No kidding."

"You mean you couldn't hear it outside? I'm sure people in China could have heard her, she was so loud."

Bart's face blanched. "That's not fun."

They went into the living room and sat down on the ladder-back chairs by the coffee table.

"The shoot went really well today," Bart said. "Do you want to see the pictures?"

"Sure. I can't wait to see how they turned out."

"There might be some wrinkles that need to be ironed out–maybe reshoot some setups, but other than that, I think they're not too bad."

Bart turned on the laptop. He removed a CD from his jacket pocket, and shoved it into the slot. A moment later, image icons popped up on the screen. James watched a slide show presentation and smiled. "You're right. They look great. You've got an eye for beauty, there's no doubt about it. Michelle pitched a wonderful idea for the Murphy account. Good job, Bart. It captures everything they were looking for."

Bart turned off the computer and shut the lid. They sat back and brain stormed for a little while longer.

* * *

Veronica's screaming could be heard downstairs. The bartender, back from his break, looked toward the ceiling and grimaced. Tom had had enough of being upstairs and was back at his spot at the bar. A few minutes later, Nicholas joined him. He nursed a beer, hoping the Dragon Lady wouldn't find out where they were. They heard footsteps on the stairs and looked over to see Michelle enter the room. She went over and put her hand on Tom's shoulder.

She sat on the other side of Tom and said, "We were wondering where you all disappeared to."

Nicholas's lips curled in disgust. "This is the Veronica free-zone."

"Gotcha."

The bartender smiled at her. "What can I get you, ma'am?"

"A glass of white wine would be terrific."

He reached for a bottle on the rack and poured it into a glass. "Here you are, ma'am."

She took it and thanked him. She sat to Tom's right and said, "Are you gentlemen discussing office politics without me?"

"No, we're talking football," Tom said.

"Anything and everything Eagles related," Nicholas added.

A few minutes later, Charles Talbot ducked as he entered the room and grinned at his guests. "I knew I'd find you all down here."

Michelle beamed at him and said, "Charles, you have a beautiful house."

"If you're a good girl, Veronica and I can give you the grand tour. In a little while."

"That would be wonderful!"

"The festivities are about to start," Charles announced. "Veronica is in a tizzy not knowing where everybody went."

"It figures," Nicholas said under his breath.

"James is about to make a speech and would like you all to be there," Charles said.

They followed him upstairs. Tricia trailed after the adults.

* * *

When everyone gathered in the living room, Tricia recorded the toast on her cell phone.

She was smiling and glowing. She looked beautiful in a gawky sort of way.

James Dobson raised his glass and said, "Here's to Veronica. May you have the best of luck!"

She kissed his cheeks and said, "Thank you so much."

Charles pecked her on the lips and said, "It is well deserved. It just goes to show what good taste the boss man has."

James Dobson laughed. "I always knew that. To Veronica!"

They clinked glasses and cheered.

Nicholas pursed his lips and said, "Congratulations, Veronica."

"It was a good try," she said. "One of us had to get the job."

"It was a lot of hard work." Nicholas nearly choked on nuts as he walked away. Mindy handed him the cell phone and he went back to shoving it in people's faces to their annoyance.

"You have a really beautiful home, Veronica," Anna McWilliams said softly.

"Thanks darling. It's taken years to get it just the way I wanted it."

Housekeeper Kelly McDougal entered the room and said, "You have a phone call, Mrs. Talbot."

"Take a message please, dear. I'm busy."

Veronica was in and out all afternoon. When it came to having parties, she worked just as hard as she did at Creative Concepts.

Michelle kissed her fiancé, Tom, and backed into Veronica.

"I'm sorry."

Veronica feigned a cheerful grin and put an arm around her. "That's okay, you're just a little clumsy and didn't know any better, dear."

She left them alone.

"Why do you let Veronica treat you like that, Michelle?" Tom asked in alarm. "It's demeaning."

"I'm okay, Tom."

"It's wrong. She treats you like dirt."

"It's okay, dear."

"It isn't right."

"That's Veronica for you." She headed downstairs to get another drink.

Bart and Craig were talking about Veronica, as she walked toward them.

"That horrible–" Craig stopped in mid-sentence.

"You know the monster story board that Dobson approved. Whose lame-brained idea was that anyway?" Bart continued, unaware of Craig's frantic looks.

Veronica stepped in between them and put her arms around their shoulders.

"Mine." She tapped Bart's shoulder as if to say, *watch your step*.

The usual friendly and talkative Bart cowered in fear at her presence. "Sorry."

Craig would not be intimidated by that woman. He stood practically nose to nose with her and gritted his teeth. "I don't care how you got your promotion, Veronica, but we all know that you pushed your way in through intimidation and threats."

Veronica eyed him coldly. "You're jealous."

"We all know what you're capable of. You stole Tom's idea and presented it to Dobson before he could pitch it. That's pretty low."

She managed to laugh and sneer at the same time. "Oh Craig, darling. Poor misguided, unappreciated Craig. If I hear talk like that again. Well, I've been planning on reorganizing the company, as you know."

Bart's eyes narrowed with suspicion. "Reorganizing? So the rumors are true."

"I suggested some changes," she replied coolly. "That includes cuts from the payroll."

"I've worked hard for fifteen years," Craig said. "Dobson would never agree to–"

She grinned and said, "I'm just teasing." Then she went to pounce on others.

Craig drew a deep breath and muttered, "She is out of control."

"You're telling me! Somebody should straighten her out about a few things."

They watched Veronica flit about the room like the Energizer Bunny. She spoke so fast, it was hard to understand what she was saying. Maybe she was buzzed. Maybe it was the excitement of the promotion combined with the party. Craig and Bart gave each other silent nods, as if to say, 'She's bombed out of her head.' As the afternoon dragged on, her gait seemed off. She seemed unsteady. Her speech was slurred. She was drunk as a skunk!

At some point, her glass shook in trembling hands and she staggered to the closest chair. She wiped a bead of perspiration from her forehead and clumsily got back to her feet again. She was not moving as quickly as she had earlier. In fact, she seemed rather dazed and confused.

Anna had the misfortune of bumping into her. The Bloody Mary spewed onto Veronica's outfit.

Anna cringed and looked down at the red stain on Veronica's dress. "I'm so sorry."

"You klutz!" Veronica shouted at the top of her lungs. "Look what you've done! My dress. You dimwit!"

"I'll get you another drink. I'll–I'll pay to have it cleaned!"

"And just how the hell do you think a cleaner is going to get this stain out of my dress?"

"I'm so sorry. I'll–I'll go get you another drink." She walked hurriedly across the room and slipped through the hidden door leading to the basement.

Dana stomped over to the Dragon Lady and practically stood nose to nose with her. "Veronica, you didn't have to treat her that way. That was a cruel display."

"Hush. I know about your cheating ways."

Dana glared at her and said, "I'll bet you do. You don't care. It's funny how you know so much about us. And how did you get that promotion anyway? Sleeping with James Dobson, wasn't it?"

Edna Dobson's jaw dropped. She glared at her husband and shook her head in disbelief. Everyone's attention was on Veronica and Dana.

Veronica gasped. "How dare you! I worked my ass off to get this promotion!"

Dana laughed. "That's not what I heard."

"I have no time for idle gossip."

"I have information about you. It's been going around the office. It's about what you did a few years back."

Veronica cringed and said, "Not that."

James Dobson intervened. "What's the trouble here?"

"It's nothing, James," Veronica assured him. "Dana was just congratulating me."

"That's not what it sounded like. What is really going on?"

"Nothing, sir," Dana said. "It's between Veronica and me."

"Maybe we should discuss this on Monday morning," Dobson suggested.

Veronica closed her eyes and yawned. "Oh my, I'm so sleepy. Charles, I'm taking ten in the study. Take care of things, please." She took Dana by the wrist and awkwardly held the glass with her other hand. "Come with me!"

She walked unsteadily across the room. Dana had to help prop her up as they exited through the double doors.

James hurried over to his wife and tried to explain. She shot him a cold look and stalked out of the room.

CHAPTER 3

Penny Lane was immediately drawn to Detective Frank Logan. This quiet but intense man had an energy about him. He was a force to be reckoned with. She felt safe whenever she was around him. Though they both told different versions of how they met, two things remained the same. He was a beat cop in Philadelphia and she was with her friends, minding her own business when their paths crossed one day. They hit it off immediately.

Penny's parents were thrilled that she was dating a police officer. He was the perfect match for her. They were both straight arrows–strong-willed and never caved in to peer pressure. While other kids drank and did drugs, they had steered clear of them. They did not want to mess up their lives. They felt they had more important things to do, though they didn't know what those things were at the time.

In high school, Penny got involved in groups that helped raise money for charities. She also volunteered at nursing homes and helped stock shelves for homeless shelters.

Frank was an orphan at fourteen. He had always dreamed of working at the same Philadelphia police precinct as his father, Francis. One dark day when he was in junior high school, Francis was gunned down in the line of duty. Two short years later, Frank's mother, Vera, was killed in a car accident. The surly teenager was forced to live with his grandfather. Their relationship was volatile in the beginning. Gramps had recently lost his wife of forty-eight years. They bonded as they grieved together.

Having lost his parents at such a young age made Frank more serious than kids his own age. His desire to make Francis proud spurred him on to become a policeman just like him. Frank made detective before his thirtieth birthday. The stress of city life got too much for him and he transferred to Townsend. The slower pace came as a culture shock. He worked at a police station with a small staff. Detectives often had to divide up their workload. There were only two criminologists and one coroner. It often took several weeks to get test results back from Philadelphia.

Though he came to like the slower pace, Frank yearned for the excitement that the city had to offer. He really missed Penny, who worked at a bank in Center City and spent weekends with him in Townsend. She enjoyed hanging out with his coworkers at Barney's, the only bar in town. When she realized that he didn't really try to fit in with her friends at the bank, she got angry. From the very beginning of their relationship, he told her he was not good at small talk, especially with people that were not in his "world." That included her stuffy coworkers, as he so unwisely told her. Weeks went by, and he did not hear a word from her. Then they reconciled over dinner one night.

Frank was happy that Penny took him back, but with every good relationship, there has to be give and take. He was not so good at the give and take. She moved in with him and made a few small changes in his apartment. She put framed pictures of her family in the living room and hung plants over the front window. She replaced the drab curtains with lacy ones.

The rest of the apartment had a definite Logan flair about it. Pictures of his colleagues at the Townsend Police Department, along with various awards and medals hung on the living room walls. Pictures of his parents were on his bedroom walls. One of his favorite framed snapshots of him with his grandfather was on the dresser. They were both in fishing getups. It was taken when Frank was about twelve.

Penny quit her job at the bank and landed a dream job at Creative Concepts. It was a long commute to and from work, but the sacrifice was worth it. So far, living together had saved their relationship, for the most part. Frank was still stubborn about some things. Sometimes he wasn't an easy man to live with. She had learned to accept it.

He grimaced as he looked at himself in the mirror. He pulled off his tie and said, "Come on, Penny, I've done what you wanted. I refuse to wear this."

"Come on, Frank. Didn't you agree that you wanted this relationship to work?"

"Yeah."

"You said you'd go to meet my friends, like I do with yours. This party is very important to me. If I'm going to succeed, I have to go to parties like this."

"A lot of snobs go–"

"I know. But it won't be so bad. I promise. Veronica is very nice to me."

* * *

Veronica Talbot shoved Dana Phillips through an arched doorway that led into the study. A love seat was at the center of the room. A marble end table was next to it. Old leather-bound volumes lined the shelves of a bookcase, and an antique rolltop desk was in front of it.

Dana stood as dangerously close to Veronica as she dared and screamed, "What right do you have treating people the way you do?"

"Oh Dana. Perfect Dana. You should talk. Carrying on the way you are with my husband."

"He needs love and affection. Something he doesn't get from you. At least the boss isn't screwing me!"

Veronica laughed sardonically. "Poor girl. I know."

Dana looked dubiously at her and said, "What are you talking about?"

"Don't be coy. What goes around comes around."

"I resent what you are implying. You're jealous. When are you going to tell Charles the truth about your financial–"

"Bitch!"

"Slut!"

Veronica shoved her. Dana slapped her face.

* * *

The caterers stopped what they were doing and exited the kitchen. They stood outside the study door and listened. They heard every word the women were saying. And so could everyone in the living room. They rushed through the double doors and snickered and whispered among themselves. The office grapevine would twist in many directions come Monday morning! Others engaged in vile innuendo.

"They're really going at it," Bart said with a twinkle of mischievousness in his eyes.

Tom Daniels laughed nervously. "Like cats and dogs."

This incident prompted Edna Dobson to get up and join the others in the hall. Her eyes darted around at the gathering. She couldn't get enough of the endless gossip. She scowled at James, wondering if the rumors were true. Had he really slept with that awful woman? He averted his wife's gaze, a sure sign that he was hiding something. He was definitely not looking forward to the long ride back into Philly.

Nicholas Bradshaw stared intently at the study door and said, "If you ask me, Veronica has had it coming for a very long time."

A naughty gleam flashed in Tom's eyes. Michelle gaped disapprovingly at everybody but kept silent. Tricia suppressed a snicker as she stared at the group. She focused her attention on Tom's bald spot. He seemed so old. What did that woman see in him anyway?

Deep ridges formed on Charles' forehead. He waved the caterers away and shot scorching looks at his colleagues. "You all should be ashamed of yourselves! You're acting like four-year-olds! Go back in the living room!" He put his ear to the door and listened intently. "What the devil is going on in there?"

"I'll go break them up," Craig volunteered.

☆ ☆ ☆

Nicholas Bradshaw was listening from the kitchen door. When everything was quiet, he peered out and saw Craig walking back down the hall with his hand around Dana's shoulder. Craig told Mindy that he needed to talk to Dana and that he would be back in a few minutes. Mindy followed everyone else into the living room.

Nicholas knocked on the study door but there was no answer. He turned the knob and slowly opened it. He saw Veronica lying on the love seat. He quietly made his way across the room and leafed through piles of sketches in the desk. He opened drawers and sifted through more papers. He glanced over at the love seat and closed the drawers. His attention turned to the laptop. An orange flash drive was next to it. He popped it into the machine and opened the files. A minute later, he groused as images popped on the screen. He opened a couple of them, his anger rising.

"I don't believe it!"

☆ ☆ ☆

On her way down the hall, Michelle saw Nicholas coming out of the study. They smiled and waved.

"She's asleep," he said. "You'd better not wake her up."

"Why would I want to wake the Dragon Lady from her lair?"

"You've got that right." He went back into the living room and rejoined the group.

* * *

Craig and Dana slipped onto stools at the bar downstairs. As the bartender got their drinks, Dana said, "Don't say a word."

Craig took a deep swig of his scotch and said, "Why would I?"

Dana was shaking so much that she had to hold the glass in both hands to steady it. "The nerve of that woman!" she sputtered.

"Talk to me. What's really going on?"

"The usual. She's didn't forget to take her nasty pill today."

"Just forget about it."

"I can't just forget about it. What she said–"

"You know Veronica. It'll blow over."

"You're optimistic." She downed her white wine in one gulp and slammed down the glass on the bar with incredible might. The bartender poured her another glassful.

* * *

Tom Daniels crept into Veronica's study. She was sound asleep on the love seat. He couldn't believe how angelic she looked when she was deep in slumber. He went over to the desk and rummaged through drawers. Hopefully, he'd find something, anything, that might shed light on what her plans entailed. He was about to put a folder back and shut the drawer when a memo caught his eye. He looked back over his shoulder to make sure the bitch was still asleep and flipped the page.

"I don't believe it," he muttered. "The little–"

He had seen enough and put the folder back in place. He gently shut the drawer and slipped out the door.

* * *

Frank slowed down as they approached the Talbots' country home. It was about ten minutes from the Townsend Police Department. He didn't know how many times he'd zipped past the beautiful white two-story house on a daily basis. He had always wondered what it looked like inside. It even had a historic marker out front. It had been built before the Revolutionary War–so it was really old. There were rumors that the basement might have been used to hide slaves on the Underground Railroad.

The sun was setting when he pulled up the long gravely road leading to the house. Penny gasped as they got closer. It was an imposing sight with its white columns and large windows with black shutters. The American flag on the post flapped in the wind.

Penny leaned against him and whispered, "I can't believe I actually know somebody who lives here!"

"Really."

Frank parked his hatch-back next to a gigantic teal Hummer, and they scrambled out of the car. A shot of crisp, fall air billowed up her coat as they walked swiftly toward the house.

"Come on, we're late!" she shouted back at him.

He groaned and said, "That's good for me."

Penny rang the doorbell and rubbed her hands together for warmth. Frank hurriedly climbed the steps and stood by her side. The door opened and Charles smiled broadly when he saw her.

"Oh, hello, Penny," he said quickly.

Her face beamed. "Hi, Charles."

He held open the door, and Frank followed her inside.

"Charles, this is my boyfriend, Frank."

He shook the detective's hand and smiled. "You're the detective? It's nice to finally meet you."

"Likewise," Frank said cordially.

"Penny has told us a lot about the exciting murder cases you've been working on."

He led them across the foyer and said, "You can put your coats on the rack down the hall." He sounded rushed. He was practically out of breath.

"What's wrong, Charles?" Penny asked.

"I don't know what's keeping Veronica," he said as he showed them into the living room. "She said she was taking a ten minute nap. That was over a half hour ago. I'll go get her."

Penny and Frank walked into the living room, and her coworkers circled in on them like vultures. Frank smiled politely as he talked to them. Penny knew that look on his face. She knew that he was probably thinking something like, "'What have you gotten me into, Penny?'" She put her arm around his shoulder and joined in the conversation.

Tricia practically vibrated from the excitement of actually meeting a real detective. She couldn't wait to tell her friends at school on Monday. "It must be pretty gruesome looking at dead bodies all day!" she exclaimed.

"It can be pretty nasty," Frank admitted. "It's not like it is on TV."

"What on earth made you decide to move out to the middle of nowhere?" asked Craig. "I'm sure Philly had all the action!"

"You're right, it does. But I really needed a break from all of that."

"So you moved out to Sticksville!" Bart blurted out.

"Yeah."

"The pace must be really dull," Craig said.

"It has its moments," Frank agreed. "At first, I thought I made the biggest mistake of my life moving out here. It's so slow, the most action we get is handing out parking tickets sometimes."

"But then somebody flips out and kills their spouse or something, right, Frank?" Penny said.

"Or we have to break up drunk and disorderlies at the only bar in town," Frank added.

Craig was about to say something when Charles came rushing back into the room. All the color had drained from his face.

James Dobson looked in astonishment at him and said, "What's wrong, Charles? You look ill."

"She's dead!" Charles exclaimed. "I--I think she's dead!"

CHAPTER 4

A sudden stab of anxiety twisted in Charles's gut as he led Logan into the study. He stared in wide-eyed horror at his wife lying on the love seat. A spasm shot across his face; his heart pounded uncontrollably. The fear was so palpable that it felt like he had been slammed against a brick wall.

"I yelled for her to get up, and she just lay there on the sofa," Charles quavered. "Then I–then I shook her, and that's when..." His breath caught in his throat, and he just gaped in stunned silence. He felt lightheaded, and his skin was clammy.

Dana Phillips patted Charles's shoulder and escorted him out.

Frank knelt down to check for a pulse, and there was none. Nothing seemed out of the ordinary. It looked like she was asleep. There did not appear to be any signs of a struggle. Upon closer examination, he noticed a smudge on her makeup and a few strands of hair were out of place. There was a reddish stain on her outfit. He glanced at the end table and saw a half empty glass of Bloody Mary. He looked around the room and made a mental note of the surroundings. Nothing seemed out of the ordinary.

When Frank went back into the foyer, the frightened guests gathered around, waiting to find out what happened. He looked at Charles and asked, "When did she go to take her nap?"

They were all talking over each other as they tried to remember.

"One at a time," Logan instructed.

"It must have been about a half an hour ago," Charles said.

"Was she under any stress?"

"She was perfectly fine," Michelle Delancey said. "She was excited about her promotion."

No one was about to volunteer the fact that Veronica was agitated. They also didn't mention that she had gotten into an argument with Dana Phillips in the study.

"Did she have medical problems, Mr. Talbot?"

"She was in perfect health," he replied gravely.

"Was she on any medications?"

"She was taking muscle relaxants. She–she had a tennis injury–it helped her when–when she was in pain. I told her not to drink when she was taking it, but she had a mind of her own!"

"Did she take any before the party?"

Charles shook his head. "She never took the meds if she knew she was going to drink. She hasn't been taking them lately, anyway."

"Was she on anything else?"

"Sometimes she took antidepressants to help calm her nerves."

Logan jotted the information in his pad that he always carried with him and looked back at him. "Right now it looks like she died of natural causes. I won't know anything more until the coroner examines the body. No one can leave the premises until further notice."

There were a few murmurs, but no one wanted to argue with a cop. They went back into the living room and waited. There was a lot of excited gossip. They had nothing better to do.

The police arrived about fifteen minutes later. Lieutenant Harry Winters walked hurriedly across the hall and met Logan at the bottom of the stairs. He was a large man with a buzz cut of solid silver and a prominent mustache. He claimed that the scar over his right eyebrow was the result of being injured while on duty. His pals said he got it busting up a bar fight at Barney's.

Detective Joe Flosky rushed in behind him. He was a scrappy five-foot-four man with an abundance of energy. He had a dark crew cut, a ruddy complexion, and a gap between his front teeth. He had lived in the Townsend area his whole life and knew the residents well. The lackluster crime rate in town often resulted in many unproductive days. Flosky often told lively stories over a few drinks after hours. He didn't let the sparse population of single women in the area get him down. He was always hopeful that he would meet his future wife at Barney's.

Coroner Stan Green was right behind them. At fifty-six, he was a beefy man with a large, round face and thinning gray hair. He had gotten used to Townsend's limited facilities. Most tests had to be sent to the lab in Philadelphia. It often took longer to get results. Technicians often bumped Stan's tests for bigger cases in Philadelphia. Townsend detectives often pressured him to get the test results and he had to constantly tell them that the tests were put on hold. Stan had lived in the area his whole life and didn't want to move to the city. He had learned years ago to make compromises. Actually, it made him feel powerful making the detectives wait. Due to their limited budget, he could not always perform expensive tests. There had to be a really good reason for doing so. He would only order tests if the death involved suspicious circumstances.

Logan gave them a brief run-down of what was going on, as Charles quietly listened. "I got here after the fact. Veronica Talbot, about fifty-five, was found dead on the love seat in the study. She was apparently in excellent physical shape."

Kelly McDougal led Stan into the study and closed the door on her way back out. She went over and stood next to Charles. Winters and Flosky went into the living room to talk to the guests.

Charles collected his thoughts before speaking. "She said she was sleepy. And she went into the study to take a nap. And about half an hour later, I found her lying there...like that."

Kelly put her hand on Charles's shoulder and offered words of comfort. "Is there anything I can do?"

Charles ran his fingers through his hair and said, "Tricia. Where is she? My God! I've been so distracted with what happened to poor Veronica, that–that–oh my God."

"That's all right, Mr. Talbot. I'll find her." Kelly went upstairs to look for her.

"Who is Tricia?" asked Logan.

"My daughter. I–I don't even know if she knows...I haven't seen her. Oh my God! What if–what if she saw the flashing lights on the police cars? It probably frightened her!"

"That's okay, Mr. Talbot," Logan said gently. "We'll have an officer talk to her."

"No! I need to do it. I mean, it's something I should tell her. If you'll excuse me." He went upstairs and met Kelly on the second-floor landing.

"She isn't in her room, Mr. Talbot. Do you want me to check downstairs?"

"No, I'll go. If you'll excuse me. I'll be back." He went past the kitchen and slipped into the little hallway that led to the basement.

Logan looked at Kelly McDougal. "Did Ms. Talbot say how she was feeling?"

"She was tired, as Mr. Talbot said. I guess the fight tired her out."

Logan regarded her inquisitively. "What fight?"

"Mrs. Talbot got into an argument with Ms. Phillips. We could hear them in the study."

"What were they arguing about?"

She shrugged her shoulders. "I don't know."

"We're going to have to collect samples of everything she ate and drank at the party. So tell the caterers not to throw anything away. And that goes for you too."

"All right."

Logan thanked her and went back into the study. Stan was down on his right knee, examining Veronica's body.

"She was arguing with one of the guests," he told Stan. "What do you think?"

He pointed to the smudge of makeup and said, "She has a mark on her face, as if she was slapped. Other than that, it looks like she died of natural causes. I won't know until I examine her body. It might have been a heart attack. It looks like she died in her sleep. Her body is still warm. The time of death was probably about thirty to forty-five minutes ago."

Logan glanced at the clock on the bookshelf and said, "That would put her death about five or five thirty."

The photographer finished shooting the scene. Charles came back upstairs with Tricia just as Veronica was being carried away on a gurney. Tricia sat on the stairs and wept as she watched them go out the door.

Kelly gently rubbed her shoulder and spoke softly. Logan walked over to the frazzled young girl. Charles reached for his daughter's hand. She was trembling.

"You must be Tricia," he said softly. "I'm Detective Frank Logan. I am so sorry for your loss."

"Thank you," Tricia mumbled. Her expression was stone-like.

"It'll be okay," he said, then wished he hadn't. A situation like this was tricky. He was not very good at breaking bad news to people. "Maybe in a little while, when you've calmed down a bit, maybe–maybe I could talk to you."

"Okay." Tricia's voice was barely audible.

"I just need to ask your father a few more questions." He followed Charles to the other end of the hallway.

Michelle Delancey and Dana Phillips came through the double doors and went over to them. Charles introduced them to the detective, and they stood quietly by his side.

"Veronica was in and out all afternoon," Charles said. "We were all in and out."

"Did she complain about feeling ill?" asked Logan.

"Only when she left to take the nap."

"That's when she left with Dana," Michelle interjected.

"You went with her?" Logan asked Dana.

"Yeah. We had a talk. It got...rather intense."

"The housekeeper said it was more like an argument. What did you talk about?"

"Business."

"Can you be more specific?"

Dana pursed her lips and huffed. "It was just the usual stuff. We're both high-strung. It's the nature of the advertising business, I suppose."

"How did Veronica seem when you left her?"

"She was tired. I guess the excitement of getting ready for the party did her in."

"Is there anything else that might be important, Mr. Talbot? Anything at all?"

Charles held his fingers to the bridge of his nose and closed his eyes. He looked back at Logan and said, "I can't think of anything."

"Well, if you do remember something just let me know. I'm sorry for your loss, sir."

Logan went into the living room and compared notes with Winters and Flosky. They told him that everybody thought Veronica Talbot was acting rather odd. Some thought she was drunk. Others weren't sure what was wrong with her.

About an hour later, the detectives had gathered as much information as they could and told everyone they could leave. Winters carefully put the half empty Bloody Mary into a container, sealed, and labeled it. Then he put the glass in an evidence bag and did the same thing.

Meanwhile, Logan and Flosky concentrated their efforts in the kitchen. Flosky groused as he sifted through the garbage.

One of the caterers pointed to large piles of uneaten finger food and told him that those belonged to Mrs. Talbot. Flosky fished them out of the trash can and shoved them into evidence bags.

"This is so disgusting!" he cried. "It had better be worth it after all this!"

Logan stuck his head out of the refrigerator a moment and said, "Preserving evidence is a dirty job, but has to be done."

"Why do you always get the easy jobs?" Joe griped.

"I'm lucky, I guess."

Logan pulled out cans of tomato juice and Tabasco sauce and put them on the island. He poured samples into plastic containers and made sure they were sealed tight. He stuck them in evidence bags and labeled them. He went back to the refrigerator and opened the vegetable drawer. He pulled out celery stalks, olives, and black peppers and stuck them in separate evidence bags. He noticed a take-out container with Veronica's name on it. He pulled it open and saw a half-eaten salad. He dumped the contents in a bag, sealed, and labeled it. A few minutes later, they checked out the basement. Flosky removed vodka bottles from the shelf and immediately ruled out the other ones. If any of them had been tampered with, a lot of guests would have been poisoned too.

He pointed to a bowl on the bar and said, "The guests were probably eating nuts in these bowls. You think we should bag them too?"

Frank shook his head. "Everybody was probably eating them. And they didn't get sick. It had to have been something that was given to her. Something separate on her food plate or in the drink that was handed to her. She was the only one who was drinking Bloody Marys."

"It's like looking for a needle in a haystack!" Joe groused. "It'll be a miracle if we find anything. Do you think the killer will walk?"

"Don't even think it!"

A few minutes later, they met Lieutenant Winters in the Talbots' bedroom. It was a large room with elegant antique furniture. A Persian carpet stretched across the floor. There was an old chest in front of a king-sized poster bed in the middle. A rocking chair was in the corner by a window that overlooked the driveway. Cream-colored lace curtains were in the windows. Domed oval portraits hung on the walls. The images looked like they were a hundred years old. Oil paintings hung on the other walls. An armoire stood prominently opposite the bed. A wall-mounted flat-screen TV was the only modern item in the room. Frank figured that Charles insisted on it.

The bathroom had all the modern conveniences. The sink was large with a brown marble top and track lighting. A comb and facial creams lay neatly on it. The shower stall was big, with powerful jet spray spigots. There was a whirlpool tub at the other end of the room. Knowing the Talbots, they probably had one of those toilets that flushed like Niagara Falls, Frank thought.

"Did you find anything?" Logan asked Winters.

Harry held up an evidence bag, which contained medicine bottles. "I checked her medicine cabinet. She was on pain killers and an antidepressant."

"I just talked to her husband about it. Maybe somebody snuck in here during the party and broke the pills up into a powder and stuck it in her drink when nobody was looking."

"Or maybe it was ground up and put in her food."

"Either way, we know she wound up getting really sick and died in her sleep."

* * *

When Logan reported to work on Monday morning, Joe Flosky handed him the medical examiner's report and said, "I've got good news and bad news, Frank."

He regarded him suspiciously and said, "What?"

"You're not going to like it."

Logan studied the report and said, "It's just as I suspected. She died of a heart attack from all her stress."

"Read on."

Logan continued reading and groaned. According to the report, Stan Green initially believed Veronica Talbot died from a heart attack. After careful scrutiny of the odd symptoms that guests witnessed, though, Green got suspicious and ordered a toxicology test to be done in Philadelphia. The results indicated that deadly toxins were in Veronica's blood and stomach contents. Further tests were being conducted to determine if the poison was in something she ate or drank at the party. Time of death was between five and five thirty, which was when she left to take her nap.

Logan flipped page after page and grimaced when he reached the last one. Flosky braced himself for Logan's shocked reaction.

"It says that the reaction time could have been anywhere from two hours or longer! Stan can't pinpoint the exact moment that exposure occurred."

"That means any one of the guests could have slipped it in her drink at the party."

"And that means someone had the perfect alibi."

CHAPTER 5

The morgue was as cold as Veronica was if she was alive. The pungent aroma of formaldehyde penetrated Logan's nostrils as he entered the room. It was the one thing that he could not stand about his job, but he knew that it had to be done. He had gotten used to seeing what used to be a living, breathing person with his or her flesh splayed open on the autopsy table, their blood and fluids draining down the hole in the autopsy table. One bloody mess.

Flosky followed him into the room and looked wide-eyed at the blood splattered surgical tools on the metal table. Stan Green held a human heart in his right hand. The glove was splattered with blood. He placed it on the scale and weighed it. Then he took notes.

Logan and Flosky ventured over to him and waited until he was ready to talk to them. After jotting notes, Stan removed his rubber gloves and threw them in a trash can by the door. He lathered his hands with disinfectant soap on the sink and led them into his office in the next room.

Logan and Flosky sat across from Stan's desk and waited for him to finish making coffee. He pulled open the door from the small refrigerator on the shelf and picked up a sub that he had ordered from the deli three blocks from the police station. He sat down, ripped off the tape and took a big bite. He wiped oil off his hands and checked his notes pertaining to the Veronica Talbot case.

"It's going to be very difficult proving who did it," Stan told them.

"I was afraid you were going to say that," Logan muttered.

"It's a tough case. I'm just showing you what I have on her."

"Does it have anything to do with the pain medication she was on?"

Stan shook his head. "There were no traces of pain medication found. But we do know that alkaloids were found in her tissues and bloodstream."

"What are they?" asked Flosky.

"They are deadly toxins that can cause cardiac arrest. If it wasn't for the odd behavior that the guests witnessed, I would have left it at that."

"But you can't pinpoint the exact time she was exposed to the poison?" asked Logan.

"Not at the moment."

"Is there anything else you can tell us?"

"It took several hours for the poison to take effect."

"That's not reassuring," Logan said.

"I know," Stan agreed.

"Well maybe you can find out something from the samples we collected."

"I hope so."

They thanked him and continued to discuss the case on the way back to the office.

"The killer must have distracted Veronica and slipped the poison in her drink when no one noticed," Logan speculated. "Or maybe it was put in a crab puff or something."

"That would have been really hard to do without somebody seeing it."

"I know. That's what's got me really stumped."

"Well, you know how things go at parties, Frank. There are a lot of people wandering around. A lot of people are talking. It's usually pretty noisy. They probably didn't even notice anything."

"She had already been poisoned way before James Dobson made his toast. And guests said she was acting odd for a couple of hours before she went to take her nap. That was way before she got into the argument with Dana Phillips. The poison was working through her system."

"That's right."

"The killer was thinking all the time, and planning to have the perfect alibi. Even still, at that time, he or she could have easily slipped out of the room. Whoever did this is knowledgeable about poisons."

"You're right."

"That's the key."

"We'll have to find out which of them knows about chemistry or poisons," Flosky said. "We'll have to check their backgrounds."

"The question is, who knows about poisons in that group?"

"I'm sure you're going to find out."

"You bet I am!"

* * *

The break room was like a miniature kitchen. There was a table in the middle with four chairs around it. A vending machine was next to a small refrigerator. Next to it there was a large shelf holding coffee mugs of varying designs and sizes. A toaster and tiny microwave oven were on the counter. There was a sink across the room from the door.

Penny Lane's coworkers were shocked to find out that someone actually thought that Veronica Talbot was a nice woman. When she showed them the obituary that was in Townsend's *Times-Sentinel* the day before Veronica's memorial service, the write-up was the topic of discussion. They sat around the table in the break room, passing it to each other after each person was finished reading it. There were a lot of raised eyebrows and grunts and groans. Of course, there was no mention of her nickname, the Dragon Lady, which had been uttered so often behind Veronica's back. The woman described in the article was foreign to them.

Dana shook the newspaper and said, "What do they print in that little town of yours, Penny? This obit is pure fiction!"

Nicholas couldn't agree more. "It's too bad the writer didn't take the time to get to know the real Veronica."

Penny looked incredulously at her friends. "Come on, be nice, you guys. How would you like it if people said nasty things about you when you're not with us anymore?"

Craig yanked the newspaper out of Dana's hand and scanned the article. He shook his head in disbelief and grumbled, "You've gotta be kidding."

"Well, at least they were right about one thing," Bart observed. "She did have impeccable taste! Their house was beautifully furnished!"

Nicholas nodded his head in agreement. "It was like a museum in there."

Bart's eyes gleamed with pleasure thinking about the furniture. "I'm sure the antique store owners just loved her. She's probably made them very rich over the years."

"Well, nowhere in this fluff piece is there anything that says that she was a pushy, high-strung bitch!" Dana exclaimed.

"Come on, you guys," Penny interjected. "She had some nice qualities."

Bart laughed and shook his head. "Oh, sweet, naive, Penny. You really haven't been here long enough to have had to really deal with her."

They all clammed up when Charles entered the room. Dana handed him the obituary and said, "It's a beautiful write-up, Charles."

"I know. They did a good job." His eyes darted around the room. He knew what they had probably been saying, but he dismissed it from his mind. He had more important things to worry about right now. "I hope you all can make it to the service."

Dana patted his shoulder and said, "Anything you need. We're always here, okay?"

"Thank you. I don't–I don't know what I would do without you all." He walked out of the room, and they headed back to work.

* * *

A sixteen-by-twenty-four inch color portrait of Veronica Talbot was displayed prominently next to an oak box with her name etched on a gold plaque at the bottom. Tricia sat between her father and Kelly, who rubbed her arm and quietly offered words of comfort to the grieving young girl. Tricia wept uncontrollably as the minister eulogized her mother. His words were a blur. The shock of her mother's sudden death was too much for her to handle. The stress of picking out the right flowers and last-minute details for the memorial service were too much for a teenager to endure.

Fortunately, Kelly was there for her. She was always there whenever Tricia was in crisis mode.

Dozens of relatives and friends filled up the pews behind them. Her colleagues took up rows throughout the church. Nicholas Bradshaw rolled his eyes when Veronica's lifelong friends said nice things about her. He was thankful no one had asked him to speak on her behalf, because, frankly, he could not think of any nice things to say about her. He settled on one positive word: ambitious. Veronica had certainly been that. And she had a lot of spunk. And she had a lot of energy.

He exchanged a knowing look with Anna. She also could not believe Veronica was as nice as these people claimed she was.

Michelle Delancey wiped away tears. Tom reached for her hand and gently stroked it. He secretly wondered which direction Veronica's spirit went in.

Dana Phillips was also surprised to hear such wonderful stories about Veronica. Clearly, there had been another side to the woman that none of them knew about. She came off as the most caring, charitable woman on the planet.

"You could have fooled me," she whispered.

Craig heard her and nodded his head in agreement.

The slightest thing anyone said released a flood of emotions for Bart. He wiped away tears with a Kleenex. Daryl reached over and caressed his hand. It felt clammy.

James Dobson didn't know the woman these nice people were talking about. Surely, it could not be Veronica Talbot. Colorful anecdotes? She was joyless, if that was a word. She drained all the fun out of any situation. When it was his turn to speak, he wiped a bead of perspiration from his bald spot and tapped Edna's hand for luck. His legs felt like Jell-O as he went up to the podium. He planned to start off with a joke–would a joke go over well at a memorial service?

He felt a sudden surge of nervousness overwhelm him. He was used to talking to clients on a daily basis, but he never had to speak about the life of someone he'd known only at work, and knew nothing much about privately.

"Veronica Talbot was like the Energizer Bunny," he began.

Everyone laughed. He smiled meekly, feeling more relaxed now.

"She was definitely a force to be reckoned with. She was a go-getter. She got things done. She would run you down if you were in her way."

There were a few nods and murmurs from colleagues who knew exactly what he was talking about.

"She did not get the opportunity to be the creative pulse of the company for nothing," he continued after a long silence. "If given a chance, I am quite certain that Veronica would have taken Creative Concepts in new directions."

He glanced at Ben Goldstein who nodded his sunburned head enthusiastically. A few weeks away from the office had done him good. He looked more calm and relaxed now, despite the current circumstances.

"Veronica, you leave behind a dynamo of a husband and a bright, shining star of a daughter." He looked at Tricia and said, "I have no doubt that Tricia will be a household name about ten years from now."

Tricia beamed with enthusiasm at the mere mention of her name.

"Veronica was the most efficient employee I have ever known. She was always on time for every meeting. She cut to the chase and got to the heart and soul of what clients were looking for. Did I mention that she was never late for meetings?"

Everyone murmured, "Yes."

"Well, if any of you ever rode with her, you know what I mean."

Shrieks of laughter erupted around the room. A few people snickered.

"She was never late for a meeting because she drove at the speed of light to get anywhere she was going."

Penny burst out laughing. She glanced over at Frank, who had a serious look on his face.

"Did I mention that she was a back-seat driver? She should have taught Defensive Driving classes."

There were more shrieks of laughter from around the room.

"Sometimes I had goose bumps on top of goose bumps when I rode with her."

Ben Goldstein laughed so hard he couldn't stop.

"Well, Veronica eventually slowed down and got the account because she got to the meeting way before everyone else."

He waved to the box and the framed photograph and blew a kiss toward her face.

"Veronica, you will be missed. Thank you for your hard work and your friendship over the years. There will never be anyone like you."

James wiped a handkerchief over his head and headed back to his pew. He sat next to Edna, who patted his hand and said, "You did a wonderful job, honey."

He smiled flatly at her.

A couple more friends engaged the mourners in lively stories that most people didn't know about the woman. Then the minister drew the service to a close.

Everyone stood for the closing hymn. The minister picked up the box and handed it to Tricia, who wept uncontrollably. Kelly put an arm around her and spoke softly. Charles looked down at the floor and closed his eyes. A moment later, they followed the minister down the aisle. The mourners filed out after them.

They stood in the narthex. The reception line snaked all the way back down the aisle.

Small talk was not Charles's forte. Veronica had been the one blessed with the gift of the gab.

He locked eyes with his daughter a moment, and a feeling of pride came over him. Greeting all the wellwisher's was taking Tricia's mind, temporarily, off the horror of the memorial service. Her face gleamed like it did when he saw her on stage. He knew she would be all right.

Frank and Penny reached out to shake Charles's hand.

"I'm so sorry for your loss, Mr. Talbot," Frank said.

"If there's anything I can do, please let me know," Penny said.

Frank looked into Tricia's blue eyes, wondering if that was the way he had looked when he lost his parents at such a young age. The pain in her eyes was unmistakable.

"How are you holding up?" he asked her.

"It's hard, but–but Kelly has been such a big help." She squeezed her hand.

"If there's anything I can do, just let me know," he said softly.

Tricia smiled faintly and said, "Thank you."

He shook Kelly's hand and said, "It's a good thing you're there for her."

Kelly smiled flatly. "I'm glad she doesn't have to go through it alone. I'm glad I'm here for both of them."

Penny reached out and hugged Charles and Tricia. Then she shook Kelly's hand. "You'll get through this. It was a lovely service."

"Thank you all for coming," Charles said in a quiet tone.

Frank and Penny offered their condolences to other family members as they worked their way down the line. Afterward, they chatted with her friends from the office.

* * *

Charles and his colleagues gathered around a small table at the luncheon that followed the service, trying to think of only positive things about Veronica.

"As accomplished a woman as she was, she was terrified of suspension bridges," Dana quipped.

Penny gasped and said, "No kidding! That's unbelievable!"

"One time she freaked out so bad when we were approaching the Walt Whitman Bridge that she had to pull to the side and I had to get behind the wheel."

"That is really unbelievable!"

"It's amazing that she was able to accomplish so much, despite her phobia."

Michelle looked at Penny and asked, "Has the coroner found out anything yet?"

"All he knows is that she was poisoned, but he doesn't know anything other than that. And as usual, Frank's getting impatient."

Michelle sipped her coffee and wiped her mouth with a napkin. "How is Tricia holding up?"

"As best as can be expected," Charles replied gravely. "It's such a shock for everyone."

Michelle smiled graciously. "It was a beautiful service. Very inspirational."

"Thank you. You'll never know how much it means to me that you all were there to help us get through it. Especially after the way she treated you all. But–but it was just her way."

Dana sneered. "She wouldn't have gotten where she was if she had been Miss Manners."

Charles sighed. "Thank God Tricia is in the middle of rehearsals for the play she's in. It's taking her mind off things, I think."

Penny's eyes lit up. She leaned forward and asked, "What's the play?"

"*Grease*," Charles replied, his eyes twinkling. "They're having a lot of fun with it."

"That's wonderful!" Michelle cried.

"It's a wonderful outlet," Dana agreed. "She can lose herself in her art."

Charles took a sip of his tea and smiled. "It's escapism. That's what she needs right now."

"When is opening night?" Penny wondered.

He shrugged his shoulders. "I don't even know."

"That's okay," Dana said. "I can't wait to see it."

"Maybe we should all go together," Michelle suggested.

"She–she's just in the chorus. I've been listening to her singing around the house for weeks. She sings in the shower. She sings just about everywhere. She's really quite good."

"Does she dance?" Penny asked.

"Yes." His face lit up at the thought of it. "She started taking dance classes when she was four-year's-old."

"Veronica would have been so pleased to see her in it," Michelle said.

"If she had gotten around to seeing it," Charles added bitterly.

* * *

About nine thirty a.m. the next day, Logan pulled up the long driveway that led to the Talbots' house. He hurriedly climbed the front steps. The weather felt crisp and hinted at a cold winter. He rang the doorbell and rubbed his hands as he looked at the beautiful fall leaves on the grounds.

Kelly McDougal opened the door and smiled broadly. "Well, good morning, Detective Logan. Can I help you?"

"It's about Mrs. Talbot's death. I need to talk to you all about it. I couldn't talk about it over the phone."

She led him into the house and offered him coffee. He said he took it black and waited in the living room.

"I'll let Mr. Talbot know that you are here." She went back out to the foyer.

Logan's eyes darted around the room. He gazed at the mammoth old oil painting over the fireplace mantel across from the double doors. Then he looked at the antique furniture.

He wished he had gotten to the party earlier. Maybe he could have seen what had actually happened. He wondered just how someone could have slipped poison into Veronica's drink or food without being caught. It would take a long time to get the results for all of the samples that they had collected. He had a very bad feeling about the direction in which the case could lead if he couldn't figure out how Veronica was poisoned. It could have been any one of the guests. There were a lot of people coming and going, but no one seemed to know anything.

He heard footsteps in the hall and looked up to see Charles Talbot in the doorway. He looked gaunt.

"Well, good morning, Frank. What–what can I do for you?"

He sat on a rocking chair facing the detective. Kelly came in and handed Frank his coffee. Then she gave one to Charles.

She started to go back out when Logan said, "Hold on a minute, Ms. McDougal. Maybe you should hear this too. I'll have to talk to you anyway, you might as well hear it now."

She sat next to them and said, "I hope it isn't serious. But the way you're talking..." She trailed off.

Logan looked at Charles and said, "I'm afraid to say that there was more to your wife's death than we originally thought."

"What do you mean? I thought the coroner ruled it as a heart attack. She was under tremendous stress."

"The coroner originally dismissed it as symptoms of heart failure, but he got suspicious when guests overheard her complaining about how bad the food tasted. Everyone else thought it was fine. A test showed that Veronica had poison in her system."

Charles gasped. "Someone poisoned her?"

Kelly's eyes widened in alarm. "My God! But how can that be?"

Logan looked from Charles to Kelly and asked, "Do you know of anyone who had reason to kill her?"

Charles was deadly silent. He clasped his hands over his face and groaned.

"I know this comes as a shock," Logan said softly. "Please take as long as you need."

Charles struggled to his feet and strode over to the front window. He gazed out at the fall leaves, lost in thought. A couple minutes later, he went back over to them and sat down. He locked eyes with the young detective and said, "Everybody in the office hated her with a passion. It could have been any one of them–oh, I'm so sorry. Except Penny! How could I have forgotten?"

"Well, we got here after the fact."

"So you think it happened sometime during the party?" asked Kelly.

"That's what it looks like, ma'am."

A look of foreboding flashed in her eyes. "Oh my," she muttered.

"I'll need a list of what everybody was drinking. And when people arrived."

Kelly drew a deep breath. "Oh, my. It's hard to say when people got here. When everybody was here, it was really quite confusing, because everybody was in and out."

"Some people were sitting at the bar downstairs for quite a while," Charles added. "I think they were just trying to get away from Veronica."

"Was anyone alone with her for an extended period of time?"

Charles and Kelly said they weren't sure.

"Wait a minute–Edna Dobson spent most of her time over there." Charles pointed to the three-corner chair. "She was planted there with a drink in her hand. She only got up a couple of times. Once when James toasted Veronica. And then she got up to listen to Veronica arguing with Dana in the study."

A feeling of shame came over Kelly. She lowered her voice. "We were all doing it."

"What were they arguing about?"

Charles shrugged his shoulders and grunted. "I don't know."

"Their voices sounded muffled," Kelly added. "Maybe you should just ask Dana."

Logan jotted it down in his pad.

Charles's face grew pensive. "Veronica had a mouth on her. If she was upset about anything, whoever happened to be around her at the time got the brunt of it. She was like a volcano, ready to explode all the time."

"Was she acting differently during the party?"

"She was practically bouncing off the walls," Kelly replied. "But she was just excited. Just before she left to take her nap, she seemed to be perspiring a lot. That was after she chewed out the poor caterers. And then she said she felt tired all of a sudden. Do you think the poison was taking effect then?"

"Quite possibly," Logan said.

Kelly shuddered at the thought. "I can't believe that somebody did such a horrible thing right under our noses! It's just awful!"

Logan looked at Charles. "Was it unusual for her to feel tired like that?"

"She had an overabundance of energy. I just thought she tired herself out getting ready for the party."

Kelly sighed in exasperation at the thought. "There was so much to do! We needed an extra day to get things ready. We rushed around at the last minute."

"Can you think of anything else?"

Charles ran his right hand through his salt-and-pepper hair. "I can't think of anything right now."

Logan pulled out his wallet and handed him his card. "Well, if you do think of anything, please don't hesitate to give me a call. Even if you think it's trivial." He got to his feet and asked, "Do you mind if I look around a little bit more?"

"Go ahead," Charles said. "I just want you to find out who did this horrible thing." He was quiet again. "Oh my God. How am I going to tell Tricia?"

"I can talk to her," Logan volunteered.

"Well, maybe we should both be with you when you do," Kelly suggested. "I've been tutoring her from home. We can go up to her room if you want to talk to her."

Logan thanked her and followed them up the winding staircase. When they reached her attic bedroom, Charles knocked on the door and said, "Tricia. Detective Logan is here to talk to you, sweetheart."

There was no response. Kelly said, "You have to knock on the door a lot harder than that, sir."

"Oh, the damned earphones!" Charles cried in exasperation. "She'll be deaf before she's thirty if she keeps wearing those blasted things in her ears!"

"Really," Logan replied sardonically.

Kelly turned the knob and stuck her head in. Her voice was soft and gentle.

"Tricia."

A moment later, the girl looked up, realizing that the door had opened. She yanked the earbuds out and said, "What?"

She saw Detective Logan in the hall and said, "What...what's wrong?"

Kelly pulled up a chair and sat next to Tricia. "Detective Logan needs to talk to you, honey."

"Why is he here?"

"He came to tell us there's more to your mother's passing, honey."

"I don't understand."

"Here. Let him explain it. It's too complicated for me to tell you."

Frank entered the room and smiled at her. "Hello, Tricia. Can I call you Tricia?"

"Sure."

"You can call me Frank." Kelly let him sit on her chair and stood by the door next to Charles.

"I know that right now you must feel really confused," Frank said gently. "I know how it feels. I lost my folks when I was about your age."

"It must have been really hard for you."

"Just as hard as it is for you, I suspect. Now to get back to the reason why I'm here. We don't think that a heart attack is what your mother passed away from."

Tricia looked intently at him. "Then what was it?"

"We think someone poisoned her."

Tears trickled down her cheeks. Kelly cradled her in her arms. She was trembling. Charles stood helplessly with his hands at his sides.

"You're upsetting her!" he shouted at Logan.

"No! No! No! It's not true!" Tricia exclaimed.

"I'm afraid it is," Logan said in a quiet tone. "I need you to do me a favor. I need you to remember everything that went on that day. From before the party to when people got here. And anything at all you can remember during the party."

Her voice sounded strained. "I remember watching people pulling up to the house, but I...but I don't remember what time they got here. My mother was rushing me to get dressed. I just wanted to listen to my music."

"You're doing a great job," Frank encouraged.

"Craig came with this beautiful girl on his arm. I remember...I remember wishing I could...look like her. A little while later, I looked out again, and there were a lot more cars in the driveway. I saw Michelle coming in. She's really got it together."

"She does," Charles agreed.

"And then I saw Bart and Daryl coming in. I got dressed and went down to talk to them. My mom and dad were irritated that I was bothering them."

"She was talking their ears off," Charles explained. "It's okay."

"I was just asking them about the modeling business."

"She wants to be a model," Kelly told him.

"Or an actress," Charles added.

"Something like that," Tricia said. "I just thought...I just thought that they might know how I could break into the modeling business."

"That's great," Frank continued. "Go on."

"They were very helpful. Bart is so nice. And he's really funny, too. He just says what other people are too afraid to say."

Charles hung his head and said, "I know."

"Then we went downstairs. Then my dad came down and said they wanted us all upstairs."

"How long were you down there?"

"About a half an hour or so. Maybe more, maybe less."

"So when you went upstairs, then what happened?"

"Mr. Dobson made a toast, and everybody was happy. And then...and then that weird lady–Anna, I think it is–"

"Tricia Jean Talbot!" Charles admonished. "That isn't very nice. Anna does great work for us."

"I'm sorry." She looked back at Logan and said, "Well, she accidentally backed into my mother and spilled her drink on my mom's dress. My mother said nasty things to her. She was like that. She wasn't a bad person. She was just...uptight."

"Then what happened?" Frank asked eagerly.

"Ms. Phillips started yelling at my mother. I don't think my mom liked her very much."

"They despised each other," Charles corrected.

Logan looked at him and asked, "Why did they hate each other so much?"

"That's a long story. I'm sure you're too busy to hear it right now."

Logan jotted a reminder to ask Charles about it later.

"My mother pulled Ms. Phillips out of the room, and everybody listened outside the door."

"I was fit to be tied!" Charles sputtered. "The very idea of grown adults behaving like school children."

"I would never act that way," Tricia assured them.

Logan looked at Charles. "Do you know what they were angry about?"

"Veronica didn't like the way Dana was handling a client's ad, and they had it out at the office. I thought they'd gotten it out of their system on Friday afternoon, but I guess it carried over to the party. She was always getting into arguments with everyone. And then by the end of the day, everything was hunky-dory until the next cat fight."

"It sounds like it happened frequently," Logan commented dryly.

"I learned to ignore it, as did everybody else. We just were glad we weren't in the fight at that particular moment."

"What happened after their argument?"

"Veronica announced that she was going to take a short nap–but she wanted to have it out with Dana first. After their fight, Dana came out looking flustered, and my wife took her nap. And then–"

"You found her on the love seat," Logan finished his sentence. He closed his notepad and said, "Well, you all have been very helpful. I wish I had been here then. Maybe I would have seen something that could help solve the case." He got to his feet and looked at Tricia. "I'm sure we'll get to the bottom of all of this. I'm sorry that I had to lay all this on you now."

"No, it's okay. I'm glad you're doing it. I want to know what happened to my mother and who did it."

"I won't take up any more of your time."

"Thank you, Detective Logan," Tricia said when he reached the door.

He looked back at her and said, "You're welcome. If you need to talk, you can reach me at the police station. So long."

She waved, and he walked out the door after Kelly and Charles. She jammed the earphones back in and listened to the music.

* * *

Logan looked around the Talbots study again. The room was the same as it had been a few days before. Nothing was disturbed. He decided to take a look in the desk. When he pulled open the drawer, he saw a yellow pad on top of a pile of papers. He picked it up and read the notes that were scrawled in Veronica's handwriting with her signature at the bottom. One addressed to James Dobson caught his attention. In it, she laid out her plans for the company which included a list of recommendations for who should go. Half of the party guests were on the list except for Craig, Michelle, Bart, and Penny.

"Hmm, that's interesting," he muttered. "She really did have a hit list."

He leafed through a stack of old letters and Christmas cards, and then carefully removed papers under the notepad. He glanced up at the framed snapshots sitting on top of the desk. They were happy family pictures from many years ago: a smiling Tricia at about two years old, and a picture taken about three years ago. They were all dressed up and smiling for the camera. No one seemed to believe that Veronica was ever that nice. But people did say nice things about her at the memorial service, he mused.

He went to take another look in the kitchen. His eyes trained on a box of rat poison on the counter below the microwave oven. It must have slipped his mind the afternoon that Veronica died.

Kelly McDougal entered the room and said, "Is there anything else I can help you with, Detective Logan?"

He pointed to the rat poison. "Was that out in plain sight during the party?"

She grimaced and said, "I forgot all about it. Yeah–it was there. I can't believe I left it out there. It's so embarrassing."

"Any number of the guests could have seen it, ma'am. Maybe somebody stuck it in her drink as a joke. Only he or she didn't realize what a deadly combination it would be."

Kelly swallowed hard considering it. "If that's what happened, I would feel awful. It would've been my fault."

"I'm not laying blame on anybody at the moment, ma'am. I'm just trying to see what poison could have been used."

"So you...so you actually think one of the guests did it?"

"That's the way it looks right now."

"You don't suppose Mrs. Talbot took her life, do you?"

"Well, I had never considered it, but it is a strong possibility. She would have been the only one who had access to her drink the whole time."

"You're probably right. But she wouldn't have done such a thing. I'm sorry I brought it up."

"No, don't be. I have to look at every angle. Was she depressed?"

"No, she was excited about the new job. She was nervous and nasty, but that was her way." She went to the utility closet and pulled out a broom and swept the floor while he spoke.

"You helped set up for the party, right?"

"I was up very early, sir. About six o'clock. Ms. Talbot was a nervous wreck about it. Poor Tricia had to listen to her raving all morning. Ms. Talbot screamed at me. And she screamed at Charles."

"She made you so angry, maybe you put something in her drink before the party started."

Her eyes flashed with rage. "How dare you suggest something like that!"

"Well, I have to examine every possibility, ma'am. You were here all day. You had ample time to arrange the poison for her to drink. Maybe you told her to drink a special tea to calm her down. Or maybe you put something in her food."

"How dare you! I am a mother! I would never do such a horrible thing!"

"Sometimes people are driven to great lengths when they are forced into certain situations. She was a really nasty boss, and you had means and the access to a lot of poisonous household items."

"Why don't you get the evidence tested and then find out who really did it?" She leaned the broom on the counter and stormed out.

CHAPTER 6

Frank looked at brightly colored flowers and potted plants on a table in the Creative Concepts lobby. He followed Penny down long and winding corridors, glancing at eye-popping posters that hung on the walls. He found the bright fluorescent lights to be annoying.

Penny beamed and said, "This is where the artists make magic happen." She pointed to Anna and Nicholas's work areas and waved at them. "Hi, guys. You remember my boyfriend, Frank, right?"

Nicholas reached out to shake Frank's hand and said, "Good morning, Detective Logan."

"It's nice to see you again."

"It's too bad it can't be under better circumstances."

Anna smiled sheepishly and asked, "Have you found out anything new, Detective Logan?"

"Right now it feels like I'm grasping at straws, to be honest."

"Well, I hope you find out something soon. It's such a shame what happened." She looked back at her laptop and continued working.

"I will need to talk to you both later, when you've got the time," Logan said.

Nicholas grinned. "Sure thing." Then he looked back at his monitor. Out of the corner of his eye, he watched Penny lead the detective down the hall.

"What's that all about?" he muttered.

"I don't know," Anna replied from the other side of the cubicle wall.

"If you ask me, I think Penny's detective boyfriend is snooping into our business too much. It's none of his business." He went back to work.

* * *

Frank stuck his head in Dana Phillips's office and saw that she was on the phone. She smiled when she saw him and waved him in. He sat across from her desk and looked at a framed family portrait that had probably been taken about ten years earlier. A boy with strawberry blond hair with a red and white striped shirt on stood to Dana's right. Her youngest son sat on her lap. He looked about two-years-old, with shaggy blond hair, and was dressed in a sailor suit. A more recent family photo was next to it. The boys had grown into lanky teens, with shocks of long blond hair. They had on soccer uniforms and were hamming it up for the camera. Logan noticed that there were no pictures of a husband or boyfriend. There was no ring on her finger, so she must have gotten a divorce.

He glanced at plants hanging in the window. It looked like she had a nice view of the city. His eyes were drawn to the modern artwork that hung on the walls. They were probably prints from famous artists that weren't at the tip of his tongue.

A couple minutes later, she hung up and motioned for him to take a seat. "What can I do for you, Frank?"

"I didn't have a lot of time to talk to you at the party, with all that was going on. Do you mind if I ask you a few questions? I see that you are super busy. It won't take long."

When he told her that someone poisoned Veronica, she recoiled in horror.

"I don't believe it! How is it possible?"

"That is what I'm trying to find out, Ms. Phillips. Can you tell me anything you can remember that happened at the party?"

"It's hard to say."

"When did you get there?"

"I got there early and helped get ready."

Logan looked dubiously at her. "That sounds a little surprising."

"What do you mean?"

"Well, the housekeeper told me that you got into an argument with Veronica just before she went to take her nap."

"Oh that. We were always getting into tiffs. And then we'd patch things up a few minutes later."

"What were you arguing about?"

"Anna accidentally spilled her drink on Veronica, and she chewed her out. I told her I didn't like the way she was treating the poor girl, and we started screaming at each other. We were always having creative disagreements. It was Veronica's way or the highway. But my parents didn't raise a wimp. I fought her every step of the way."

"It sounds like an unpleasant work environment. Penny never mentioned the fights."

"She hasn't been here long enough, I guess."

"Did you see anything suspicious during the party?"

"Not really."

"Was there any time during the party that someone could have slipped something in her drink?"

"It was all so confusing. We were all wandering around from one room to another. Veronica was flitting about like a flea! It seems to me it would have been pretty noticeable if... somebody did such a horrible thing like that."

"So you were the last one to see her alive?"

"I guess so."

"Maybe you were so angry with her that you stuck something in her drink."

Dana's eyes were wild with rage. "Now, wait just a minute, Frank. Just because we had disagreements–doesn't mean...that I wanted to do her in!"

"Well, it's just a thought."

"It wasn't always like this, you know. We used to be good friends when we started working with each other. At least, I thought we were friends. And then I saw her true colors. She was just using me like she used everyone else."

"What did she do?"

"She stole my ideas. She pitched them to clients before I could talk to them!"

"It sounds pretty cutthroat."

"We used to work well together to start with. But then we had to be separated! So, Michelle and I were partnered. Veronica went to every means to make me look bad. She constantly sabotaged my campaigns. Ask around–they'll give you an earful! She stole my ideas. She stole my jingles right out from under me–she dashed to James before I could talk to him. She did it with everybody. She was that competitive."

"How did you put up with her?"

"It was extremely difficult. I was at the edge of my patience, that's for sure."

"It sounds like plenty of reason for wanting to permanently put an end to her."

He thanked her and left her shocked and dumbfounded at her desk.

"I don't believe it!" she cried in disbelief. "He actually thinks I did it!"

* * *

Nicholas Bradshaw's family was close-knit. His parents told everybody they knew that he worked at an advertising firm in Philadelphia. They were supportive of everything their boys did. His father, Christopher, was a high school chemistry teacher. His mother, Jessica, was a Realtor.

Nicholas and his older brothers, Mike and Bob, were close in age. They were as thick as thieves when growing up and had constantly gotten into mischief. Nicholas emulated his older brothers. Their parents had flexible schedules and took turns being at home after school. That meant that one of them would be there to make sure that the boys didn't get into trouble, which was quite often. Christopher knew how to deal with his high school students. When it came to his teenage sons, though, he had difficulty getting them to do what he wanted. Fortunately, Mike and Bob were preoccupied with sports after school and they spent less time together.

Raging hormones created an unpleasant mixture when girls entered the picture. Christopher laid out strict rules for what his sons could do and not do around the opposite sex. Girls were not allowed in their bedrooms under any circumstances. Car dates were strictly forbidden. If they were going to go out, they had to do it in groups. There was to be no drinking under any circumstances.

When they started dating, Mike and Bob ignored their little brother. When Nicholas got into high school, he found that he had not been blessed with the charm and sophistication that they possessed. When he was finally old enough to date, Jessica told him to be nice and respect girls and not to be overly aggressive. His brothers and friends told him the opposite. His first date was a disaster. He was riddled with self-doubt. He didn't know if he should kiss the girl or hold her hand. The girl kissed him. His awkwardness sealed his fate with women for all eternity. They broke up after a few weeks, and he wondered why.

He used humor like a defense mechanism to ease his awkwardness in social situations. Though he was not as skilled in wooing women like his brothers, he made up for it in his artwork. He gained confidence in his artistic abilities working at Creative Concepts.

Success came at a price. Like so many of his colleagues, Nicholas worked long hours and had little time for a social life. If he did go out, it always consisted of after-hours cocktails with his coworkers. His brothers were married and had children. His family kept asking him if he had found the right woman yet. His mother constantly reminded him that he was in his late twenties, and "time marches on." She was tired of hearing him say, "I work long hours and don't have time to date." His parents were afraid that he was wasting too much time fooling around with his friends after work and not seriously thinking about settling down.

Nicholas was a fool for love. He really did want to settle down and have kids. If he ever found the right woman, he wouldn't do anything stupid to jeopardize the relationship. He didn't really like going out with his friends after work, but it was better than going home to an empty apartment. Quite frankly, he was tired of hearing Craig Holloway complain about the women that he sent to the trash bin. He thought Craig purposely sabotaged his relationships for some unknown reason. Nicholas was a one-woman man. He would never treat a girl like that.

The only woman he was in constant contact with was Anna. It seemed like they spent their entire working lives together. They had gone on a couple of dates and decided that they would remain good friends. If he went on dates that went south, he'd always ask Dana what he had done wrong. She always told him to be himself and stop making jokes.

He thought that Penny was the light of the office. She was so positive and enthusiastic, much needed new blood in an office full of tension created by Veronica Talbot. The Dragon Lady's bitchiness had been bringing everybody down until Penny came to work there. If the circumstances had been different, he could see himself dating her–if Detective Frank Logan hadn't seen her first.

At that moment, he looked up to see the detective coming toward him. He eyed him quizzically, not knowing what to expect.

Logan whistled when he saw the images of fire-breathing dragons and flying horses hanging on Nicholas's cubicle walls. They were set against dazzling backgrounds like castles and mountains, with otherworldly background colors. They could have been on book covers or movie posters. Squeezed in between his art work, there were posters from *Harry Potter, Star Wars*, and the *Lord of the Rings*. There was one family picture in the mix. Nicholas had attached their heads to the bodies of wizards and super heroes. Logan noticed there were no pictures of Nicholas with a wife or girlfriend.

Nicholas led Frank into an unoccupied meeting room so they could talk privately.

"I was angry," Nicholas admitted. "Wouldn't anybody be angry? I've been at Creative Concepts for seven years, and I deserved that promotion. I have a lot of really great ideas, but nobody listens."

"Revenge is a powerful motive, Nick."

"That's true, but I didn't kill her. I swear."

"I can't believe that James Dobson would have passed you over for promotion, with your background."

"It's on account of the argument. James said I can't control my temper, and it's true. It doesn't seem fair, though. Veronica was always losing her temper."

"We all have our ways of handling upsetting situations. It does seem a little odd. Maybe there was another reason why you didn't get the job."

"James said he didn't think I was ready to handle all the responsibilities, or something like that."

"Do you know anybody who might have wanted to kill her?"

"We were all angry with her, so that's a hard question to answer," he admitted.

"Did you see or hear anything suspicious during the party?"

"I spent most of the time at the bar downstairs, just to get away from her."

"What about during the toast?"

"I played nice for a couple minutes, and then, all of a sudden, she dragged Dana into the study, and we ran to hear them arguing. They were really going at it!"

"That sounds pretty childish."

Nicholas grinned like a Cheshire cat. "I know, but I couldn't help myself. When we're here all day–doing what we do–little things like that tend to relieve stress."

"I understand. When it gets dull around the station, my pal Flosky and I toss around a Nerf ball and talk about cases."

"It was pretty stupid what we did, but it was just something we did."

"What were they arguing about?"

"Dana was angry about the way Veronica treated Anna. And then–" He giggled and said, "I heard Charles's name mentioned. Veronica got upset that Dana spends so much time with him at work–or something like that. If you ask me, I think Charles and Dana are doing it. If I had to live with the Dragon Lady, I wouldn't feel the least bit guilty for messing around with another woman."

"I don't respond to rumors."

"Well, you wanted to know what I heard. It's not like we haven't all been talking about them behind their backs."

"Did she say anything nasty about you?"

Nicholas's eyes widened. "It's no secret that we had creative differences. She was constantly criticizing my work. Could you work with somebody like that?"

Logan shook his head.

"She was constantly breathing down my neck, complaining that I didn't get my work done fast enough! It was really a stressful work environment." He pointed to his designs on the cubicle walls and added, "I admit that I'm a perfectionist, but take a look at what I can do. She was just a pain to work with! It's a wonder it took somebody so long to do away with her."

"It sounds like you were pretty angry with her."

He wiped a bead of sweat from his forehead and said, "That's an understatement!"

"It sounds like a powerful motive for wanting to poison her."

CHAPTER 7

James Dobson had been married to his work for decades. With one failed marriage behind him, he was making the same mistakes with his second wife. Edna complained that he didn't spend enough time with her. His son Tim from his first marriage, was twenty-four now and had a life of his own. James had worked so much that he'd missed out on a major chunk of his son's childhood. Father and son were like strangers. They had nothing in common.

James would never admit that he was just as much of a workaholic as his father, Richard, who had worked long hours as a newspaper reporter. Summer family trips were rare. Quality time was squeezed into a few short days, not a week or two, like a lot of friends James's age. Richard developed a drinking problem. He often drank to calm his nerves after deadlines. He hid bottles in his desk. After years of suffering and loneliness, his wife, Marian, divorced him. She increased her hours working as an R.N. at a doctor's office. She would come home and tell James stories about patients with all kind's of maladies like snake bites, accidental poisonings, cuts and bruises. Sometimes the patients had unusual problems that she could not talk about until her boys were older.

James had a close relationship with his brother David, who was three years older. They were basically in the same boat. They helped their mother out as much as they could after their father moved out. Requests to spend time with Richard fell on deaf ears. He was always on deadline. He was always in a rush. He never had time to settle down and relax. He was not suited for fatherhood. David and James thought he never should have gotten married in the first place. He never took an interest in things they did. Later on, when he left work for a while to be treated for his alcoholism, Richard was filled with regret for not being there for his boys. David and James were that much closer because of it.

After high school, James got a job as an ad man for the *Philadelphia Inquirer*. He inherited his father's workaholic tendencies. A few years later, he got a job at an advertising firm a few blocks away. He worked his way up to become owner of Creative Concepts, and hired the best people in their fields. He was proud of what he had accomplished. But success came at a cost. Not only had he alienated his ex-wife and son, he made Edna angry too. It had gotten to a point where he spent more time at work to avoid problems at home.

After dealing with all the stress that Veronica Talbot handed him on a daily basis, it was a refreshing change not having her around. He did feel bad that she died, of course. He wondered how she had gotten away with not being murdered years ago.

He was hovering over a pile of paperwork when there was a knock at the door. He looked up and saw Detective Logan standing in the doorway. James smiled politely and invited him in.

Logan's eyes were immediately drawn to the window. There was an excellent view of the buildings in the distance. Brightly colored posters of ads and awards and medals hung on the walls. A print of Monet's "Water Lilies" was next to the door. James's eyes darted back to the paperwork that he had to attend to.

Frank apologized for the interruption and promised not to take up much of his time.

James launched into a brief discussion about the advertising business like a true salesman.

"I started here when the company went by a different name," Dobson beamed. "I worked damn hard on my way up the ladder, and I didn't play games like I've seen other people do in that amount of time. I see what goes on. That's why I am where I am today. I've always been careful."

"How so?"

"I'm not ashamed to admit it. I'm a mediator. I don't ruffle feathers. I give the public what they want without offending anyone. That's how I got to be where I am today. I worked many long hours and sacrificed a lot to be the head honcho at Creative Concepts. Twenty-somethings know half of what I know. On the other hand, sixty-four-year-old's don't know digital and electronics as well as they should these days."

"Did Veronica play games?"

"Of course she did. She was ambitious. That's what made her a successful woman. Unfortunately, her ambition killed her."

"Were you threatened by her?"

"Of course not."

"She was an attractive woman. She was close to getting everything she wanted."

"She did all that by resorting to ruthless tactics, that I quite frankly, found rather unsettling. Ben Goldstein left because of her."

"And you gave her his job."

"She was right for the position."

"I heard that she spread rumors about people to get the promotion."

"I knew that."

"And you let her get away with it?"

"She was still the best in her field."

"Others would say the opposite. Nicholas and Dana said she stole people's ideas."

"Creative people often come up with similar ideas. Especially when they're in brainstorming sessions."

"Were you having an affair with her?"

Dobson slammed his fist on the desk and glowered at him. "Now wait just a minute, you're way off base! Everybody assumes that a successful career woman has to sleep her way to the top. I'm a happily married man. Veronica Talbot was a married woman. End of discussion."

"Thank you, Mr. Dobson. You just confirmed something for me."

James looked at him incredulously and said, "What?"

"You don't want your wife to know something. You're covering up."

"Logan, we can replace your girlfriend. Remember that."

"Is that a threat?"

"You can take it any way you want."

"If Penny loses her job, I'll have a talk with your wife. Check-mate."

* * *

Bart Sullivan grew up in a small town near Tulsa, OK. He never at any time felt okay. He knew he was different at an early age, but kept his feelings bottled up inside. He couldn't put his finger on what was wrong with him. The small town he lived in left few options. He was not athletically gifted like his brothers. He was quite the opposite. He was athletically challenged. Like so many other escapees from America's heartland, he yearned for the excitement that city life offered from the other side of a corn field.

His parents were strict disciplinarians. He always did what they wanted until he reached puberty. Then he started questioning life around him and what the town had to offer, which was absolutely nothing! His father, Clay, was a blue collar automobile factory worker. His mother, Bonnie, was a fifth grade school teacher. They meant well, but they did not understand Bart. Clay watched all sports–anything with a moving ball.

Bart always felt like he was adopted. He did not fit in at all with his siblings. His older brothers, Shawn and Jeff, were just as obsessed with sports as their father. They were far from athletically challenged. Girls flocked around them. Bart could be any guy's wing-man. Girls would look past him to his friends.

Little sisters Mary and Rachel had problems of their own. They wanted to look *hot* to get boys interested, but their parents forced them to wear plain clothes, which added to the conflict in the household. Bart's father took a backseat and let Bonnie deal with the girls–except when it came to dating. Clay was very strict about whom the girls went out with. Clay and Bonnie did not want their daughters dating when they were in high school. The girls got upset, because they knew Shawn and Jeff were not only dating, but sleeping around behind their parents' backs. They kept those thoughts to themselves. The Sullivan kids always kept secrets from their parents. They did not know what their dad would do.

Bart knew what was expected of him. He would get a part-time job when he was old enough. When he graduated from high school, he would work to support himself while attending college or trade school. It did not matter what trade it was, as long as he made enough money to eventually support a wife and children. It was a dead-end life. There was no way to escape from the town. Everyone stayed there. They were all equally miserable, working dead-end jobs.

Though his siblings were unhappy in "Dullsville," and though they did not totally get Bart, they privately supported him in his desire to go to the big city. Rachel and Jeff even gave him some money after high school. They wished they could go too. Jeff and Shawn knew that they would never be any better than they were as high school football heroes. They got jobs as car salesmen at a dealership. They got married, had a lot of kids, and went to the same church they had gone to since they were kids. Rachel and Mary found the right guys, upon their parents' approval, got married, and became housewives.

Although Bart's siblings admired him for getting away and doing what he wanted to do, the road to freedom was not so easy.

He waited tables at various restaurants to put himself through art school in Washington, D.C. Later on, he interned for a fashion photographer in Manhattan. Bart's name got around, and he wound up at Creative Concepts. He lost himself in his creativity and shone as a studio photographer. He could be himself, without the judgmental eyes of despicable townspeople. Back home, there were swarms of busybodies and old lady gossips, judgmental religious zealots and hypocrites.

Bart studied the faces of the children in the anti-bullying advertisement that he was photographing. He knew that they were just models, but wondered if any of them were being bullied. After the shoot, he would take the time to study the photos. Usually the eyes revealed the pain on the subject's face, even though they kept their feelings bottled up inside like he had done for so long. The anti-bullying campaign brought back painful memories.

Out of the corner of his eye, he saw Detective Frank Logan enter the room. Logan looked in awe at the studio setup and quietly watched Bart take pictures of the children.

Bart glanced over his shoulder and said, "Oh, hi, Frank. Can I help you?"

"I know you're busy, but I'd like to ask you a few questions about Veronica Talbot."

"That's okay. We were about to take a break anyway."

Bart told the children to go to the break room and get sodas. They darted out of the studio. Bart and Frank sat on stools on the set.

"What can I do for you, Frank?"

"How long have you worked here, Mr. Sullivan?"

"Two years. And you don't have to be so formal. Bart is fine."

"Okay, Bart. Is it true that Veronica Talbot cozied up to James Dobson?"

"It's hard to say with her."

"That would put her in a better place to get the promotion."

"It looks that way."

"So, I guess Nicholas Bradshaw was pretty upset that he didn't get the promotion."

"If it wasn't for his temper, I'm sure Nick would have gotten the job. He tends to lash out at people when he's under stress. He's usually perfectly fine after he's had time to blow off steam. He'd never admit it, but he has the same tendencies as Veronica. It's to be expected. This is a really stressful job. We all just have our own ways of dealing with the pressure."

"I understand that Veronica spread nasty rumors about people here to get ahead. Did she say anything about you?"

"She had no reason to. I'm pretty open about everything. So I don't really have any secrets that she could expose and twist around in the ugly way that she did to everybody else. I had no reason to want the job in the first place. I'm just not that competitive. I do my work and go home. I try not to piss people off. She knew I couldn't beat her. So, as you can see, I have no motive for killing her."

"Everyone has a reason. And everyone has a part of themselves they would rather keep secret."

Bart waved his hands and said, "I have a clean record, Frank. I've never been in jail. You can check my high school year book. I was in the National Honor Society. I'm a hard worker. And I got where I am at twenty-five by producing. I have no reason to screw up my life."

"You seem very confident. Tell me more about office gossip."

* * *

Craig Holloway did not have a clean record. He had been in jail for misdemeanors when he was a teenager. His mother, Donna, had just graduated from high school when she gave birth to him. At nineteen, her husband, Sam, had not been prepared for fatherhood. He was too busy hanging out with his buddies at the local watering hole than to spend time with his wife and baby. At the bar, Sam and his pals chased any skirt that walked by. They never grew up.

Sam got a job as an electrician, while Donna worked at a hair salon.

Craig always knew that he was an inconvenience to his father.

Sometimes Craig felt more like the adult. He swore that he would never be like his father, but it must run in the blood.

Donna knew about Sam's carousing ways. She finally got fed up and tossed his clothes out on the street one afternoon when Craig was thirteen. She worked long hours at the hair salon to make enough money for them to live on. Sam's child-support payments were intermittent. Craig watched and overheard them arguing with each other prior to and post divorce. She had to take Sam to court several times for delinquent child support payments. Alternate weekends with his dad turned into disasters. Sam would be hung over, and Craig had a lot of free time on his hands. Meals consisted of pizza and Chinese food takeouts and deli orders.

Sam eventually married a woman named Tammy, who was just out of college and a "knockout." She was definitely a lot smarter than Sam. Friends warned her not to get mixed up with that jerk, but she didn't listen. Sam didn't change his ways. It didn't take Tammy long to figure out that he was a loser. Their marriage crumbled, and Tammy freed herself from the train wreck of a marriage.

Donna eventually met and fell for Lance Freelander. She was in her mid-thirties when they got married and settled in Philadelphia. He was about six years older and was much worldlier. He was a photojournalist who had a sense of adventure. He had covered war-torn Middle-Eastern countries. His love of adventure rubbed off on Craig. They enjoyed hunting and fishing and camping and rock climbing and anything that got the adrenaline pumping. Every time they went off on an adventure, Donna cringed. She didn't want either of them to get hurt or killed. They just shrugged her concern off with a hearty laugh.

Craig was fifteen when they had a son named Scott. Craig wasn't sure if he'd like being an older brother at his age, but he got used to it. He was a senior in high school when his mother gave birth to another boy, named Eric.

For many years, Craig had unresolved feelings about his father. To him, Sam was just a sperm donor. Fortunately, he didn't have any other children. His second wife dumped him, and he commiserated with his beer buddies at the bar, searching for another beauty queen to settle down with.

Craig looked up to Lance as a real father figure. Over the years, they had formed a tight bond. Unfortunately, Lance was killed covering the Iraqi war. His death was a devastating blow. At that point, Craig had a good job and sometimes lent his mother some money to help her out. He always felt bad that he was so busy when Eric and Scott were little kids. First, he was in high school, then he went away to college, and then he worked at jobs in different cities. He wasn't there to watch them grow up. He tried to carve time out of his busy schedule to do things with them to help keep their minds off the death of their father. Once or twice a year, they went camping or mountain climbing.

Fortunately, their father had been nothing like Sam. Craig had to deal with that demon on his own.

He was making a lot of money now. His love of adventure and his insatiable appetite for beautiful women, which he inherited from his biological father, combined for an unhealthy mixture. He gave women expensive things and drove around in fancy sports cars to impress them. He sweet-talked them into removing their clothes so he could photograph them in nature. Some of his best work was exhibited in galleries in New York City. His images graced the pages of *Vogue* and *Sports Illustrated.*

For nearly a decade, he had endured the wrath of Veronica Talbot. It was no secret that he despised the woman. And she despised him. In an odd, twisted sort of way, they worked out their personal differences and produced thought-provoking ads that helped their clients sell millions of dollars' worth of merchandise. Whatever that truly awful chemical mixture was, it seemed to work.

After learning that the old crow had been poisoned, Craig knew he was probably number one on the suspect list. He stared intently into Logan's eagle-like dark eyes and blew a stream of cigarette smoke toward the ceiling.

"Veronica and I didn't work well together. I guess it's because we are two of a kind. Out for one thing: success. I might not look it, but I'm ambitious. She did things to eliminate the competition, and so did I."

"What did you do?"

"I shot the best ads. People remember them. They get your attention."

"When I searched the Talbots' study, I looked in their rolltop desk and saw some notes Veronica made. Did you know that she was thinking of making major changes around the office once she took over creative control?"

"There were a lot of rumors floating around," Craig admitted.

"Well, several names were on that list. People she was thinking of getting rid of."

"That's not a surprise. Like I said, there were a lot of rumors."

"With Veronica out of the way, who stands to get her job now?"

"It's hard to say. Dobson will choose. He's usually unpredictable. But I've been with Creative Concepts for about ten years. Longer than Bart the Wonder Boy. I doubt old man Dobson would consider him after..." He mixed sugar in his coffee and said, "Nah, Bart's too nice a kid to be dragged in the mud. Veronica was capable of many cruel things. But what she did to him was one of the most vile things I've seen in a long time. Her lust for power nearly destroyed the kid. She treated him like the office whipping boy. He's acting like nothing's wrong, but inside he's a time bomb."

"What happened?"

"She hurled gay slurs at him. Sometimes behind his back. And sometimes right in his face."

Logan shook his head and whistled. "That's not nice."

"Dobson reprimanded her. I'm surprised she got away with all that she got away with." He leaned toward Logan and lowered his voice. "If you ask me, Dobson should've tossed her out on her ass a long time ago."

Logan regarded him curiously. "Why didn't he?"

"Nobody really knows. There have been a lot of rumors why he didn't, that's for sure!"

"How did Bart handle her cruel remarks?"

"Not well," Craig recalled. "She eventually apologized. Bart was a good sport about it, but I don't think he ever really got over it." He rolled his eyes and scoffed. "After that, we all had to go to a sensitivity workshop. It wasted a lot of time. I don't care what he does. I'm no saint myself. I've had a lot of girlfriends. And I look at Bart and his pal, Daryl. They've got a tight bond. Veronica probably was thinking those awful thoughts. She just screamed at other people for other reasons. Everybody was on edge because of her! The stress eventually got to poor Bart, though. I think he was about to go bananas and took a leave of absence."

"That was probably a good idea," Logan agreed.

"This is a highly stressful job, and people burn out a lot. I feel for the kid."

"But you cared more about the job opening."

"Wouldn't anybody want to better themselves?"

Logan nodded and grunted. Then he changed the subject. "I've checked into your background, Mr. Holloway. In high school, you were arrested a couple of times for getting into bar fights."

Craig smirked and said, "Those were wild and crazy days."

"It's a wonder how Veronica had time to work around getting dirt on you people."

"She couldn't get anything on me. I've laid the cards on the table with Dobson. He knew I wasn't an angel when he hired me.

He also knew talent when he saw it and was willing to take a risk. So far, I've made a bundle of dough for the company."

"So, with Nick's job on the chopping block, Bart nearly destroyed, and Veronica dead, it looks like you might have a shot at the job opening."

CHAPTER 8

Michelle Delancey had always been drawn to older men. Maybe it was because they were more experienced and wiser. Maybe she needed the security that older men provided. They did not have to struggle to establish themselves in their careers. They had money and knew what they wanted in life. Maybe older men filled a gap that had been missing in Michelle's life for a very long time.

Her parents were high school sweethearts. After graduation, they got married, and Rob went into the US Marine Corps. Michelle was two-years-old when he went to Vietnam. The only memories she had of him were from snapshots that he had sent to the family. When he came home on leave, Rob tried to jam in a year's worth of experiences into one short month. He was around long enough to fix things around the house and shovel snow during blizzards. When Michelle was a little girl, he was killed on the battlefield. Single mother Noreen worked long hours as a waitress to take care of her children.

Michelle and her older brother, Jake, shared a tight bond. They were both overly protective of their mother. When they were old enough, Michelle and Jake got part-time jobs and helped contribute to the monthly bills. Going to work made them independent. They stayed at home when they went to college, and balanced classes around their work schedules.

A few years later, Noreen married a commercial artist named Everett Weaver. He had two grown sons, Donald and Keith, who were just getting established in their careers. Donald was a mechanical engineer, and Keith was a sportscaster for a radio station. They spent a lot of time at work and with their wives and children. Michelle and Jake always felt like they were at an arm's length behind them, never quite able to catch up.

About twenty years later, Michelle finally caught up to and surpassed her step-brother's careers. She made significantly more money than they did, balancing a career and a family. Her husband, Brendan, was killed in Iraq. Their son, Jeffery, was five when his father was killed. While she was torn up inside, Michelle struggled to be a strong mother for her grieving child. Her family helped her through that difficult time in her life.

Jeffery was in college now and had a girlfriend. Michelle worked long hours and did not have time for a social life. Maybe it was just an excuse. Her family constantly badgered her to meet a nice man and settle down. She just brushed it off or changed the subject.

Michelle's career path eventually led her to Creative Concepts, where she met and fell in love with Tom Daniels, a much older man, who had lost his wife several years earlier. They had an old-fashioned kind of relationship. Maybe he was like the father she never had. They enjoyed talking to each other every day. No one would ever guess that there was such a big age difference. They shared common interests and just loved talking to each other. Their friends and coworkers secretly cheered them on.

Michelle was consulting with a client when she saw Detective Frank Logan enter the room. He smiled brightly at her and said, "Excuse me, Ms. Delancey. I know you're busy, but do you think I could talk to you for a few moments?"

She smiled back at him. "That would be fine, Frank. In about five minutes?" She looked at her client and said, "Is that all right, Mr. Peterson?"

He nodded, and she finished her presentation. She whipped out her cell phone and punched numbers. A minute later, a pencil-thin woman walked hurriedly over to them, clip-board in hand. Michelle instructed her to take notes and said she would be back soon. She escorted Logan to an unoccupied meeting room and pulled up a chair across from him.

"What can I do for you?"

"I just have a few questions about Veronica Talbot."

"I figured you would. What's on your mind?"

"I understand that several people in the office were vying for a plum position, including Veronica."

"You bet she was."

"What happened to the person who had the job before her?"

"Ben Goldstein? He burned out."

"That's a shame."

"He worked himself too hard. He put in long hours. His wife was going to leave him. Or maybe he was just trying to avoid being around her. Whatever it was, he went over the edge. This is an extremely stressful job with a high turn over rate. I don't blame him for quitting." She leaned forward as if she was revealing a secret and said, "But if you ask me, I think Veronica Talbot was one hundred percent the reason why he left. She drove him nuts!"

"It didn't take long for everyone to fight for the job."

"You've got that right. There was a lot of competition to have creative control of the company. We all walked on egg-shells around here for weeks before Mr. Dobson made his decision. We were all fearful that we'd lose our jobs. We didn't know what Veronica would do."

"It sounds like it was an unpleasant time around here."

"That is an understatement!" she exclaimed.

"Why didn't Ben Goldstein just take a leave of absence?"

"Dealing with Veronica Talbot on a daily basis was enough for him."

"What led up to his decision to leave?"

Michelle laughed nervously. "Are you sure you really want to hear all the office gossip?"

"Sure. I'm game."

"It was a matter of creative differences. Dana Phillips got into a nasty argument with Veronica over an ad that Craig was filming."

"What was it about?"

"It was a pro-choice ad. It was a lucrative account. Dana was in charge of the project. They were halfway into it when she suddenly turned a one-eighty! Veronica was livid! She would have killed to do that ad!"

"Did Ms. Phillips say why she changed her mind?"

"She's totally against abortions. That's her choice. She tried to get the clients to film an alternate ad with opposing viewpoints.

When she ran the idea by them, they got so angry that they threatened to sue the company if we didn't give them their money back! It would have been a nasty contract dispute. They threatened to go to our competitors. Mr. Dobson had Dana and Veronica in his office–behind closed doors–for almost two hours! We could hear a lot of screaming from all the way down the hall."

"It sounds like it was pretty nasty."

Michelle bristled and said, "It was enough to make your blood curdle!"

"What happened?"

"Veronica demanded that Dana be fired! But Dana isn't the type of woman that sits and takes a licking. She gave as good as she got."

"So what happened?" he asked eagerly.

"Ben Goldstein walked out! He said something like, "Life is too short.' And he walked out just like that! Dana stormed out of the office in tears! Anna and I tried to console her, but she was furious. Mr. Dobson caved in, and Veronica put her claws into the project. James appeased the clients, and Craig finished the shoot. After all the turmoil, I don't blame Ben for leaving in the least."

Logan nodded in agreement. "Neither do I."

"If you ask me, Dana never should have been in charge of that campaign. She knew going in that she was opposed to it. She should have said something from the beginning."

"That would have been a help."

"But it's a minor detail. She tried to make a compromise, but our clients wouldn't go for it. And it didn't help that Veronica stuck her nose in it. She was an unpleasant person to work with. We've lost half our staff in under a year because of her."

Logan whistled. "You don't say."

"I've probably said too much. Now you're not going to want Penny to work here."

"Don't worry about her. She's a tough bird. She has to deal with me, doesn't she?"

"Really?" Michelle was astounded. "She only says the nicest things about you."

He grinned and said, "That's good to know the next time we have an argument. Which is usually never. Well, anyway, when did you start working here?"

"About ten years ago. If you can believe it, Veronica gave Mr. Dobson glowing recommendations for me. You see, we used to work together in the Big Apple. We trained together at an advertising firm there."

His eyes widened. "Really?"

"She wasn't as nasty back then, if you can believe it. We were actually friends then."

"And then what happened?"

"She turned into the aggressive bitch that everyone despised so much."

"What made her so hostile?"

Michelle shrugged her shoulders. "I'm not really sure. But she did have a Type-A personality. And her drive for success was just born in her. I don't think she could help herself."

"That is a kind way of looking at it."

"I try to be a forgiving person. I know she had problems. Something must have happened between the time we were in New York and the time we got here. But I never pried. She was an extremely private woman."

"Who seemed to make it a hobby of exposing people's secrets."

"That's true."

"I'm sure you two must have talked a lot when you were in New York City. Did you ever share secrets?"

"Maybe once in a while."

"Did she have anything on you?"

Michelle smiled. "I'm a fairly open book, Frank. What you see is what you get. I lost my husband in Iraq and raised our little boy all by myself." She pointed to his picture on the desk and beamed. "Can you believe he's in college now?"

"Time flies," Logan agreed. "I'm sorry about your husband."

"I kept busy so I wouldn't have to think about it."

"What made you decide to come to Philly?"

"I needed a change of scenery," she admitted. "There were too many reminders of Brendan in New York City."

"I understand."

"We needed a fresh start. And Philly has so much to offer. I'm glad I decided to come here."

Frank nodded in agreement.

Her eyes gleamed. "If we hadn't moved here, I wouldn't have met Tom. It's hard not to fall in love when you're working so closely with a man for so many long hours."

Frank nodded his head in agreement. "That's understandable. People don't have much social life in that kind of a situation."

Michelle glanced at her wristwatch. "Is there anything else you want to know, Frank? I need to get back to my client."

"Well, maybe there is one thing. Why didn't you apply for Goldstein's position?"

She thought about it for a moment and said, "It would have been a great job, but a lot of responsibility. I'm happy consulting with clients and making pitches."

"Were you afraid Veronica might spread rumors about you?"

"Of course not. I don't have anything to hide."

"We all have secrets. Maybe she threatened to expose something you did a long time ago. Did she threaten you in any way?"

Her lips quivered. "Don't be ridiculous!"

He took note of her facial twitch. "Is something wrong, Ms. Delancey?"

"No!"

"Have I struck a nerve? What are you hiding?"

"Nothing, I tell you!" she snapped.

"Veronica had something on you, didn't she? If you don't tell me now, I'll find out. What did you do?"

"I had to—I had to get rid of a problem," she said after a long, awkward silence.

"You got an abortion!"

She lowered her voice and said, "I didn't want anyone to know. It was a mistake. I wasn't ready to have a baby at that point in my life. The guy I was with panicked and I never heard from him again. I couldn't tell my parents. They would have—they would have been so disappointed."

She reached across the table for a Kleenex and wiped her tears. She sat in stunned silence for a little while.

"Are you okay?" he asked gently. "I didn't mean to upset you."

"Please don't tell Tom!" she implored. "He wouldn't understand. He'd never marry me if he knew. He can be judgmental."

"Did Veronica know about it?"

"She was the only one who knew. I told her about it when we were actually friends. That was a long time ago."

"Is that why you didn't apply for Goldstein's position?"

"Yes. I didn't want Veronica to tell Tom what I did."

"I understand she was really good at spreading rumors."

"That was one of her strategies for getting ahead. She always had to hold the better card. Well, this time she played the wrong one. Somebody killed her, and I'm not ashamed to say that I'm glad she's gone. She was a miserable witch and hurt too many people."

"Where were you when Veronica was taking her nap?"

"I was in the living room."

"The whole time?"

"Yes–well, I went to check on Dana, but she had already left."

"Did you go into Veronica's study?"

"No."

"Did you see or hear anything?"

"I saw Nick coming out of the room. We waved, but didn't say anything."

"What time was that?"

"About five thirty."

"Before she went to take her nap, how did she seem?"

"She was more cranky than usual," Michelle recalled. "I think she had a little too much to drink. She seemed really animated. She was flitting about like mad. And then, a little bit later, she seemed to slow down a bit. When she started to get tired."

"Was she feeling okay?"

"Well, she was perspiring a lot. And she said she felt chilled. At the time, we thought it was kind of strange."

"Anything else?"

"She was complaining that the food didn't taste right. We heard her chewing out the caterers. The poor women. We all thought the food tasted great. Tom kept stuffing his face with crab puffs. I told him that he should watch it, or he'd bloat up like a pig!"

"Thank you, Ms. Delaney. I'd better let you get back to your client. I'm sorry that I upset you."

* * *

Tom Daniels found it difficult to get back into the dating scene, despite the urging of his children. It had been about six years since he lost the love of his life. Julia died of a heart attack, three short months before their forty-fifth anniversary. He had spent many lonely nights after work at the bar around the corner. Mondays were fried chicken night. On Tuesdays, fish and chips. On Wednesdays, it was steak night. The other nights it was either hamburgers or cheese-steaks. He spent as little time at home as possible. During the day, a neighbor came in to feed the cat. He would get back about ten o'clock and read a book on his favorite easy chair, with the TV blaring in the background to keep him company.

Working long hours saved his life. Consulting with clients and coworkers on a daily basis helped him stay sane. Veronica Talbot was the exception, of course. He tried to steer clear of her if it was humanly possible but had to on occasion work with her. She sucked all the joy out of life. Sometimes he looked at Charles and wondered why in hell he had stayed with her all these years. Didn't he know that she had demasculinized him? He seemed to be a gutless man–too scared to stand up to her.

For six long years, Tom stuck to a routine that had become a pattern. That all changed when he and Michelle Delancey started working together at the firm. Though their ages were far apart, they had a lot in common. They both had lost their spouses. In time, they began eating out together. They enjoyed going to plays and concerts. It was as if they had always been together. The age difference didn't seem to matter.

Tom was in the middle of casting the right actor for a voice-over for a radio ad. He had spent the morning listening to a stack of actor demos and narrowed the list down to five really good male voices. They had used each of them before, so it would probably not be too hard to make a decision. When he narrowed it down to three, he would ask Michelle for her opinion. Later on, he would make recommendations to his client, who would listen and make the final decision.

Now all he had to do was select the right female voice. He had just started listening to some demos when there was a knock at the door. He looked up to see Detective Logan standing in the doorway. He pushed stop and said, "Oh, hello, Frank. What can I do for you?"

"I just have a few questions to ask about Veronica Talbot, if you don't mind. I know you're busy, so I'll make it quick."

Tom waved him in, and Logan sat down. He made a cursory look at the stacks of CDs and the notepad on Tom's desk. His eyes were drawn to the framed photos of his late wife. There were other pictures of his children and grandchildren. He glanced at the trash can by the door. It was overstuffed with take-out containers and empty Chinese food cartons. Awards hung on the wall. Prints from old magazine illustrations hung on the opposite walls.

Tom grinned and said, "What's on your mind?"

"Your coworkers have told me what a miserable woman Veronica was. Do you know why someone would want to kill her?"

"She was a bitch," Tom answered coolly. "That's what they say. I've always done my job and never bothered anyone. That's the way I get ahead. I don't suck up. I don't make waves. I know people who suck up–including Michelle. That's her one bad trait. Please don't tell her I said that. I keep telling her Dobson likes me because I don't suck up. I'm more like a referee. I'm neutral like Switzerland." He laughed nervously.

"James Dobson said the same thing."

"We are alike in many ways. I think he noticed that in me. I knew I didn't have to suck up to get on his good side. I'm pleasant and don't get involved in office politics. I believe hard workers are rewarded in the end. It may be a naive philosophy, but that's what my father always told me when I was little. Dobson and I are from a fading generation, I suppose. Now everybody expects things to be handed to them, if you know what I mean."

"Did Veronica say anything negative about you?"

"Yeah, she said a lot. But I didn't let it get to me, like Bart. Poor guy. He was really shaken up. He hasn't acted right since then."

"Oh, yeah, that's right. He had a break-down, right?"

"It was on account of something nasty she said about him."

"What did she say?"

"It was when she was having one of her tirades. She made a gay slur and there was a lot of tension around here for weeks. She eventually apologized to him, and then the Dragon Lady went back into her lair. He just stood there and took it, didn't try to stick up for himself. I wish he had just told her off. I would've respected him more if he had."

"What did she say about you?"

"It isn't important."

"It might be. What did she have against you?"

Tom rolled his eyes and grunted. "She basically said that I'm old school, if you catch my drift. Dozens of talented twenty-somethings fresh out of art and design colleges come through these doors every year. I'm not so good with the modern stuff. And she thought that I wasn't as sharp as I used to be when I'm dealing with clients who are up on all the technological wonders!"

"I imagine you must have been pretty angry with her."

"I've dealt with people like her for decades, Frank. I've seen them come and go. They eventually get what's coming to them in one way or the other."

"Or maybe a disgruntled coworker decides to poison them," Logan observed.

Tom glared at him. "I hated her with a passion, but I would never have done a thing like that. That is what you're implying, right?"

"I'm just trying to figure out what happened, Mr. Daniels."

"Well, good luck, Frank. A lot of people hated her."

"Did you feel threatened that she was going to take creative control of the company?"

"Well, we were all on edge. We didn't know what that crazy bitch was going to do when she took over." He adjusted his glasses and grunted. "There's not much she could do to me. I did my work and I ignored her. With all her talk, it seems funny nobody ever got dirt on her."

"So true," Logan agreed.

"If you ask me, Dobson should've fired her years ago."

"I wonder why he didn't."

Tom leaned forward. There was a glint in his eyes. "Believe me, there's been a lot of talk around the office about that! We think she had something on him."

"You don't say."

"At the party, Dana blurted out that the Dragon Lady was sleeping with him! And his wife got really upset."

"I need facts, not just rumors, Mr. Daniels. Can you think of anything else?"

Tom was quiet a moment and then shook his head.

"I looked in the roll-top desk in her study, and guess what I found?"

Tom pretended not to know, but it didn't go over too well. "What?"

Logan told him about Veronica's chopping-block list. "Your name was on it."

"I'm not surprised. She probably thought I was slowing things down because I'm technology challenged."

"If I were you, I'd be pretty upset about it."

"As I said, I'm not surprised."

"One last thing. Where were you during the half an hour when she was napping in her study?"

"I was in the living room. At first, I was listening to her argument with Dana. We were all listening from the hall. Then, I went outside to look for Michelle. After that I went downstairs to get a drink."

"Thank you, Mr. Daniels," Logan said as he got up and left the room.

CHAPTER 9

Anna McWilliams had not had a man in her life for quite some time. She spent more time at work than at her apartment. The only social interaction she had lately was with coworkers. There were not too many men to choose from at work. Most of them were old and married. Bart was gay. Craig went from woman to woman without a thought. Nick didn't even know she existed.

Her parents, Greg and Catherine, had been overprotective of their daughters. They would not let them watch the filth on TV or at the movies. Greg was tyrannical about the boys they dated. Danielle, Maggie, and Anna had to obey them or else.

At sixteen, Anna had yearned to pull free of the prison she lived in and explore the world. She craved excitement and could not wait until she could get out and be on her own. But she played nice. She was the good girl. She always tried to please her parents. She knew full well what would happen if she disobeyed her father. She had seen what he did to her sisters. He was abusive. Everyone up and down the street must have heard their family squabbles. She wondered why no one had ever offered to help her.

Anna got a scholarship and studied art in Philadelphia. She flourished in her creativity. City life offered her freedom from the tormenting thoughts of the past. The pain never quite went away, though.

She maintained a cool distance from her father. He was no longer a part of her life. She only saw him at weddings and funerals. She did not want anything from him.

She pitied her mother. All the years of mental abuse had taken a toll on her. Catherine finally had the courage to leave her husband. Over the last decade, her drinking had gotten so out of control, Catherine soon hit rock bottom. After her fifth rehab attempt, she finally picked up the pieces of her broken life. She moved into a halfway house, got a part-time job in a department store, and worked one day at a time to recovery. She lived pay-check to pay-check, was careless with her finances, and could not balance her check-book. Anna lent her money to help her out whenever she could.

Anna tried really hard to erase these painful memories from her mind. She lost herself in her work. Any distraction was helpful.

At the moment, the death of Veronica Talbot was all the distraction she needed. She was designing an advertisement for a restaurant on Broad Street when she saw someone approaching out of the corner of her eye. She looked up to see Frank Logan.

She smiled wryly at him. "What can I do for you, Detective Logan?"

"I just needed to ask you a few questions about the afternoon Veronica Talbot died. If you don't mind. I can see that you're pretty busy."

"Feel free to ask anything you want. I needed a break anyway."

He sat on a swivel chair next to her desk and glanced at family pictures hanging on the walls. One showed Anna with an older woman–her mother, he figured. Next to it, there was a snapshot of Anna clowning around with two other girls. He figured they were her sisters. Pictures of babies and toddlers were in the mix. There was a portrait of a happy, smiling baby with the name "Lily" scrawled in red ink. There were Sears portraits of Anna's nieces and nephews and their parents. Anna was in a lot of the photographs with the little kids. He noticed that there were no pictures of Anna's father. There were also no pictures of Anna with a boyfriend. He looked at how things were neatly stored in the cubicle's cubbyholes. She was the kind of person that had a place for everything.

She grinned and pointed to the images of her oldest nephews and nieces horsing around in the snow. "Can you believe they're in college now?"

"It looks like they're having a good time."

She beamed and said, "They have so much fun that they tire their parents out."

"I can just imagine." He studied the image of a coffee pot on the laptop screen.

"I'm working on an ad for a coffee house. It's going to be on posters and buses all over the city."

"It must be exciting seeing your artwork all over the place."

"It's a lot of fun. But it can be exasperating, trying to get it done on time and making sure to hone in on all the fine details. Well, anyway. What do you need to know?"

"It looks like somebody poisoned Veronica."

Anna gasped and clutched her face. "Oh my God! Who would do such a horrible thing?"

"That's what I'm trying to find out. What time did you arrive at the Talbots' house the day of the party?"

"A little after three. But I don't see what's so important about that."

"I have my reasons."

"Oh, I get it. You're trying to figure out when the killer slipped the poison in her drink."

"Well, it could have been in something she ate. Samples of everything she had to eat and drink a few hours before she died were taken to the lab. We should find out soon enough how the poison was administered."

"It sounds so technical."

"It's a fascinating field, I must say."

"Scientific stuff goes over my head," she admitted.

Logan smiled. "To tell you the truth, it goes over my head too. I have to trust that the lab techs know what they're looking at. Well, anyway, did you notice Veronica acting oddly before she went to take her nap?"

Anna told him about the same odd symptoms that her colleagues had told him about earlier.

"Where were you about an hour or so before Veronica Talbot took her nap?"

"I was having a drink in the living room. I have a hard time concentrating on what people are saying at parties. There's too much noise. So I just sat there and everybody came to me."

"Did you see or hear anything out of the ordinary?"

Anna shrugged her shoulders and shook her head. "Everybody was having a good time. A lot of the guys decided to go downstairs to have drinks at the bar. If you ask me, they were just trying to get away from Veronica."

"I understand that she was hard to get along with."

"That is an understatement!" exclaimed Anna. "After a while I got bored just sitting there trying to think of meaningful small talk, so I wandered around for a little while."

"Where did you go?"

"I explored the rooms. I know I shouldn't have done it, but I think we were all curious. And then I looked around outside. The grounds are just gorgeous! If I had had time, I would have taken a walk along the pond. The trees are so beautiful this time of year."

"I know."

"When I went back inside, James was gathering everybody together to toast Veronica's success. That's when I accidently bumped into her. She chewed me out for spilling her Bloody Mary. It got all over her dress. I went to get something to clean it up, and when I came back in, she was arguing with Dana. And then, all of a sudden, Veronica said she was tired and was going to take a nap. And then she pulled Dana into the study with her."

"How long did you know Veronica?"

"For about five years. That's how long I've been working here."

"I've heard a lot of negative comments about her from everybody here."

"Well, there are a lot of people around here who couldn't stand her."

"Was Ms. Talbot your supervisor?"

"Yes. I worked closely with her. I know she had a temper and she often chewed me out, but I just took it."

"Why did you continue to work under those conditions?"

Anna adjusted her glasses and said, "To be honest, I had no choice. I had a rough time getting started. I was a late bloomer, you might say. I got the job here a couple of years after college. Mr. Dobson has been very good to me. Without him, I would still be waiting tables with an art degree behind me. For a while I worked at a radio station. But it didn't last long. I wasn't that good at it."

"Can you remember anything at all about the events leading to her death?"

"She was wired, that's for sure. She wasn't on drugs or anything...not till the unfortunate incident. The advertising industry is extremely stressful. Some people need pills to help get them through it. When she got nervous, she tended to get wired. She was in and out all afternoon, flitting about like a social butterfly. She was talking a lot. She had too much to drink. I knocked into her and spilled my drink on her dress. She was furious and yelled at me. That's when Dana defended me. They had words, as you probably know. You could tell something was going on between them. But everyone was angry with her. I spent most of the time in the corner trying to avoid her. She really scared me sometimes."

"Did you apply for the promotion?"

"No."

"Why not?"

"I wasn't in a position to do that." Her voice was barely audible. "I made a mistake. A huge mistake."

"What happened?"

"It was a lucrative account that I lost for them. I didn't check my copy before it went to print. I misspelled the company's name!" She hung her head and looked down. "It was just awful. I can't blame them for being upset. It's a wonder I didn't get fired right then and there. A few months before, I caused another mistake. I neglected to type the contact information in the ad. And no one noticed it. I cost the company a long time client. Veronica could have had my head on a platter, but Mr. Dobson gave me another chance. I've tried to stay clean and work hard, but this time–I knew I blew it big time."

"You weren't the only one who didn't catch the error," Frank pointed out. "Everybody makes mistakes. You shouldn't blame yourself."

"That's what my shrink tells me. I can't blow this job–not now. It's taken me years to get to this level. By the time I got the job here, women my age were above me, and I had to work that much harder."

"So you didn't apply for the job."

"No, but I agreed to help Veronica get it. She promised to put in a good word to Mr. Dobson. She said she would butter him up about the mistake I made. That never happened, of course. I found out later that Veronica tried to get me fired. But Mr. Dobson kept me on. He told me he saw talent in my work and that I was an asset to the company. He said he made mistakes earlier in his career too."

"That was nice of him."

"He's so kind and understanding."

"Were you angry with Veronica when you found out that she tried to get you fired?"

"I was livid!" Her voice shook.

"Maybe you were so angry with her that you poisoned her."

She recoiled in horror. "I could never do something like that!"

"Did you have skeletons in your closet that she could threaten you with?"

Anna looked at the floor to avoid his penetrating gaze.

"I take that to mean that you do have something you are hiding. What happened?"

She wiped away tears. "Mr. Dobson saved my life. Before I came here, I scrubbed floors and waited tables. I did it all. I've come too far to end up like I was...scared, vulnerable, and desperate. I was really lousy at everything I tried to do, until I came here. Without Veronica, I'd be nowhere. I learned everything about the business from her. I just learned to put up with her...warts and all."

"I've heard that you were all worried about what she would do when she took over creative control of the company."

"We were on edge for weeks. It was an unpleasant time."

Anna did not look at all surprised when he told her about the list he found in the roll-top desk in Veronica's study.

"It's as I suspected," she said.

"Maybe you were so upset that she wanted to fire you that you decided to poison her," Logan suggested.

"I swear, I didn't do it! Maybe–maybe she would've done me a favor if she had fired me. I could've just started over again. I would've just moved onto a job with a friendlier work atmosphere."

"Well, you don't have to worry about it with her out of the way."

She breathed a sigh of relief and said, "Thankfully not."

"If you can think of anything else about the afternoon of the party, please give me a call." He slipped her his business card and stood up. He thanked her and headed down the hall.

She stared at the image on the laptop screen, concentrating hard on correctly typing the coffeehouse's name.

CHAPTER 10

It was the noon rush at Pinelli's Bistro in the neighboring town of Angola. The head chef did not have time to talk to a detective. She looked coldly into his dark beady eyes and snarled, "We carefully screen all of our caterers. Random drug tests always come out clean. There is no way that Svetlana and Dora could have done what you are accusing them of."

"We're just trying to explore all possibilities, ma'am," Detective Joe Flosky assured her.

"Well, you're barking up the wrong tree! I run a clean operation here! I have a lot of happy customers. We run a professional catering service."

"Maybe I could talk to them?"

"We're busy!" she snapped. "Come back in an hour or two."

"A young girl lost her mother," Flosky reminded her. "Surely, they can take a couple of minutes to talk to me."

"Fine, fine. You've got five minutes."

"I'll need to talk to them separately."

"Fine."

"I really appreciate this, ma'am. I promise I won't take up much of their time."

The chef went out, and he glanced at the various awards and framed newspaper writeups that boasted of the restaurant's success. He heard clanking metal from the kitchen and people talking over each other.

A minute later, a petite brunette stood in the doorway. Her eyes were wide with apprehension. She looked at Flosky and said, "You wanted to see me, sir?"

"Yes. Yes."

She sat at the desk and stared at him in disbelief. "What can I do for you?"

"You catered the party at the Talbots' home last week, right?"

She regarded him suspiciously. "Yes, what do you want to know? Dora and I didn't have anything to do with what happened."

"I believe you, but I'm just trying to get some information. We think that the poison was either put in her food or her drink at some point during the party. I was wondering if you saw anything suspicious. Did you see anybody near the food trays or the drinks?"

She shook her head emphatically. "The hors d'oeuvre trays never left our hands until they were empty. Then–then we put them back in the kitchen."

"What about the drinks?"

"We didn't serve the drinks. The bartender did."

"Did you see Veronica Talbot leave her glass unattended at any time during the party?"

"I was so busy, I wasn't paying attention. She was all over the place. Talking to the guests and yelling at us to get more hors d'oeuvres." She leaned forward and said, "Off the record–she wasn't very nice to work for."

Flosky rolled his eyes and huffed. "I've heard horror stories about her. What else can you remember?"

"She got into an argument with a woman. They went into the study. We were all listening to them."

"Could you hear what they were saying?"

"From the kitchen, I heard something about somebody's guy being stolen."

Flosky's eyebrows arched. "So it was a love triangle?"

"It sounded something like that."

"Do you remember anything else?"

"She chewed us out about how bad the crab puffs and shrimp tasted. We assured her that there was nothing wrong with the food, but she insisted that we were lying! She threatened to have a talk with our manager. I was shaking by the time she got through with us."

"Did you serve any other kinds of hors d'oeuvres?"

"Yeah. The usual. Swedish meatballs with toothpicks. Cheese puffs, stuffed mushrooms, and ham. Shrimp. Crackers and dip."

"Did anybody else think the food tasted bad?"

She shook her head.

"Did anybody act suspicious during the party?"

"I was too busy to notice much of anything...except...well, the guy that came with the blonde woman. He's really good-looking." She lowered her head and said, "It isn't my place to say. Sorry."

"That's fine."

"Mrs. Talbot seemed kind of jittery all day. I guess she was nervous. I overheard people say that she was always like that."

"Anything else?"

She shook her head.

"If you remember anything, give me a call at the station."

She got up and headed out. Dora came in next. She was of medium build and was plump around the thighs. She had short strawberry-blonde hair and freckles. She smiled widely at him and sat down.

"What can I do for you? I'm really busy right now."

He told her the nature of his visit and asked her similar questions. She remembered a lot more than Svetlana.

"Ms. Talbot needed a chill pill." She lowered her voice. "She was a total bitch! I hate working for people like her. They aren't satisfied with nothin' and they always take it out on the help. We don't make much money for the long hours we put in at these things. It's just a few extra bucks to help put food on the table, if you know what I mean."

Joe nodded his agreement. "It must be rough."

"My feet are really sore when I get home, that's for sure."

"Do you think it's possible that somebody could have slipped something into her food or drink sometime during the party?"

"We were always carrying the trays, so it would have been impossible for that to have happened."

"I understand that the bartender handled the drinks."

"Right. They had to go downstairs for more variety, if you know what I mean."

"Did either of you take a break at any time during the party?"

"Yeah–but not at the same time. I took a smoke break. Then Svetlana had to sit down a little while later."

"Did you see any of the guests go into the kitchen?"

"Yeah." She was lost in thought. "But it was just curiosity. They were looking around the house."

"Who was it?"

"That wild-looking guy and his girlfriend. And then I saw that redheaded woman go take a look. She's really well put together!"

"Anybody else?"

"Those gay guys stuck their heads in. I think I heard something about them wanting to renovate their kitchen. The African American guy was really excited about the antiques around the place. It's a beautiful home. Ms. Talbot had good taste!"

"Anything else?"

"Well, Ms. Talbot tore into us about how bad the crab puffs and shrimp tasted. We tried them ourselves, and there wasn't anything wrong with them. We asked around. The guests couldn't get enough of them. Maybe it was just her."

"Maybe you're right," agreed Flosky. "It could have been a side effect of the poison."

"Then it wasn't our fault?"

"I don't think so. When did she yell at you about the food?"

Dora closed her eyes, deep in thought. "Around four o'clock or so. I'm not sure. I'm sorry, I don't seem to be of much help."

His eyes lit up. "Oh, no. You've been a lot of help."

"It doesn't really seem like I said much."

"We usually start out with the tiniest puzzle pieces and end up cracking the case."

"Well, I've got your number. Can I call if I remember anything?"

He smiled and said, "Please do."

"Well, I really gotta get back in there before Mrs. Pinelli breathes fire down my neck."

He followed her out and watched her dash into the kitchen. Did she really just ask permission to call him? It sounded more like a personal call than one relating to the case.

* * *

Logan went to track down the other guests from the party. Mindy Sawyer had just met Veronica Talbot that afternoon. She never would have stepped foot in a house like that if Craig Holloway hadn't invited her to go with him. They had been seeing each other for less than a month. It didn't take long for their relationship to go south.

"I caught him checking out another woman," she told Logan. "What a jerk!"

"Some guys are like that, I'm sorry to say."

"Well, I knew it wouldn't last long anyway. I just had that feeling about him. He promised to take pictures of me at the park and make me look really glamorous–told me that I'd be in a magazine. I bet he says it to all the girls."

"He probably does," agreed Logan. "Did you see or hear anything unusual at the party?"

"I was kind of nervous. Being in that big house! Meeting all the people he worked with. Just being around Mrs. Talbot is enough to make your skin crawl! I could definitely sense a cold vibe around the place. Real chilly!"

"Did you notice if Mrs. Talbot ever set down her drink for a minute or two? Or did she set her food plate down anywhere?"

Mindy couldn't remember. There had been too much confusion, especially when everybody raced out into the hall to listen to Mrs. Talbot arguing with that other woman.

A few minutes later, Logan realized the interview wasn't going anywhere and thanked her for taking time out to talk to him.

* * *

Logan went to the Dobson's house in Bala Cynwyd and talked to James's wife, Edna. He had a little better luck with her. At least she knew all of her husband's colleagues. She told Frank that as soon as they arrived at the Talbots' home, she admired all of the beautiful antiques and congratulated Veronica on spotting just the right furnishings for that time period. For many long years, she had heard horror stories about that awful woman. James would come home and lament about the Dragon Lady. She didn't believe that anybody would want to sleep with that despicable woman. But the office rumors were so believable, she wasn't so sure. James spent long hours at work. Was it possible that he was sleeping with the enemy?

"Do you think it's true that James was having an affair with Veronica Talbot?" asked Logan.

Edna's face was emotionless. She stared back at him with just as much intensity and said, "Of course not. He would never hurt me that way."

"Do you know anyone she worked with that would have had reason to poison her?"

She laughed, much to Logan's surprise. "They all despised the woman."

"Including your husband."

"James was under a lot of stress because of her."

"Did you see or hear anything suspicious the afternoon of the party?"

"I usually feel so uncomfortable at social functions that I tend to sit by myself. I watched people come and go all afternoon."

"Did Veronica act differently that day?"

"She seemed more flustered. She flitted about like a flea. And then...she acted erratic."

"What do you mean?"

"Her face was flushed and she was sweating."

"What time was that?"

"Oh...about a couple of hours before Anna bumped into her. The poor girl! Veronica wasn't very gracious. She chewed her out for a simple mistake. And right after that, Veronica and Dana went into the study and screamed their lungs out at each other! Before that, Veronica seemed really tired all of a sudden. It just came on her out of the blue! She didn't look good at all. I thought she was drunk or something."

"Did she ever leave her drinks or food unattended?"

"I was sitting in the corner and saw her go into the hall a few times. I couldn't see her from my point of view–but sometimes she did put her plate down when somebody came in the living room. She got so excited that she threw her arms around people when they came in."

"That wouldn't have been long enough for somebody to slip something in her food or drink," Logan noted.

"Perhaps not," Edna agreed.

"Can you think of anything else?"

"Not really. But if I think of anything, I'll give you a call."

Logan thanked her and headed back to his car.

* * *

Daryl Forster's suite was on the eleventh floor with an excellent view of the Delaware River. Priceless marble statues of Greek soldiers holding swords and shields lined the expansive entryway. Logan glanced at gigantic oil paintings on opposite walls as he followed Daryl into the living room.

The living room was bright and airy with more expensive-looking oil paintings hung on beige walls. A portrait of Bart and Daryl was on the end table. They were all dressed up for a wedding or something. Logan looked at the window and whistled. He went over and admired the view.

"It's beautiful!" he cried.

"It's hazy today. On a clear day, you can see New Jersey."

Logan returned and sat on a beige leather chair. It was overstuffed and really comfortable. Daryl sat across from him.

"Coffee?" he asked the detective.

Logan nodded his approval. Daryl slipped into the kitchen for a couple minutes and returned holding a mug. He handed it to the detective and sat back down.

"What can you tell me about the events the day that Veronica Talbot passed away?"

"She berated Bart, as usual. I tell him to quit all the time. No job is worth dealing with somebody as miserable as that woman. I'm fortunate enough not to have had to deal with her on a daily basis. I barely knew her. I'm usually in four different cities in one week."

"It sounds like being a model keeps you really busy," Logan said.

Daryl drew a deep breath and laughed. "I'm busier than busy. And Bart doesn't like it one bit. I can't really blame him. I get to go out and do all these exciting things and he's stuck working long hours in a stressful job with a woman like her!"

"It sounds like a really good reason to want to bump her off."

"You saying I did it?" Daryl asked in alarm. "I barely knew the woman!"

"Well, it's just a thought. Maybe you did it to protect Bart. Or maybe he did it because he couldn't take it any longer."

"Man, you got it all wrong!" Daryl protested. "You don't know Bart like I do. He wouldn't hurt a flea. He's sweet and gentle. And I don't got time to mess around with people like her! We just got to the party. And if you ask me, she was acting strange the whole time we were there. We just thought she was nervous–but after she died, I got to thinking and it does seem like she wasn't...right."

"How do you mean?"

"Well, she said her drink didn't taste right."

"Really? When was that?"

"About an hour or so before the big fight. And she was complaining that her food didn't taste right. She was bawling out the poor ladies with the trays. And she was asking everybody if their drinks tasted all right, and we said they did. And then she told Charles to say something to the bartender."

"How was she acting when you got there?"

"She seemed okay to start with, but then she started acting wired."

"Maybe that's because one of you slipped something in her food or drink."

Daryl looked wild-eyed at him. "I can't believe you think that we are capable of such a horrendous thing!"

"I'm sorry if it sounded like I was accusing you of something. I'm just trying to piece it together."

"I can't believe you could've thought I would do such a thing like that! Maybe you're at a dead end and are just accusing people like the police do when they don't know what to do next."

Logan was afraid to admit that Daryl was right. He just stared blankly at him until he finished ranting.

Logan got to his feet and said, "I'm sorry that I upset you. If you remember anything else, just give me a call."

"That's no way to treat people!" he heard Daryl shout in the background. "You need to work on your people skills, man!"

* * *

Ben Goldstein's three week vacation on Saint Croix did wonders for him. His complexion was a golden brown. He was totally relaxed now. He was happy that he didn't have to go to that cess-pool of an office anymore. His wife noticed a sense of joy that had come back into his life. He actually smiled now.

Except when Detective Logan showed up to ask him about Veronica.

He cringed at the mere mention of the Dragon Lady's name. The thought of Veronica Talbot sent chills down his spine. When Logan told him what happened, he shook his head in disbelief. He couldn't believe that it hadn't happened a long time ago. He was glad that he hadn't been in the country at the time. He very well could have been a suspect.

He provided Logan with a fountain of information. Goldstein didn't really tell Logan anything he didn't already know, but he volunteered to call him if he could think of anything else. Logan thanked him and was on his way.

* * *

Pete Vogel acted cagey with Logan. He had been tending bars at many dives for close to thirty years. He smelled trouble the moment the detective sat at the bar. He knew that he would have to answer a lot of questions after what had happened to Ms. Talbot. His answers were vague, but Logan wasn't leaving until he got answers.

"I was behind the bar most of the time," he told the detective.

"But you did go out for a smoke break at some point, right?"

"Yeah."

"So anybody could have gone behind the bar and slipped something into one of the ingredients used to make the Bloody Mary. Was anybody there when you left?"

"Yeah. The old dude."

"Which old dude?"

"Kind of heavyset. Thinning red hair."

"Tom Daniels?"

"Yeah…that's right. I went out front and saw that gay guy and then the old dude came up from the bar. The little shrimpy guy said his name. The old dude was looking for his girlfriend. She's a knockout."

Logan reached in his jacket pocket and held a picture of Michelle Delancey in front of him. He pointed and asked, "Was it this woman?"

Vogel nodded his head and grunted. "Yeah, her. Well anyway, the blond kid went back inside. And then I went back to the bar."

"How long were you gone?"

"About ten–fifteen minutes."

"Was anybody at the bar when you got back?"

"Not till later. Then everybody went to toast the lady of the house. I heard muffled voices. Couldn't make out what they were saying, though."

"Did you notice any changes behind the bar when you came back from your break?"

He scratched his rough crew cut and said, "Well…it seemed like one of the bottles of scotch didn't have as much in it as it did before I left."

Logan's eyes widened. "Really?"

"Well, it could've just been my imagination, but doing this as long as I have, I really get to notice these things. Especially if there's nobody to take over for me."

"Gotcha."

"The old man seemed like an honest guy when I left him there by himself."

"Did you see anybody tampering with Ms. Talbot's drink during the party?"

"Not really. She didn't come down much. It was mostly just the guys. They can't stand her. Just being around her for a few minutes, I can see why. She was a nasty woman!"

"If you remember anything else, please let me know."

Pete nodded his head and swabbed the counter with a bar towel.

* * *

Back at the Townsend Police Department, Logan and Flosky compared notes. The only thing that Joe seemed to get out of his interviews was how well he got along with Dora. She seemed really into him. Maybe he would ask her out. Maybe they could go to Barney's on Saturday night.

Logan was more interested in finding out what the women had to say–not about Flosky's troubled love life.

"What about the bartender?" Joe asked.

"He wasn't really a fountain of information."

"Do you blame him? He doesn't want to be blamed for anything."

"I did find out one important tidbit. It turns out that Tom Daniels was alone at the bar when Pete Vogel went on his smoke break."

"Maybe he put something in one of the vodka bottles?"

"If that was the case, whoever had vodka would have been poisoned too. Damn, I wish I had remembered to ask all the guests what they were drinking." He jotted a note to check later.

"You can't think of everything, Frank."

"Well, Tom was alone for quite some time. Maybe he went behind the bar and tampered with one of the Bloody Mary ingredients. The bartender said he brought his own supplies. Maybe we'd better collect samples from the stash that he had at the party."

"That's a good idea."

"I hope we can find out something when the test results come back."

A few minutes later, they were poring over photos that Veronica's coworkers had taken at the party. Logan had made copies from each person's smart-phone and digital camera images and labeled them with the photographer's name. Lieutenant Winters came over to give them a hand.

Logan glanced across at Flosky. "See anything?"

Flosky grunted. "No. How about you?"

"Not a thing."

"This is a waste of time," Harry Winters groused. "Do you really expect to find anything this way?"

"You never know," Logan said.

"Let's take another look at the video taken with Nicholas Bradshaw's digital camera," Flosky suggested.

They hunkered around the laptop and watched the unedited footage of the party.

"At least we can see what went on before Penny and I got there," Logan said.

"It's pretty much like they said," Flosky noted. "Can you feel the tension?"

"Veronica Talbot was as cold as ice!" Winters exclaimed.

"Shh, listen!" Logan said. "Pay close attention to what Veronica does with her plate and glass."

Sometimes the footage was shaky. They saw Veronica wander in and out of the room. Her voice could be heard, greeting guests from the foyer. Unfortunately, he could not see around the double doors from that angle to see if she put down her plate and glass long enough to shake their hands.

They watched the camera pan to Edna Dobson and Anna McWilliams. The camera panned over to Veronica and James. They looked up and smiled. They continued looking at images that Nicholas shot of all the rooms. It stopped when he went downstairs to have a drink.

Logan picked up Tricia's phone and they looked at everything that she recorded with it. Footage shifted to the time James made the toast. The image was shaky, but they could see everyone in the room.

Logan looked at the glass of Bloody Mary in her left hand. He grumbled and shook his head in disbelief. "This isn't getting us anywhere!"

"Just be patient," Winters advised. "We'll see something."

"Are you sure about that? I say it's a big waste of time." Logan got up and walked over to the coffee machine. He poured a cup and sat back down. "What are we missing?"

Joe shrugged his shoulders. "I don't know. Let's keep watching."

"I've been through it a couple of times and it's the same old thing," Logan said. "The men were downstairs most of the time. Nicholas's footage pretty much ended when he went down there. He took a few shots at the bar and then started drinking. About an hour later, he went upstairs, and we see James giving the toast to Veronica. Do you notice anything different?"

Joe Flosky shook his head. Harry Winters wasn't sure either.

"It was right about here that Anna accidentally bumped into Veronica, and she chewed her out."

They rewound the footage about a half a dozen times. There was no magician's switch of the hand tricks. They saw Dana go up and start yelling at Veronica. They saw Anna rush out to get something to clean Veronica's dress. They watched Veronica pull Dana out of the room. Muffled shouting could be heard in the background. Nicholas turned the camera around, and Anna's face was a bright red color as she stood in the doorway holding a rag. Her eyes were tearing up.

In the video, Bart patted her shoulder and said, "Don't worry, Anna. You know how she is."

"She's a bully!" Anna cried.

"It'll blow over," James assured her. He went back and sat next to his wife.

Bart looked into the camera and laughed to lighten the mood. "It's just another fun time at an office party!"

They watched everyone talking over each other about what just happened. The footage stopped a few minutes before Frank and Penny arrived.

"It's too bad Nicholas stopped filming then," Logan muttered.

"I didn't see a thing," Flosky said.

"There's got to be something we're overlooking."

Harry Winters grunted. "Good luck finding that out, pal. I think you should face facts. Without enough solid evidence to go on, you're looking at a cold case here."

Logan was afraid to admit that Harry was right. He stared at the photos spread across the desk and groaned.

"I just hate to think that somebody might get away with murder."

"I know," agreed Flosky. "You'll find something, Frank. You always do."

* * *

Frank pecked Penny on the lips after a long day of interviewing Veronica Talbot's coworkers.

"Fill me in on the office gossip," he said.

Her face brightened. "What do you want to know?"

"She knew their business. Why didn't they try to get back at her sooner?"

"I can't say for sure. So many things were happening. I didn't have time to listen to gossip."

"Was Veronica really that bad?"

"She was that bad. If she liked you, she liked you. But some other people I work with are hard to get along with too. Anna, Tom, and Bart are the only ones who keep their mouths shut."

"Anna seems awfully mousy."

"She's very shy. But she's nice. I think she has a hard time meeting men, though."

"That's too bad."

"She works really well with Nicholas."

"I hope you're not going to play matchmaker again. It usually ends in disaster whenever you get involved."

She laughed. "Not all the time."

"Well, it seems like most of the time."

"Give me one example."

"How about your friends Judy and Mike? They're divorced now, aren't they?"

"Well, what about Grace and Peter? They're still together after...How long has it been? Six years?"

"Well, Tom and Michelle seem like an unlikely pair."

"Opposites attract. But I think they have more in common than what they don't."

"He's old enough to be her father. What can they possibly have in common?"

"She lost her husband. And he lost his wife."

"Wouldn't her husband have been Tom's son's age?"

"Maybe."

He kissed her again and said, "Well, what about us?"

She kissed him back and said, "We break every rule."

"Your parents probably still think you should hook up with a guy who works in the bank or something."

"They've warmed up to you, Frank."

"But I know that you've been having talks with them."

"And every time I talk to them, I am always in your corner. I just tell them that you're the way you are and that you'll never change."

"And what do they say to that?"

"I usually change the subject by then."

"Well, at least you've got my back like I've got yours. Can you do me a favor?"

"What?"

"Could you be an office spy for me? Get some information."

"They know you're my boyfriend."

He gently rubbed her shoulders and said, "That's true. Well, just open your ears."

She pulled her ears and saluted him. "Office spy, reporting for duty."

He laughed and kissed her again. The TV blared in the background.

CHAPTER 11

Tears welled in Anna's eyes as she looked at the cuts and bruises on the little boy's face. At the bottom of the image she typed "Bullying doesn't have to go this far. Report abuse." And then she typed the telephone number for a shelter for abused women and children.

She knew in the back of her mind that it was not real. The children in the ads were just models. But they were so realistic. The makeup department had done an excellent job. She knew it would really get people's attention. Maybe it would save some kids' lives.

She thought it was too bad that Veronica Talbot wasn't around to see these ads. Maybe it would have made her a nicer person. Maybe it would have made her stop bossing everyone around.

She quickly dismissed that thought. Nothing would have changed Veronica's behavior. She was a bully, plain and simple. If she hadn't been poisoned, Anna doubted that she would have ever changed.

Anna wished there had been somewhere her sisters could have gone years ago, when they were dealing with their abusive father. While he beat them up, their mother had just taken a back seat. Why didn't she step in and tell him to stop it?

Anna knew that her sisters had sneaked behind their parents backs when they got to high school. She was very good at keeping secrets. When she was about thirteen, her father caught Danielle with a boy from the wrong side of the tracks. Darren was a wild child, a boy that Greg and Catherine did not approve of.

"What did I tell you?" Greg had screeched. "That boy is a dirt bag!"

"I love him!" Danielle had shouted over her tears.

"We told you not to go out with him!"

Danielle had looked over at her mother, pleading with her eyes. Catherine stood helpless with the girls. What happened next was like out of a nightmare.

Greg beat Danielle repeatedly. Her screams were horrendous.

Catherine finally had gone over to him and waved her hands. "Stop it! You're hurting her!"

Greg had pushed his wife out of the way. She had fallen and hit her head on the end table. She lay there helplessly watching. Greg raved like a madman.

"Go to your rooms! This does not concern you!" he screamed.

"But Dad!" Maggie protested.

His face had turned a purple color. "Get the hell out of here!"

Catherine got to her feet and herded Maggie and Anna upstairs. She looked over her shoulder and shuddered. Anna sat on her bedroom floor and bawled while her mother comforted her. She had closed her eyes, trying to block it out, wanting it to end. Her mother spoke gently to get her mind off the horror that was unfolding downstairs.

The beatings sounded louder. Anna had cringed as the sounds of Danielle's horrendous screams drifted upstairs.

Catherine had run her hands through Anna's hair and said, "It'll be okay. Your father is just upset. It'll pass. And then–and then we can sit down and have a good long talk with her."

"But he's hurting her!" Anna had protested. "Shouldn't–shouldn't you call the police?"

"It's something we need to handle ourselves, honey."

"But he'll hurt her!"

Catherine pulled her closer and waited it out. She knew Anna was right but was too frightened to make the call. She didn't know what Greg would do. Anna could not believe what a coward her mother was. From that moment on, she and Maggie vowed to not let the abuse happen to them.

Life at home had become intolerable for Danielle as the weeks went by. She skipped town six weeks shy of her high school graduation and moved in with Darren's parents. She got a job at a lingerie shop at the mall and soon found out that she was pregnant.

When Greg found out that she was having a baby, he tracked her down at the mall. Anna stood helplessly by as she watched her father pounce on her. They argued so loudly that shoppers stopped what they were doing and watched the spectacle unfold in front of them.

"You've made a lot of horrible choices!" Greg screamed. "Moving in with that cretin!"

"Please, Dad, you're embarrassing me," Danielle said in a quiet tone. She looked around the store. Her coworkers wondered what in the hell was going on.

"I didn't raise a little slut!"

The manager stepped up to them and said, "What's the problem here? Sir, I'm going to ask you kindly to leave. If you don't, I'll call security."

Greg paid no attention to the woman. He glared at his daughter with a look that could kill. "You're a stupid cow! How could you be so careless? You don't got squat to live on and you're having a baby out of wedlock! You stupid, stupid girl!"

By now, shoppers were gathering around. A heavyset woman said, "Who do you think you are, mister? Leave her alone!"

"What right do you have to lay into her like this?" someone else said.

"Leave me alone! This is none of your damned business!"

Two security guards entered the shop and said, "Sir, leave the young lady alone. You are causing a scene. We can discuss it quietly in the office."

Greg waved his hands and shouted, "This isn't over!" He stalked out.

Anna had watched as the manager put her arm around Danielle and they disappeared into an office.

Anna cringed when her father stomped toward her. She looked around, praying that no one was watching, but they were. She shrank into herself and hoped no one would recognize her. Who was she kidding? All her friends went to the mall. They'd see her. She'd be humiliated. She wouldn't be able to face them on Monday morning.

Then she thought about how selfish she was. Especially after the way her father had treated Danielle like dirt for everybody to see.

After the incident, Darren's parents gave them some money to rent a room at the boarding house on Main Street, which had individual rooms converted into efficiency apartments. Danielle gave birth to a son that they named Vincent. Maggie and Anna often visited them so they could see the baby. Anna even volunteered to babysit whenever Danielle was at work.

Anna had been just a naive teenager until her father started in on Danielle. Up until then, she'd seen only the good in people. She did not know people had dark sides. That all changed when her father acted like a dictator. Anna wished she had been a little wiser.

Her feelings of being trapped intensified. She could not wait until she graduated from high school. She would flee the town and experience life.

* * *

Bart had dealt with similar familial problems when he was growing up. He was about sixteen and starting to figure things out–though he didn't want to admit it to himself at the time. It was a typical Friday night. He knew where his brothers were and what they were really doing. His little sister Mary was in one of her moods again. He glanced at the outfit she wanted to go out in and reluctantly agreed with his parents. The low-cut blouse might make her popular with the boys, but they weren't the right kinds of boys she should want to date. His father was more blunt.

"If you go out in that you'll get raped!" Clay shouted. "You look like a whore!"

"It's like a prison here!" Mary screamed at him.

They heard a car door slam. A moment later, the tall and rugged figure of Todd Price appeared at the door. Bart recognized him. He was on the football team and had only two things on his mind: sex and drinking. Todd probably didn't know he existed. He had no idea how much Bart looked up to him. He hung out with the cool kids. His interest was in Mary and only Mary.

"You are not going out with him dressed like that!" Clay shouted. "Change into something more appropriate."

Mary flashed an angry look at her mother, who came to her husband's defense. Clay's eyes were wide with rage. "Do it!"

"Fine!" Mary shouted as she stomped out of the living room. She uttered profanities under her breath as she pounded up the steps.

Bart went into the kitchen and pulled open cabinets to rustle for some snacks. He heard his parents talking. "She looks like a tramp!" Clay cried. "We didn't raise her to look like a hooker!"

"It's what all the girls are wearing these days," Bonnie said.

"What's the world coming to? You try to bring them up right. And what do you get in return? Back talk! She gets that from all those kids that go to Lincoln High. That boy is no good for her!"

Bonnie looked to see if Todd could hear them. He stood obliviously on the porch.

Bart popped open a Coke lid and started back into the living room with a bowl of chips. He stood in the entryway and listened to his parents talking about him.

"Bart is the kind of boy that Mary should be going out with," his father said. "He's harmless."

"He wouldn't hurt a flea," Bonnie agreed.

"Just because a boy is nice like that doesn't mean nothing. He's still a guy. Maybe he's just putting on the 'boy next door' act so he can nail a pretty girl that pays attention to him."

"We don't have to worry about Bart doing anything like that. He's a good boy."

"I just wish he would ask a girl out or something. He's not shy. He don't seem to show any interest–he's too wrapped up in himself. He needs to have some fun. He hasn't been hanging out with the kids down the street lately."

"Maybe he's going through a phase," Bonnie suggested. "He'll snap out of it."

Bart waltzed past them and plopped on the sofa. Mary came downstairs wearing a glittery blouse and blue jeans. She glared at her father on the way out. They cringed when they heard the engine backfire as Todd sped down the street.

"That kid is trouble," Clay muttered.

Bart concentrated his attention on the TV.

CHAPTER 12

Penny went into the break room and waved at Anna. She made some tea and asked, "Is this seat taken?"

"No, go ahead."

She sat across from her. "How are you?"

"I'm better."

"You weren't before?"

"The pressure is getting to me."

"I feel the same way."

"Everybody's on edge. Michelle just told me that Mr. Dobson was real close to firing me after I screwed up that ad. She stuck up for me. Veronica wanted to get rid of me."

"It's nice to have somebody who's willing to look out for you at work, don't you think?"

Anna nodded. "It's so cutthroat around here. I've seen a lot of people come and go. If I make another mistake...Mr. Dobson has been very patient–but, I don't think he'd keep me here–if I screw up again. There are too many talented people here."

"Don't put yourself down. You need confidence."

"If I had confidence, I would have applied for Ben's position." She sipped her tea. "Your boyfriend asks hard questions."

"I know, but he usually gets what he wants. I tell him if he were nice, he'd get better results. It's a source of constant debate. He does care about people, though. He just wants to set things right in the world."

"He's cute enough. How did you land him?"

Penny's face lit up at the thought of it. "It's a long story."

"Don't worry, I've got time. I'd love to hear it."

"All right, but I just don't want to bore you with details."

Anna tapped Penny's arm and said, "That's fine. Bore me with the details."

Penny took a few more sips of tea and wiped her mouth with a napkin. "I met him when he was a beat cop fresh from the police academy. He pulled me over just as an excuse to talk to me. Apparently, he'd been stalking me for some time before he worked up the nerve to pull me over for a bogus traffic violation. He let me off with a warning. He didn't think Penny Lane was my real name. He thought it was a fake ID or something. I get it all the time. So does my sister. I bet you can't guess what my parents stuck on her for life. Take a guess."

Anna thought about it a moment. "Is it...oh, no. Lois?"

Penny squealed with laughter and nodded her head enthusiastically. "Bingo!"

"I can't believe your parents stuck you with those names."

"Our brother got away unscathed in the name game. He has a normal name. Steven. We got stuck with names of a super-hero's girlfriend and a Beatles song."

Anna snickered. "That's so funny. I bet his story is different, though. In his version, he's probably not so fearful about talking to you. I think it's a romantic story, anyway."

Penny leaned forward. "I couldn't stand him at first. He kept annoying me, and for some reason, I dated him. Now I'm glad I did."

"He seems a bit abrasive, though."

"He is to start with. That's part of his subtle charm."

Anna adjusted her glasses. "My folks would have gone for Frank. They couldn't stand my boyfriend, Max. They hated him! You see, they're staunch Catholics and sent me to this strict all-girl Catholic school–Holy Angels. Oh, I hated it. I had to wear an ugly uniform."

"I had to wear a uniform at my school too. Wasn't it just awful?"

"Oh, I know!" Anna exclaimed. "But I rebelled when I got out of high school."

Penny's eyes lit up. "Really?"

Anna smiled wryly and took a sip of her coffee. "I dated him to get back at them. I haven't thought of Max in years."

"What happened?"

"I think you can get the picture. Frank would not have liked him."

She finished her coffee and excused herself. Penny sipped her tea while reading the newspaper. A few minutes later she went back to work.

CHAPTER 13

The fall leaves made crunching sounds under the weight of the horses' hooves. Red trotted across the corn field that had just been cleared by the farmer. A few leaves clung to tree limbs. Tricia pulled in the reins, and Red slowed down. She craned her neck to wait for her best friend, Cindy McDougal, who was riding on Avalon. When they caught up, Tricia guided Red toward the woods.

The path eventually led up to the pond across the road from her parents' house. Colorful leaves floated on top of the water. Pretty soon it would ice up, and they could go skating.

Cindy was like the sister Tricia never had. They enjoyed doing a lot of things together. She could tell Cindy things that she couldn't tell her parents. Tricia spent more time with Cindy and her mother than she did her own parents. Sometimes she and Cindy would hang out with Kelly. Kelly was more than just a housekeeper. Sometimes Tricia wished Kelly was her mother. She thought of Cindy as her adopted sister. Whenever Tricia had a problem, Kelly was always there for her.

Tricia's parents were so busy that she really only saw them on weekends. They were always so rushed during the week that if Tricia was having a problem, they agreed to talk about it later, which usually never happened. Tricia might see her parents come back from work late at night, or maybe she wouldn't. They were always stressed out and on deadline. Sometimes Tricia wondered why they bothered having her in the first place.

The two hundred-year-old mausoleum of a house she lived in loomed in the distance. She should have been happy living in such a large house with all its surrounding farmland, but she wasn't. She felt lonely in that big house. She often told Kelly and Cindy that it was like living in a museum with all the antique furniture and paintings. The only bright spot was the den in the basement, with its big-screen TV and sofa. It would have been awful if she had to sit on the uncomfortable furniture in the living room all the time. Her father had converted the attic into her bedroom. It had a great view of the pond and woods, but had a lot of drawbacks. She was growing so fast that she often hit her head on the slanted ceiling when she was not thinking about it. The floors were creaky. In the winter, it got really cold upstairs. And in the summer, she had to keep the windows open and have two fans on when it got really hot. It was better than sleeping on the antique beds in what were now Kelly's and Cindy's rooms. Her bedroom offered escapism from her mother's constant rants.

As they got closer, she saw a blue mini-van next to her father's red Hummer in the driveway. She knew whose car it was. Dana Phillips had been at the house a lot lately.

Her mother hated that woman with a passion. And the feeling was mutual.

Tricia maneuvered Red into the barn at the rear of the house. Cindy followed on Avalon. They dismounted and led the horses into their stalls.

* * *

Dana and Charles were on the sofa in the den holding wine glasses. After a stressful week, it felt good to unwind on Sunday afternoon. They glanced at the TV when they heard a female reporter mention Veronica's name.

"Veronica Talbot's death is still a mystery," the reporter was saying. "At this time, investigators have not been able to discover how she was poisoned. Coworkers reported that she was feeling flushed and tired at a party at her home a few minutes before she went into her study to rest. A few minutes later, her husband found her body..."

Charles turned his attention back to Dana. "I wish they would just give us some privacy!"

She rubbed his hand and said, "You're an important man around here. It's a major news story."

He took a deep swig of his Merlot and looked into her eyes. "This can't be good for Tricia."

"She's a strong girl. I think she can take it."

"She's an emotional wreck. You never know what mood she'll be in one moment from the next. That's a trait she definitely inherited from Veronica."

"When are you going to tell her the truth?"

"About us?"

"Not that."

"It would hurt her more if she knew. I hoped it would never come to this. I dread the day that I might have to actually tell her."

"Frank Logan is snooping around. You'd better tell her before she finds out. It'll be worse finding out from a stranger."

He frowned and turned away. Dana took his hands in hers and pulled him close.

He sighed and said, "I'll have to tell her."

* * *

After settling the horses in their stalls, the girls tore into the back of the house and opened the basement door. As they pounded the rickety wooden steps, they heard the TV blaring in the background.

"Veronica Talbot's colleagues thought she was a power-hungry dragon lady," the female reporter was saying. "The murder investigation has made the tension around the office a lot worse. Reporting outside the Creative Concepts building, Angie Matteo, Channel Five News."

Tricia saw her father and Dana sitting too close, in her opinion, and gave Dana a dirty look. She marched in front of the TV and glared at him in horror. He moved away from Dana a little bit, unprepared to explain what his daughter had just walked in on.

"Why are they saying such awful things about, Mother?" Tricia demanded.

Charles got up and held her tight in his arms. "I don't know, sweetheart. Life is often cruel. You've got to toughen yourself up. Don't listen to the news." He turned off the TV. He kissed Tricia's cheek and said, "Go study, honey. I have to talk to Dana."

Tricia and Cindy darted across the room and hurried upstairs.

Dana folded her arms and said, "When are you going to make an honest woman of me?"

He pulled her close and said, "Soon."

"When are you going to tell Tricia?"

"It's hard."

"You have to tell her. She's old enough. She'll understand."

"Will she understand what a rotten woman her mother was?"

Logan descended the steps and entered the room. He glanced at the wine glasses on the end table, then smiled at Dana and Charles. They looked guilty of something.

He said, "Hello, Mr. Talbot. Don't worry. Tricia let me in. She's a lovely girl. I just found out that the Bloody Mary didn't have the poison in it."

Charles looked at him blankly. "Really? Then what happened to her?"

"We still don't know," Logan admitted. "We're still waiting for more test results."

"How long will that take?"

"Your guess is as good as mine. I'm so sorry that it's taking so long."

"That's okay. Just as long as they do their job right. There's no sense in making sloppy mistakes because they're in a hurry."

Logan nodded his head in agreement. "I guess I caught you at a bad time. You must have been in the middle of something when I came down here. Something about Tricia. I didn't mean to listen in. How rotten was your late wife?"

"We were just discussing what the news people have been saying about Veronica."

"As you know, I've been talking to your coworkers. A lot of them weren't too happy with her."

"She was a bitch to work with. Hell on wheels!" Dana looked at Charles and said, "Sorry."

"That's fine," Charles said flatly. "I know how you all felt about her."

"Were you jealous of your wife's success?" asked Logan.

"Of course not!" Charles snapped. "She was just a high-strung woman, that's all. People had to learn to steer clear of her when she was in a foul mood."

"What does Tricia need to know?" Logan wondered.

"About the affair," Charles mumbled.

"She knows," Dana assured him. "She's not dumb."

Logan's eyes darted from Charles to Dana. "I get the feeling that there's something else you aren't telling her. What else does she need to know? If you don't tell me, I'll find out."

"Tell him," Dana urged.

Charles's lips twitched. "Oh, very well. Tricia was adopted."

Tricia had been eavesdropping from the top step, out of view. They heard her scream.

"Are you satisfied now?" Charles shouted as he went after her.

Dana waited until he was gone and said, "Veronica was infertile. Oh, God! Charles is going to be really upset when he finds out I told you."

"It doesn't matter. I would have found out anyway."

"It wasn't my place to tell you something that's so personal."

"That's okay. If I'm going to get to the truth, I need to know everything. You certainly know a lot about the Talbots' private lives."

"Sometimes Charles told me things that he couldn't even tell Veronica. They tried for years to conceive."

"And that's where you came in?"

"Yeah. He talked to me. Confided in me. That's about the time her anger manifested itself. She was even more of a witch back then."

"Why did they keep it from Tricia?"

"They were on the verge of splitting, and there was a lot of tension around here then. They decided to wait till she was old enough to understand."

"What's so hard to understand about that?"

"Let's just put it this way. They adopted her to save their marriage. As you can probably tell, they weren't that happy. Veronica wasn't the easiest person to live with. I'm so thankful that he put in the good word for me at Creative Concepts."

"Where were you before? I can't remember if you mentioned it."

"I was in LA. My ex-husband got a job here and we moved back, oh, about ten years ago."

"How did you know Charles?"

"We often crossed paths at conferences and whatnot. Well, despite having to deal with the Dragon Lady on a daily basis, I think moving to Philly was the best thing in the world for me.

I think it's been the happiest time of Charles's life. I only wish things could have been different–that he had married me, instead of that opportunistic bitch!"

* * *

Tricia looked coldly into her father's eyes and folded her arms. "I would have understood. Why didn't you tell me?"

"You were a child."

"You had no right lying to me. You lied to me!"

"I've never been good at expressing how I feel, you know it, honey. I keep everything inside. It was hard for us to tell you. We did what we thought was the right thing to do at the time."

"You lied to me!"

"Honey."

"Get away from me!" She ran off.

"We always loved you like you were our own!" he shouted after her. "I believed it in my heart."

She paused and turned to face him. "Go away!"

Charles left her alone.

* * *

Logan was not happy with how the Veronica Talbot case was headed. There was still no word from the Philadelphia forensics lab. He had no leads. To make matters worse, there was a front-page story in Townsend's weekly newspaper, the *Times-Sentinel*, which highlighted his lack of evidence. The headline read: "TALBOT MURDER STALLED."

By Kim Weston

Townsend police still have no solid leads in the Veronica Talbot murder investigation. Ms. Talbot, 50, of 38 Old Hickory Lane, was found dead on her sofa in late October. At first, Coroner Stan Green suspected she died of a heart attack. Further tests proved that she was poisoned.

The Talbots were hosting a party at their home the afternoon she died. She had recently been promoted to a high-ranking position at an advertisement firm called Creative Concepts in Philadelphia.

Several of her guests reported Ms. Talbot exhibited odd behavior during the party.

According to lead detective Frank Logan, samples of everything she ate and drank at the party were collected after the police arrived on the scene. The poison was not found in the Bloody Mary that Ms. Talbot was drinking. At this time, he does not believe the finger food contained the poison. No one else thought the food tasted bad. Logan believes that the poison must have been in something else she ate, so he collected samples of everything that was in her refrigerator. Further tests are pending.

"All of the guests are suspects," said Lieutenant Harry T. Winters of the Townsend Police Department. "It is difficult to determine who could have done it. Everyone was coming and going during the party."

Frank growled and tossed the newspaper on his desk. He looked over at Joe Flosky and said, "Did you see this?"

He nodded and grunted. "At least your name is spelled right."

"It makes us look like dopes!"

"Don't worry, Frank. We'll find out what happened."

At the moment, he did not agree. "It's looking like a cold case right now."

"Don't worry. The other test results will come back soon. And then we'll be one step closer to cracking the case."

He rolled his eyes and grunted. "I wish I shared your optimism."

"What else can we do but wait?"

Logan stomped across the room and got a cup of coffee. A couple minutes later, he sat back at his desk and compiled a suspect list.

BART SULLIVAN–Talented artist/photographer. Veronica treated him like the office whipping boy.

TOM DANIELS–Salesman/ad writer. Worried that Veronica might fire him because he's not fast enough with all the technological changes. He's worked for over 30 years in the business and resented her for possibly wanting to get rid of him.

CRAIG HOLLOWAY-Photographer. James Dobson knew about his police record in high school, so Veronica Talbot could not have used that against him. He seems too sure of himself. Confident he would get the job.

ANNA MCWILLIAMS-Graphic artist. She was on Veronica Talbot's chopping block. She made some mistakes that cost the company mega bucks. James Dobson kept her on, despite Veronica's insistence that she should be fired.

MICHELLE DELANCEY–Advertising representative. Competitive and ambitious. She didn't apply for the job opening. She didn't want Tom to find out about her abortion. Veronica knew about it. Was that reason enough to kill her?

DANA PHILLIPS-Ad representative. The last person to see Veronica alive. She went to LA for a few years. Having an affair with Charles Talbot? Spends a lot of time at the Talbots' home.

JAMES DOBSON Generous boss. Has been in the industry for 40 years and worked his way up to becoming owner of the company. VT was a possible threat to his power. VT rumored to have blackmailed him. She apparently told him she would tell his wife about their alleged affair. If they had one is beside the point. Veronica said nasty things about people at the office that should have gotten her fired. Nobody seems to know why Dobson kept her on. Did she have something on him, besides the alleged affair? (After doing some digging around, it turns out that his mother was a nurse. Maybe she told him about poisoning cases?)

NICHOLAS BRADSHAW Graphic designer. Everybody knew he hated VT. He was on her chopping block list. Is he hiding something? (After some poking around, I found out that his father's a chemistry teacher. Maybe Nicholas has some knowledge about poisonous chemicals).

CHARLES TALBOT-VT's henpecked husband. Was he having an affair with Dana? He found Veronica's body. He could have slipped the poison into Veronica at any point before the party.

PATRICIA TALBOT-Charles and Veronica's adopted fifteen-year-old daughter. Never knew she was adopted.

KELLY MCDOUGAL–The Talbots' housekeeper. She could have slipped poison into something VT ate several hours prior to the party.

DARYL FORSTER-- Bart's model boyfriend. He was fortunate enough not to have worked with Veronica Talbot too much. Maybe he killed her to protect Bart?

Logan drew a circle around Nicholas Bradshaw's name and said, "It's too obvious. Everybody knew he hated her. That leaves us with six prime suspects: Charles, Dana, Tom, Anna, Bart, Dobson...maybe Bradshaw."

"You'll never prove who killed her," Joe said.

"Don't tell me that."

"I think they're all lying or covering for each other. I wish I could help."

"There's got to be something I'm overlooking."

* * *

It was a typical Friday night at Barney's. It was so loud that everybody had to shout over each other to be heard. The ball game was on. Men at the bar yelled when their team scored.

Penny looked from Frank to Joe, who were in a loud disagreement about the case. They had been discussing theories for about an hour. Frank was too distracted to notice her. She might as well have been invisible. It had gotten so much for Meg Winters that she nudged her husband, Harry, onto the small dance floor when a Kenny Chesney song started playing.

"Come off it, man!" Frank shouted. "Now you're going to tell me that an alien poisoned her!"

"There wouldn't have been time for anyone to have done it," Penny interjected. But they didn't hear her.

A little while later, Frank said, "There really wouldn't have been time for anybody to have done it."

Penny clutched her hand over her mouth and laughed hysterically. Frank eyed her suspiciously and asked, "What's wrong?"

"I said that five minutes ago, Frank!"

"You did?"

"You don't even know I'm here!" she protested. "And you're breaking the rule. No talking about work at Barney's."

"I'm sorry that you aren't having a good time."

"Sorry, Penny," Joe said.

"That's okay. I enjoy listening to your theories. Maybe I can use them to write a mystery. Maybe I'll become a best-selling author!"

"Well, you work with them," Joe said. "What do you think? What are your impressions of them people?"

"That's a lot to tackle, Joe."

"Who do you think did it?"

"You're asking me? You're the detectives. I have no idea."

"According to Edna Dobson, Veronica did put down her plate a few times during the party," Frank said.

Joe shook his head defiantly. "But only long enough to greet guests as they were arriving."

"That wouldn't have been enough time for anybody to have slipped the poison in," agreed Penny.

Meg pulled Harry back to the table. She gave them a troubled look and said, "You're still talking about the case? You're breaking the rule. Who can arrest you guys?"

Penny got her up to speed on the latest theory. Meg agreed. There wouldn't have been time for someone to have done it.

Harry seemed to be lost in thought. He guzzled down his beer and looked at Logan. "There were no witnesses. If the killer slipped the poison in while she was distracted, somebody would've seen it."

"Maybe she did herself in," Meg suggested.

Harry grunted his approval. "That is a distinct possibility."

Penny regarded them skeptically. "But why would she have wanted to kill herself? She worked hard to get that promotion. She was happy. She got what she wanted for a long time. She wouldn't have done it. There were a lot of people angry with her."

"The only other explanation is that one of the caterers did it," Frank said.

"But they told me the trays never left their hands," Joe reminded him.

"Did it ever occur to you that one of them might have been lying?"

"They had no reason to kill her!" Joe insisted.

Meg leaned her elbows on the table and looked intently at her husband. Then she looked at Frank and Joe. "Then maybe it was the housekeeper. She could have put something in the food before the party."

"Charles and Tricia live there too," Frank reminded her. "Maybe they could have done it."

Penny looked wide-eyed at him and gasped. "You actually think her own daughter could have done it?"

"I'm just trying to throw out possibilities. We know that she was upset with her mother."

Meg looked incredulously at Frank for even suggesting it. "Everybody gets mad at their parents, Frank. And parents are mad at their kids. But that doesn't mean that they..." She couldn't even finish the sentence.

"Well, Charles had a lot of reasons to want to get rid of Veronica," Harry interrupted. "She was a pain in the ass!"

"You should hear the rumors flying around the office," added Penny. "People are saying that he was having an affair with Dana. They're talking behind their backs."

Frank nodded enthusiastically. "And she's been hanging out a lot at the house. I saw her there one day when I went to talk to Charles."

"She could have spiked the food before the party," Harry volunteered.

Frank strongly disagreed. "But if that were the case somebody else might have eaten it by mistake."

"Maybe she wasn't the intended victim," Harry countered.

Frank thought about it a moment and shook his head. "Maybe the killer put it aside and added it to her plate when she wasn't looking."

"Then it would have had to have been somebody who had prepared it hours before."

Meg cleared her throat, and they all looked at her. "Come on, you guys, you're talking in circles! You're not accomplishing anything. We came here to have a good time. And you're all being a drag!"

"Meg is right," agreed Harry. "I don't want to even think about it anymore. Maybe by the time we come back to it on Monday, we'll have some fresh input."

Frank looked at the women and said, "You're right. I'm sorry we bored you. How's it going at work, Meg?"

CHAPTER 14

Logan looked fondly at framed portraits of former Philadelphia officers of the law hanging on the long corridor walls that led to the squad room. He stopped a moment and smiled with pride at the one of his father, Francis, staring back at him. It had been taken about ten years before his father was gunned down in the line of duty. He looked so sharp in his uniform. Beneath the picture, there was a plaque with his name on it in gold letters. He was a legend at the station.

The old familiar din came crashing back to Logan as he strode across the squad room.

Detectives took statements from harried witnesses, while their colleagues busily processed hookers, thieves, and punks off the streets. The rancid aroma of a homeless man burned his nostrils. It was a combination of cheap booze and urine-soaked sweat pants. He glanced at the man on his way across the room. He had on a holey T-shirt and had long hair and a beard that reached down to his chest.

Logan recognized the young detective who was taking the derelict's statement. In the few short years that Frank had been gone, Officer Thomas Moore had become a detective. He looked up and grinned as he watched Frank walk by. Moore turned his attention back to the homeless man, who couldn't give him a positive identification of the man that mugged him for the measly five bucks that he'd collected on his street corner of choice.

Frank walked past endless rows of desks and checked the name on an office door at the other end of the room. Sergeant Avery Cox was leaning over a mound of paperwork. He was an African American in his mid-thirties. He and Frank went way back. They had gone through the police academy together and started out as rookies. They had each other's backs then. Cox looked up and shook his head in disbelief.

"Look what the cat dragged in!" He got up and shook Frank's hand. "What the hell are you doin' in these parts, man?"

"I'm working a case at an advertising agency down town."

"The one that your girlfriend just happens to work at?"

"How'd you know?"

"I hear things. Sure you aren't just making an excuse to see her?"

"A little of both," Frank admitted with a gleam in his eyes.

Cox shoved papers off the chair, and Frank sat across from him.

Frank glanced behind his desk at the window covered in mesh wires. He could see a puke-colored brick building across the street.

"You've moved up in the world," Frank noted. "You've actually got a little bit of a view."

"If you call that a view. I usually keep the blinds closed so I don't have to look at it."

Frank looked at the paperwork and asked, "So are you working on any exciting cases? Any shootings or stabbings? Decapitations?"

"Just grand theft auto. I'm tracing it right now. Part of a bank robbery getaway."

"Really?"

"We'll get 'em. So you're still seeing Penny?"

"We moved in together."

"No shit? How's that going, man?"

"It was rough at first, but she hasn't changed the apartment totally–yet."

Cox erupted into a fit of laughter. "You never were one that was good at changes."

"No, I guess not."

"When are you gonna come to your senses and come back here? Your vacation out in the sticks is over. We got a spot opening up soon. Captain DeAngelo's retiring in a few months."

Frank's eyebrows shot up. "Really? Vinny's leaving? I never thought he'd retire. I thought he'd go out in a blaze of glory."

"That's what we all figured. His ticker's on the fritz."

"I'm sorry to hear that."

"You seen him yet?"

"Not yet."

"You gotta go up and see him, man. He'd be surprised to see you."

"I don't want it to be that big of a shock–what with his bad heart and all."

"If he keels over, we can blame you, man."

Frank shook his head. "So Tommy made detective. Good for him. When did that happen?"

"About a year ago. He's as sharp as a tack, that kid. He's handled some pretty nasty drug busts."

"No kidding."

"Don't mess with that dude. He's tough!"

They reminisced about their toughest cases. When one of them couldn't think of something, the other was right there to pick up the slack. It was just like it was at the academy. Then Frank got back to the reason for his visit.

"I've got a problem with this poisoning case."

"What's wrong?"

"Well, the woman was poisoned at her home out in my neck of the woods. She worked at the same company that Penny works at here in Philly, actually."

Cox nodded his head. "Right."

"We did a thorough sweep of her house and sent the samples to the lab."

"The one that's not in your town."

"Yeah, our limited resources. I get it, pal. It turns out that it wasn't in anything she ate or drank during the party."

"So you came to me 'cause you need to search the offices, right, and you need me to hold your hand doing it 'cause it's not in your area?"

"You got it."

"So when is this search gonna take place?"

"As soon as you can get the ball in motion."

"I'll make some calls, and then we're in action, baby!"

"Good, good. I thought you might see it my way."

"But I get to call the shots, remember?"

"Sure."

"I like telling you what to do."

Frank grinned and said, "I know."

"Have you talked to some of your old buddies here?"

"I haven't made the rounds yet, but I will."

"Maybe we can go out to lunch," Cox suggested. "We can kick back some beers and shoot the shit."

"I can't wait."

"And maybe I can talk you into coming back here. We miss you, man."

"Don't count on it."

"What do you do out in the country, anyway? You've been on vacation too damn long, man! You probably aren't as sharp as you used to be."

"It's not as slow out there as you think."

"Yeah, yeah, I heard. Something 'bout a star basketball player at that fancy private school being murdered. Something like that."

"He had a promising future. It was a shame."

"And somethin' about a lawyer bein' knocked on the noggin?"

"Yeah. It was a sad situation. The family was all torn up."

"And now Penny's moved in with you." Cox laughed uncontrollably. "This I gotta see."

"Then come over, and we'll give you a sweeping tour of Townsend with its only traffic light in town and its only bar. You might like it so much, maybe you'll decide to stay. We can always use another uniform to hand out parking tickets."

"You gotta be kiddin', man! I'm where the action is! You've probably gotten soft in your ways. I'm just sayin'!"

"Isn't it the other way around, Cox? Maybe you've gotten soft without me around cracking cases."

"We'll see when we do the search for you. We'll see."

"I'll figure it out first. I always do."

"Wanna bet?"

They laughed and talked for about ten more minutes. When the telephone rang, Cox had to take the call. Frank wandered through the squad room and chatted with former colleagues that were not busy at the moment.

CHAPTER 15

James Dobson was not at all happy to see the swarm of detectives and their entourage of criminologists file into his office with a search warrant. It was an invasion of privacy.

"I realize that this might seem like a major inconvenience, Mr. Dobson, but it's necessary," Sergeant Cox said. "We promise that we won't take up too much of your time."

"Well, do whatever you must. I want to find out what happened to Veronica, for our sake and for Charles's. But please don't let our clients see you all wandering around. It's not good for business."

"I understand that, sir, but these people need to be here to help with the investigation."

"Well, try to be discreet about it."

"We can have them go to the areas where your clients wouldn't be sitting in," Cox said. "Just let us know where those places are."

"Okay. I'll just have them stay in the conference rooms. Do your searches there after they leave. How long will it take?"

"It depends," Cox replied. "We can't really say."

"Fine. Just find something that will help us know what happened to Veronica."

They all filed out. James picked up the telephone and dialed his home number. "Honey, you won't guess what's happening..."

* * *

Criminologist Maria de Jesus concentrated her efforts on the break room. She pulled open the refrigerator door and saw a half-empty bottle of grape juice on the lower shelf. Soda cans were in the door. Leftovers from restaurants were on the shelves. Microwave containers with names scrawled on them were sandwiched in between other items. Water bottles were on the top shelf. She picked them up and examined them for signs of puncture marks.

Cox pulled open cabinet doors and dumped samples of spices into evidence collection bags. Then he gathered unopened sugar and herbal tea bags into other ones. Logan placed Veronica Talbot's mug into a bag and labeled it.

Michelle Delancey stood in the doorway with her hands on her hips. "I thought Veronica was poisoned at the party. Do you really think that somebody slipped something in her drink while she was here?"

"We are looking into every possibility, ma'am," Frank said without diverting his attention from the task at hand.

"It makes you wonder how much you really know the people you work with."

"It's true," Cox agreed. "I don't mean to be rude ma'am, but we're busy."

"Fine." She marched out.

"What do you know so far?" Cox asked Logan.

"It wasn't in anything Veronica Talbot drank or ate at the party. Our coroner, Stan Green, believes that it took several hours for the poison to take effect."

"That's interesting. So what do you think?"

"The person who did this knows things about poison and chemistry."

* * *

Charles unlocked Veronica's office door and let the detectives in.

"It's as she left it just before the party," he said. "It gives me an eerie feeling every time I come in here for something." He pointed to the date book on the desk and said, "She penciled in dates to meet with clients. They have since been reassigned to other people."

"Did she always lock her door?" Logan asked him.

"Usually. But not all the time."

Maria went over to the little refrigerator on the counter and pulled open the door. A stack of bottled water took up most of the lower shelf. A plastic container of yogurt was on top. Apples and oranges were in a bin at the bottom. Maria collected samples of everything inside, and went on to examine the tea bags on the counter.

While she was doing that, Logan and Cox took notes.

"When do you think you'll know anything?" Charles asked Frank.

"It depends on how long it takes at the lab. It'll probably take a while for the samples to be analyzed."

"But why are there so many?"

"We're just trying to find out what the poison could have been put in."

"Didn't the coroner tell you what kind of poison it was?"

"He told us that there were toxins in Veronica's system that contained alkaloids, which are highly poisonous. But we don't know what it could have been from. We still don't know how your wife ingested it. Or who did it."

"How long till you know?"

Logan shrugged his shoulders. "I don't know."

Charles let them get back to work. He was halfway out the door, when he paused and turned to look back at Frank. "Would you like anything to drink?"

"No, I'm fine."

Charles walked hurriedly down the hall. When Maria finished collecting samples, Logan followed them out and locked the door. They went to Charles's office next.

"Why are you searching my office?" Charles asked in bewilderment. "If anything was tampered with in here, I would have been poisoned too, don't you think?"

"We're just checking to make sure everything is okay," Frank assured him. "Someone might try to get you too."

Charles's face blanched. "Oh, I see. Well, I better let you concentrate on your work. I don't want to distract you." He headed on out.

They continued collecting samples and taking notes. Meanwhile, Maria concentrated her efforts on everything she could find in the lobby.

* * *

Family pictures hung on Bart's cubicle wall. There were a lot of snapshots of babies on Bart's lap. In the middle, there was a photo of the entire family. There was another one of just Bart and his parents. Most of the pictures featured the love of his life, Daryl.

"You've got a big family," Logan commented as he yanked open desk drawers.

"Yep. We were just one big happy dysfunctional family."

"I was an only child," he commented dryly.

"Sometimes I wished I could have been one."

Logan saw prescription bottles in one of the drawers. He pointed and said, "What are these for?"

"They're antidepressants," Bart admitted. "I wouldn't be able to manage without them around here."

"What about these?"

"Painkillers for the migraines."

"And these?"

"Those keep me on an even keel. If I didn't take those I'd bounce off the walls or flip out. They were very helpful for being around Veronica."

Logan jotted the names and increments of the medications in his pad and closed the drawer. He glanced at breathtakingly beautiful nature scenes hanging on the cubicle walls.

"Those are beautiful," he said. "Did you shoot them?"

"Yeah."

"You've got quite an eye for beauty."

"Thank you. It's a gift from God."

"I go jogging in the park every day and don't ever see things like that."

"You have to really look," Bart said. "Well, I don't think I'd have the stomach for looking at dead bodies like you do."

"You're probably right."

"We all have our talents."

Logan apologized for the inconvenience and headed out.

* * *

Cox trained his eyes on images of scantily clad young women on Craig Holloway's office walls. Snapshots of Craig with his friends hung next to them. They all looked filthy, with various degrees of stubble. Tents were behind them. There was another one of Craig climbing a mountain.

"You're quite the adventurous one," Cox commented.

Craig grinned. "I love it! Ever try it?"

"Hell no. I'm a city boy."

"You ought to step out into nature."

"I probably should."

Craig leaned back in his seat and regarded Cox skeptically. "And just what are you looking for?"

"I'm not sure." He looked at empty plastic food containers scattered across the desk's surface. The trash can was filled to capacity with empty water bottles and paper cups and take-out cartons.

"I'm on deadline, so you need to wrap things up," he informed the detective.

"Fine."

Cox opened the little refrigerator on the floor and saw more bottles of water. He took them out and examined them.

"What are you doing?"

"Checking to make sure nobody's trying to get you too."

"What do I say? Thanks?"

Cox concentrated his efforts on obtaining evidence. Then he apologized for inconveniencing him and moved on to Tom Daniels's office.

* * *

Nicholas Bradshaw did not appreciate the interruption at all. He glowered at Logan, an edge of growing impatience creeping into his voice. "I told you what you wanted to hear. Why are you doing this? I've got work to do!"

Logan told him that the poison had not been in anything Veronica Talbot ate or drank at the party and that they had to look around the office.

"So you think I had something to do with her death? Is that what you're saying?"

"I'm just doing my job, Mr. Bradshaw."

Nicholas bristled when Frank moved closer to his desk.

"What the hell are you doing?" he snapped.

"I just need to take a look in your desk. It won't take long."

"This is a total invasion of privacy! It's like living in a police state!"

Anna peered over the cubicle wall and gave her colleague a stern look. "Come on, Nicholas. Don't be such a baby. Let him do his job. They're looking at all our stuff. They won't be here long."

Nicholas gave her a sideways glance and groaned. "Thanks, Mary Sunshine."

Logan pulled open the top desk drawer and thought Nicholas was going to have a coronary.

Nicholas shouted, "What the hell are you doing? It's not your business."

Anna rushed over to his side of the cubicle to see what was happening. Her eyes trained on the unflattering graphic representations of Veronica Talbot that Logan was sifting through. They were of a rather violent nature. Most of them depicted Veronica with her mouth wide open like she was screaming at someone. Blood spurted out of her chest in one of the images. Another one showed her head exploding. Nicholas was a predominant figure in one of them. He had on armor and was riding a white horse. Veronica's head was pasted onto a dragon. A sword was plunged into her chest.

Anna gasped and looked wild-eyed at Nicholas. There was a long, uncomfortable silence. "You should find better things to do with your free time, Nicholas," she said at last. Then she went back to her side of the cubicle.

"So drawing pictures of the murder victim is something you do for kicks, Mr. Bradshaw?" asked Logan.

"What I have in my desk drawer is really none of your business!" Nicholas shot back.

"Well, if you did it on office time, I would think it would matter to James Dobson."

"Please don't tell him."

"Did Veronica know about these?"

"Of course not!"

"Why did you do them?"

"It was just a joke. Something to do to release steam after she'd chewed me out for something. I didn't mean anything by it."

Logan grunted and said, "Well, I beg to differ." He pulled open the middle drawer and noticed an inhaler in the mix. "Do you have asthma?"

Nicholas nodded. "It's not as bad as it used to be. Sometimes I need it when I get anxious, which was quite often being around Veronica!"

Logan shut the drawer and started to go when Nicholas said, "Please don't mention the drawings to Dobson."

"I won't say anything, but word gets around."

Nicholas wiped a bead of sweat from his forehead and sat back in his swivel chair. He was too wound up to concentrate on the design he was working on, so he got up and headed toward the break room.

Logan poked his head around the cubicle and smiled at Anna. "I'm sorry to bother you."

"Oh, it's quite all right. How is the investigation going?"

He kept her up to date on what was happening and why it was necessary to look around Creative Concepts.

"Do you mind if I take a look in your desk?"

"No, go ahead. You won't find anything that interesting. Just office supplies. Staples, paper clips, and what not."

He took a quick look and immediately agreed that she was right. He closed the drawers and looked around.

"I hope you don't think that Nick is a psycho or something."

"I don't think anything at the moment."

"That's Nicholas for you. He didn't mean anything by those pictures. He just has a warped sense of humor. I guess we all have ways of relieving stress."

"I guess you're right." He thanked her and apologized for the intrusion.

A few minutes later, he met up with Cox in the lobby after all the offices had been searched. They compared notes and took their samples to the forensics lab. Later on, they met for drinks at their local hangout in Center City, and talked about old times.

* * *

"Your boyfriend must be getting pretty desperate if he had to come here with his gang of buffoons and go through our things the way they did," Nicholas Bradshaw said huffily.

"It had to be done," Penny replied in a calm tone. "If you have nothing to hide, then you shouldn't worry about it."

"It's an invasion of privacy."

"What are you hiding?"

"Did he tell you to snoop around in our business?"

"Come on, Nicholas. What do you expect? Veronica was murdered. He's not doing anything that he wouldn't be doing in any other case, which is asking suspects a lot of questions."

"I told him everything he wanted to hear. Why did he have to look through my stuff?"

"What are you hiding?"

"Nothing!" he insisted.

"Then let Frank do his job!"

"I hope they find out who did it soon. It's giving me the creeps knowing that somebody we work with every day could have done it! It's really a weird feeling!"

"We're all on edge," she said in a rather calm tone.

"I can't concentrate with all the distractions!" He walked hurriedly out of the break room.

She blew a deep breath out and muttered, "I wonder what's bugging him?"

CHAPTER 16

Dana Phillips never in a million years thought that she would be a murder suspect. She thought the whole thing was rather ironic. She always believed that every life was precious, and still couldn't believe that Frank Logan had accused her of murdering the Dragon Lady. After a short time with Veronica, the kindest, sweetest person on earth would probably want to murder her.

If it hadn't been for the abortion ad, she and Veronica wouldn't have gotten into the nasty argument that forced Ben Goldstein to resign. Veronica would never have been placed in a position of power, reeking havoc around the office. Things would have been different if Veronica had never hosted the party at her country home. Everyone hated her. Dana wondered if she still would have been poisoned at the party.

The mood around the office had been somber since Veronica Talbot's passing. The cold chill that everyone felt when Veronica stalked around the office, was lighter now. As the days went by, they were on edge, knowing that Frank Logan was delving into their personal business. It was ironic that the woman she worked so closely with was dating the detective who was asking so many questions.

Dana was not in the mood to talk to Marcus Campbell, owner of Liberty Bell Brewery. He was a large man with an overpowering voice. When they weren't discussing advertising campaigns, he had a raucous sense of humor. He always had them in stitches. Dana's mind drifted for a couple of minutes. Fortunately, Tom Daniels picked up the slack. Penny stared at her and knew that something was on her mind.

That was the way it had been for the past few weeks. Their minds were on the investigation. Without saying a word, everybody was wondering if the person they spent more time with than their families could possibly have slayed the Dragon Lady.

After the meeting, Dana rushed to the editing bay and sat next to Charles, who was concentrating on the counter at the bottom of the laptop screen. They had been working closely together for two years. Their personal relationship had intensified after they had gone out for drinks after work one night. That led to quick breaks from editing, which meant either take-out Chinese or pizza. Their little weekly cocktail ritual at the bar down the street led to spending more time with each other out of the office.

One day, Dana looked up from the footage that flashed across the screen in time to see Veronica scowling back at them from the door. She said nothing, but looked as cold as ice.

"What's her problem?" Dana asked Charles.

He looked up in time to see his wife march back down the hall.

"It's a long story. Trust me. You don't want to know."

"It must be so hard working with your wife."

"It has its advantages and disadvantages. If we worked at separate jobs, we would have split up years ago. We wouldn't have ever spent any time together."

"But you still have a daughter," she reminded him.

"I know."

"Well, I'm in the same boat with my boys. At least you've got somebody to look out for Tricia after school. I never know what the boys will get into. And they're getting to the age where they might experiment with sex and drugs."

He sighed and said, "It's a really hard thing to deal with." Then he took one last bite of his General Tso's chicken and tossed the carton in the trash can by the door. He turned his attention back on the two screens and rewound the footage about twenty seconds. "It's going to be hard knowing what to cut."

"I know."

"Let's just hope the Timkos won't be upset."

"I'm not as worried about upsetting the client. I'm more concerned about how Veronica will feel about it."

As the weeks went by, the Talbots' marriage grew more frigid. Charles spent more time with Dana after work. They timed their dinner meetings when they knew Veronica was swamped with work. One night, they had a few drinks too many, and one thing led to another. They wound up at his private suite in the Creative Concepts building. He and Veronica kept clean clothes there in case they worked late and didn't want to drive back to Townsend.

Dana and Charles were worried that people would find out, so they tried to be careful about their after-work activities. At first, Dana never stayed overnight. She had to get back to the boys. Then she got more daring. She planned nights with Charles when the boys were staying with friends. She felt like a hypocrite telling them that they couldn't fool around with their girlfriends when she was doing the same thing with Charles, but she didn't care! Time with Charles melted away her uneasiness. Then they weren't as careful.

A million thoughts rushed into her mind when she lay in Charles's protective arms. When would he dump Veronica? She hoped the boys would like Tricia. She thought they could blend into one happy family. The only thing that stood in her way was Veronica. God, Dana wished he would leave the woman! He was such a wimp for not standing up to her!

Everybody at the office knew that Charles had been staying at the suite a lot lately. Tom Daniels reported seeing the duo at the bar down the street. The grapevine twisted into many sordid rumors, basically because people had nothing better to do than to dissect the Talbots' crumbling marriage in minute detail. They whispered behind Charles and Dana's backs.

Now Veronica was finally out of the way, but it wasn't supposed to end up like this. If he had just divorced her, no one would have pointed fingers at her. She was the last person to see her alive. They all knew they had been arguing. But what difference did it make, anyway? The poison was already coursing through her veins while they argued.

Frank Logan was making her nervous with all his questions. And just what exactly was he looking for at the office?

She patted Charles's knee and watched the minutes and seconds flash across the bottom of the screen as the footage played out.

"It's running thirteen seconds long," he reported without looking at her.

"What should we cut?"

"I don't know."

"Maybe we could cut out the ending. Maybe put the voice over a little sooner. When the little boy comes running toward the foreground."

"And cut to the information."

He made her suggested cuts, and they watched the timer again.

He grimaced. "Now it's about six seconds long."

"Does it really make that much difference? It'll ruin the meaning of the piece if we cut out too much."

"It has to be thirty seconds." He drummed his fingers on the keyboard, lost in thought.

"It's Craig's fault. He shot too much footage."

"Well, I can't help it if Mr. Diamond can't make up his mind what he wants in it."

"Maybe I'd better go talk to James. Maybe Tom and Michelle can take a look."

"Too many cooks spoil the brew."

"Well, it wouldn't hurt to get their opinions. Michelle has impeccable taste. I'll be right back."

She got up and dashed out the door. Charles stared blankly at the screen and groused to himself.

CHAPTER 17

Anna McWilliams remembered how heavy the big fat man had been on her. His breath smelled of cheap booze and cigarettes. Occasional flashes of those horrifying eight minutes haunted her till this day.

She was fifteen that summer. Temperatures rose above ninety degrees, and her clothes clung to her moist skin. She was at her sister's apartment at the boarding house. She was babysitting while Danielle was at work.

Anna had seen the fat man down the hall a few times. She never thought he would force himself on her. She managed to fight him off. Thank God he didn't rape her.

She remembered the nice police lady who had tried to calm her down. Detectives were examining evidence all over the place. Blood was everywhere. On the floorboards. On the sofa. On that horrible man! The broken bottle that she had smashed on his head. He was taken to the ER and lived. If he had died, she would have gone to prison, Anna was sure of it.

Her parents sat with her. She cried with her mother. Her father blamed himself. They all blamed him. If it hadn't been for his ferocious treatment of Danielle, the whole ugly nightmare would not have happened.

It took her a long time to get over what had happened. It affected her relationships with others. She despised abusive people.

She knew just how wicked Veronica Talbot could be. She was a bully. Many years ago, Anna had vowed to get even with bullies.

When her temper tantrums were over, Veronica could pass as a nice person. She was just hyper. That was the nature of the business.

Anna didn't mean to screw up so much. Maybe it was just being around Veronica that distracted her. Maybe it was a subconscious thing. She didn't make mistakes with anyone else's projects, just Veronica's.

Nicholas Bradshaw was the only man that she felt safe around. She often watched him from across the room and envisioned a romantic relationship with him. He had an energy about him. Yes, he was as cocky as could be. He was childish and stuck on himself. But their brother-sister relationship prevented them from wanting to go any further. It was better to just keep things on a platonic level. They would just be really good friends.

She sipped her green tea and stared at the screen. She triple-checked her copy and made damn sure the client's name was spelled correctly this time before she printed it. She felt a sense of power knowing that a few days later, her design would be on buses and taxis all over the city.

CHAPTER 18

The drive to and from work gave Charles Talbot a lot of time to think. Years of working long hours in a stressful job were getting to him. Maybe he should get out of the advertising business and spend more time with Tricia. They certainly needed time together after the traumatic events of the past few weeks. He could start his own business in the Townsend area. It wouldn't be big-city advertising revenue, but it would be enough to keep him closer to home. It did not matter if it was a big city or a small town. Wherever people lived, there were businesses. And wherever there were businesses, owners and entrepreneurs needed to advertise so the public knew who they were and what they did.

His parents grew up during the Depression and expected their children to work hard. They never wanted to hear them belly-ache about their problems. After the hell that Stewart went through in WWII, he was not going to have wimpy children. Charles and his siblings were too scared to screw up in school or horse around in public for fear of the wrath of their father–what little they saw of him. Stewart's harsh life experiences affected everyone around him.

When he was sixteen, Charles spent the summer working at the local newspaper. He worked the graveyard shift at the printing press. It was a hot, stinky job. He went to work at 4 p.m. and came home exhausted after 6 a.m. His hair, clothes, and skin were black from newspaper ink. He worked there part-time when he was in college. After the first semester, he dropped out to work full-time. His parents were livid. They wanted all of their children to go to college. But he ignored them and worked his way up from the press room to the news room. He covered local high school sports events as a cub reporter. He knew what he wanted to do and wasn't turning back.

A couple years later, the very wise and prudent editor at the time suggested that Charles try working in the sales department. He proved to be a natural at advertising and eventually landed a lucrative position in the magazine industry. It wasn't long before a prestigious advertising company in the Big Apple lured him away from all of that. He helped the company take millions of dollars from the pockets of happy clients. The fast-paced lifestyle was in his blood. He got an adrenaline rush every time he worked on a high-priced project on deadline.

Charles sacrificed a happy family life for his career. He often regretted not spending as much time with Tricia as he should have. He let work interfere with personal relationships every time. At least, he could spend time with Veronica every day on the job–if that could really be considered a blessing.

He knew people wondered why they stayed together. Veronica was cold and callous. She constantly berated him in public. Yet, he just took it. So it was really no surprise that he'd struck up a friendship with Dana Phillips at the bar down the street during an extremely stressful day. He didn't know if he was just stressed out over an assignment or if it was all Veronica's doing. After being with her for five minutes, it would make anybody want to smoke or jump off a building.

Their talks moved to chance meetings at the gym. Dana was so sexy in her leopard-spot leotards, though she probably didn't think she was at that moment. He was on the treadmill. She was catching up on the latest Hollywood gossip in *People* magazine while she was on the exercise bike.

She flipped a page and said, "Having a bad day?"

"The usual."

"Why do you let Veronica do it?"

"I don't know."

"You are a saint to put up with her. I would've divorced her by now if I were you."

Then she launched in on her ex-husband. What a jerk!

Charles went over and sat at the exercise bike next to her. "Your ex-husband sounds like a louse."

"He's not at all supportive of the kids' needs. I don't mean to talk your ear off."

"It's okay." He reached for his towel and wiped a bead of sweat from his forehead.

"Rob is selfish and manipulative. Ohhhh. He makes me so angry! When I'm working late, he can't even step up to the plate and make sure the boys get home from soccer practice okay."

"At least we've got Kelly."

"I wish I had a Kelly. Anybody."

"What do you do when he doesn't help out?"

"I scramble around at the last minute and try to get a neighbor to pick them up. Sometimes they get rides home with their teammates' parents. What ticks me off the most is that he could do it. He just doesn't want to. He just wants to make my life as hard as it can be."

"You're better off without him. You deserve better than that. There are a lot of nice men out there. He's a lemon."

"You certainly don't deserve Veronica. Why do you stay with her?"

"Because of Tricia, for the most part. But sometimes...sometimes she still excites me like she used to. We both get a thrill from all the excitement. I know she can be a bitch at times. But she's high-strung. It's a fast-paced business we've gotten ourselves into."

Dana sighed and said, "I know."

"Maybe Rob is jealous of you. He can't compete. You make way more money than he does and maybe that makes him feel like half of a man or something. I don't know."

"I could've saved myself a fortune in therapy sessions if I had talked to you before."

"Well, I'm always around if you need to let off steam."

They were quiet for some time. She concentrated on a talk show. He was more interested in what the Dow was doing on the Fox Business channel on another TV.

She looked back at him and said, "Say, would you like to get a drink sometime? Maybe when my boys are with their dad? If Rob will let me."

His eyes narrowed. "Well...it would have to be a quick one after work. Depending on how late we go. I don't want to be too late for Tricia."

"She is a terrific girl!"

"Thank you."

"She is so talented."

"She wants to be an actress. Or a model. Or maybe a singer. She wants to do something like that."

"Well, good for her."

"I feel bad for her. I'm doing to her what my father did to my brother and sister and me."

"He was a workaholic too?"

He nodded and grunted. "We didn't see a lot of him when we were kids. He saw some horrible things in WWII. He was in the Philippines with the navy."

"I'm sure he had stories to tell."

"Actually, he didn't talk much about things that happened. He...he bottled things up. But when he got older, he started talking about those things. And then we couldn't get him to keep quiet about it. He drove my mother crazy. Every time someone mentioned the war, he'd open up and start talking about it too much."

"It must have felt good getting it out of his system."

"I think it was the dementia."

A couple weeks later, they met for lunch at a nearby bar. Over drinks, Charles told her about more things that had happened when he was growing up. Then she told him about her family. They talked so much, they didn't realize that an hour had gone by.

He glanced at his wristwatch and said, "Whoa! We'd better get back or they'll wonder where the hell we are!"

She smiled. "I'll see you in a few minutes."

Who knew that a simple, harmless drink could turn into much more? Choosing times and places to meet in secret was difficult, but made it that more exciting. They did not know how much they needed each other. Their relationship was escapism from their horrible lives at home. Dana needed a distraction from her creep of an ex-husband. Charles found Dana a welcome change of scenery from his witch of a wife.

Life with Veronica had grown increasingly chilly as the months went by. Charles knew what Dana wanted. He was seriously considering divorcing Veronica weeks before she was poisoned.

* * *

After rehearsal, Tricia filed out of the auditorium after the rest of the cast. Leading man Marty Pierce flashed his pearly white teeth and waved good-bye to them as he marched off with his arm around Jenna Riley, his leading lady on stage and in real life. Tricia watched them zip toward the parking lot, admiring him from a distance. He probably didn't even know she existed. No wonder they were so terrific playing their parts. They probably got a lot of additional one-on-one practice when their parents weren't at home.

The crowd thinned as kids with cars sped out of the school parking lot. The other students climbed in back of their parents' vehicles. Kelly was behind schedule today. She preferred it when Kelly picked her up.

When she had finally returned to school after the party, Kelly had driven her back and forth from school. It was a lot less stressful without her mother taking out her anger on the road.

Despite the pain that had been inflicted on her on a daily basis, Tricia realized that her mother couldn't help the way she acted. For some strange reason, she missed her. Home life was less stressful now. It was too quiet.

Concentrating on the play was the perfect distraction from all the horrible events of the past few weeks.

Tricia leaned against a pole and gazed at the road. She couldn't believe that her father had had the nerve to hang out with Ms. Phillips so much. Dana had been hanging around the house too much lately.

She thought about the fight her parents got into a few months ago. It was about Dana.

She could hear them screaming all the way up in her bedroom. It made it hard to concentrate on her homework.

"Keep your goddamned mitts off that woman."

"What are you talking about?"

"Don't deny it. You're sleeping with her!"

"You're drunk."

"You know damn well what I'm talking about. I see the way you look at each other at work, and it makes me sick!"

"Get a grip, Veronica."

"I will make you sorry you ever laid eyes on her."

"You can't scare me with your idle threats!"

"Maybe she should be transferred. I'll talk to James in the morning."

"You wouldn't do that."

"I'm so sick of you!"

"You need to calm yourself down before you have a stroke."

"I'll send her back to LA where she belongs! Maybe she'll fall into the earth!"

"If you send her to LA, then I'll take Tricia and go out there with her."

"You wouldn't dare!"

"Maybe it would be good for her. If she wants to be an actress, maybe she can make connections out there."

"You won't go."

"Try me. I have put up with your tirades for years! It's no wonder I wound up with Dana. Maybe if you had shown me an ounce of love or affection, maybe, just maybe–I wouldn't have cheated on you! That's right. We are doing it. We've hooked up with each other, and I don't feel the least bit guilty about it. She treats me with love and respect. Things I don't get from you!"

Tricia flinched at the sound of breaking glass. It was hard to make out what they were saying now. Her mother was cursing at him. A few moments later, she heard the car door slam. She went over to the window and peered out. She saw her mother speed out the driveway in their red jeep.

Tricia darted out of her room and stood at the balcony at the top of the steps. She looked forlornly at her father in the hallway.

"Just go back to your room," he ordered.

"I didn't say anything."

"Go on! You know how your mother is. Just give her some time to blow off steam."

Tricia started to go, but stopped in her tracks. "Are you and Mom going to get a divorce?"

"I don't know. Just go to your room. We'll discuss it later."

Tricia went back to her room and slammed her textbook shut. She spent the next two hours listening to music instead of studying. She didn't care if her mother gave her a lecture about it.

A car horn jarred her out of her bad thoughts. She looked at Kelly and smiled. She walked hurriedly to the car and sat next to her.

"Did you have a good day?" asked Kelly.

"It was okay."

"How is the play going?"

"It's a blast! We're having so much fun!"

"Well, I can't wait to see it." Kelly glanced to her left and right before pulling onto the hilly road leading to their house.

CHAPTER 19

Tricia was beaming as she followed her cast mates into the lobby. It was as if they had stepped out of the 1950s with their hair and outfits. She saw her father in the crowd and rushed over to him. He handed her a bouquet of red roses and gave her a big hug.

"You were terrific, honey! I'm so proud of you!"

"Thanks, Dad!"

She looked at Dana, who stood next to him, and they hugged each other.

"Way to go, baby!" Dana cried.

A throng of people clamored to have their pictures taken with "Danny" and "Sandy." Tricia stood next to her friends and soaked in the attention. There was so much commotion that it was hard to hear what people were saying.

Nicholas Bradshaw and Anna McWilliams were among audience members who wanted to shmooze with the cast. He was decked out in a blue button-down shirt and wine-colored cords. Anna looked a lot better than she usually did at work. Her hair had a certain bounce to it, and she looked quite attractive with a little bit of makeup. She had on a snug-fitting maroon dress and a beaded necklace. The high heels she was wearing made her look much taller. She would have looked a lot better if it hadn't been for her glasses.

Nicholas reached out to shake Tricia's hand and said, "You were just great!"

"I was just in the chorus."

"You had so many parts to play!" Anna chimed in. "You did a great job!"

"Thank you, Ms. McWilliams."

She smiled coyly. "You don't have to be so formal–call me Anna."

Nicholas sized up the cast's costumes. "It must have taken a lot of work to get this together."

Tricia's face lit up. "It took weeks, but it was a lot of fun!"

"Well, keep up the good work," Anna said. She reached in her jacket pocket and pulled out her digital camera. "Here, Nick. Take our picture with Tricia in her costume!"

Nicholas took the picture. Then he got a high school boy to take a picture of all three of them. They continued down the line and got their pictures taken with the other actors. People swarmed around "Danny" and "Sandy." Nick waited patiently to get a chance to talk to them. While he waited, he grinned at Charles and Dana from across the lobby. He finally got his chance to talk to the stars. Then he stood in between them as Anna snapped a couple of shots. Then somebody else took a picture of all four of them.

"Maybe I should get a leather jacket," muttered Nicholas as he merged with the crowd. "Women go crazy for them."

"There's something about leather jackets that make guys look really cool," agreed Anna. "You shouldn't have to wear one to impress women, though. Just be yourself."

"Whatever."

They met up with Charles and Dana and talked about how wonderful the kids were in the play.

Dana's eyes gleamed as she looked over at Tricia. "I think she's found her true calling."

Charles was glowing. "Indeed."

When the crowd thinned, Tricia invited them to the opening night cast party at a pizza place a few miles from the high school.

The stars of the show sat at a long table with their family and friends. At the next table, Tricia sat at the center with the adults, while the kids sat at the other end. Dana was so busy talking to Charles that she wasn't paying attention to what her boys were doing. Kyle and Kevin were texting so much that they were oblivious to what was going on. They had barely said a word after the play to indicate whether they liked it or not. Cindy constantly hollered across the table to get Tricia's attention, commenting on her most favorite parts of the play. Kelly put her finger to her mouth and told her daughter to be quiet.

Nicholas Bradshaw sat at the other end and babbled, thinking the others could hear him. "I wasn't in the cool crowd in high school. The cool kids would walk right past me like I was invisible. My folks laid out the most embarrassing rules when we were with girls." He started cackling uncontrollably. Everybody turned to look at him and then continued their private conversations. "It's only just now that my brothers have been leaking out juicy tidbits from when they were out with their ex-girlfriends.

They had all the charm and sophistication. And what was I left with?" he asked with a wave of his hand.

Anna tapped his hand and said, "You need a shot of confidence, Nick."

"How could any guy have confidence with older brothers like that? And then–and then–my dad would always say, 'There's a girl for you,' every time we went somewhere, for crying out loud!"

"Maybe he was just trying to help you."

Nicholas sat up straight and brushed his hair back. "I don't need help." He took a few sips of his beer and set the mug on the table. "And they're always on me about settling down."

Anna sighed. "I know. I'm not looking forward to going home for Christmas. I get that speech all the time."

Nicholas nodded his head enthusiastically. "I know, isn't it annoying? They say I'm in my late twenties. I should be married with a few kids. I try. I go out and have a few laughs with some girls I like. It's not my fault it doesn't work out."

"Maybe you should ask yourself why that is," Anna suggested.

"I really don't have a clue. They think I'm a laugh riot. But then something always goes wrong to foul it up."

"That's why you've got me. We stick together like glue."

Nicholas howled like a hyena.

Everyone stared at him in astonishment and went back to their conversations.

"What's so funny?" Anna asked him.

"My folks think we should get married!"

Anna's face turned bright red. "Really? They said that?"

"All the time. They ask me, how is Anna doing? And I tell them, she's fine. Does your mom ask about me?"

"Sometimes."

"Well, anyway, I never fit in with the cool crowd in high school. I guess I just didn't have it in me to be so bad, like the kids in the show. I was kind of a geek."

Tricia turned and smiled vaguely at him. "That's too bad." Then she turned her attention on what her father was saying.

"I wish your mother could have seen you, honey."

"I think she was probably looking over you," Kelly said.

"She was probably pointing out all my mistakes," Tricia added.

"Girls never looked at me that way in high school," Nicholas continued. "Maybe I'm just a bit self-conscious. Maybe that explains a lot. My brothers are married and have kids by now. And so do a lot of my friends."

"Well, maybe you should do something about it," Anna suggested. She turned her attention on Tricia and asked, "Is this what you want to do?"

"You bet!"

"Have you talked to your dad about doing ads at the company?"

"We've talked a little bit about it."

"I really think you should. You don't know how lucky you are having a father who works in the advertising business."

Dana could not have agreed more. "A lot of kids can only dream of catching a lucky break. We cast hundreds of actors all the time. None of them have a father who's in the advertising business like yours."

Tricia's eyes were bright with enthusiasm. "Do you think I could be in a commercial?"

"I'll definitely run the idea by your dad," Dana assured her.

"My mother wouldn't let me do it. She said I wasn't old enough."

"We use infants in our ads!" Dana cried.

"That's what I kept telling her. She wouldn't let me do anything."

"She let you do school plays," Anna said. "You've got to start somewhere."

Tricia looked at Anna and asked, "Can you say something to my dad about it?" She did not want Dana to be involved.

"Sure, but maybe Dana would have more clout since she's more directly involved with casting parts for commercials."

Dana grinned and said, "I'll talk to him."

"Thanks."

CHAPTER 20

By Thanksgiving, the Veronica Talbot case was leading nowhere. Test results of the samples collected at Creative Concepts were slowly coming back. He hoped that forensics would find the poison in one of the samples they had collected at the office. If they didn't find anything, he was afraid the murderer would walk.

Bright and early that morning, Frank and Penny picked up Gramps and drove to her parents' house in Glenside. It was the same house that she had grown up in. The neighbors were friendly and looked out for each other. They hung their American flags on every holiday. Sometimes it seemed like they competed with each other to see who had the most elaborate Christmas decorations. It was close enough to Philly that Penny could have fun with her friends when they got older.

George and Maribeth Lane were always supportive in everything their children did. George was a social worker, and Maribeth was a nurse. George spent a lot of time working with underprivileged children and kids from broken homes whose parents were strung out on drugs. Sometimes one or both of them were in jail. Their children were often put in separate foster homes when Child Protective Services stepped in. Some of the kids were abused by alcoholic parents.

It was difficult to have a quiet, "normal" family life when George was getting emergency telephone calls. He was often called out in the middle of the night to help a battered wife and her frightened children. It was such a depressing job, that he burned out. At Maribeth's urging, he quit his job to spend more time with his family. He opened a private practice in their home and dealt with alcoholic or drug-dependent clients, couples with marital problems, and teens who questioned their sexuality.

Penny learned two valuable lessons from her parents: you have to help people who can't help themselves, and keep on the straight and narrow path. You would think this no-nonsense attitude would have made Penny serious, but she always had a zest for life–a "live to party" attitude, in a clean way, of course. Though George was never able to talk about his clients' problems, Penny had heard bits and pieces of stories. Maybe that was what had made her the caring woman she was today.

George and Maribeth always instilled in their children the importance of helping those in need. Maribeth's capacity for kindness and nurturing as she cared for sick patients, motivated Penny to help with charitable organizations. Her parents were so proud of her when she got involved with groups that raised money for suffering people.

With her parents at work a lot, Penny helped around the house. When she was in high school, she made sure she was home in time to get dinner for her little brother, Steven, and her sister, Lois, if her mother was working late hours or if her father was helping a poor family deal with a traumatic event. George and Maribeth had told them horror stories about what happened to kids their age, whose parents beat them up. Those kids were not as fortunate. They had to live with total strangers in foster homes. Sometimes, kids from broken families missed meals. Their parents were shooting up and did not feed them, and they looked like skeletons. The only meal they got was at school.

The stress of dealing with drug addicts and children from broken homes had taken its toll on George's health. He was now recovering from bypass surgery. Maribeth cut back her hours at the hospital to care for him at home. He had not been the nicest of patients, and she had not been the kindest of nurses when it came to caring for her husband. When he felt up to it, he went back to work but only dealt with couples with marital problems and teenagers and their issues.

They were really pleased the day Penny brought Frank to meet them for the first time. He was the perfect match for her. He was a straight arrow and tried to help people. But he was also a workaholic, and they were concerned that he did not spend enough time with her. It was a constant source of irritation for Penny. Every time they brought it up, she ignored them.

Fortunately for Frank, the football game would be on and there would be little, if any, talking.

The football game blared in the background. Penny helped her mother prepare the turkey in the cramped kitchen, while the men gathered around the TV in the family room. Every so often, they heard screaming and cheering. When things weren't going so great, one of them would scream, "Oh come on!"

After a hectic week at the office, Penny felt relaxed working with her mother. It gave them a chance to catch up. Maribeth talked about church and the neighbors. Penny talked about happenings in Townsend and at work. Then Maribeth mentioned the unmentionable topic.

"How is Frank's case going?"

Penny grimaced. "Not well."

"I'm sorry to hear that."

"He's hit a dead end, and he isn't sure if he'll be able to crack this one."

Maribeth stirred the mashed potatoes on the stove and said, "A bump in the road has never stopped him before."

"But there are so many ways that the poison could have been slipped to Veronica. The tests take a long time–all the samples they collected."

"Well, yes, it can take a while to gather the information," agreed Maribeth. "But once they've got it, they'll be able to pinpoint what they're looking for. And then Frank will have a better idea of what happened."

"I hope so."

Penny pulled open the cabinet door and carried the fancy china plates with the floral designs to the dining room table. They were the ones that looked beautiful but were only used for special occasions.

"Oh man!" her father shouted.

She looked in and smiled at them. They looked so happy in their element. Even Gramps seemed happy. It did him good being around people. Well, this was definitely the perfect diversion for Frank, Penny thought. Maybe being away from the case for a few days would clear his head.

Their eyes met. She winked at him and continued placing the plates around the table.

During a commercial, he entered the kitchen and scooped silverware into both hands. He craned his neck in the direction of the family room and helped her set the table.

He leaned in to give Penny a kiss and said, "It smells great! When is dinner? I'm starving!"

"In a couple of hours!" Maribeth shouted from the kitchen.

He helped Penny fold the cloth napkins, and they set them next to the plates. When the game came back on, he bolted back to his spot on the sofa next to her father.

"Deserter!" Penny yelled into the family room.

"Yeah, yeah!" Frank exclaimed.

Gramps beamed at their lively banter. George was too preoccupied with the game to notice.

* * *

The football game was just a blur in the background. Tom Daniels's attention was shot.

Judith stared blankly at her son. He looked to see if there was any recognition, but there was none. Michelle pressed his hand as he averted his eyes from his mother's gaze. Her face was pallid. Her eyes were bright red. Her shoulder-length silver hair was matted and in her eyes.

She seemed frail and helpless.

Framed snapshots of a lifetime of fond memories hung on the drab nursing home walls. Some days she looked at them and felt temporary happiness. Other days it was like looking at strangers in a bus station. Her late husband, Henry, was a complete stranger to her. They had been married for fifty-six years.

"Who are you?" Her voice sounded weak.

"It's Tom, Mother."

"Who's he?"

"I'm your son."

She looked inquisitively at him and said, "I have a son?"

"You have two sons, actually. Me and Ron."

"Hmmm." Judith Daniels drifted into a trance-like state.

"I want you to meet Michelle. She's my fiancé."

Judith glanced over at Michelle. It was like she was looking right through her.

"Hello," Judith said simply.

Michelle smiled brightly. "It's so nice to meet you, Mrs. Daniels."

Judith did not say anything. She just stared past them. Tom fumbled for things to talk about, but it was hard. Michelle did most of the talking.

"It's such lovely weather we're having," Michelle said. "It's nice and crisp. Just like fall is supposed to feel like. Isn't that right, Mrs. Daniels?"

Judith did not say.

A short time later, Tom said, "Well, maybe–maybe we better let you get some rest, Mother."

He rose unsteadily to his feet and leaned down to kiss her on the forehead. She jerked forward at his mere touch.

"Who are you?" she screeched. "Help! Help!"

An attendant entered the room to investigate. Tom explained what happened and waited till things calmed down before they left.

Michelle reached for his hand, and they slowly walked down the long, winding corridor. "She isn't getting any better."

Her grip tightened. "I'm so sorry, Tom."

"It really isn't fair. She was so vital. So alive. To be reduced to...that?"

"It's so sad. But thank you for sharing this part of your life with me. It must be so hard to manage things on your own–what with your brother on the West Coast."

"Ron means well. But I'm pretty much the primary care giver."

They went past the cafeteria and saw residents sitting with their loved ones at tables, eating a Thanksgiving feast.

"I had thought about eating in here with my mother, but..."

She tapped his hand. "It's okay."

"She wouldn't remember anyway. It–it wouldn't be meaningful to her."

They walked out the entrance, and he told her to wait at the curb while he went to get his car. It was really just an excuse. He didn't want Michelle to see him choke up. He sat in the driver's seat and wept like a baby.

It was the same ritual every time he left the place. Working here must be so depressing, he thought. He imagined there was a high turn-around rate.

When he'd had time to calm down, he stuck the key in the ignition and started the car. He pulled in front of the building, and Michelle got in. No explanations for why it had taken so long were necessary. They rode in silence until he pulled onto I-95. About forty-five minutes later, he pulled in front of his son Andrew's house.

The second hardest part of the day was now underway as he drove to the cemetery. They got out and walked to the grave stone. Michelle stood at a safe distance and let them have their privacy.

They put a rose on his late wife Julia's grave and stood in silence a moment. Then Tom said, "Michelle and I are getting married. I'm sure you won't mind. You'll get to care about her after you get to really know her."

Andrew patted his father's shoulder and said nothing.

Tom looked at the gravestone and said, "Now here's the bad news. I'm a murder suspect. Can you believe it?"

* * *

During another commercial, Frank went into the kitchen and carefully picked up a gravy boat, holding both ends. He went into the dining room and came back for the basket of rolls. Penny stood in the entryway and handed him a bowl of cranberry sauce. He set it on the table and made a bee-line for the counter. He swiped a couple of pieces of white meat and darted back into the den. They watched the game in silence as the final seconds ticked down. Then it was time for dinner.

"Are you working on any interesting cases, Frank?" asked Penny's little brother, Steven.

Frank briefly went over the details of the Veronica Talbot investigation, but did not want to admit that it was steadily going downhill.

"I think it's so exciting what you do."

"Well, it's not always that exciting. There are a lot of slow times in Townsend."

George poured a little too much gravy on his mashed potatoes in his wife's opinion. She shook her head and looked at him disapprovingly. He got the message and tried scooping some of it back into the gravy boat. Penny handed him a bowl of green beans, and he dumped them in between his meat and the stuffing.

George looked up at Frank and said, "So why don't you just move back to Philly? It would make things a lot easier for Penny."

She tapped her father's hand and said, "There has never been a time when my life has been simple. Things would be totally boring if I didn't have all the excitement."

George grumbled and shook his head. "If you ask me, I think you're creating a lot of stress for yourself, Penny."

"Now, Dad, you promised you wouldn't mention it. We just moved in together. Isn't that good enough for you?"

"Come on, you guys," Steven cut in. "Let's eat in peace, okay?"

"Is it like this all the time?" asked Frank.

Steven chuckled. "Sometimes it's worse!"

Penny snickered. "It was a lot worse when we were kids."

Steven nodded and smiled, thinking about some of their most colorful Thanksgiving incidents. He wiped his mouth. "We were always yelling at each other."

George grinned mischievously and said, "Until I put them straight."

Steven looked at Frank and groaned. "He scared us with tales from the streets. We thought we'd starve to death or something."

George laughed heartily. "It got your attention, didn't it?"

"It certainly did," Penny agreed.

"Well, you look good, George." Frank was quick to change the subject.

"He looks a lot better than he did after the heart surgery," Maribeth said. "But he hasn't been the best patient! He just put all my years as a nurse to the test!"

Everyone laughed except George.

"I keep reminding him how lucky he is to be married to a nurse."

"Oh, I know. The doctors said if I hadn't gone to the emergency room the night that I was experiencing heart attack symptoms, I would've been gone like that," he said with the snap of his fingers.

"It was the most frightening night of my life," Maribeth reiterated. "And I've dealt with a lot of trauma patients at the hospital."

"Sometimes it's easier dealing with strangers than with your own family members," Frank said.

Steven's eyebrows furrowed. "He's lost so much weight. We're really lucky he's still with us."

"It makes you appreciate your family more when something like that happens, doesn't it?" Gramps said.

"Especially when they aren't there anymore," Frank added.

"So when are you two going to settle down?" George asked.

"When the time is right," came Frank's tried and true response.

Penny laughed and said, "If we did get married, Frank would probably be called out on an emergency on our wedding day!"

They all laughed.

Frank was introspective about it. "I wouldn't let that happen, babe. That's what Flosky is for." He looked at Maribeth and said, "The stuffing is great!"

* * *

Charles Talbot did not feel at all like eating Thanksgiving dinner at home, so he took everyone out to a quaint restaurant about ten miles from Townsend. Tricia spent most of the evening jabbering with Cindy McDougal. She practically ignored Dana's sons who were about her age.

Eating out in public with her boys was a rare occasion for Dana. She was busy at work, and they were busy at school. They never had much time to spend together.

Talk about the murder investigation was strictly forbidden.

"Going through Veronica's personal effects has been so tiring," Charles said. "I don't know what I'd do without your help, Kelly."

"I know how hard this has been for you both," she said.

"I don't even know what to do with it all."

"I can help you put it in piles to keep and piles to get rid of," Dana volunteered. "Maybe we can have a yard sale or something."

"Veronica didn't do yard sales," Charles said. "Isn't it ironic?"

"Well, you can't keep everything."

"Well, we don't want her brother to get his greedy mitts on her things. The antiques that she collected over the years are worth a lot of money. He would probably sell them..." He looked at the kids and edited himself. "For unscrupulous activities."

"What are you guys talking about?" Tricia asked.

"I'll explain it when we get home. Are you enjoying your dinner?"

"Very much. It's delicious!"

Dana's eyes sparkled as she looked at Charles. "I have always loved coming here."

"When you two were sneaking around?" Tricia blurted.

Charles looked dumbfounded at his daughter and said, "Patricia Jean Talbot!"

"It's okay, Dad. You don't have to sugarcoat things. I'm not a little kid. I know what's really going on." She pointed to the boys. "And so do they."

Kyle cocked his head at his mother and said, "Huh? What's she talking about?"

Dana looked him square in the eyes. "I will discuss it with you later."

Kelly changed the subject. "I can't believe it's almost time for Christmas. I haven't even started shopping yet."

"I can't wait!" Cindy exclaimed.

Dana looked at Tricia and said, "Well you were terrific in the play."

"We had a blast doing it!"

Kelly's face glowed. "Maybe someday we'll see your name up in lights on a Broadway marquee."

"Or on the cover of a fashion magazine," Dana added.

"Mother never encouraged it," Tricia said. "She thought I was too flat-chested!"

"You look fine," Kelly encouraged. "I keep telling you that, but you won't listen."

The boys sized her up and said nothing.

"She said she'd pay for me to get a boob job," Tricia blurted out.

The boys snickered and cried out in unison, "Really!"

Charles stared at his daughter in stunned silence for a moment. "She did not tell you that," he said finally.

"She did."

Kelly nodded her head. "I heard her."

Charles rolled his eyes and said, "It figures."

Kelly leaned down and spoke in a tone that was warm and gentle. "What I don't understand is why you can't just be happy with the package that God gave you, sweetie?"

"Because I could look so much better with a boob job." Tricia got up and walked hurriedly across the room.

Charles started to go after her, but Dana motioned for him to stay put.

"Excuse me." She got up and off she went to catch up with Tricia.

"Why can't she just be happy with the way she looks?" Charles asked in bewilderment. "She's beautiful!"

Kyle smirked and said, "That's not what the kids on Facebook and Twitter say."

Charles's eyes flashed with rage. He turned his attention to Kyle. "What do you mean?"

Kyle handed him his smart phone and showed him the latest nasty comment a girl from her school had made. Charles was shocked and horrified when he read the messages. Her head was superimposed on pencils and broomsticks with taunting names like "Titless Tricia" and "Amazing Invisible Girl." "GO IN A CORNER AND DIE, FREAK!"

Kyle yanked the phone out of Charles's hand. "The other ones are so bad, maybe you shouldn't look at them right now."

"They might make you toss your cookies on the plate," Kevin said.

Charles shook his hands and shouted, "They are savages! How can anybody be so cruel? What's wrong with kids these days? I'm going to have a little talk with their parents. By the time they're through with me, they'll wish their monsters had never been born!"

He shoved his half-eaten meal aside. He had lost his appetite.

Tricia seemed to be in a much better frame of mind when she came back with Dana. They sat back down at their seats and Tricia said, "Dana just told me there's a spot open for a kid in an ad that they're shooting in a few days!"

"That's wonderful!" Kelly cried.

Dana looked at Charles and said, "I told her she could do it as long as it's okay with you."

Tricia's eyes gleamed as she looked at her father. "Can I do it? Please. Please."

"I think it would be a really good thing for you to do. It'll give us more time to spend together. Did you thank Ms. Phillips?"

"Yes! Thank you."

Dana grinned. "You're welcome. I hope you have fun with it."

She told Tricia what to do on the day of the filming, and then the boys talked about their soccer team. And then Cindy jabbered on about school.

Charles concentrated his attention on his troubled daughter and wondered how he could get through to her. At least filming the TV commercial was something that would take their minds off the investigation.

* * *

James and Edna Dobson spent a subdued Thanksgiving dinner at a restaurant on City Avenue. His son, Tim, was busy and couldn't bring the kids this year. They barely spoke. Normally, the holidays were their only chance to catch up on their hectic lives.

James really couldn't blame him. He had worked long hours when Tim was growing up. After he divorced his first wife, James saw even less of him.

Edna and James ate in silence. The room was filled with other families who had chosen to eat out on Thanksgiving rather than cook for their own reasons. She looked sadly at the people who were eating alone and figured they must have missed a plane or had to work. Why else wouldn't they be with loved ones tonight?

James dreaded eating out with Edna. They had run out of things to talk about. The wind had gone out of the sails of their marriage. They had been drifting apart for some time now and were afraid to admit it to each other.

"I would think you would have had better taste than to get mixed up with Veronica Talbot," said Edna out of the blue.

He met her gaze. "What?"

"I know what the office gossip is, James. I don't think you were foolish enough to mess around with that horrible woman."

"We never–she just always came to my office to cause a problem for whomever she was upset with at the moment."

Edna cut a piece of turkey. "The white meat is so moist. It's wonderful."

"It's good–but not as good as the way you make it."

"It's not bad though. We should come here more often. You're always so busy."

"I know. I'm sorry."

"Are you having an affair?"

He shoved a pile of mashed potatoes on his plate and took a bite. He looked up at her and said, "Yes."

"Who is she?"

"A woman I met a few months ago. Not from the office."

Her face took on a stricken look. There was a long, painful silence.

"What are you going to do about it?" she asked finally.

"I don't know," he admitted.

"Did Veronica know about it?"

"Yes."

"Did you kill her?"

He glared monstrously at her. "Of course not? What would make you think such a thing?"

"I can't believe you! How long were you planning on sneaking around? Were you ever planning on telling me?"

Patrons stopped what they were doing and stared at them in astonishment. He was quiet for a moment. He shoved a forkful of white meat in his mouth and said, "I don't think so."

She waved her hands, her voice growing louder. "So you were just going to string me along! Is that what you're telling me?"

He reached for her hand, but she pulled it away. "Please, you've got to understand. It had just gotten to a point where I couldn't talk to you anymore."

"Don't you find me attractive anymore?"

"Yes. But we're total strangers now. We don't have anything in common anymore."

"So what are you saying?"

"I want a divorce."

Tears streaked her cheeks. People were still looking at them. She wiped her moist eyes and sniffled.

"I didn't want it to turn out like this," he tried to explain. "I wanted to tell you, but I didn't know how to do it."

"So you just waited till I heard the vile rumors at the party! How could you do this to me? I deserve a lot better!"

"I'm sorry. I didn't mean for it to happen this way."

"Is this how it happened with your ex-wife?" She got up and stormed out.

A woman across the room gave him a disapproving look. He concentrated on his meal.

* * *

The football game was on, but Craig Holloway spent more time ogling the pretty brunette on the other side of the bar. It wasn't the best way to spend the holidays, but it was better than being alone.

Mindy Sawyer had given him his walking papers a while ago. They had fun while it lasted until she saw him flirting with a beautiful model, and that was that.

He never had trouble finding an attractive woman to keep him company.

He sat next to the brunette at the bar and stared ravenously at her as they made small talk. A few beers later, they wound up at his apartment.

She temporarily filled the void in his empty life. In the morning, she would be gone, only to be replaced by another woman who would eat up his empty promises of photo shoots on the beach or other exotic locales.

CHAPTER 21

When Anna was in high school, she hoped that her parents wouldn't find out that her sister, Maggie, was hanging out with the partying crowd. Sometimes Maggie was so stoned that she told her parents that she was too sick to get out of going to church. Then, it happened. Greg went into her bedroom and found pot stashed in her bureau.

He stomped down to the den and waved the baggie in her face. "What the hell is this?"

"What do you think it is?" Maggie asked in defiance.

He smacked her on the head and shouted, "What the hell is wrong with you?"

Anna was a lot bigger now and refused to stand idly by and watch this time. She went over to break them up, but her father pushed her onto the floor.

"Stay out of this, Anna!"

"No, I won't!" Anna's voice shook. "Leave her alone!"

"Get out!" he shouted at the top of his lungs.

Catherine helped Anna up and pulled her out of the room. They stood in the doorway, so frightened they couldn't move. Greg struck Maggie repeatedly.

Her fingers trembled as she dialed 9-11. Maggie was taken to the emergency room.

Greg was arrested for child abuse and did time in jail.

After all that had happened in her life, Anna was not one to judge others for their mistakes. She was a deeply forgiving woman, except where her father was concerned.

* * *

"It's so nice that you two could finally find time to have supper with us," Helen Ferguson said.

Penny grinned. "It's always so hard to find the time. You never know when Frank is going to be called out at night to investigate something."

"That's the life of a detective, I guess." Helen's face flushed with happiness as she looked at them.

"The spaghetti is really good, Mrs. F.," Frank said. "You should open a restaurant."

"How is the Talbot case going?" asked her husband, Gus.

"It's challenging," Frank admitted. "But I can't really talk about it."

"He's always tight-lipped about these things," Penny explained.

"I just don't want to look like a fool if my theories don't pan out."

Helen gushed and said, "I can't believe you actually stepped foot in the Talbots'house! I've always wondered what it looks like inside."

"It's beautiful!" Penny exclaimed. "It's just like you step back in time when you go inside. You should see the antique furniture!"

Helen pointed at their modest furnishings. "It's probably better than what we've got."

"The same with us."

Helen sipped her tea, her eyes sparkling. "I bet Mrs. T. was very precise with her decorations."

"I heard her talk about the house at the office from time to time. She had an eye for detail. She was quite the perfectionist professionally and at home. She wanted the furnishings to match the period."

"Our furniture matches the period all right," Gus said with a roll of the eyes. "Some of our junk is probably fifty years old."

"Then maybe they're antiques," Penny quipped.

"I wouldn't call what we got antiques. Let's just say it's lived in."

Helen leaned toward Penny and said, "I've been begging him to get rid of the reclining chair for years! You've seen it, with all the springs hanging out."

"It's a classic. It's perfectly contoured to the shape of my butt."

They all laughed.

Frank took a bite of his bread and said, "That's what I tell Penny when she wants to toss my stuff."

"What is it about men and their things?" Helen wondered.

Mirthful crescents formed around Penny's eyes. "It's a mystery that we'll never figure out. I guess I wouldn't make a very good detective."

Frank reached for her hand and gently stroked it. "You would make an excellent detective." He looked from Gus to Helen. "She is my eyes and ears at the advertising firm."

Helen's eyes flashed with interest. "You don't say. What are you finding out?"

"That she's working for a bunch of treacherous people," Frank answered for her.

"They're not that bad!" Penny insisted. "They've got their secrets, and so do we."

Frank chomped on the bread and said, "The bread is really good, Mrs. F."

"I'm glad you like it. I slaved in the kitchen all day for that."

"She spent hours at the store preparing for tonight," Gus commented dryly.

Helen shook her head. "It wasn't that long!"

"It just seems that long."

"How is your grandfather doing?" Helen asked Frank.

He twirled noodles onto his fork and took a bite. He looked at Helen and said, "He's had a set back. He–he had a fall after Thanksgiving and had to go to a rehabilitation center."

"Oh, Frank, I'm sorry to hear that."

"I feel so guilty about not being there for him as much as I should."

"You shouldn't blame yourself, Frank."

"I know."

Penny rubbed Frank's hand, her eyes flashing with concern. "I tell him that all the time."

Frank grimaced. "It's been one thing after the other, and we haven't had time to see him as much as we'd like."

Gus had a pensive look. "It's a tough situation. It's a really hard thing to see your parents or grandparents get older."

Frank drank his tea. "He's always been so independent. And now, he's just upset that he can't get around on his own. He has to ask staffers at the rehabilitation center to take him places. I know he doesn't want to be a burden on me."

"We've been talking about having him move in with us," Penny added.

Gus and Helen exchanged surprised looks.

"Won't it be pretty cramped in your apartment?" asked Helen.

"Well, we've been talking it over," Penny said. "Maybe we should move closer to Jenkintown."

"It would be a little closer for Penny to get to work," Frank said. "Sometimes she doesn't get back till real late. And then she has to get up real early to go to work."

"You live in your car, Penny," Gus said. "I used to do the same thing."

"Sometimes it can be pretty rough," Penny admitted.

"We can make it work," Frank said after a long silence. "We could find someplace that's handicapped accessible, and Gramps could move in with us. I don't mind a little bit of a drive to work. It's the least I can do. He raised me after I lost my parents. And believe me, I was a real nasty bastard at the time. I gave him a run for his money."

Helen looked in awe at him. "It's amazing that you can live in the same apartment building with people for years and not know what they went through. I knew you had trouble back then, but I didn't know how bad it was for you."

Penny reached for Frank's hand and said, "It made him a stronger person."

Helen wiped her mouth with a napkin. "Well, we don't want you to leave, but sometimes you do what you've gotta do. Does anybody want any more tea? I hope you saved room for the apple pie."

Penny got up and followed Helen into the kitchen.

* * *

The TV blared in the background as Frank and Penny prepared dinner three days later. They cherished the moment. It was the first time in days that they could eat dinner together at the same time. Their momentary relaxation was short-lived unfortunately.

His cell phone on the coffee table rang and he went to answer it. She watched his face change from relaxed to nervous.

"That's terrible!" he exclaimed. Then he hung up.

Penny rushed over to him, her eyes wild with horror. "What's wrong?"

"Gramps apparently caused a commotion at the nursing home!"

CHAPTER 22

Frank swerved around the hairpin turn a little too fast. The wheels screeched as he slowed to better negotiate the turn. His thoughts were on his grandfather. He had to get to Jenkintown as fast as he could.

He was overcome with feelings of guilt and dread at the same time. Frank felt bad that he was so busy that he couldn't get over to see Gramps as much as he should. The man who had raised him since he was a surly teenager was now in need of his help. Gramps had always been independent. Now he depended on Frank.

He knew full well that Gramps did not want to be in the nursing home. Frank knew that even if he only had to stay there long enough to recover from his fall, Gramps would feel like a prisoner.

Gramps would rather be fishing on a nice sunny day. Frank wished they could both be in their favorite spot. It would be an escape from reality. An escape from thinking about Gramps's long-term needs. An escape from realizing that the once vital man that raised him to adulthood was slowing down.

Frank tried to ease his guilt of not visiting him enough lately by concentrating on the Veronica Talbot case. It was better than watching Gramps slowing down. If there was anything he could do to help, Frank would do it, but he didn't know what to do. His only option was to just help him as much as he could when he visited him. The trip back to Townsend was always heartbreaking after watching Gramps' painful decline.

How could he get Gramps to listen? He was a stubborn man. But Frank could be just as stubborn if he had to be. He would treat Gramps like one of his suspects. He would be tough, but firm. He would lay the cards out on the table and tell it like it was.

This time it would be different. Gramps would listen to him. Frank knew it would take a miracle for that to happen.

He cranked up the volume on his radio and sped down the road.

* * *

"I'm not sorry I did it," Gramps said. "How would you feel being cooped up inside all day?"

"Gramps, I'm supposed to take care of you. You can't walk away from here. You might end up in the hospital."

"It was worth a try. I'm sorry to put you in this position, Frank. I don't want anyone to be responsible for me. You have a life and I'm interfering."

"You aren't interfering, Gramps. You've always been there for me. It's my turn to take care of you."

"Don't do it at Penny's expense. Don't let her go this time."

"I won't. But you can't keep trying to escape."

"As long as I'm able, I'll do it."

"Would you like to live with me? We've talked about this before. Penny and I have been talking about moving somewhere about half way between Philly and Townsend. Something a little bigger."

"I'd interfere. I've always been open-minded. But, I don't think Penny would like it if she came out in her underwear or something."

"It won't be like that. We'll talk about this next time. I need to get back to the case."

"How is it going?"

Frank grimaced and said, "Not well."

He gave him a brief run-down of what he had found out recently as they headed back to the main desk. They rounded a corner and went past nurses and residents as they walked down the long corridor.

"It doesn't sound like Veronica was a very nice person. Everybody she worked with hated her."

Frank nodded and grunted. "It isn't the kind of place Penny should be. I keep telling her that. But getting her to listen is as impossible as getting you to listen, Gramps. It's a highly stressful job with a high turn around rate. And she works long hours."

"I agree. There are other jobs."

"But she loves it."

"Well, all that stress can't be good for her health. Plus, your job is extremely stressful."

"I know, but if I wasn't out there putting bad guys away, who else would?"

Gramps beamed. "Nobody is as smart as you are."

"Well, maybe other people are smarter, but they don't go the extra mile like I do."

"And that is most of your problem, Frank. You and Penny aren't spending enough time together."

Frank blew a deep breath out and said, "Boy, don't I know it."

"You two need to go on a vacation or something."

"That would be nice, but–"

"No buts," Gramps interrupted. "You two make too many excuses."

"We're doing the best we can."

"It doesn't look that way to me."

"We need to talk about your living arrangements when you blow this joint."

"We'll have to talk about it later."

"Now who is making excuses?"

Gramps dismissed his comment with a sigh and a wave. When they reached the lobby, Frank hugged him and watched a staffer help Gramps back to his room. Frank felt drained as he walked back to his car.

CHAPTER 23

Bart was full of excess energy. His eyes were red and his face was puffy. He was going on little sleep and a lot of coffee. Assistants scurried about the set with lightning speed. The technical director took extensive notes, making sure everything was good to go. Set decorators rearranged furniture for the living room set.

Tricia practiced her one and only line while the "parents" rehearsed in a quieter section of the studio, if that was possible. Dana walked hurriedly into the studio, holding a clipboard and talking to her colleagues.

"Is everything set?" she asked Bart.

"It's getting there!"

She went over to Tricia and asked, "Are you ready?"

"Yeah! I can't wait!"

"Good. If you need anything, I'll be around."

"Thanks, Dana!"

"Don't thank me until we see the finished product." And then she dashed out of the room.

The crew was ready to start filming, but then there was a problem with one of the lights. Fifteen minutes later they were ready to roll.

"Action!" Bart shouted from behind the camera.

Charles watched from the back of the studio. Tricia only had one line, but she was bound and determined to make it the best one ever. The children were gathered around a fake fireplace while their "parents" sat next to them. Meanwhile, in a sound stage two floors up, an actor recorded a voice over with the lines: "What if something bad happened to you? What will happen to your children? Do you have life insurance?"

* * *

About two hours later, Tricia followed Bart into the break room.

"You can have anything you want in here, as long as it doesn't have a name on it," he said quickly.

"Thanks, Bart."

"Anytime. Sorry I can't talk now. I'm so rushed!"

"That's okay."

Bart poured another cup of coffee and darted out of the room. Tricia pulled open the refrigerator door and grabbed a Pepsi can. She pried open the tab and sat at the table.

About five minutes later, Dana came in and heated up a mug of water. She dropped in a bag of green tea and stirred it briskly. She sat across from Tricia and took a few careful sips.

"Everything is going just fine," she announced.

"Super!"

"I know that it was hard for you to ask me to help you out with this."

Tricia didn't say a word.

"I'm sure you feel uncomfortable, seeing me with your father. I get it. You're mad at me."

"I'm not mad at you. It's just weird seeing you two together so much."

"I know."

"I heard my parents arguing about you once. She got really upset with my dad. I would've been upset too. You were sneaking around behind her back."

There was a long, uncomfortable silence, and then Dana said, "We didn't want to hurt your mother. Maybe someday you'll understand. It just happened."

"She wasn't the easiest person to live with."

"I can't blame her for being angry with us."

"Were they going to get a divorce?"

"I couldn't stand being the other woman. I finally convinced him to break up with her."

"I see." Tricia was eerily silent. "That must have been why she was so upset with you at the party."

"It was part of the reason. We just couldn't work well together."

"She couldn't work with any of us," Anna said as she entered the room. "I didn't mean to interrupt."

Dana turned and smiled at her. "No, that's okay."

"Why did you guys let her step all over you?" Tricia wondered.

Anna went over to the sink and reached for her mug on the shelf. "You gave as good as you got, Dana."

"Well, she wasn't so nice to you either."

Anna poured water into her mug and heated it up in the microwave. "I'm just not as good at standing up for myself as you are, Dana. Well, anyway, we shouldn't be discussing this in front of her."

"No, I'm the one that brought it up," Tricia said.

"We all have different ways of doing things, I guess. How is the filming going?"

"It's a blast!" Tricia exclaimed.

Anna grinned. "That's terrific. I'm glad you're enjoying yourself."

"Thanks for telling me that I should do the commercial."

"Well, I'm just glad it's working out for you."

Tricia was still jabbering about the commercial when the microwave oven beeped. Anna opened the door, put the mug on the counter and dunked a bag of herbal tea in it. She stirred it with a spoon and added sugar. Then she pulled up a seat and sat next to them.

"Bart is in rare form today," Dana observed. "He's bouncing off the walls."

Anna blew on her tea. "He didn't take his nerve pills today, I guess."

Dana reached in her jacket pocket and pulled out her cell phone. "I'll be right there!" She got up and poured the rest of her tea in the sink and looked back at Tricia. "Bart wants me right away! I'll see you in a few minutes."

Tricia grinned and said, "Okay."

Dana walked hurriedly out of the room. When she was gone, Anna and Tricia sat in silence for a little while.

"Have you ever thought about going to LA?" asked Anna.

"All the time!"

"I think you should definitely try it."

"My dad would never let me do it. My mother never wanted me to do it either."

"You've got to go out there if you want to get noticed."

"My folks said I'd be eaten alive out there."

"It's true, there's a lot of competition, but it's worth a shot."

Tricia pointed to herself and frowned. "My mother said I didn't have the right looks. She said it all the time."

"It figures she would have said something like that. It's not kind."

"Tell me about it." Tricia added something about the ugly duckling becoming a beautiful swan.

"Your mother actually said that?" Anna asked in alarm.

Tricia nodded but said nothing.

"She had no right being a mother! There are a lot of women out there that can't have babies. It's a crying shame!"

"I didn't believe it when she kept saying it. I got sick and tired of hearing her."

Anna tapped Tricia's hand. "You are beautiful. I hope you don't let what your mother said stand in your way."

"She said I could get a boob job when I turn eighteen. She would've paid for it."

Anna's mouth was agape. "You're fine just the way you are."

"That's what our housekeeper always says."

"Well, she's right. Believe me, there's nothing wrong with you."

"Well, my mother wouldn't agree with you."

"You think you had it bad with her–well, my folks were extremely overprotective! It was like living in a police state." Then she told Tricia about some of the horrible things her father had done. She neglected to mention that he wound up in jail for beating up her sister, though.

Tricia's eyes welled with tears. They sat there sniffling.

"It was awful," Anna admitted. "Oh, my. I really shouldn't be telling you this."

"No, that's okay."

"It wasn't so bad after I graduated from high school. I went to art school and met a lot of friends. It was a lot of fun. And then I wound up working here." By now her tea had gotten cold. She shoved it aside and looked back at Tricia. "So, you're not as bad off as you think. Whatever issues you're going through now will pass. You'll have a lot more freedom when you get out of school."

Dana came back in and gawked at them in disbelief. "I've only been gone a few minutes! What–what's wrong? Look at your face!"

"We've been talking about something sad," Tricia told her.

"Well, go back to the makeup department! Hurry up about it!"

Tricia darted out of the room. Dana shot Anna a look.

Anna's face was drawn. "It was my fault. I was trying to cheer her up, but it didn't go very well."

"I should say not!" Dana walked hurriedly out of the room.

Anna dumped the contents of her mug in the sink and went back to work.

CHAPTER 24

The news that Logan had been waiting for finally came to him late that afternoon. It was like an early Christmas gift. The results of the toxicological tests came as a bit of a surprise, though.

"I don't believe it!" he exclaimed.

Flosky stared in astonishment at him and asked, "What's wrong?"

He handed Joe the report and waited for his reaction.

Flosky shook his head and grunted in frustration. "Monkshood," he muttered. "What the hell is that?"

"It's some kind of plant," Logan said with a wave of the hand. "I don't know. It's toxicity level is number six—the highest one for poisons."

"And it was in Veronica Talbot's salad? She didn't even eat any salad at the party."

"You're right. That means she must've eaten it before the party. And that's something we can check." He dialed the Talbots' home and asked Kelly McDougal a couple of quick questions. When he hung up, he grinned enthusiastically at Flosky.

"What did you find out?" Joe asked quickly.

"The housekeeper just told me that Veronica was nibbling on some salad she brought home with her from work on Friday afternoon."

Joe slapped his forehead and cried, "No kidding! And all this time we were looking at everything she ate and drank at the party!"

"It explains a lot. I don't believe it!"

"What does it mean?"

"It means that we need to concentrate our efforts on the office itself. Somebody there chopped up Monkshood leaves and slipped them into her salad! It was right there in plain sight. Anybody could have done it."

"It looks like we're back to square one, right?"

"It looks that way," Logan grumbled.

* * *

Penny waved at James Dobson in the first floor lobby when she got to work about eight thirty Tuesday morning. He punched the elevator button, and they chatted amiably as they watched the numbers rise.

"How is the Henderson account coming?" he asked.

"We're finishing up some lose ends, but I think you will be pleased with the results."

He beamed and said, "That's what I like to hear." The door opened, and passengers disembarked while others got on.

His eyes darted around the cramped space. He looked back at Penny and asked, "How is Frank coming along with the murder investigation?"

Everyone gasped and looked wild-eyed at them.

"He found out that the poison wasn't in anything she had to drink or eat at the party."

James grimaced and said, "That's odd. Then how did she die?"

"He said that somebody at the office stuck a poisonous plant in her salad. It came from one of the flowers in the lobby."

Passengers seemed to hang on their every word. Their eyes darted from James to Penny. When the door opened, they hated to leave them.

The door opened on the twenty-first floor, and they got out. They continued their conversation as they walked down the long marble-tiled hallway.

"It's rather disconcerting to know that somebody I hired might have murdered Veronica, as unpleasant as she was."

"Did Veronica really think you were cheating on your wife?"

James stopped dead in his tracks and stared coldly at her. "Did Frank put you up to this? He came here and asked a million questions and got you to pry further into our lives? Is that what this is all about?"

Penny waved her hand in the air. "Of course not!"

"This investigation is making us all nervous. When we aren't at our best, we don't produce good results. So I suggest that you do your work and stop asking everyone the probing questions. You don't think I notice things, but I do. Have a good day!"

He walked ahead of her. It didn't take her long to catch up.

"I don't think a few harmless questions are going to hurt anyone," she said.

He turned and faced her. "Just concentrate on the Henderson account. I expect results by the end of the day." Then he waddled toward his office.

* * *

CHAPTER 25

Bart Sullivan had come a long way since leaving small-town life behind. But he had to go back home for Christmas. This year was going to be challenging, and he needed to mentally prepare for it at least two days beforehand.

He knew he could handle his siblings' endless questions about where he'd met Daryl. He didn't know how his father would react. It was bad enough that he was bringing another dude home to meet the family, but an African American! There weren't even any interracial *straight* couples in Dullsville. Despite the modern way of thinking, townspeople's attitudes had not changed with the times.

Bart spent the majority of the trip prepping Daryl for what to expect. It would be a testament to their relationship if Daryl could withstand the probing questions and outright hostility coming from Clay Sullivan. Bart hoped and prayed that a fight wouldn't break out before dinner like it usually did. Or maybe during dinner. It wouldn't just be about Daryl and Bart.

Bart didn't know what he did to deserve Daryl. He wished he had been in his life a long time ago. Maybe things would have been different when he was in high school.

Daryl had gone from having nothing to being a successful model. He was always traveling from one city to another, but he was at the right place in his life now.

They had decided to get married after Thanksgiving. Bart thought it would be best to let his family get to know Daryl before they announced their engagement. Bart braced himself for the sparks to fly. He hoped no one would wind up in the ER.

As he drove down the lonely streets leading to his childhood home, Bart could not believe how little had changed there. Other than the fact that Christmas decorations were hanging up and down Main Street, the shops looked the same.

Before going to his house, he decided to take Daryl on the grand tour of the town. He drove past his high school, which was built in the 1940s. Daryl glanced at the football field behind the building. In his hey-day, Daryl made his high school proud as a star quarterback. A lot of girls had looked at him in admiration, but he wasn't interested.

Bart thought about all the pain he had endured in that building. Daryl sensed his mood and reached for his hand. Bart had not told him everything about those horrible years at Lincoln High School.

Back then, Bart was a gangly kid who dreaded going to gym class. He went straight to his next class without showering first. After some time, gym teacher Mark Hendrickson sat him down, and addressed the problem.

"Is this really necessary?" Bart could hear his voice squeak. "I take my showers at home. What's the big deal?"

"Kids are starting to talk," Mr. Hendrickson said. "I shouldn't have to tell you what to do. At your age you should know these things."

Bart rolled his eyes and said, "Fine! I'll do it here."

"Do you have a problem...in there?"

Bart wanted to say yes. He wanted to shout it out. He wanted to tell him that the kids were roughing him up and calling him awful names. Instead, he lied and said, "No. I just don't want to be late for my next class."

"I thought it was something like that. If you need anything, you know where I am."

Showering was only a minute part of Bart's problems at Lincoln High School. He waited till the boys finished up before he took his own shower. Then his algebra teacher complained that Bart was always late for class.

When word got to his parents, Bart did not have a good enough explanation for his recent wave of tardiness. Clay and Bonnie sat him down for a long talk.

"What's going on here?" Clay asked. "Why are you late for class so much?"

Bart hung his head and said, "I don't know."

"You don't know?" Clay asked angrily. "How the hell do you not know?"

Bonnie patted her husband's hand and said, "Come on, Clay. Don't act so nasty. I'm sure Bart has a perfectly logical explanation."

"The kids are horrible!" he cried. "They–they say things."

"What do they say, honey?" she asked softly.

"They're monsters! They–they start in on me and call me horrible names like 'shrimp' and–and things I don't want to tell you, Mom. They knock me down and hit me with their towels."

Bonnie shook her head in disbelief. "Why do boys that age have to be so mean?"

"They all do it," Clay said. "You need to learn to toughen yourself up, son."

Bart burst into tears and told them that some bullies pushed him into a bathroom stall and stuck his head in the toilet.

After a long, painful silence, Bart blubbered, "Please...please don't make me go back there...I'd rather pee my pants than go back in there!"

Bonnie had had enough. "I'm going to speak to the principal. This goes way beyond roughhousing."

Clay strongly disagreed. "What good will that do? Kids can be mean. He's gotta learn to defend himself."

Bart wept uncontrollably. Bonnie pulled him toward her and felt his entire body shaking.

"We'll do something about this," she promised. "We'll put a stop to it."

Bart cried till his tears dried up. He spent the rest of the night in his room. When he came back downstairs, he heard his parents talking quietly with the TV on in the background.

"If you make waves, it'll only make it worse for him," Clay said. "I know how these things work."

"I don't care what you say! He's suffering. Our boy is a victim. If we let it go, it'll only get worse! Do you want him to end up in the ER?"

"Of course not."

"Good. Then, for once, you actually show signs that you care about your son!"

"That's not fair!" Clay shouted. "I do care about him!"

"It doesn't look that way to me." She got up and rustled around in the kitchen.

Clay looked up and saw Bart standing in the entryway. Bart said nothing and wandered silently back upstairs, acting ghost-like. He felt like he was barely there.

As the weeks went by, there was little improvement even after Bonnie complained to the principal. Her clout as a teacher did not seem to make any difference. Bart's gym grades were abysmal. He skipped class all together. When word got back to Clay, it was war in the Sullivan household. Bart's brothers and sisters were nowhere to be seen. It was just Bart and his father.

Clay looked sharply at him and said, "I don't get it."

"I suck at sports!" Bart cried. "Why do I have to be forced to do something I hate so much? The kids make fun of me! Please don't make me go to gym class! Can't I take something else instead?"

"You need to take gym to graduate," Clay replied in a harsh tone. "Just suck it up."

It was like arguing with a brick wall. Neither of them would give an inch. Bonnie, as always, was the referee.

Clay loved sports just as much as his older boys. He didn't get Bart at all.

Bart spent the rest of the day moping in his room. He angrily flipped the pages of a teen magazine. He focused his attention on the boys, not the girls.

He hadn't told his parents the whole story. He wouldn't dare tell them the main reason the guys were so awful in that hell-hole of a locker room!

Whether it was true or not, they accused him of being gay and looking at them in a certain way. They hurled the worst possible slurs at him. Some of them hit him–with Mr. Hendrickson a few feet away in the confines of his office.

If he survived to graduation, it would be a miracle. He vowed that if he died before then, he'd come back to haunt his father and all the bullies for the rest of their lives.

* * *

Christmas was supposed to be bright and cheery. Neither Charles nor his daughter, was in a festive mood. The atmosphere around the house was somber. Charles would have settled for a smaller tree this year, but he got a bigger one for Tricia's sake. It was about fifteen feet tall and stood in the middle of the living room. He had to climb a ladder to secure a thick wire to it from the wall to prevent it from falling. Kelly and Cindy put red and gold ribbons on it. Nobody had the energy to put the ornaments on. They remained in their boxes in the storage room.

Charles was so busy at work he didn't have time to put up the lights outside. Maybe he used work as an excuse. He really didn't feel like doing it anyway.

Tricia had kept busy with school, which was a good thing. It took her mind off missing her mother and thinking of the horrible thing that happened to her. It seemed odd not having her mother there, yapping at everybody. She was always in charge over the holidays. Maybe Tricia had gotten used to all of the noise and confusion and missed it. The house was eerily quiet, and it was starting to get to her.

Dana helped Kelly and Cindy decorate around the house. Brightly colored packages under the tree did not help improve the mood.

They exchanged gifts with Kelly and Cindy. Later that morning, Dana arrived with her two boys. Everybody was laughing except father and daughter. Dana and Kelly exchanged concerned looks as the boys tore open their gifts. They shrieked with excitement at the sight of the latest electronic gadget.

"Awesome!" Kyle cried. "I didn't think you'd get it!"

Dana beamed and said, "I can't believe I actually fooled you."

He threw his arms around his mother and shouted, "You're the best mom ever!"

Tricia regarded them coolly.

Cindy got on her hands and knees and pulled out a large red package addressed to Tricia from Kelly. She picked it up, her legs buckling under as she walked over to Tricia.

"This one's for you!"

"Thank you," Tricia said. Her expression remained detached. She pulled off the paper and opened the box. It was a gray London Fog coat. "Thanks, Kelly. It's really nice."

"It'll keep you nice and warm this winter," Kelly said.

"You bet." Tricia made an effort to be happy, but her limited acting skills weren't enough to help her pull off a cheerful mood.

Cindy squealed when she opened a box and saw ice skates. "Cool! I can't wait to try them out when the pond freezes up!"

"Just be careful," her mother warned.

Cindy and the boys made so much noise that no one seemed to be paying attention to Tricia or Charles. They sat in silence, watching the world go on around them.

* * *

The sounds of little kids squealing with delight filled the living room, drowning out the Christmas music in the background. Everybody was laughing and talking over each other. Anna quietly watched her little nieces and nephews ripping open gifts and hogging all the attention.

She had gotten used to the awkwardness of coming alone to family gatherings. Fortunately, her mother and sisters had stopped asking if she was seeing anyone lately. It was awkward for everybody.

In less than two hours, the presents under the tree were gone. Anna's mother, Catherine, scooped up shreds of wrapping paper and put them in a trash bag. The kids went outside to play, and their parents drank their adult drinks and found quiet spots around the house to collect their thoughts.

Late that afternoon, Catherine's daughters helped out in the kitchen. They sang cheerful Christmas songs while getting everything ready. Eleven-year-old Rory darted through the room and yanked a chocolate chip cookie from the jar.

Maggie swatted her hand and said, "What did I tell you about eating too many snacks before dinner?"

Rory shoved it back into the jar and raced out of the room.

"And don't run in here so much!" Maggie shouted back at her. She looked exasperated at her sisters and said, "That girl is going to be the end of me!"

"And she isn't even a teen-ager yet," Danielle said.

"Don't remind me!"

Catherine suppressed a smile, and then broke into uncontrollable laughter. When she calmed herself down, she said, "I thought you girls were the limit, squawking at each other like you did."

"I was the perfect child," Anna reminded her.

Catherine kissed Anna's forehead and said, "And you still are!"

Vincent strolled into the room nonchalantly and asked, "When's dinner?"

"Soon," Danielle told her son. "Now scoot!"

He ducked his head as he went out the entryway.

"He's gotten so tall!" Anna exclaimed. "What are you feeding him anyway?"

"Plenty of vitamins, I guess," Danielle said.

"I can't believe that little baby I babysat for way back then is in college now."

Danielle's eyes practically lit up the room. She had a dreamy look about her. "Time flies," she said.

"His girlfriend seems nice."

"She's wonderful!" Catherine cried.

"She helps keep him grounded," Maggie added.

"And we don't have to lay down the law like Dad did." Danielle glanced at her mother and was quiet a moment. "Sorry."

"Why should you be?" Catherine's smile seemed forced. "It's ancient history."

Danielle looked at Anna and asked the forbidden question. "Are you seeing anybody?"

Anna smiled sheepishly and said, "I'm so busy at work that I don't have a social life anymore."

Catherine groaned and shook her head in disbelief. "Not that sorry old excuse, Anna. Time marches on. You need to get out and have a good time once in a while."

"I know."

Catherine's tone sounded softer now. "What about Nicholas? You like him, don't you?"

"He's all right. We go out sometimes. He's a lot of fun to be around."

"Then why aren't you two a couple?" Maggie pressed.

Anna opened the cabinet door and pulled out a stack of plates. "It would never work out. He's so childish." She went into the dining room and set the table. She took her time, hoping they would start talking about something else while she was gone. Unfortunately, that was not the case.

"I think you two would make a great couple," Danielle said when she returned.

"It's purely platonic," Anna was quick to point out. "I'm like his older sister, constantly telling him to behave."

"Some people need to be told what to do," Catherine said.

"There are no sparks. Believe me."

"Well, maybe you just haven't tried hard enough to make it happen," Danielle said.

Anna pulled open the silverware drawer and scooped up forks, knives, and spoons.

She feigned a cheerful grin and said, "Well, maybe it will someday. You never know." She went back into the dining room and continued setting the table. When she went back into the kitchen, they were talking about the kids again.

A few minutes later, Maggie asked, "How is the murder investigation going?"

Anna's voice raised an octave. "Detective Logan is asking us a lot of questions and snooping into our personal things. It's making us all a bit jumpy. I wish he'd get it over with."

"Does he know who did it?" asked Danielle.

"I don't think so."

"It sounds awfully stressful, if you ask me," Catherine said. "Who would want to do such a terrible thing to that poor woman?"

"Well, there are a lot of people around the office who couldn't stand the woman, Mom."

Catherine's eyes narrowed. "She wasn't very nice to you."

"I despised her!" Anna grabbed a bowl of green beans and walked hurriedly into the dining room again.

* * *

Nicholas Bradshaw had been too busy to get back to Baltimore to visit his family at Thanksgiving, so Anna had invited him to her mother's apartment. He knew they were whispering to each other. He knew that her family thought that he was Anna's boyfriend. He and Anna had a brother-sister relationship. There was no possibility that their relationship was going to go any further. They were strictly coworkers who occasionally enjoyed going out with their friends or colleagues after hours or for late-night parties.

He had remained tight-lipped about his activities over the past two months. His parents didn't know if he had been dating. His e-mails and Facebook postings revealed little information about things that were happening in his life.

After the usual mass confusion opening Christmas gifts that morning, the family gathered around in the den and watched football. Little communication took place that afternoon. At dinner, they all talked over each other, as usual. Then there was a lull in the conversation.

"I'm a murder suspect," Nicholas announced to his family's shock and horror. "Please pass the mashed potatoes."

His older brother, Michael, handed him a large bowl and asked, "Did you do it?".

"Of course not!" Nicholas slopped a large heap onto his plate and set the bowl on the table.

Jessica eyed her son suspiciously, not believing him for one minute. She never knew what would come out of her son's overactive imagination. She had grown to detest his warped sense of humor. "Are you pulling our legs?"

"No. I'm totally serious, Ma."

"Why didn't you say anything?" she asked in alarm.

"It's really no big deal."

"It's no big deal?"

Nicholas laughed like a hyena and said, "I've got nothing to hide. You really think I did it?"

"Who was murdered?" they asked in unison.

"Veronica Talbot, the Dragon Lady."

His father choked on his wine and beat his chest until he felt better. They all sat in stunned silence.

"She was poisoned at a party a couple months ago," Nicholas continued after they had a chance to calm themselves down. "And the detective searched through our stuff. It was kind of annoying that he got into our personal things. And he asked us all kinds of questions. I didn't think he'd ever leave! You should see her house. It's huge! It's a mansion! It's out in the country near this little town near Lancaster, Pennsylvania. It's unbelievably beautiful out there."

His mother looked dumbfounded at him. Then it dawned on her. "Is this some kind of joke?"

Christopher Bradshaw looked sternly at his son and said, "You can be so childish sometimes. Maybe that's why you're not in a serious relationship."

"What Dad is really trying to say is that you act like a jerk around women," Michael quipped.

"Maybe if you would stop horsing around like a four-year-old, women would take you more seriously," Christopher admonished.

Nicholas sipped his wine and said, "I don't need any advice about women." He was about to utter his famous "I'm too busy for dating" speech, when his mother beat him to it.

"You're too busy messing around to think seriously about what direction you want your life to go in," she said.

"I don't need this, Ma," Nicholas protested. "It's Christmas! Let's enjoy ourselves. Spend time with each other. No criticism. I am seriously taking my career into consideration. Benny Goldstein quit a few months ago–and I applied for his job."

Christopher stared at him like he had three heads. "And you mention this now?"

Nicholas wiped his mouth with a napkin. "I didn't get it, or I would have said something. It was kind of a big deal at the time. But with the investigation and all–it sort of isn't such a big deal anymore."

"Why didn't you mention the murder?" his father asked incredulously.

"Because I knew it would upset you. That puts negative energy into things. Everybody should be happy."

His father shook his head in disbelief.

Nicholas looked at Michael and said, "Pass the stuffing, please."

* * *

Penny snuggled in Frank's arms. They lay on the couch in the dark and admired the twinkling lights of their first Christmas tree. A feeling of serenity emanated around the living room. After the usual hectic festivities at her parents' house, they were happy to end the day together at the apartment.

Thoughts of the Talbot case were temporarily on hold. At least, Penny hadn't heard Frank muse about it to Gramps or her family. Knowing him, he would keep his thoughts mulling around inside until they burst out of him in one big gripe about how the investigation was leading nowhere fast.

It would do no good to tell him that it would come to him. She knew full well what he was thinking. He was kicking himself for not being at the party until after the fact. She knew he was upset that he had missed something. The murderer was among them and would probably get away with it. The number one question was, how did he or she pull it off?

"You've been a good boy today," she said.

"I'm always good."

"You didn't mention the case one time. Even when everybody kept asking about it. You sort of just growled a little and looked like you could chew nails."

"You covered up nicely for me. Talking about the people you work with." He leaned in and kissed her. "One of them is a killer, you know."

"I know."

"How can you stand working with them?"

"It's fun."

"You really don't know much about the people you're around on a daily basis."

"Bart and Daryl are getting married."

"Well, good for them."

"At least my dad wasn't pressuring you to pop the question this time. I guess my mom talked to him after Thanksgiving."

"He's just being a good father." He stroked her arm. "He must've done something right."

"I'm worried about Gramps. He seemed a little wobbly. More so tonight than a month ago."

Frank didn't appear to be listening. He concentrated his attention on the blinking lights. He did not want to accept the inevitable.

"Do you talk to him about–"

"Let's not spoil the moment."

"You two need to talk about it."

"It" was what most people did not like to discuss with an elderly relative.

"You don't have the training to be his caretaker, Frank."

"I know."

"What are you going to do if he falls down again? You can't be there to help him when you're way out here."

Frank stared at the lights. He could not deal with it. He could not face the fact that the man who raised him from the time he was a bratty teenager needed him now. They had both lost so much over the years. For the longest time it was them against the world. And now that world was getting increasingly smaller. Thank God, Frank had Penny now.

"We'll discuss it later." Frank got up and went into the bedroom.

"Maybe we should find a bigger place," she yelled back to him. "He could move in with us. Maybe–maybe a caretaker could move in too."

* * *

The thing Bart most dreaded was coming to an end soon. A weekend of endless questions about the upcoming nuptials. His father's cold stares. His mother tried to be understanding, but was not pulling it off. She tried to be gracious, at least.

Daryl had taken it a lot better than Bart thought he would. On the way back to Philly, he glanced at him and said, "You passed the test with flying colors."

"This is new to them," Daryl said. "Of course they have a lot of questions."

"I was so relieved that my sisters were more interested in your modeling career than us."

"Your brothers are nice. I'd go out and drink with them."

"I think my dad was impressed that you've met some supermodels."

Daryl erupted into an uncontrollable fit of laughter. It was loud and thunderous like a lion's roar.

"So were your brothers!"

"I shoot pictures of these women all the time, and they're impressed with you?"

"It's more exotic coming from somebody they don't know." He gazed out the window and watched the endless farmland zip by. "I thought that your brother Shawn was gonna bust a gut when I told him that I started out dressing nude women when I broke into the modeling business!"

Bart laughed like a fiend.

Daryl patted Bart's knee and said, "So you don't gotta worry now. They like me."

"I'm so glad. After all the tension to start with."

"And now, very soon, we'll be on a tropical island drinking margaritas...."

CHAPTER 26

It had been a hectic morning. Actors lined up to try out for a part in a TV commercial. Michelle Delancey had keen instincts when it came to casting the perfect actor for a part. She put stars next to the ones that she was interested in. The weeding-down process would take all day.

She glanced at her clipboard. Six more actors to go. Then lunch. She, Dana, and Tom were going to the diner a couple blocks down the street. She would collect her thoughts then and finish casting the commercial by the end of the day.

Most of the actors were fresh out of acting school and hungry for their big break. With bit gigs here and there, they managed to scrape by. Michelle was looking for a certain spark in their eyes. Something that set them apart from all of the others.

About one o'clock, she glanced at the clock on the wall and smiled at the young man across the room.

"Thank you for coming in," she said. "We'll be in touch."

She looked over at Dana and Tom and pointed to the head-shots of the ones she liked the best. They talked about it over lunch, eventually settling on the top three.

"Who do you think the Beckets would like the best?" Tom wondered.

Michelle pointed to the picture of the Latino model and said, "There's something special about the Delgado kid."

Dana nodded in agreement. "He seems to want it more than the others."

"He lights up with enthusiasm."

"And it's not just because he's hot," Dana chided.

Michelle's face brightened. "Well, he's really good too. I think we should go with him."

"I respect your judgment," Tom said.

Dana took a deep breath and said, "Now all we have to do is find a girlfriend for him."

"Oh joy!" Michelle cried.

Tom winked at them and said, "Hopefully, we can start shooting in a couple of days. I know Chris Becket is really picky, but I think he will be pleased. Craig will do a good job with it."

Dana's eyebrows shot up. "I thought Bart was doing it."

"He backed out at the last minute," Michelle told her.

"Well, nobody told me!"

"Gosh, I'm sorry. I've been so swamped with work I forgot to mention it."

"What's with him lately, anyway? It's the third time he's backed out of a shoot."

"I don't know. I guess he's got a lot on his mind."

They discussed the budget for the ad, and then the waitress served their food.

They ate their meals in silence. Michelle sipped her iced tea and looked at a young woman across the room who seemed to be having an intense conversation with the girl across from her.

Michelle listened closely to what was going on.

"I'm pregnant," the girl told her friend.

Instead of being overjoyed, she seemed to be distressed. Pregnant women shouldn't be in tears, Michelle thought.

The pregnant girl sobbed and said, "I don't know what I'm gonna do."

The other girl patted her hand and spoke softly. Michelle couldn't hear what she was saying. She imagined the girl reassured her friend and told her it would be all right.

About twenty minutes later, Michelle followed her friends out. As she went past the two girls, she overheard the pregnant one say, "I'll go to a clinic to get rid of it."

Michelle paid her bill and followed Tom and Dana outside.

That afternoon, Michelle's mind was on the poor pregnant girl and not on the eager actresses who were vying for the "girlfriend" role.

Michelle knew full well what that pregnant girl was going through. She had faced those same fears when she found out she was pregnant when she was in college. At that time, she was alone and confused. She was young and wanted a career. A baby would slow her down. She wasn't ready to think about having a family, so she decided to get an abortion. It seemed like the only thing she could do.

It had been raining for a solid week the day she went to the clinic. Her raincoat was soaking wet. She sat in the waiting room, studying the expressions of the other girls who were in her situation. Late night out with friends at the club. A few drinks and one thing led to another. They made love either in his dorm or her apartment. It didn't matter where the action took place. The baby presented a major problem for all of the college women in the waiting room.

She couldn't tell her family. They wouldn't understand. She had always been on the straight and narrow path. She was 100 percent goal oriented.

Then one night Michelle went out with her friends to a bar. The booze had gone to her head. The really cute guy on the dance floor was flirting with her big time, and she was eating him up.

She hadn't really been thinking about anything. She wasn't thinking about the consequences.

They wound up in her bed together. And then the next morning, he was gone. She thought she'd never see him again, and then she found out she was pregnant.

She met him at the same nightclub to tell him. He freaked out. He didn't want to be a father at that point in his life. She was on her own.

She was so emotionally fragile that most of what happened after she was in the waiting room was a blur. She remembered the nurse walking her into one of the examination rooms.

The doctor explained what was going to happen.

"I didn't mean for this to happen," Michelle said repeatedly. "It was just one big stupid mistake."

"I know," the nurse said gently. "I bet he was really hot, wasn't he?"

Michelle nodded her head reluctantly. "My mom and dad won't understand. This will be...this will be a secret, right?"

"It's strictly confidential," she assured her.

"Good."

The nurse held her hand as Michelle listened to the doctor's instructions. Everything he said was a blur. She wondered if it was too late to back out.

CHAPTER 27

Frank didn't know what to expect when he entered the art gallery hand in hand with Penny. They thought the event was a bust at first. It seemed like they were the only ones there. They wandered around looking at breathtaking color nature photographs from the top of mountains and landscapes from out west.

"She's the only one that has clothes on!" someone shouted from the next room.

They walked hurriedly into the next room and suddenly realized why everyone had gravitated in there. Pictures of nude women were on every wall! Frank looked across at Bart, who was laughing and pointing at a picture of a stunning woman with long, flowing black hair wearing an ivory silk nightgown. The faded morning light seemed to cascade on her. She had smoldering dark eyes. The only other color in the picture was her bright red lipstick.

Daryl leaned over Bart's shoulder and asked, "Where does he find all these gorgeous women that are willing to take off their clothes?"

"He has to liquor them up first," Bart quipped.

A crowd gathered around Craig Holloway, the guest of honor. He was decked out in a white tux with a white tie. He actually shaved for the occasion. His work looked great under the track lighting. People milled about holding champagne glasses in one hand and plates of hors d'oeuvres in the other.

Frank made a cursory look around the room and whispered in Penny's ear, "Why are we here?"

"To show support for one of my friends." She pulled him in the direction of the hors d'oeuvres table and handed him a plate.

A woman walked by with a tray of champagne. She handed him a glass and he took it.

"This is the way I wish it had been the night that Veronica Talbot was poisoned," Frank said. "If we had been there before it happened, maybe I would have seen something."

"You can't be so sure of that," Penny said.

"Maybe they'd better be careful or the killer might strike again."

They all heard him and looked at their drinks.

Craig grunted and said, "Nah, it was just a fluke. We couldn't stand her!" He glanced over at Charles and said, "Sorry."

"No, no. You're honest. That's what I like about you, Craig. You don't keep things to yourself. And neither did she. I know Veronica did things that made people upset. But she got results, and that's all that is important in the end, right?"

Craig drank his champagne and said nothing.

Bart went over to Craig and said, "You've got a terrific eye for beauty."

Craig winked at him and said, "Maybe you should try shooting nudes, pal. It might turn you straight."

"It would take a miracle for that to happen." He reached for Daryl's hand and added, "I'm quite happy with the package that God sent me." They pushed through the crowd to look at the images across the room.

James and Edna Dobson went up to Craig and raved about his work. "You are so talented," she said.

"Thank you, Mrs. Dobson. It's a lot of hard work getting it all together."

"I can imagine."

"I was up all last night hanging them."

"You must be getting by on very little sleep," Dobson noted. "You didn't leave the studio till about eight o'clock last night."

"And I was up till about four this morning hanging them. Thankfully, some buddies gave me a hand."

Edna pointed to a black-and-white image of a woman lying on a beach.

"Her eyes are so haunting. She's beautiful!"

"It's one of my favorite pieces. It's one of my earliest images."

"You do magnificent work."

He pointed to Nicholas and Bart and said, "Well, they're really good too."

Nicholas brushed up to them and said, "Did I hear somebody talking about, *moi?*"

"You should put a show up in here, Nick. You're so vain you'd eat up all the attention."

"Maybe I should. I love hearing people saying nice things about me."

"You're not that good."

"Oh my God!" Bart shrieked.

Everybody stopped what they were doing and stared at him once again. He pointed to a gigantic image of a nude blonde lying on a four-poster bed.

Bart laughed hysterically and shouted, "It's Veronica!"

They all rushed over to take a closer look. Then they all began talking over each other.

"Oh my God, he's right!"

"What a rack on her!" someone cried.

Charles stood in stunned silence as he gazed upon a much younger version of his late wife. She was beautiful and captivating. Her expression was alluring and inviting. She did not appear to be the cold, manipulative bitch that everyone said she was. She looked very much like the woman he had once found so attractive.

Charles got up in Craig's face, clenching his fists. "What the hell were you doing with my wife?"

Everyone stood with their mouths agape. They looked back and forth from Charles to Craig, bracing themselves for a fist-fight. Thank goodness an officer of the law was nearby in case he had to step in to break them up. Frank eased his way toward them and eyed them intensely.

"It was taken a long time ago, Charles," Craig said.

"I can gather," Talbot replied angrily.

"I was just a kid at the time–about twenty. Fresh out of photography school. I interned at a studio in Manhattan."

"Veronica worked there then," Charles said coolly.

"And so did I." He waved his hand in a placatory gesture. "Hey look, man, it was a long time ago. I'm not ashamed of what we did. It was a short little fling. Didn't last long. I'm not sorry we did it."

Charles was eerily silent. He glared at Craig with such intensity that everyone backed away. Frank stepped in and said, "Maybe you gentlemen had better step outside and get a breath of fresh air. We don't want any trouble tonight."

"After all these years, Veronica never one time mentioned that she was messing around with you way back then!"

"It's really none of my business why she didn't tell you. It's not like she was trying to protect me from you. I didn't really care if she said anything one way or the other."

Charles snarled and popped him one. "You disgust me!" he shouted through clenched teeth. Then he marched out of the gallery. The wall shook as he slammed the door.

No one knew quite what to say.

"Well, the dip is just fabulous," Michelle said, trying to lighten the mood.

"I love the cups of lobster bisque," Dana added.

They looked uneasily at Veronica in all her glory.

"She was a beautiful woman back then," Dana said at last.

"And she was till the end," agreed Michelle.

They went on to look at the other women in Craig's collection. They stopped and stared at one of a woman with light brown hair nursing an infant.

Dana gawked. "Who is that?"

Craig brushed up next to them and said, "She's my ex-girlfriend. And he's my son."

CHAPTER 28

As winter dragged on, Tricia's attitude toward Dana changed. She appreciated that Dana had helped her get the part in the TV commercial, however brief it was. She'd had one line, and the other kids didn't have any.

Tricia's interest in pursuing an acting career was at a fevered pitch. It was all she talked about. Every week, she asked her father if there were future ads needing kids. His answer was always the same: "If a part comes up, I'll let you know. But you'll have to audition like the other kids. You don't want people to think you got the part because of me, do you?"

"No."

"You can do it as long as it doesn't interfere with homework."

"It won't, I promise."

"Okay." He glanced at the newspaper and scanned the page. "You were good in the one we just did."

"Thanks." She leaned down and kissed his cheek. Then she scurried upstairs.

Kelly picked up his empty plate and said, "Now that she's tasted a little stardom, she'll get a swelled head."

"For that bit part? I doubt if anybody would even recognize her."

"It's really exciting!"

"I know. I actually got to see her for more than a couple of hours that day."

"Maybe you can go somewhere, just the two of you, on Easter vacation."

"We deserve it."

* * *

After the holidays, Tricia landed another bit part for an ad Craig Holloway was filming. This time, however, she had no lines. She didn't care. It was the experience that she craved.

About a week later, she was quiet during dinner. Charles stared at her and said, "You haven't said a word for a long time. What's wrong?"

"I'd like to go out to LA to talk to agents during my break."

"What did your mother and I tell you about going out there?"

"That they'd eat me alive."

"You are too young to get involved with that rat race. You can go out there when you are eighteen. When you have finished school. Maybe you could apply to UCLA."

"Well, maybe since I've done a couple of ads for you all, it might be a foot in the door. That's what Dana said."

"What makes you think that a couple of bit parts in local TV ads will land you a job in the big leagues?"

"I just thought–"

"Well, you thought wrong. There is no way I'll let you go out there."

"Please. I never ask you for anything. I just thought it would do me some good to get away."

"Well, we all should go somewhere. I was just talking to Kelly about it. Maybe we could go to a Broadway show. Anything you want. It's so nice in New York in the spring. If you want to act, you need to be on Broadway. It would be closer to home. If you go out to LA, we'll never see you and I'll miss you."

"And I'd miss you too, Dad."

"If you go to Broadway, I won't have to worry about you falling into the ocean."

"Oh, Dad."

"You can go out west when you're older. It can be your graduation present."

Tricia's eyes lit up. "You mean it?"

He nodded his approval and said, "What have I gotten myself into?"

She sprang to her feet and threw her arms around him. "Oh, Dad, you're the greatest!"

"Well, maybe by then you can shoot some more local ads. Maybe even try some ad agencies in New York City. Get your name out there. And then you'd have more to show to agents on the West Coast. And maybe I can go out there with you to make sure you stay out of trouble."

"All right." Tricia liked that idea even better.

* * *

"You look upset. What's wrong?"

Dana blew a strand of hair out of her mouth and looked up at Penny. "It's the ex, as usual."

"What happened?"

"It's supposed to be his weekend to take the kids, and he's spending it with his girlfriend. I already made other plans. I guess I'll have to call my folks."

"It must be a real pain."

"You don't know the half of it!" she exclaimed.

"Is he always this hard to get along with?"

Dana nodded her head and said, "So you can see why we ended up splitting up."

"It was probably for the best."

"It would be nice if everybody could have a relationship like Tom and Michelle."

"They seem so good for each other," agreed Penny. "And I don't even think it matters about their age difference."

"Well, you and Frank seem to work well together too."

"We're not that perfect, Dana. Believe me, we've had our moments."

"It doesn't seem that way to me." She drank tea and glanced at the headlines on the front page of the newspaper.

"We've had to really work hard to make it work. He's so pig-headed at times. But I knew that going in. He'll never change. We broke up a couple of times. He was so busy putting bad guys behind bars that I dated a guy from the bank I used to work at."

Dana's interest was piqued. "I bet that made him pretty damn jealous."

"I think so. I think it got his attention. He really did try to change. We got back together briefly."

"What happened to screw it up?"

"We went to the Poconos and I found out he was spying on somebody for a case he was working on."

"Oh, good God!" Dana exclaimed. "I bet you were good and frosted when you found out."

"I was irritated, but realized that he had to do it to help solve the case. Our arguments usually centered around his work. I told him he was working long hours and didn't have enough time for me."

"It must've been really frustrating."

Penny nodded her agreement. "I enjoy going out with his friends, but I got really ticked off when I tried to get him to go out with my friends."

"What happened?"

"We got into a big fight after an office party one night. I got so mad that I didn't speak to him for weeks, and he was pretty upset. He kept calling me all the time and I refused to call him back."

"Good for you! It serves him right!"

"We eventually patched things up and decided to move in together."

"But are you happy doing what you're doing? It can't be easy making the commute back and forth from Philly to that little town you're living in."

"It's not so bad. It's a nice quiet drive, and I can collect my thoughts after a stressful day here."

Dana smirked. "Oh, the scenic route." She finished off her tea and went to get some more. She sat back down across from Penny.

"Don't knock something that seems to be working."

"He seems like a man that sticks to a routine," Dana observed.

"That's Frank to a tee."

"I think a lot of cops are like that. Regimented. If that sounds right. How is the investigation going?"

"He's hit a bit of a dead end. I hate when he gets stuck with a case. He gets frustrated. And I get frustrated not being able to help him."

"But eventually he comes up with the solution, right?"

"Yeah."

"I don't think I could handle doing what he does. Looking at dead bodies on a daily basis must be so depressing."

"I know, but I think the police and medical examiners are trying to help the families they leave behind. It's a good thing that those people are doing it."

"I just don't know how they could figure out something like this. How can they pinpoint the poison that killed Veronica?"

"I understand that it's extremely time consuming, with all the different tests that have to be done."

"Something like that isn't simple. Whoever did it has to have some knowledge of poisons and how they work."

"That's what Frank says."

"It really makes you wonder, doesn't it? Who knows about that sort of thing around here?"

Penny shrugged her shoulders. "I don't know."

"She pissed off everybody here. Frank has his work cut out for him, that's for sure."

"I'm sure some major clue will come up. It always does."

There was a long silence. Penny reluctantly started a new conversation.

"Is it true what I've heard people saying about you and Charles? Oh...maybe it's not my place to ask."

Dana's facial muscles stiffened. Her lips trembled. "Those were rumors that Veronica started."

"But I heard you two fighting a lot. And Charles's name came up. People said they heard you two shouting his name in her study the day of the party."

"We're just really good friends. That's all. I suppose Veronica couldn't handle it. She didn't like the idea that her husband could have such a close, personal relationship with another woman that wasn't sexual in nature. We have a lot in common. We both have kids that are about the same age. He's just a very good listener. And believe me, you need somebody like that when you're having a bad day."

Penny nodded in agreement.

"We go back many years," Dana continued after a long silence. "Our paths crossed frequently at conferences when I was in LA.

"Oh really? I didn't know that."

"We used to go out for drinks. When my ex-husband was transferred to the Naval Yard here in Philly, Charles put in a good word for me with James."

"That was nice of him."

"That was about ten years ago. My marriage to Rob might've gone south, but my friendship with Charles has remained constant."

"It's nice to have a steady influence in your life."

"I guess Frank is your anchor."

"I guess so."

Dana glanced at her wristwatch. "I guess I'd better get back to the drudgery. It was nice talking to you."

"Likewise. I didn't mean to upset you about those awful rumors."

"It's not like I haven't heard them before. Ciao."

Penny finished her coffee and tossed the cup in the waste basket.

* * *

Dana didn't like lying to Penny about her relationship with Charles, but she didn't want everybody to think that everything Veronica had said was true. Penny was right about one thing. The arguments were always about Charles. Veronica was jealous, plain and simple. It would have been so easy if Veronica had been out of the picture. She and Charles could start over and have a good life together. Their kids were the same age, and would make the perfect step-siblings, if she was ever lucky enough to have Charles ask her to marry him.

With Veronica out of the way, her dream of marrying Charles was closer to reality than ever before.

If Frank Logan would stop asking so many questions, Charles's mind would be more at ease. He was so worried about the investigation that he wasn't thinking about a future with Dana.

Dana knew she would have to wait. Patience was not one of her virtues.

CHAPTER 29

Michelle Delancey was ashamed that she had terminated her pregnancy when she was twenty-one. The decision scarred her for most of her life. She often wondered what her unborn baby would have become. Those thoughts haunted her waking hours and her dreams.

She had felt a tinge of guilt when she worked on the abortion ad last fall. She probably should have pulled herself from the project like Tom did, but thought that it might help educate young women who were as frightened as she was at their age.

She kept the abortion a secret for a long time. Then, years later, she had opened up to Veronica Talbot when they worked together in Manhattan. It was a time when they were friends, before Michelle knew what kind of person Veronica really was.

"I got an abortion when I was in college," Michelle said one night at a nightclub. "Oh, God Almighty, I...I didn't mean to come out with that."

Veronica was understanding about it. She patted Michelle's hand and said, "It's okay. I won't tell anyone."

"I can't believe I told you."

"It must have been very painful for you."

"It was the most horrible experience you can imagine. Why did I tell you?"

"Because you needed to get it off your chest. I imagine it must be a relief to tell somebody about it."

"It feels like a weight has been lifted off my shoulders," Michelle admitted.

"I'm glad." Veronica finished off her Bloody Mary and waved her hand to get the waiter's attention. "I've got my own share of secrets."

"Everybody has secrets. What did you do that's so bad? Sorry. I really shouldn't have asked. It's none of my business."

Veronica leaned closer to her and said, "I posed in the altogether for a photographer."

Michelle's jaw dropped. "You're kidding!"

"He's such a sweet kid–in a raw, sensual way."

"You slept with him!"

"He's wild and needs taming. It's a work in progress."

"So you're having an affair!"

Veronica pressed Michelle's hand and leaned toward her. "Please don't tell Charles. It was a mistake, and I know it. And I'll end it with him as soon as I can. Charles and I hit a rough patch, and Craig was there. He's so wild and free, I just wanted someone to talk to, really. And then we wound up in bed together."

Michelle knew that she was in no position to judge. She sat and nursed her white wine as she listened to Veronica talk about her troubled love life.

"So are we agreed?" Veronica asked a few minutes later.

Michelle reached across and they shook hands.

"We won't tell anybody about our dirty little secrets?" Veronica asked.

"Nobody will ever know."

They clinked their glasses in agreement.

Little did Michelle know that she had made a pact with the devil that night. It was years before Michelle met Tom Daniels. When they started dating, Michelle knew that she was vulnerable. Veronica Talbot was capable of just about anything. What if she told him about the abortion? If he found out the truth, he would never understand. It had taken a very long time to find a man as kind and compassionate as he was, and Michelle was not willing to give him up.

She could have told everybody she knew about Veronica's affair, but she was not willing to go that low. It was not in her to be that nasty. There were other ways she could have gotten leverage on Veronica.

CHAPTER 30

It looked like Bart was getting by on very little sleep. He hadn't shaved in two days. His eyes were red and his face was blotchy. He sat across from Penny in the break room, drinking yet another cup of coffee. She wondered how he did it. How many cups had he consumed so far that morning? She flipped through a coupon newspaper, pulling out ones she could use, listening to him ramble about his upcoming nuptials while she ate her Stouffer's Lean Cuisine pasta dish. He was talking really fast.

"I guess you're excited about the wedding," she said.

"I'm psyched, but I'm a nervous wreck at the same time!"

"I bet you are."

"Everything has to be just right. I'm so worried that something will go wrong. Tending to the last minute details is a bear!"

"It will be just fine."

"I wish I shared your optimism, Penny."

"How did your parents react when you told them that you were marrying a guy?"

"I was nervous at first when I introduced Daryl to the whole family. It was as I expected. There was a lot of tension. But then they warmed up to him."

"I'm so happy for you. You really deserve it after what you've gone through lately."

He patted her hand and said, "Thanks, I'm so glad to have somebody as nice as you are in my corner."

"It couldn't have been easy for you growing up in that little town."

"You've got that right!" It didn't take much for him to spill like a fountain. A few minutes later, he apologized. "I didn't mean to talk your ears off."

"No, that's okay."

"Sometimes I'm ashamed about the things I did before I got to this point in my life."

"Hey, nobody's perfect, Bart."

"I'm sure you were a cheer-leader and never caused any problems. You landed a detective for a boyfriend. I know his type. He's a goody-two-shoes kind of guy."

"He has his moments. But he's not as perfect as you might think. And neither am I."

"Well, you seem perfect to me."

"That's so sweet. I'm sure, that whatever you did when you were a kid can't be as bad as you think."

"I was so scared that people would find out that I was into guys and that they wouldn't understand, that I got this girl named Amanda to pretend to be my girlfriend. I called her my fake girlfriend. We went out for a little while when I was in eleventh grade. She served her purpose. She temporarily distracted my parents from suspecting that I was gay. I feel so ashamed of myself for doing it. I feel like I was using her."

Penny was quiet for a moment. "Did she know?"

"Of course she knew! She was such a great girl. Instead of making out like straight couples, she just let me vent. I told her things I couldn't tell anybody else. I guess she felt sorry for me. I told her how trapped I felt, and she agreed to pretend for a while. A few months later, she started going out with a jock from the basketball team. We still talked once in a while. I don't think I'm that good an actor."

"What do you mean?"

"Well, I don't think I pulled off the romantic boyfriend role very well. It had to have been pretty obvious that we were faking our relationship."

"That's hard to say because I wasn't there. But your parents didn't go out on dates with you two. They were probably just happy that you had a girlfriend at the time."

"Well, they weren't happy with a lot of other things I did in high school."

She tapped his hand and said, "You were just a kid. All kids do really dumb things."

"Sometimes I wonder whatever happened to her. The last I heard she had a baby girl. That was years ago."

"Maybe you should try to get back in touch with her online."

"Maybe." He got up and poured another cup of coffee. He plopped back in his seat and asked, "How is Frank's investigation going?"

"He's working very hard on it. The forensics people discovered that the poison was in Veronica's salad."

Bart's eyebrows shot up. "No kidding!"

"Frank is getting upset because he can't figure out who did it."

"It must be frustrating."

"It is." She took a sip of her tea. "Especially since it could have been somebody here."

He was quiet a moment. "It's kinda creepy, isn't it? Not knowing if somebody we work with for hours on end is a killer!"

"It's especially hard because everybody here hated her."

"You hadn't been here long enough to hate her."

"But I'm sure I would have if...she hadn't been murdered."

"Well, I'm glad that the Dragon Lady was put in her place. Whoever did it did us all a favor. Veronica was a vile woman. The things she said about me–" He couldn't even finish the sentence. He looked up at Penny and said, "What does that say about me, to say something like that?"

"You're just upset. Everybody couldn't stand her."

"The things she did to people!" His voice shook. "I'm an open book. It must've been really frustrating for her, knowing that she couldn't get anything on me. I'm out in the open about everything. I don't have secrets that she could use against me."

"But other people do?"

"Everybody has secrets, Penny. And Veronica was good at exposing them. Don't ask me how she found out these things."

"Why didn't Mr. Dobson just fire her?"

"She must have had something on him."

"What do you think that might have been?"

"That's what everybody wonders around here. But they wouldn't tell it to Mr. Dobson's face, of course."

There was a long silence. Bart studied her a moment and grinned. Penny eyed him quizzically.

"You should be the detective," Bart said at last. "Did he ask you to get the dirt on us?"

"I won't lie," she admitted. "He might have suggested that I talk to you. But you volunteered the information on your own."

"That's true," he agreed.

"Please don't tell the others."

"I don't like to keep secrets."

"Please."

"Well, okay. Maybe you should become a detective."

There was another long silence. Penny finished eating her lunch.

"What kind of poison was it, by the way?" Bart wondered.

"Monkshood. I think that's what he said. The really creepy thing is that it came from a plant that's in the lobby."

Deep lines formed on Bart's forehead. He looked pale all of a sudden. "That means it happened right in front of our eyes, and we didn't notice a thing."

"That's right."

"It's really freaky." He got up and dumped the rest of his coffee in the sink. He rinsed out his mug and put it on the shelf. Then he rushed out of the room.

* * *

A blast of frigid air smacked against Craig Holloway's face as he approached the tiny tombstone of his two-year-old boy. As he got closer, he noticed that someone had put a bootie in front of it. He knelt down and rubbed grass off the little grave.

"Well, Matthew, Christmas has come and gone," he muttered. "Oh, we had such fun on Christmas, didn't we? I just wish you could be here to enjoy it now! You'd probably be driving me nuts wanting to borrow the car keys by now..."

He placed a red bow on the ground in front of the marker, feeling bad that he was doing it after the holidays.

"You know I'm not much into talking to a stone...maybe... maybe things were supposed to work out the way they did. I don't know why...I'm just sorry that you didn't get to do all the fun stuff I wanted to teach you like...like rock climbing and camping and white-water rafting..."

His eyes moistened, and he wiped a tear.

"Maybe you're like my little guardian angel or something..."

He rubbed his fingers on the dates that Matthew had lived. Two short years. Not enough time.

Maybe it was his fault. Maybe he was being blamed for his bad-boy behavior. Maybe his mother was right. Maybe he wasn't responsible enough to raise a kid. Hell, he could get his girlfriend pregnant. That was the easy part. Raising a baby to adulthood was the tricky part. But he didn't get it right. Matthew didn't live to adulthood.

He stopped questioning why it happened. The numbness that swallowed him up for years had dissipated over time. Now he just drank to forget. The meaningless relationships he had with women was his way of escaping the loneliness.

If only he had done things differently that day...then everything would have been okay now. If he could step back in time–he'd change the outcome.

He had learned very early on that people have no control of what happens in their lives, unless they choose not to do certain things. He had chosen the wrong path for way too long and suffered the consequences. Was it too late to start over again?

The wind picked up, and he tightened his scarf. He got up and rubbed his hands on the tombstone.

"Well, sleep tight, little buddy. I'll be back."

He walked hurriedly across the graveyard and hopped behind the seat of his sports car.

He wiped away tears and sped off.

CHAPTER 31

Penny sat with clipboard in hand taking notes, her attention on Tom Daniels as he made his spiel to the potential clients. Every so often, she looked at them, then back at Tom. They smiled politely as they listened to his ideas for their ad. He was too busy talking to realize he had lost them. Their target audience was a younger and hipper age group. Tom had no idea what kids wanted nowadays. His market research was outdated. The clients didn't have to say it. Penny could practically read their minds.

After speaking for nearly twenty minutes, Tom reached for a glass of water and took a couple of sips.

Maddy Pierce whispered something to her business partner, Roy King, and then looked back at Tom.

"I don't mean to interrupt," Maddy said. "But you haven't dazzled us with what we are really looking for."

"We thought you would do a Power Point demonstration," added King.

Penny was quick to help Tom out of the jam. "We figured you would like to see the final product, as we envision it, on the cards and posters we've shown you."

"It's better to actually see the physical product than on an impersonal computer program," Tom said.

Roy and Maddy weren't so sure. They whispered to each other once again, before announcing that they had to talk privately for a few minutes. Tom and Penny left them alone in the meeting room.

In the hall, Tom wiped a bead of sweat from his forehead and looked nervously at Penny. "They are extremely picky. I doubt they'll go with us."

"You did a great job pitching to them."

He grimaced. "Sometimes I think I'm losing my magic touch. I know how to read people's faces. They think I'm old. They want hip. I'm not hip."

"You said it yourself. They're picky. Picky people are hard to please."

"Maybe Veronica was right. Maybe–maybe I am old school."

"You're not old school," Penny assured him. "I'm sure you know things that these people don't know."

"Gadgets come and go."

"I know."

"They're investing a lot of money for a product that will be obsolete in a year or two. It's just so frustrating. I used to be up on the latest things kids would be interested in. Now, I haven't a clue what they're into, and it shows."

Penny patted his shoulder and said gently, "Maybe I'll go back in and see if they're ready for us."

She went back inside. A moment later, she waved for him to come back in the room.

Maddy did all the talking. She smiled broadly and said, "We think your presentation was really good, Mr. Daniels, but we feel that Creative Concepts just isn't going to meet our target audience. There is another company we've been talking to as well. Their presentation was that much better."

"We're sorry for wasting your time, Mr. Daniels," added Roy King.

"Maybe if you want to appeal to a younger audience, you should consider updating your computer skills," Maddy suggested.

Maddy and Roy thanked them and got to their feet. They put their laptops under their arms and headed out.

"How do they not drop those things?" Tom asked incredulously.

Penny grinned. "It's a bit of a challenge, isn't it?"

"At least they didn't think I was that bad. But, on second thought, they were probably just being polite. They didn't want to hurt my feelings because they think I'm old."

"Just be glad that we don't have to deal with them. They would be a pain to work with."

"I've had my share of Maddys and Roys, believe me! People like that can never make up their minds. And just when you think you've gotten everything just right, they always change their minds at the last minute! I'm glad they are going elsewhere. To tell you the truth, I'm too old to deal with people like that."

"Did it make you nervous thinking that you might have been on Veronica's list?" Penny asked out of the blue.

He looked sharply at her and said, "Of course it did! But you know what? I didn't really care if she kicked me out. I probably would have left at some point anyway. Life is too short to deal with a woman like her. Sometimes I don't know why she got so upset about things. Sure, it's a stressful job. But there was no reason why she had to act like that."

"I know."

"I've been in this business a long time, and I know how to survive. Veronica was just one of many self-obsessed people that I've had the displeasure of working with over the years. And the Maddys and Roys of the world don't bother me. I've come across people like them for years too. Maybe we'll get clients that have more exciting projects to offer."

"That's a positive way of looking at it."

He smiled and winked. "That's the key. It's how you win them over. You got it?"

She laughed. "Yeah, thanks for the tip, Tom."

"Don't mention it."

* * *

Craig sat in the break room reading the newspaper. Penny sat across from him, drinking coffee. She took a sip and said, "I really liked your exhibit."

"I'm glad you liked it," he said without looking up from the newspaper.

"I've been meaning to say something, but I've been so busy."

"I know how it is."

She reached for a *Time* magazine and flipped through the pages. "I didn't realize that you'd gone out with Veronica."

He rolled his eyes and grunted. "That is ancient history."

"You don't have to be so defensive. I was just striking up conversation."

He apologized and flipped the page. "I don't know what Charles got so worked up about. It's not like I did it on purpose. It just happened. Get it?"

"Well, she wasn't the easiest person to deal with."

"She was actually nice back then, if you can believe it."

"I wonder what happened to make her so..."

"Bitchy?"

Penny nodded.

"It was probably a culmination of a lot of crap that was thrown at her. It's none of our business."

"You're right." She could sense that he did not want to talk about his tryst with Veronica. She wished she had Frank's skill of pushing people to get information. "Did she ever tell you things about herself?"

"She kept things private. I didn't pry."

Penny picked out a fashion magazine and pointed to the woman on the cover. "She has beautiful eyes."

Craig glanced at the image and said, "Mesmerizing."

"It gets your attention." She sipped her coffee and added, "You would have done a much better job."

"You've got that right."

Changing tacks, she said, "Your little baby is so adorable! You never mentioned that you had a boy. What's his name?"

"Matthew."

"That's a nice name. How old is he?"

Craig folded the newspaper and laid it on the table. He looked coolly into her eyes and said, "He was about six months old in the picture." His eyes moistened, and his voice rose an octave. "I lost him when he was two."

Penny stared at him in astonishment, not sure what to say. "I'm so sorry," she said at last. "What happened?"

"He had a real bad temperature and didn't make it. I took him to the ER. The doctors did everything they could."

"Oh, Craig, I'm so sorry. I wish you had told us."

"What's there to tell?" He got up and headed out the door. "I've got to finish a shoot. See you."

Penny's eyes widened as she watched him go out. "Poor guy," she muttered.

* * *

Bart Sullivan didn't think that his father would show up to the wedding, but he did.

Neither of them said a word. Clay tied the knot on his son's tie. The strong man that he was, Clay could not hold back his tears.

"Thanks, Dad."

Clay patted Bart's shoulder and said, "Now, come on, let's go."

They entered the small chapel and met the justice of the peace at the altar. Valentine's day decorations were hanging all over the place. Bart craned his neck to see his family rooting him on. His coworkers were scattered around the room. All of Bart and Daryl's gay friends took up the remaining seats and cheered them on with thunderous whistles and clapping.

He reached for Daryl's large hand and squeezed it. His protector. Daryl would jump tall buildings for him.

Frank's grip on Penny's hand was tight. She nudged him to lighten up a little. He stared intently at the action taking place at the altar. There was something off about Bart, but Frank could not put it together. It wasn't just wedding day jitters.

Bart wiped a bead of sweat off his forehead when the justice of the peace said, "Now, does anyone have reasons why these two should not be wed?"

Bart glanced at his father, who nodded his head in approval. Tears welled in Bart's eyes. His mother was bawling.

"I now pronounce..."

Bart teetered to the right and fell down the steps, flat on his face.

"Oh my God!" somebody shouted.

CHAPTER 32

Bart stared at the bland decorations in the examination room. He was slowly coming around. Daryl sat by his bedside, holding his hand. His parents were there too. He didn't know what had happened or why he was there.

His thoughts drifted to another hospital room, a part of the past he didn't like to think about too much.

He remembered how bleak the surroundings were then, too. He could not look at the pained expression in his mother's eyes. His father just stared incredulously at his son.

No one spoke.

Then finally his father asked, "Why did you do it?"

"I don't know."

"It would've ripped us up inside if–if anything happened to you," Bonnie said through her tears, her face twisting in agony.

Bart rocked to-and-fro and said, "I've been trying to tell you but you won't listen!"

She reached over and held his hand. "I know it's been hard for you. We've talked to the principal. Something needs to be done."

Bart's voice was barely audible. "It wasn't the nasty kids' fault this time, Mom."

"Then why?" his father pressed.

"I'm different."

Bonnie pushed strands of Bart's beautiful blond hair out of his eyes. "That's what makes you special, honey."

"I don't fit in."

"None of that matters," she said softly.

"Maybe I forced you to do things too much," Clay said. "Things that you aren't interested in. I'm sorry. I know you're bad at sports. I just thought if you hung out with your brothers that they'd be able to teach you how to play better. I didn't realize that you really weren't into it."

"Don't feel bad, Dad." Bart's lips curled into a big grin and he laughed. "It rhymes."

Bonnie smiled weakly. She knew Bart's weird sense of humor was shining through. Maybe that was a good thing. Maybe it was a sign that he'd be okay. "Whatever it was that made you do this...Things can't be that bad." She rubbed her son's hand, and tears rolled down her cheeks. "You know you can tell us anything, and we'll understand."

Tears welled in Bart's eyes. "No, you won't."

Clay teared up too. "Try us."

"You get mad at the girls a lot."

"I promise I won't get mad," Clay reassured him.

"I really like Lucas."

Bonnie rubbed Bart's shoulder tenderly. "Well, that's what best friends are for. I'm glad you have him in your life."

"Well...I like him like...you want me to like girls."

They were quiet for a few moments.

Bonnie squeezed Bart's hand and said, "It's really confusing at your age. You're just figuring things out. Hormones are running wild."

"That's...that's why I don't want to take showers after gym. They–they say mean things about me."

Her grip on Bart's hand tightened. "What...what do they say?"

"They call me a fag!"

* * *

Bart opened his eyes and saw his parents across the room. Her eyes were heavy from lack of sleep. Daryl sat holding his hand by his bedside.

"What happened?" Bart asked as if in a daze.

"They don't know yet," Bonnie answered in a quiet tone.

"You gave us a real scare," Daryl said.

Bart gave him a puzzled look. "Did we–are we? Married? Why...why am I here?"

"You fell down just before the justice of the peace was about to pronounce you married," his mother told him.

"Really?" His voice sounded faint.

"The doctors are trying to find out what happened," Clay said. "He should have the results any time now."

At that moment, the doctor entered the room and asked the others to leave. He sat next to Bart's bed and said, "There are so many pills in your system, it's a miracle you're still with us, Mr. Sullivan. Why is that?"

Bart rubbed his eyes and said, "I needed something to pep me up at work. It's a highly stressful job. And then—and then

I needed something to help calm me down. I didn't mean for this to happen. I just needed something to get me through the day. If I didn't take the pills, I wouldn't be able to function at work..."

* * *

Bart looked plaintively into his sister's eyes and said, "I'm sorry. I guess you're not so proud of me now."

Mary shook her head in disbelief. "Why didn't you tell us? How long has this been going on?"

"For months."

Bonnie gave him a disapproving look. "My God, Bart! Why?" was all she could get out.

"You don't know how hard it is at work. Everything–everything's so fast...deadlines...long hours..."

"If it's that bad, you should have just quit," Bonnie admonished.

"I know, Ma. I know."

Mary just sat and listened.

"I promise it'll never happen again."

"We were so proud of you when you went to the city," his mother said after a long silence. "We even loaned you some money to help you out when you were struggling to pay rent. And now this! Were you doing drugs with your friends?"

"No, Ma."

"Where did you get the drugs?" Mary asked.

"One day I was bouncing off the walls, I was so stressed out. Mrs. Talbot gave me a pill to help calm me down."

Bonnie and Mary exchanged nervous looks.

"It really helped calm me down. After that, I went to a clinic and got a prescription. It didn't take long to get hooked. I just had to have it to help me get through the day."

"Why didn't you tell anybody?" Bonnie demanded.

"I didn't want to let you down."

Bonnie waved her hand defiantly and glowered at him. "You have the nerve to say that, after all–after all that you've put us through?"

"It was because of all the crap I put y'all through. I didn't...I didn't want to upset you. It kind of just snowballed. I needed it to cope."

Mary patted her mother's arm and said, "Come on, Ma. Maybe he needs some rest. Let's grab a cup of coffee at the cafeteria or something."

Bonnie stared at Bart in stunned silence a moment. "No job is worth this. Did Mrs. Talbot pressure you to use these awful pills?"

"Not really. But she didn't say I shouldn't use them, either."

Bonnie rolled her eyes in disgust and marched out after her daughter.

* * *

Logan sat at Bart's bedside and listened to him lament about being cooped up in the hospital room.

"You could have died, you know," Logan said at last. "You're lucky you were in a roomful of people when it happened."

Bart's eyes narrowed with shame. "I messed everything up. I don't think Daryl will ever forgive me!"

"I think he will," Logan said in a quiet tone. "Why did you do it?"

"I was really uptight about the wedding. I knew my family would be there, and I was scared."

"That doesn't mean you should have taken the pills."

"I just needed to feel relaxed. I was bouncing off the walls! I needed something to calm me down!"

"How long have you been on the pills?"

"For months. This is a very stressful job. The guy that left burned out, you know. They help keep me on an even keel. Without them, I'd be bouncing off the walls!"

"Wasn't Veronica on the same kind of medication?"

Bart nodded and grunted. "She strongly suggested that I take the pills or I'd burn out."

"I guess you needed the pills to deal with a woman as nasty as she was."

"You've got that right!"

"It must've been extremely stressful dealing with a woman that said such horrible things about you."

"It was just awful. Sometimes I don't know why I just didn't quit. I could've gotten a job anywhere."

"I bet you could have."

"It's scary knowing that somebody I work so closely with could have done it."

"I bet you wouldn't blame them though, would you?"

"Of course not. Whoever it was did us all a favor. If I was on the jury, I'd vote for acquittal."

"The thing that I can't wrap my brain around is who could have stuck the plant in her salad."

"It makes you wonder," agreed Bart.

"Just one simple little plant leaf looks so much like something you'd see in a salad. Who would have ever guessed that such a beautiful flower could be so deadly. It contains a lethal poison. Did you know that?"

"I can't believe it was in plain sight like that and none of us had a clue."

"Any one of you could have done it."

"Well, I hope you're not going to pin this on me!" Bart snapped.

"I'm just trying to figure things out, that's all. You knew her habits, right?"

"Yeah, but what does that have to do with anything?"

"Well, maybe you slipped it in her takeout carton when she wasn't looking. You had motive. And everybody knew how much you hated her. She treated you like dirt."

Bart eyed him intently, anger rising in his voice. "I resent what you are implying, Frank. I didn't do it."

"Whoever did it had the perfect alibi, wouldn't you say?"

Bart nodded his head and grunted.

"Can you think of anything that happened the week that she died–anything unusual or out of place?"

"Not really."

"There must be something."

"Well, she made everybody feel like jumping out of their skin."

"You were all worried about getting sacked."

"That's right. She called us all into her office, one at a time, like a shark circling around its prey."

"Well, it's an awfully big coincidence that you were alone in her office the day before the party, don't you think?"

"I don't like what you are insinuating, Frank. I swear I didn't do it!"

At that moment, a nurse entered the room and shouted, "What's going on in here? Is this man bothering you, Mr. Sullivan?"

"I was just trying to get some information," Logan said before Bart could say anything.

The nurse knew that Bart looked upset. "Get out!" she barked. "You have no right coming in here and upsetting the patient like this!"

At least if he had to be booted out, Frank left knowing that Veronica had been talking to her colleagues one-on-one prior to the party.

Thoughts swirled around in his head as he walked hurriedly down the corridor. He had figured out how the plant could have been slipped into Veronica's salad. Now all he needed to find out was who did it.

CHAPTER 33

About two weeks after the incident with Bart, a snowstorm blanketed the tri-state area. Penny rubbed her hands as she sat next to the fireplace. Her mother sipped a cup of hot cocoa and gazed at the flames. George was asleep on the reclining chair. A newspaper was on his lap. Penny reached over for her mug of cocoa on the end table and took a sip.

When the Weather Channel's Local on the 8's came on, they looked at the TV. It was going to get a lot colder overnight. The roads would be like an ice skating rink come morning. Shoveling the snow would be that much more difficult.

"I'm glad you decided to stay with us tonight," Maribeth said. "I don't like you driving on those back roads at night anyway, but it really isn't safe in this kind of weather."

"I know. I was tired too. It was a long day!"

Maribeth asked her how Frank was coming with the case. Penny told her that the poison came from a flower in the lobby and that someone put it in Veronica Talbot's salad the day before the party.

"That's unbelievable!" Maribeth cried. "I bet he's relieved to finally know how it happened."

"Well, yes and no. They might know how it happened, but everybody at the office had access to that plant. It could have been any one of them."

"It must be very frustrating for him."

"You're right. And you know how he gets when nothing is coming together."

"He'll figure it out. He always does." Maribeth took another sip of her cocoa. "Well, if he can't find iron-clad proof that somebody stuck it in her salad, it's going to be a cold case, I'm sorry to say."

"I hope you're wrong, Mom."

"Well, there were a lot of people who hated her."

"Luckily, I wasn't there long enough for her to stick her claws out at me."

"How is Frank's grandfather?"

Penny frowned. "The same."

"That's too bad."

Maribeth smiled when Penny told her that they were looking for apartments closer to the city. A few minutes later, Penny got up and went to look out the front door. The snow was coming down in gigantic chunks now. The mailbox could barely be seen. She went back into the den and gave her mother the latest weather report.

"It's really coming down now. Just like they said it would."

"It looks like we're snowed in for the duration."

"It looks that way." Penny picked up her digital camera off the drop leaf table and sat next to her mother on the sofa. "We got so busy over the holidays, that I forgot to show you pictures of the office Christmas party. It was a lot of fun."

Maribeth adjusted her glasses and watched Penny flip through the pictures. They burst out laughing at the images of Nicholas clowning it up for the camera.

"He's really funny. He keeps us laughing all the time."

"It's really nice to have a person like that in a stressful job. Every office should have a Nicholas."

"And there is Anna. She's really quiet, but nice. I like her." She flipped to the next shot. "And there's Tom. He's really nice too."

"It's great that he's taken you under his wing."

"He looks out for me. He looks out for everybody."

Maribeth's eyes trained on an image of Charles Talbot. "He looks so sad. You can see it in his eyes. They reveal so much."

"And there are Bart and Daryl. Don't they make a cute couple?"

Maribeth pointed to Daryl and said, "That man is gigantic!"

"Bart calls him his Big Black Teddy Bear. They're really good for each other. I think that Bart had some problems when he was growing up. But he doesn't like to talk about it."

"Well, he seems to be doing just fine now."

"Well, he isn't doing so great right now." Then she told her about what happened at the wedding.

"That's too bad," Maribeth said. "I hope he'll be okay."

"So do I."

Penny showed her some more pictures. They laughed at the one of Penny with the Santa Claus hat on.

"You wear that every year, no matter where you're working at the time."

"It's tradition."

George stirred from his seat and looked over at them.

"You've got to take a look at these pictures, honey," Maribeth said. "They're a scream!"

Penny showed the rest of the pictures to her mother and got up to hand the camera to her father. He scrolled through the files a little faster.

Maribeth looked back at the fire and rubbed her hands together. Penny took another sip of her cocoa.

"Frank works too much," Maribeth said after a long silence.

"We've been through this before, Mom. But at least we're living together now. I can see more of him."

"Not when you work such late hours. But I guess it's not as bad as when you were still in Philly. At least you can see him long enough to kiss him good night."

Penny shot her mother a disapproving look. "I don't want to get stuck here if you're going to lecture me."

Maribeth fixed her gaze on her daughter. "It still doesn't seem like he fits you into his schedule."

"It's better now that I'm there all the time. He's more relaxed when we're together after a hard day at work."

"Well, maybe if you find a place closer to work, then you might have more time to spend together."

George looked up at them and grunted. "Not if he's trying to crack a case. He'll never change."

"Just look at the pictures, dammit!" Penny's voice shook.

"I'm finished. They're really good."

"Thanks." She got up and went over to get the camera. She put it back on the table and marched out of the room.

George looked over his glasses at his wife and shook his head. "She will never learn."

"They're working it out, but Frank still needs to lighten up a bit."

"What's the latest about the storm?"

* * *

It was about three in the morning. George hadn't been able to sleep for almost a week. He sat in his reclining chair and read for a little while. Then he worked on a crossword puzzle. He glanced at Penny's digital camera on the table and went over to get it. He sat back down and turned it on.

He slowly went through the pictures, one after another. He didn't know why he was looking at them again. He didn't know those people. But there was something that had been nagging at him since dinner, although he didn't say anything.

When he finished looking at the files, he started over again. He paged through them, more slowly this time. He went ahead a couple of shots, then went backward until he saw it.

"Hmmm, that's interesting," he muttered.

He pressed the magnifying glass icon and stared at the enlarged image. "She looks familiar. I know I've seen her somewhere before."

CHAPTER 34

By morning, cars were buried under the snow. As usual, people up and down the block would have to dig out to get to their vehicles.

Penny peered out her bedroom window at the winter wonderland below. The snow looked so beautiful as the sun glistened off the tree limbs. She heard her cell phone ring and dug it out of her purse. She lay on her old bed and talked to Frank for about fifteen minutes. Then she called the office and told James that she would not be able to make it in to work today. Then she put on her thick winter attire and went downstairs.

She smelled bacon cooking on the stove as she entered the kitchen. Her mother was busily preparing breakfast. Penny pulled out plates and mugs from the cabinet and set them on the island. Then she helped her mother.

"I'm sorry I got so mad at you last night."

"I shouldn't have lectured you," Maribeth said. "I think Frank is doing better. Moving in with him was a major step in the right direction."

"I know you're right. But it's just his way. He'll never change. You just have to take him as he is."

"Well, your dad has his faults too. And I suppose he thinks I do too. Nobody is perfect, but if you love each other, you just learn to adapt–or you conk each other's heads like the cavemen did."

"Thankfully, none of us are that bad."

"Sometimes your dad comes down looking like a caveman in the morning, you know. He's usually grumpy till he gets his first cup of coffee."

Penny pointed in the direction of the den and said, "It seems awfully quiet in there. It's almost nine o'clock. He's usually up by now."

"He had a rough night. He hasn't been sleeping well lately."

"He should take something to get him to sleep."

"He usually just comes downstairs and reads. When I come down in the middle of the night, I find him asleep in his chair and put a blanket on him."

"Maybe he's worried about a client."

"That's usually the case when he can't sleep."

Maribeth finished stirring the pancake batter and spread it out onto the griddle. Penny poured orange juice into glasses. George emerged from the hall entryway. He kissed his wife and smiled brightly at his daughter.

"It's so nice to see you here for a change," he said.

Penny's face brightened. "It's nice to be back in my old room. I'm glad you didn't turn it into an office or something."

"I seriously thought about it."

"What stopped you?"

"It was too expensive." He plopped down at the table and unfolded the newspaper. He grunted as he read about the abysmal economy.

"Another murder," he grumbled. "Theft. A rape. Three house fires. A stabbing. Drug busts."

Maribeth turned and cocked her head at him. "Isn't there ever anything pleasant in the news?"

"That would be nice." He glanced at the local section and whistled. "Would you look at that?"

They went over and he pointed to the pictures. "That's something nice," Penny said as she peered over his shoulder. "Kids having fun in the snow."

Maribeth's face glowed as she looked at the pictures. "It looks like they're really having a lot of fun." She went over to the stove and flipped the pancakes. She scooped them up with a spatula and put them under a plate to keep them warm. Then she ladled more batter on the pan.

Penny apologized to her father for how nasty she had acted the night before. He said he didn't mean to upset her.

"I'm sorry you're not sleeping right, Dad. Are you uptight about a case?"

"Something like that."

"You should take sleeping pills."

"Nah. I usually just come downstairs and read until I get drowsy." He flipped to the sports section and read articles of interest. Then he checked the stats.

Maribeth laid a plate of pancakes on the table and sat down.

"Mmm, they look delicious!" George exclaimed. He set the newspaper on the empty chair, plopped a stack of three of them on his plate, and dug in.

Maribeth gazed out the window and said, "Well, at least it stopped snowing."

"I called in to work and said I couldn't make it. And I told Frank that I'm snowbound. I haven't played hooky in a long time!"

George looked at his daughter and asked, "Did they get much snow in Townsend?"

"Not as much."

There was a long silence.

"I looked at your pictures last night," George said finally. "I got this nagging feeling that I had seen one of the women you work with before."

Penny's eyes widened. "Really? Who?"

"I'm not sure. She has mousy hair and stupid-looking glasses."

"Oh. It must be Anna. She really could make herself look more attractive. It's there, but she doesn't show it off. Where did you see her?"

George chopped up his pancakes and said, "I'm pretty sure it was in family court years ago. Child protective service agents were called in to take her out of an abusive family situation."

Penny's jaw dropped. "You're kidding!" she cried.

"I helped put her into a foster home. I only worked with her for a couple of weeks, but I'm sure it's her. She didn't have glasses back then, but I'm certain that it was the same girl."

CHAPTER 35

After the roads had been plowed, Penny was able to get back to Townsend. She was getting dinner when Frank strolled in about seven o'clock.

"Well, hello, stranger." He reached over and kissed her.

She giggled and said, "Howdy."

"When did you get back?"

"A couple hours ago."

"Did you make it to work?"

"No, I decided to take the whole day off."

"Well, you needed a break anyway."

"Maybe you should take a day off once in a while."

"You're probably right. But not right now."

She huffed and said, "What difference would it make, anyway? You still can't figure out who killed Veronica."

He pulled away from their embrace and stalked across the kitchen floor.

"I'm sorry, but it's true," she said. "You work too hard. You need to take a break once in a while."

"Well, so do you." He walked hurriedly into the living room and plopped on the reclining chair. He turned on the news and whistled at the sight of a four-alarm house fire that had killed two people. Then the footage shifted to a deadly car accident. The cars were smashed beyond recognition. There were no survivors.

"The news is so depressing," he muttered. "I bet it was a kid texting while driving or something."

A moment later, the reporter announced that the driver had been texting.

He groaned. "They'll never learn!"

A few minutes later, he got up and helped set the table in the kitchen. They sat down and ate fried chicken and pasta in silence.

He was the first to speak. "How did it go with your parents?"

"It was really nice. We were nestled in for the duration, just like when I was a kid. We had popcorn and cocoa and relaxed by the fireplace."

"You really needed a little break like that."

"It felt good to help out around the house. My dad insisted on shoveling the sidewalk and my mom got mad at him. I know it's been months since his heart surgery, but he really shouldn't be over exerting himself. Well, at least he's able to get up and around to do it. A few months ago he couldn't get out of his seat!" She paused, thinking about Gramps. "I'm so sorry. I should have thought before I spoke."

He shot her a puzzled look. "What's there to be sorry for?"

"Well, you know, Gramps isn't as independent as he'd like, you know?"

"You shouldn't have to apologize. I'm thrilled that your dad is up and around now. Don't worry. Gramps is feisty. He'll be just fine."

"We've been so busy that we haven't gone to visit him as much as we should."

Frank sighed. "I know."

"Maybe we could see him this weekend. We should keep on him about moving in with us. I was looking in the want ads and saw a great apartment for rent. It would be perfect. It's almost halfway between here and Philly. It would be perfect. It's got two bedrooms and plenty of kitchen space. Maybe we should take a look?"

"Maybe." His eyes looked dreamy for a moment.

She wondered if her hard-nosed detective boyfriend was becoming sentimental about his old apartment. Maybe his thoughts were on the case. That's the way he got when he was trying to solve a homicide investigation.

"Maybe we should," he said again after a moment.

She drank some tea and said, "When I stayed overnight with my parents, my dad told me something interesting."

"What?"

"He thinks he worked with Anna McWilliams when she was in high school."

Frank's eyes lit up. "Really?"

"She was put in a foster home."

* * *

Logan jotted notes as he talked to Penny's father on the phone. About ten minutes later, he asked, "Is there anything else you can think of?"

"Her father was arrested for assault and battery," George told him.

"Really? That's interesting."

"He wasn't a very nice character. It was an abusive situation."

"Well, thanks, George. I'll check arrest records."

"I hope I was of some help."

"Believe me, you've been a big help." He hung up and got online. He typed MCWILLIAMS, GREG, and the name popped on the screen. He made a printout and read the arrest report. When Anna was about sixteen, her father had been arrested for hitting her sister, Maggie, in a domestic dispute. Child protection service agents had arrived on the scene and put the girls in a foster home. Greg McWilliams spent six months in jail. When he got back home, he was upset that the girls were still in the foster home.

Logan checked family court records from that time period. He typed MCWILLIAMS and scrolled down until the name flashed on the screen. Social worker George Lane was assigned to the case. He testified that Greg McWilliams was an unstable man and that the girls were not safe living with him. Child protection service agents described the trauma Greg had put his daughters through. The judge ordered the girls to stay at the foster home for another six months while Greg sought counseling.

* * *

Logan went to Holy Angels in Norristown and made a copy of Anna's yearbook senior class portrait. She was an attractive girl back then with long sandy-colored hair. If her name hadn't been under the picture, he would have continued flipping pages. She looked a lot better without the glasses and mousy hair. He even wondered if the printers had switched pictures with another girl by mistake. He studied her eyes for a moment and did not see any hint of the pain and suffering that she had been going through. Back then, she was far from the Plain Jane adult that she had become.

He drove over to the college she attended and did some nosing around. Over the past ten years or so, thousands of students had come in and out of the school's doors. He did not have any expectations that any of the professors would remember her, but it was worth a shot. Some teachers had left to work at other colleges. Some had retired. Four out of the five remaining professors simply didn't remember her. But then he struck gold in the graphics art department.

He checked the room number again and knocked on Matt Wallace's door.

"Come in!"

Frank popped his head in and saw a man with long gray hair hovering over his laptop. He looked up and said, "Can I help you?"

Logan introduced himself and explained the reason for his visit. For a moment, he didn't think the man was going to be of any help. Then he noticed Wallace's eyes light up as if in recognition of something.

"I remember a girl who was real shy. I'm not good with dates. Sometimes things happen a lot longer ago than you remember, you know."

"I know. Sometimes it seems like things happened recently–but it was much longer ago than you think."

Wallace nodded his head enthusiastically and said, "Exactly."

"She was a lot better looking back then," added Logan.

Wallace pointed to his flabby belly and said, "Well, none of us are in as good shape as we were in our prime."

"And sometimes people keep in surprisingly good shape."

"I wish." Wallace pushed his swivel chair over to a shelf across the room and stood up. He ran his fingers along portfolio cases stacked in order of dates and years. He pulled open a book and laid it on his desk. He opened it at random and leafed through it. Polaroid pictures of each student were included. Their project statements were at the bottom, along with Wallace's critiques of their work. He continued leafing through the pages until he reached the years that Logan was asking about. Wallace smiled as the memories came flooding back. Some of his students had gone on to do great things and he was proud of them. At long last, he tapped a page and nodded. He turned the book around so the detective could get a better look.

"There she is," Wallace said. "Now that you mention it, she was a very quiet girl. Stuck to herself a lot when she first got here. But once she got acclimated, she came out of her shell. Her parents were overprotective. I think it came out in her artwork. But then she came into her own. She started going out with her friends and meeting people. I was kind of relieved that she was having a good time. I was worried about her for a while. She showed a lot of promise. And then she dropped out of school."

"Well, she did have a lot of personal problems."

"That's right. Her father was arrested for beating up her sister. It was just awful!"

"Did she ever tell you anything else about her childhood?"

"She told me that her oldest sister couldn't handle living with her father and moved to a little apartment in a nasty section of town."

"That all came up in the family court records I was looking at," Logan noted.

"Anna clammed up about it," Wallace went on. "But it eventually came out in her artwork. It was so dark and disturbing. One day, I asked her what it was all about. She eventually told me that she had been babysitting for her sister when she was a teenager. She was all by herself when some man forced his way into the place and tried to rape her!"

"Oh my God!" Logan exclaimed.

"Well, she fought back."

"Good for her!"

"She hit him on the head with a bottle. The police arrested him. It took her a long time to get over it."

"Do you really ever get over a thing like that?"

"After she told me, I saw a big difference in her work. It was as if she blossomed overnight. And then she quit school."

"Did you ever hear from her again?"

"She came back a couple years later."

"Did she ever say where she had been all that time?"

Wallace shook his head. "No, she was as tight-lipped as she was when she started as a freshman. It was as if she reverted back into herself. She told me that she was helping her mother. Some kind of family emergency. Her work changed drastically."

"Do you know if she hung out anywhere with her friends?"

He nodded and smiled. "The college hangout back in the day was O'Brian's on Walnut Street. She hung out with a girl named Samantha Hughes."

Logan jotted it down and said, "Can you think of anything else?"

"No, not really."

"Well, if you remember anything, please give me a call." He handed him his business card and got to his feet.

Wallace closed the book and said, "I'm happy to hear that Anna is doing well."

"Well, she isn't doing that well, I'm sorry to say. She is a murder suspect."

Wallace stared at him in stunned silence, his mouth agape. Logan thanked him and headed out.

* * *

Bruno Santos had seen college-age clientele come and go for about two decades. When he was a busboy at O'Brian's, it was the in place to go for the partying crowd. He was their age. He was old enough to be their father now, though he didn't want to admit it. He was a lot heavier around the middle, and had a lot more tattoos than he did back in the day. His once shoulder-length hair went through many transformations over the years. When his hair started thinning, comb overs didn't conceal bald spots anymore. His scalp showed here and there. For a while, he sported crew cuts. Then he had to shave his hair.

He didn't know how many eager students had celebrated their first drinks in the bar the day they turned twenty-one. There were too many of them to count. His least favorite job at the place was cleaning up the vomit in bathroom toilets or on the sticky floors. He had tossed out his share of drunken idiots when he was a bouncer. He had worked his way up to being manager. Being around twenty-something's made him feel younger.

It was the slow period after the noon rush. He was wiping down the bar when he saw an intent-looking guy walk briskly toward him and sit down.

"What can I do you for?" He grinned like he had known Frank Logan his whole life.

Logan asked for seltzer water with a lemon. Bruno handed him a glass. Logan drank heartily and set the drink on the bar. He introduced himself and explained why he was there. "I've been asking around. You've worked here for a long time, right?"

Bruno eyed him dubiously. "Yeah. Am I in trouble for something, Detective?"

"Oh no. No. I just thought you might be able to help me out with something." He fished in his jacket pockets and produced the copy of Anna's picture. He handed it to the man and asked, "Does she look familiar?"

Bruno stared at the picture and shoved it back toward the detective. He shrugged his shoulders and grunted. "Never seen her before."

"Really? Well, I've been told that she frequented this place with a girl named Samantha Hughes. They went to the art college."

"Yeah, sure," Bruno replied noncommittal. "You know how many kids come in and out of here every year?"

"A lot. I just figured if you had been working here then that you might remember her." He started to get up when Bruno motioned for him to sit back down.

"I don't remember the girl in the picture, but I do remember Samantha."

Logan breathed a sigh of relief. "Oh, good!"

Bruno's face was aglow. "She was a wild chick, that one."

"You don't say."

"That whole bunch. They were just out to have a good time! I'd come in on my nights off just to try to score with her friend, Monica something. She was stacked! She had long, kinky hair. Nice and dark. Looked like she stepped off a runway. She was so much fun! We danced the night away. I wanted a piece of her. Every guy here did." He winked and said, "She wasn't shy, if you know what I mean. I loved them days! I loved every one of them gals. Their boyfriends were such jerks, though. Always getting drunk and causing problems I had to deal with. I had to toss 'em out on their keisters more than once. I knew them girls were using fake drivers licenses, but I just looked the other way."

Bruno took another long look at the photo and said, "Well, now that I think about it, there was one girl that hung out with them girls. She was kind of quiet. The guys tended to stay away from her. What was her name?"

"Could it have been Anna?"

"Well, it could have been. I remember they used to call this one girl Annie."

Logan feverishly jotted notes in his pad.

"Now that I think about it," Bruno continued after a long silence, "I think the girl you're talking about is her." He pointed to the picture.

"Now we're getting somewhere. What do you remember about this girl?"

"She seemed naive to start with, like she really didn't want to be here. I've seen the type a lot. But liquor 'em up a little bit, and they're really hilarious to watch. Cracks me up every time I watch people get drunk! It's a riot!"

"Yeah, it's a real riot," Logan said dryly. "Do you know how I can get in touch with Samantha?"

Bruno scratched his beard and grunted. "I don't know where they go after they graduate. They're just replaced with another group of kids–and quickly replaced by another group of kids. The styles change. The fads change. But one thing's always the same. They all just want to get drunk and get laid!"

"Do you know where the other girls wound up?"

He thought carefully a moment and said, "One of them works in Germantown. Lisa something. Sorry I'm not much help. But you know, I keep up with some of the guys on Facebook. We used to pal around years ago. We were total jerks back then, and we still are. Oh God, the fun we used to have! We had a blast!"

Bruno launched into loud and colorful tales from his illustrious youth. Then he whipped out his Smart phone and called a buddy who might know what happened to the women they were just talking about. Five minutes into the conversation, Bruno grinned and gave Logan a thumb's up. Then he hung up and jotted the name and address of the insurance company that Monica Halpron worked at on a bar napkin.

He handed it to Logan and asked, "Why is it so important that you find Annie?"

"She's a murder suspect."

* * *

Monica Halpron was not the way Bruno Santos had described her. She had put on weight as the years went by, and her once long and luscious hair was cut short now.

Frank explained the nature of his visit and showed her Anna's picture. It did not take long to recognize her friend.

"Anna McWilliams. I haven't thought about her in years!"

"You don't know how glad I am to hear you say that."

"Why would a detective be so anxious to find out about her? What has she done?"

"She works at an advertisement agency down town and a woman she worked for was murdered."

Monica gasped and looked at him in wild-eyed horror. "Oh my God. Do you think she had something to do with it?"

"I'm just trying to investigate everyone that worked with the woman. What can you tell me about Anna?"

Now Monica seemed guarded. Logan expected that she wouldn't want to say bad things about her friend.

"She was quiet to start with," Monica recalled. "It took a long time for her to come out of her shell. I got her to go out on the town with me and the girls. She felt totally awkward in the bar scene. To tell you the truth, we thought she was a real drag to start with. I felt sorry for her. She just sat there not saying a word while guys came up to talk to the girls and me. We tried to get her to talk, but she didn't say much. We spent a lot of time together in the art studio. I told her all about myself. And then I was finally able to get her to open up." She leaned forward and met Logan's gaze. "She had such a rough childhood."

"That's what I heard."

"Her father was abusive. They arrested him for beating up Anna's older sister. The horrible man! She and her sister were put in a foster home!"

"Did she ever tell you what it was like there?"

Monica took a deep breath and said, "It was horrible! Anna was extremely unhappy. I think that a lot of her pain and anger came out in her artwork. You should've seen it. She lived a sheltered life when she was a kid. One night at the dorm, the girls and I decided to give her a makeover. God, you should have seen how good she looked afterward! She looked like a totally different girl! I think it was a major step in the right direction. It boosted her confidence in public. And with men! Guys couldn't take their eyes off her! And when she got used to the taste of beer, she took a liking to it. She was a lot more chatty when she had a few drinks in her."

"A lot of alcoholics say that's why they started drinking. I think shy people want to be someone that they're not for a little while."

Monica nodded her head enthusiastically. "Exactly. I think that was the case with Anna. She drank like a fish! She was a real party girl! It was as if she was a totally different person. I think she was just doing it to get back at her parents."

"She was rebelling."

"Right."

"Can you remember anything else?"

"She started hanging out with this guy. I can't remember his name. They were hot and heavy the minute they met each other. I had a bad vibe about him. So did the girls. We tried to tell her not to see him anymore, but she wouldn't listen."

"Then what happened?"

"The school year ended. When we started back up in the fall, we found out that Anna had dropped out. We were kind of irritated because she didn't return our calls!"

"It must have made you angry."

"We were upset, sure. But then we got busy with our classes. I figured she dropped out to help her mother. There was a lot of drama going on in that house."

"Did you ever see her again?"

Monica nodded and said, "Yeah, sure. She showed up a couple years later. Didn't say a word about where she'd been or what she'd been doing. She was cool and aloof, so I just dropped her. She quit hanging out at O'Brian's. At that point, I couldn't have cared less."

"I don't blame you."

"Well, I'm glad to hear that she's got a good job–despite the investigation. Whatever her personal demons are, I'm sure she wouldn't hurt anyone. If you talk to her again, tell her I said hello."

"I'll do that," Logan said as he got to his feet. He thanked Monica for taking time to talk to him and headed out.

CHAPTER 36

The mood around the meeting room was tense the last Monday in March. They all suspected something wasn't right. James Dobson was about to announce some major changes, and he was twenty minutes late. They tensed up when they saw him enter the room with the company's accountant. Their expressions were grim.

For close to an hour, they discussed Creative Concepts' dire financial situation. Nicholas Bradshaw clenched his fists. Michelle's eyes darted around the room. Tom scowled at James. Charles folded his hands on the table and appeared statuesque. Craig shook his head in disbelief. Bart bit his nails. They were all waiting for the two ugly words employees in every field around the world could all identify with: "budget cuts." When they were finally spoken, there were loud groans around the room.

James frowned and said, "I will let you know who is staying and who is going within the week. I'm so sorry about this. I know you are all hard workers. This is truly the most difficult decision I've had to make in a very long time."

He was thankful when the meeting was over. He waited until they had all gone, gathered his papers, and locked himself in his office.

* * *

Nicholas Bradshaw was shocked and horrified when he received the e-mail three days later.

"You've gotta be kidding me!" he shouted. "Seven years and for what?"

Anna peered over the cubicle wall and looked despairingly at him. "Oh, Nicholas. I'm so sorry. Is there anything I can do?"

He waved his hands and groaned. "There's nothing you can do!"

"I'm sure I'll be next."

"I don't believe it!" he shouted over and over again.

A little while later, he wound up in Dobson's office. Screaming emanated from down the hall. Everybody cringed as they listened to them argue.

"I've been here seven years!" Nicholas yelled. "And this is how you repay all my hard work?"

"I'm so sorry, Nicholas. If there was any other way, you know I'd keep you on."

"I don't believe it!"

They heard a door slam and cleared out of the way when they saw Nicholas marching back toward them, full of rage. He sank in his chair and yanked open his desk drawers. He started shoving things in a box.

Penny went over to him and said, "Oh, Nicholas. I'm so sorry. Is there anything I can do?"

He was too busy cleaning out his desk to respond.

"Did Mr. Dobson give you a reason why he's letting you go?"

"He said I do great work, but that I'm too slow and I miss deadlines!" he snapped. "It doesn't make any sense!"

"I'm so sorry." She quietly listened to him rant.

"I thought Veronica was bad, but geez!"

"It's not so bad. You've got loads of talent. Another company will grab you up in no time!"

"All the time I put up with the Dragon Lady–and now this? Gimme a break! I can't believe it!"

She rubbed his shoulders and spoke in a soft, gentle tone. "If you wanna talk, just give me a call, okay? I'm a really good listener."

He was too preoccupied to comprehend what she just said. "Well, maybe," he muttered.

Everybody else hid in the confines of their offices and cubicles. If it could happen to him, they wondered could they be next?

* * *

Penny kissed Frank and said, "You'll never guess what happened today."

"Try me."

"Nick was fired, and he didn't like it one bit."

"Oh, that's too bad."

"He got into a nasty argument with Mr. Dobson and cleaned out his desk. I've never seen anybody so angry in my life! He stalked out in a fury! I tried to talk to him, but he didn't want to listen to anybody."

"Do you blame him?"

"No."

"I'd be pissed off!"

"It's such a shame."

"He probably won't have that much trouble finding another job."

"He's a terrific artist."

Frank seemed introspective.

"What are you thinking?" she wondered.

"Disgruntled employees usually can tell you everything you want to know."

CHAPTER 37

Logan felt like he stepped into a science-fiction film when he entered Nicholas Bradshaw's apartment. Brightly colored fantasy murals hung on his living room walls. They were brighter and bolder than the ones that used to be hanging up at work.

"I'll tell you anything you want to know," he told the detective.

"I want information on Dobson and Veronica. Is it true that they were having an affair?"

"Dobson was having an affair, but I think it was with someone else."

"Uh huh?"

"He was building a cottage on Long Beach Island for his wife. I think Veronica threatened to tell her that they were having an affair. It was amazing how fast she got the promotion. Veronica was cozying up to old man Dobson right in front of his wife. Boy, did he look hot under the collar! She had the job right after that. It's a real shame that she didn't fulfill her duties."

"I understand that you got angry when James Dobson gave Veronica's position to Dana Phillips."

"Well, wouldn't you be upset if you were passed up for promotion twice?" he asked with a wave of the hand.

"I believe so," agreed Logan. "Is that why you and Dobson got into the argument?"

"It was part of the reason. My big mouth is another part of it."

"Why did he fire you?"

Nicholas glowered at him. "He told me that I'm temperamental, if you can believe that! I admit that I'm a perfectionist, but you've seen my work."

"You do put a lot of detail into your work."

"He said that I've missed deadlines because I'm so picky, and I got really upset. And then–and then he showed me the door! It really doesn't seem fair. I put in seven good years at Creative Concepts. I just can't believe it!"

"Well, maybe you should learn to curb your anger a little bit," Logan suggested.

"Maybe I should."

"Bart told me that Veronica called people into her office the week before she died."

Nicholas rolled his eyes and grunted. "Oh, that!"

"What do you mean?"

"The Dragon Lady was calling us into her office to decide whose throats she wanted to slit!"

"Do you remember who went to talk to her on Friday?"

"I was pretty busy with my design...but I do remember that Anna was gone for quite a while. And when she came back, she was visibly upset."

"You don't say."

"Veronica told her that her job was on shaky grounds and that she would decide in a week or so whether or not she was going to fire her. Tom was furious that the Dragon Lady planned to sack him after all his years in the business. He was livid when he came out of her office! Dana was angry, but she's always angry. And...and she expected it from the Dragon Lady."

"Is there anything else you can tell me?"

Nicholas was unusually quiet for a moment. Then, he said, "Well, yeah. A few days before the party, Veronica and Charles got into a nasty argument. I was really surprised, actually. I didn't know he had it in him."

"What was the argument about?"

"I'm not really sure. It had something to do with Tricia. Maybe it was something about Dana. Maybe–maybe Veronica thought Dana was spending too much time with Tricia or something. Or maybe Veronica was upset that Charles was spending too much time with Dana. There were rumors floating around the office about them, you know. Maybe Veronica got so upset with Charles that she finally burst! She got so angry with him that she stormed out of her office and took out her anger on poor Bart and Anna."

"Really?"

"Anna was in tears, and it took forever to calm her down."

"What about Bart?"

"He just stood there and took it. You know, sometimes I just wish he would stand up for himself for once."

Logan nodded his head in agreement and checked his notes while listening to Nicholas lament about getting fired.

"Michelle told me she saw you coming out of Veronica's study the afternoon of the party. Maybe you were checking to make sure the poison killed her."

"How dare you accuse me of such a horrible thing!" Nicholas cried. "Sure, I hated the woman, but I wouldn't kill her!"

"What about your artwork? It's full of violent images. It suggests a pattern of thinking."

"Hey, look, man! It's just a healthy way to vent, is all."

"Well, I don't agree. And neither will jurors if it turns out that you killed Veronica. Maybe you stuck the leaves in her salad to get back at her. Maybe you did it as a joke. Maybe you didn't know they were poisonous."

"You're just grasping at straws, and you know it!" Nicholas snapped. "You can't figure out who did it, and you're getting desperate."

"What makes you think that I don't know who did it?" Logan asked as he got to his feet. "I'm getting very warm."

CHAPTER 38

Dana smirked at the twenty-somethings crammed together like sardines in the bar. It was a typical Friday night. Everybody had to shout to hear each other over the loud music. Men and women of varying ages and ethnicities sat at the bar and watched the basketball game, shooting the breeze with their buddies. Dana looked across at Michelle and asked, "Were we ever that young?"

"In another lifetime."

"I'm way beyond that now."

"Well, you're the one who said we should have a girls' night out."

Dana grinned, not wanting to admit that Michelle was right. She swigged her Coors Light lustily. It had been a bad week at work. "It's too bad about Nicholas."

Michelle frowned. "I know."

"I wonder who will be next."

"We just went through the trauma of worrying what Veronica would do when she took the job, now this!"

"Did you try to talk to Nicholas after he stormed out?"

"He's not returning my calls. I'm just hoping that when things get straightened out around the office Mr. Dobson will hire him back."

"I'm sure that Nicholas will have a more lucrative paying job by then."

"I hope so."

Dana waved and grinned. Michelle turned to see Anna maneuver her way through the crowd. It took a lot of coaxing to get her to go out on the town with them, but she finally relented. She looked stunning in a halter top and blue jeans. She had replaced her glasses with contact lenses, and her hair was long and bouncy. With just the right makeup, the Ugly Duckling had been transformed into a beautiful princess.

Dana and Michelle gasped and silently sized her up. Anna waved and smiled as she pulled up a chair across from them.

Michelle grinned and said, "You look terrific! Who knew all this was hiding behind what we see at the office?"

"That's just for work," Anna said. "Do you really think I want people to see me like that in public?"

Dana and Michelle exchanged looks but said nothing.

Anna looked around the crowded room and then back at her friends. "There are a lot of gorgeous women here. I'm surprised Craig isn't here, snuggling up to them."

"I'm sure he'll be here," Michelle assured her. "Just give it time."

The waiter came up to them, and Anna ordered white wine. It was way too loud to maintain a conversation. They had to constantly ask each other to repeat themselves. They only heard half of what the others were saying.

Dana spotted Penny pushing her way through the crowd. Her eyes lit up when she saw Anna sitting with them. She almost didn't recognize her at first.

"Anna? You look beautiful!"

"Thank you," she said softly.

Penny sat next to her and ordered a beer. "Did I miss anything exciting?"

"We were talking about Nicholas a little while ago," Dana told her.

Penny's face twisted in anguish. "It's a shame what happened."

"If it could happen to him, it could happen to any one of us," Dana lamented. "And don't think you're too good at what you do, to not be let go. God, I'm gonna miss that guy!" She lifted her glass and said, "Here's to Nick, you've made me what I am today. Sarcastic and bitter."

"You were bitter to start with," Michelle corrected. "But it wasn't your fault. Your louse of an ex-husband was partly to blame."

They clinked their glasses together and took sips of their drinks.

Dana gazed at a bunch of young people at the bar. They were rowdy but having a good old time. She looked back at the girls and said, "Did you ever do anything wild and crazy like that when you were younger?"

Michelle laughed and said, "I still do!"

Dana leaned back in her seat and laughed. "I was a naughty girl. Maybe I had a little bit too much fun back in college. But my mother always told me to grab what I wanted, and that's what I did. I fought for Charles."

"Was he going to divorce Veronica?" Michelle wondered.

"It was a source of tension between Charles and me. I kept pressuring him to leave her. He wouldn't for Tricia's sake."

"I'm sure that it must have been really upsetting for her," Penny said.

Dana's eyes moistened. "You don't know how bad I feel about it. I know Tricia has had a hard time accepting me, but you don't know how good I feel when I'm around Charles."

The girls nodded their heads in agreement.

"The old googly eyes," Penny observed. She looked at Michelle and said, "Just like with you and Tom."

"Oh, come on, Penny. We're not in grade school. We're acting like little girls gossiping about boys we like."

"But it's fun!"

Dana swilled her beer and looked across the crowded bar. A moment later, she said, "How is Frank coming with the investigation?"

"I think that he'll put the pieces together pretty soon. I'm sure of it."

"What a relief!" Michelle exclaimed. "Charles will finally get the closure he needs."

"And then we can get our lives back together," added Dana.

The band took a break and it was a lot quieter now. The only other sounds came from the basketball game that blared in the background. Every so often, fans would holler with excitement. Dana looked up and saw Craig ogling a woman across the bar. They quietly watched. The normally smooth operator was not as smooth as they thought. The woman turned him down and stalked out of the room. He concentrated his attention on his beer and watched the basketball game.

"Can you believe Craig had a thing with Veronica?" Dana said.

"That was a long time ago," Michelle reminded her. "She was actually a nice person back then. That's when she was just starting out."

"That's right, you worked with her in the Big Apple?" Penny asked.

Michelle swished the wine on her tongue and swallowed. "That's right. We both got our start there."

"Did you know she was mixing it up with him?" asked Dana.

"Not at the time. We went out for drinks one night, and she told me she was having an affair with a photographer. I figured out that it was Craig. She swore me to secrecy."

Dana's eyes widened. "You mean to tell me that you actually had something on the Dragon Lady, and you didn't use it against her?"

"I'm not vindictive that way."

"I'm surprised that Craig never mentioned it," Anna interjected.

"Maybe he didn't want Charles to get upset if he found out. I don't blame him for keeping quiet about it."

Penny looked at Michelle and asked, "Did Veronica have anything on you?"

Michelle eyed her disapprovingly. "Look, Penny, I agreed to come out tonight to have a good time, not be given the third degree by a detective's girlfriend. Did he put you up to this? Did he ask you to snoop on us?"

"That's right!" Dana cried. "You have been asking us a lot of personal questions lately. Maybe you're just trying to get information about us."

"I won't lie about it," admitted Penny. "I promised Frank that I'd help him a little bit, but he's found out the important information all on his own, I swear." She looked back at Michelle and apologized for asking such a personal question.

Michelle told her she was sorry for snapping at her. "It's just the stress of the investigation and all. We're not at our best."

"It is pretty stressful," Dana agreed.

Anna leaned forward and grinned. "Enough about that. You wanted me to join you tonight for a fun night out. So far, it's been kind of a drag. No more talk about the investigation or work, okay?"

"Anna is right," Michelle said. "We came here to let our hair down."

Penny turned her attention on Anna and asked, "What ever happened to the boyfriend that your parents couldn't stand?"

Anna bristled at the thought of it. "We broke up when I went to art school."

"I guess your parents were relieved."

"My mother was. My dad was in jail."

Dana gasped. "No kidding! What did–what did he do?"

Anna told them the sad tale of how she and her sister had wound up in the foster home. By the time she was finished talking, they were all in tears.

Dana sniffled and said, "We're really not very good at these girls' nights out. We're liable to drive the customers away!"

Michelle was very quiet. She stared at Anna with an eerie intensity and said, "But everything worked out, right? You went to art school."

Anna took a healthy chug of her beer and wiped the froth off her lips with a napkin. "It was fun while it lasted."

Dana cocked her head in surprise. "What do you mean?"

Anna was silent.

Dana leaned forward and stared intently at her. "What happened?"

Anna sat there as if she was contemplating something. Could she trust them?

"You know, whatever you say will never leave this room," Dana said. "Come on, you know you can tell us anything, right?"

Tears streaked down Anna's cheeks. "You're right–we're not very good at these girls' night's out."

"What happened?" they asked in unison.

"I got pregnant the first year I was at art school." Then she couldn't stop talking. They listened intently. "I had a skunk of a boyfriend. My parents were right, but I wouldn't listen."

"What did he do?" asked Dana.

"He deserted me!"

"Poor girl," Michelle said. "What happened?"

"I didn't know what to do. I was flat broke. And I didn't have it in me to get an abortion, so I dropped out of school and moved back home until the baby was born. It was a girl. And then–and then I had to give her up!"

Dana patted Anna's hand and said, "You, poor thing."

"What happened when you told your parents?" asked Penny.

"I didn't tell them at first, but then I pretty much had to. My mom was upset at first. My old man didn't understand when he found out."

Michelle looked wide-eyed at her. "How could they not have known?"

"I wore clothes in layers, and it just looked like I got a little chunky from eating too many cakey things."

Michelle gasped and shouted, "That's unbelievable!"

"Poor thing!" Penny exclaimed.

"It broke my heart to give her up...but I needed the money. My life ended when she was taken from me..." Anna's face twisted in anguish, and she wept uncontrollably.

Penny wrapped her arm around her. "There, there. You'll be okay."

"I just didn't think it would be so hard to give her away!" Anna shouted through her tears.

Patrons stared at them a moment and then went back to what they were doing.

"You did the right thing," Dana said.

"I wish I had done that," Michelle mumbled.

They all looked at her and asked, "What did you say?"

Michelle had uttered the words without even thinking. She said them just as easily as Veronica had revealed her affair all those years ago.

She didn't have to repeat herself. Dana looked wild-eyed at her. "You were pregnant too?"

Michelle's eyes moistened with tears. Her breathing was shallow. She swallowed hard and nodded her head. Her face flushed. She held her hand on her forehead and averted eye contact. "It was something that happened years ago. When I...when I was in college. If Tom ever knew I was pregnant and...and got rid of it..."

Dana patted her shoulder and said, "Oh, Michelle."

Penny's voice became hysterical with grief. "It must have been so painful keeping it bottled up inside. What happened–what happened to the baby?"

"I got an abortion!" Michelle wailed.

They talked over each other.

"Did Veronica know about it?" asked Penny.

Michelle nodded and wept. "It was the biggest mistake I ever made. It...it was just awful. So cold and clinical. It was just awful. I often wonder what my baby would be today. I'll never know. Tom would never forgive me. He wouldn't understand. But I had to do it. Understand? He'll abandon me at a time when I need him the most!"

She looked across the room, and her eyes took on a hunted look. Tom was sitting with a client. He shot her a scorching look. He said something to the client and rose unsteadily to his feet. He shook his head in disbelief at her and pushed his way through the crowd.

Michelle clutched her hand to her mouth and gasped. "Oh no! Do you think he heard?"

Dana reluctantly nodded her head. Michelle started to go after him, but he had already pushed his way out the door.

The always level-headed Michelle Delancey was reduced to a bundle of nerves. She shook her head and moaned. "He won't understand."

"He loves you, Michelle," Anna reassured her. "I'm sure he'll understand. Just give it some time."

Michelle shook her head defiantly. "He's strictly against abortion. He's talked about it."

"I'm sure he's done some things he isn't proud of himself," Penny said.

Dana remained silent and just listened. She felt uneasy discussing it with her. Michelle knew how she felt about the subject.

Michelle wiped her tears and sniffled. "Let's not do girls' nights out again. We're really bad at them."

"Yes, we are," Dana said finally. "Did you ever do anything wild and crazy, Penny?" she asked, to change the subject.

"Well, yeah. One time my friends and I–"

* * *

Penny got back to the apartment at about 1:30 a.m. Frank was asleep when she got in bed. About eight o'clock, he was eating Honey Bunches of Oats and drinking coffee while reading the sports section. He was so busy concentrating on what he was reading that he didn't notice when she entered the room. She went over and wrapped her arms around him. She kissed his cheek and went to get a mug out of the cupboard. She was in such a rush that she just ate a granola bar while she drank her coffee.

"I think I've got some news," she announced cheerfully.

He looked up from the newspaper and asked, "What?"

When she told him about Michelle's abortion, he told her he had known about it for some time.

"It's hard to believe that Michelle got an abortion when she was in college," Penny said. "She was really torn up about it."

He told her how upset she got when he was asking her questions a few weeks earlier.

"If Veronica knew about what she did, it gives Michelle motive for wanting to kill her."

"That's right. She didn't want Tom to know. It was so awful! He was right there in the bar and heard everything!"

"Uh-oh. What happened?"

"He got really upset and stormed out."

"That's a shame."

"They make such a great couple. It's too bad she couldn't have told him in a better situation. I doubt she would have told him, though."

Conversation switched to Anna McWilliams.

"What else did Anna say?" Frank pressed.

"She was so desperate, she gave her baby up for adoption."

"It was a girl, right?"

"That's right. You truly are amazing. How did you know?"

For a moment, it was as if she could see the mechanisms in his brain turning. She thought she heard him mumble, "It's just a hunch," as he exited the apartment. She looked out the window and saw him pull out of the driveway. He was a man on a mission!

* * *

It felt like the world had come crashing down at Anna's feet the day she found out that she was pregnant. She had a good cry with her childhood friends, Jeannie and Patty. They discussed options. She could not bring herself to abort the baby.

"What are you gonna do, honey?" Patty asked her.

"I don't know. It was such a stupid thing I did. My dad is gonna kill me!"

"Then don't tell him," Jeannie advised. "He never has to know."

"What am I supposed to do with the baby? It's gonna be noticeable in a few weeks. And I can't just dump it on my dad's doorstep."

"I've got a couple hundred bucks," Jeannie said. "It's not much, but it's yours if you want it."

"And I've got three hundred," Patty said. "You can pay us back later."

"Thanks, you guys. You don't have to do that."

"But we want to," Jeannie said. "What are friends for?"

"Did you talk to your mom about it?"

"Not yet." Anna wiped away tears with her hands.

"How about your sisters?" asked Patty.

"They're busy with their own kids."

"I'd definitely talk to them," Jeannie suggested. "They'll understand."

"You should go to a counselor or something."

"That's a good idea. I'll take you to the one on Main Street if you want to. We can go with you if you want."

"Maybe that's a good idea," Anna said through her tears. "Thanks, you guys. I don't know what I'd do without you."

Patty drove them to the center, which was about ten minutes away. Anna spoke to a kind woman who discussed her options. Anna decided it would be best for the baby if she gave it up for adoption. When the time came, a happy couple would be able to give the baby all the things that she could not. It was the right decision.

* * *

Anna was about six months pregnant. Standing on her feet all day was getting harder for her. She was waiting on fewer tables and getting fewer tips.

She had seen that couple at the diner a lot lately. The man was tall and thin with thick, dark hair. His wife was worldly-looking with a swan-like neck and strong features. Anna felt sorry for the man. His wife always told him what to do. For once, Anna wished he would stand up for himself. But he never did.

Mrs. Talbot was the kind of customer waitresses couldn't stand. Nothing ever pleased Her Highness. Anna despised the woman and was always grateful when they left.

Anna was already having a bad day when they arrived for lunch during the noon rush. She needed to take more breaks to get off her feet. Mrs. Talbot was in a hurry, like she so often was, and breathed down her neck.

"There is no reason why it should take so long to get a hot turkey sandwich."

Anna smiled meekly and said, "I'm so sorry, Ms. Talbot. It's been a hectic day."

"I don't need to hear excuses. I expect results. Now make it snappy, or I'll have a word with your manager."

"It won't happen again." Anna walked as quickly as she could to the kitchen to find out what the hold up was.

Charles scowled at his wife. "Was that necessary? You're not in that much of a hurry. I think you owe that girl an apology. She's pregnant, for God's sake. Cut her some slack."

Veronica did not dignify that with an answer. She stirred her coffee and drank it a little bit too fast. It burned her lip, and she howled in pain.

"Ouch!"

"That's what you get for being in such a hurry." He snatched the newspaper from the table and said, "Sometimes you can be a real bitch."

She snarled at him. "I just don't like lousy service."

"She's doing the best she can, for crying out loud!"

Anna came back and apologized for the hold up. "It should be out soon."

"I'll count the minutes," replied Veronica sardonically.

A cold chill shot down Anna's spine as she moved to the next table.

Charles just shook his head and continued reading. If Veronica opened her mouth, he was too busy reading to care.

"She shouldn't be allowed to get away with it," Veronica said.

"Oh come on!" Charles cried in exasperation. "Will you get off it?"

Anna was glad to see them leave. The other waitresses congratulated her for keeping her cool around the Ice Queen. Anna was sure that the woman had a lot of nicknames. Mrs. Talbot was a bully!

For the remainder of her pregnancy, Anna only saw the man come into the diner.

One day, they struck up a conversation about the baby. Anna admitted that she had no one to help her after it was born. She didn't want her father to know. She would eventually have to tell him. That thought terrified her because she didn't know what he would do to her.

"That's too bad," Charles said.

"I'll get by."

"You shouldn't have to be in this predicament. It's a bad situation to be in."

"I'm gonna give it up for adoption. I'm sure there's a couple out there that really wants to have a baby and can't. More coffee?"

"Please."

She poured a cup and started to walk off when Charles said, "Maybe when you go on break, I could talk to you about your situation."

Anna looked dumbfounded at him. Why would a man she barely knew care about her problem?

About thirty minutes later, she sat across from him, and he said, "I think I can help you."

"I don't know what you mean."

"My wife and I are having trouble conceiving."

Anna couldn't believe he would tell her such a personal thing. There really were no secrets anymore.

"I'm sorry to hear that, sir."

"My wife is desperate to have a baby. She is so upset about it that she isn't acting like herself. She can be a real bitch at times, but that's just her frustration taking over. Fertility treatments aren't working. It really pains me to see her struggling so much. Maybe we could adopt your baby. We'll give you one hundred and fifty thousand dollars. That should be enough to help you make a better life for yourself."

"That's a lot of money. But she-but she doesn't act very nice. I don't want my little girl to be raised by somebody that acts like that."

He leaned forward and said, "I know what you mean. She acts upset when she's on deadline. She's high-strung, you see. You're only seeing her when she's having a bad day. She would never act that way around a child."

"The money could really come in handy right about now."

"We'll take the baby, and you won't have anything to worry about any more. And don't worry about Veronica. She'll be a lot nicer when she has the baby she's been wanting for so many years."

"If I agree to do this, would it be possible to see my little girl? I would want to be able to see how she's doing once a year or so."

"I'll make sure that my lawyer puts that in the agreement with the adoption agency."

"You don't know how much this means to me. I really didn't know what I was going to do."

Charles grinned. "I'm so glad that you can help us out. It's a win-win for both of us."

It wasn't such a win-win for Anna. As soon as she gave birth to her daughter, she didn't see her again for about fifteen years.

CHAPTER 39

Logan thought of everything that happened since he first saw Veronica Talbot lying on the love seat in the study of her home last fall. Several people heard her yell at the caterers about how bad the food tasted. Stan Green confirmed that it had tasted bad only to her, which meant that the poison was taking effect. For weeks, he and his colleagues believed that someone slipped the poison into her food or drink at the party. To make matters worse, the poison came from a plant in the lobby at Creative Concepts. Any one of them could have chopped up the Monkshood leaves and stuck them in her salad when she was talking with them individually the day before the party. He was back to square one.

Then he thought about the list that Veronica Talbot had hidden in the desk drawer of her study. Apparently everybody was eager to find out what she had had in mind when she took over creative control of the company. There had to be something in the desk that he overlooked. He strained his brain, trying to remember.

He went back to the Talbots' home to take one more look in the study. He went over to the roll-top desk. He pulled it open and found Veronica's list on top of a stack of papers. He sifted through them and read personal notes in her handwriting. He pulled open a door on a little cubbyhole and saw a manila envelope stuffed inside. He pulled it out and dumped out the contents. There was a pile of old letters and notes. Several of them were Hallmark cards still in their envelopes with a New York City post office stamped on them. The dates were from the time Charles said they lived there. One of them had their Philadelphia address at the time written on it. He removed the card and saw a picture of a baby Jesus in a manger. "Please take care of Lily "was scrawled in red ink below the greeting. There was no signature.

The other cards were from their friends and colleagues in New York City and Philadelphia. Then his interest piqued when he saw an envelope in Veronica's handwriting addressed to Craig Holloway. A "Return to Sender" stamp was on it. There was no information about his forwarding address. He opened the envelope and read her note:

> Dear Craig, I'm sorry it didn't work out. It was fun while it lasted. Hope you aren't mad. Charles and I were just going through a rough patch. Think of the good times we had together.
>
> Fondly, Veronica.

"Fondly?" He shook his head in disbelief and grunted.

He put the contents back in the manila envelope and shut the little cubbyhole drawer. He pulled off the lid of a small box that was beneath the stack of papers. He sifted through old snapshots of when Tricia was a little girl. There was a faded Sears portrait in the mix. She couldn't have been more than two days old. Something seemed familiar about it. His eyes trained on Tricia's baby picture on top of the desk. The pictures were identical. He turned the faded photo around. "Tricia, One Day Old" was written in blue ink in the middle. Some handwriting was scratched out at the bottom. He held the picture under the lamp on top of the desk and tried to make out what was being covered over. He couldn't.

He reached for the framed picture on top of the desk and carefully slipped the photograph out of the frame. Then he removed the cardboard backing and looked at the handwriting scrawled in red ink behind the photograph.

"Oh my God!"

* * *

Tricia wasn't hungry. She shoved aside her half-eaten ham sandwich and glanced at the clock on the cafeteria wall. It was twelve forty. She felt bad about leaving without saying anything to her father and Kelly, and hoped that they would forgive her.

She knew how he felt about her going out to LA. But this was a once in a life time opportunity. Maybe he would eventually understand.

Tricia hoped her father would not be upset. Then she worried that he wouldn't take her out to Hollywood after she graduated from high school like he'd promised. She tried to dismiss it from her mind to ease her guilt. She decided that sometimes you just have to take a chance.

She fumbled with her cell phone. Should she at least send him a text to let him know what she was doing? She started to send him a message, but decided against it. He would just tell her not to do it.

About twenty minutes later, she filed out of the cafeteria with students in a rush to get to their next classes. She lugged her unusually overstuffed book bag down the crowded hallway. Instead of going to her English class, she made a bee-line for the front door.

She checked to make sure that no one saw her, and leaned against a pillar that was away from the doors. She fished through her purse and pulled out her cell phone. She decided she had to at least tell her father something, so she decided to text him. There was no signal, so she didn't have to feel as guilty. She darted across the parking lot, and saw Anna sitting in her blue Honda. She climbed in the front seat and looked to make sure no one saw her.

Anna grinned brightly and said, "Are you ready to have some fun in the sun?"

"I can't wait!"

Anna pulled out of the exit and sped down the country road.

* * *

Tricia's stomach was churning as she gazed out the car window. She wished she had had time to say something to her father or Kelly. In the back of her mind, she wondered why there was such a need to hurry.

Over the past few weeks, she had gotten to be really good friends with Anna on Facebook. They had opened up about a lot of things that were bothering them. Anna had gone through similar issues when she was growing up. Tricia could tell her things that she couldn't even discuss with Kelly.

She thought about how excited she was the day Anna posted the message: "Just talked to my friend in LA. She said you would be perfect for a film that is set to start shooting in four months. She needs to know soon!"

Tricia clasped her face and repeatedly screamed with excitement. "Oh my God! Oh my God! Oh my God!"

Anna beeped the horn, jarring Tricia back to reality.

She looked over at Tricia and grinned. "It's a beautiful day for a drive, isn't it?"

"My dad is going to be furious. We shouldn't have just picked up and left like that. I should have told him what I'm doing."

"I'm sure he'll understand." She glanced at the rearview mirror and floored the accelerator.

"You're going too fast!"

"I just want to make sure we get there on time. Just relax."

Tricia fumbled through her backpack and pulled out her cell phone. She started to send her father a text when she realized that there was still no signal.

"Damn!"

"That's all right, honey. I'll give him a call when we get to the airport."

Anna glanced over at Tricia and wondered how such a terrific young girl could have been raised by such a wicked woman. Every day that winter she had looked forward to Tricia's Tweets and Facebook posts. Facebook had really helped Anna come out of her shell. It pained Anna to read the horrible things that classmates were posting about Tricia. Anna would do anything to protect

Tricia. If she knew how to stop the online taunts, she would, just like she had managed to do with the other bullies in her life...

* * *

Kelly McDougal glanced at her wristwatch and frowned. She watched students scramble out of the doors and board school buses. Then, one after another, the drivers pulled out of the parking lot. She stared intently at the doors. A feeling of uneasiness came over her when she saw kids ride off in their parents vehicles.

She slipped into a parking spot and walked hurriedly into the building. She made a bee-line for the office and spoke to a woman behind the counter.

"Maybe Tricia told me she was staying after school for an extra-curricular activity today, or something. Can you check?"

The woman looked at the schedule and said, "I'm sorry, Ms. McDougal. Her name isn't on any of the lists."

"She hasn't mentioned any new show rehearsals. Where is she?"

"We'll help you look."

They rushed out of the room.

* * *

Anna slammed on the brakes to avoid hitting the car in front of her. Traffic was backed up for a mile ahead of them.

"I think we've made a big mistake," Tricia said. "If you had just talked to my dad, he would have let me go with you. What's the big hurry, anyway?"

"Just relax, girlfriend." Anna's eyes were on the road. There was bumper-to-bumper traffic as they got closer to Philadelphia International Airport.

"I changed my mind. When we get to the airport, I'm going to call my dad to come get me."

Anna's cheeriness was wearing thin. She looked over at the girl and said, "What do you mean? I thought that you wanted to come with me."

"I do, but not like this. Something–something doesn't feel right about it."

"Don't you trust me?"

Tricia hesitated a moment and said, "I guess."

"What do you mean, you guess?" She practically slammed into the car in front of them. "This is something you really want to do. You might never get a chance to talk to an agent again."

"Sure I will."

"Mac told me the part is just right for you. After I told him all about you, of course. It's a quick decision thing. There are a couple of other girls that they're talking to. I just don't want to see you blow it."

Tricia hesitated before answering her. "Well...maybe you're right. I wish I had gotten my dad to go with us. He's good with things like this."

Anna drummed her fingers on the steering wheel as they idled in traffic. "He's too busy at work...and with Dana. She's really good for him. It serves your mother right after the way she treated him all these years. She wasn't a very nice person. If you ask me, she got what she deserved."

Tricia stared frigidly at her. "What do you mean? Somebody poisoned her, and you think that was a good thing?"

"I didn't mean it that way. I just mean...maybe we're better off without her."

"I don't believe you!" Tricia's voice shook. "I miss her a lot! And you–you can say something so horrible? I thought we were friends!"

"We are friends, honey." Her voice was warm and gentle.

The traffic loosened up and motorists honked at them. Anna sped to catch up.

"Take me back!" Tricia demanded.

"It's too late, we can't go back now. We're almost there."

Signs for the airport loomed ahead of them. Anna pulled off the exit and drove the winding road leading to the airline terminals and the parking lots.

"Is there really an agent?" Tricia asked finally.

"Of course there's an agent."

"I don't believe you!"

"It really hurts that you don't trust me."

There was a long, uncomfortable silence. Then the words that Anna feared most hurled out of Tricia's mouth.

"Did you kill my mother?"

Anna eyed her coldly. "Why would you say something like that? Of course I didn't kill her."

"Well, you just said you're glad that she's dead! I just thought–"

"A lot of people hated her."

Tricia's face contorted in agony.

"I'm sorry, but it's true," Anna was blunt. "She didn't deserve to have children. There are a lot of couples that really would love to have a baby and can't. She–she just needed to be taught a lesson."

She eyed a spot and pulled into it. Tricia reached for her backpack at her feet and scrambled out of the vehicle. While Anna leaned down to get her luggage out of the trunk, Tricia darted across the parking lot. Anna dragged her bag and struggled to catch up. Tricia had almost reached the entrance, when Anna caught up to her.

"Not so fast!" Anna shouted, out of breath. She wrapped her arm around Tricia's waist, while lugging the bag with her free hand. "This way! Hurry up, we don't have much time! We'll just walk in there, nice and calm, okay? We don't want to make the security guards suspicious, okay?"

"If you don't let me go, I'll scream! Then security will come!" She pulled an arm free and walked hurriedly in front of her.

Anna struggled to catch up.

A long line of cars and taxis were in front of American Airlines. Tricia pushed through the revolving doors and stared wide-eyed at all the people in line at the check in counters. She looked to her left and right, hoping beyond hope that she would see her father and a dozen security guards. There was nobody around.

Anna came up from behind her and shouted, "Come on, we've got to hurry!"

* * *

The pieces of the puzzle were firmly in place. Logan was feverishly poring over his notes, when a desperate Charles Talbot called him at about four o'clock.

"What's wrong, Mr. Talbot?" Logan asked in a calm voice.

"It's Tricia!" he sputtered in exasperation. "I don't know where she is."

"What do you mean?"

"Kelly McDougal went to pick her up and she wasn't there! I'm at the school now! She's nowhere to be seen! Teachers have looked all over the place for her. She isn't here."

"Do you have any idea where she might have gone?"

"No, that's why I'm calling you. I'm heading back to my house right now. Can you meet me there in about thirty minutes?"

"Sure. Just try to stay calm."

"She always tells me what she's doing!"

"It'll be okay. I'll see you in a few minutes."

* * *

Anna leaned down and whispered, "You'll walk alongside me like nothing is wrong, got it?"

"What makes you think I'm going to do that?"

"I really don't know why you are making such a fuss. Didn't I tell you that I have connections in LA?" She ran her fingers through Tricia's mussed long hair and said, "Talent agents would be really interested in a girl as beautiful as you."

"Is that what this is all about?"

"I'm just doing it for your benefit, honey. That's all. I guess it was a colossal lack of communication or something."

"Sure. Does this agent really exist?"

"You think I'm lying?"

"Yes!" Tricia folded her arms, pouting all the way down the long path that led to the first security gate. Tricia looked to her left and right, her heart pounding the closer they got to the metal detectors. She saw the agents frisking people. Others were removing their shoes and belts and placing them in plastic tubs with their belongings and bags.

"They'll know something is up," Tricia said.

"Not if you just keep your cool."

"When we get up there, I'll tell them what you're doing!"

"Do you want me to do your father in too? He's a thorn in my side. Without him in the picture, you'll be all mine."

"What–what do you mean?"

Anna glanced at her wristwatch as they stood in line waiting to go up to the conveyer belt.

"Come on! Come on!"

Tricia locked eyes with a female security agent and secretly pleaded with her to help.

The woman told them to empty their pockets and searched Anna's handbag. She examined their boarding passes, then directed them to stand to have their bodies scanned. After all that, Anna and Tricia gathered their luggage and proceeded to their terminal.

* * *

Logan pulled into the Talbots' driveway and walked hurriedly toward the house. He rang the bell and Kelly led him inside. Charles pounded down the stairs and met him in the foyer. The living room doors swung open, and Dana Phillips rushed over to them.

"Have you found out anything?" Logan asked.

Charles was practically out of breath. "It's as if she vanished off the face of the earth!"

Logan looked over at Dana and asked, "What are you doing here?"

"I was with Charles when he got the call. We dropped everything, and he drove as fast as he could to meet Kelly at the school."

"And the teachers have no idea where she went?"

"I did some asking around," Kelly replied. "Her homeroom teacher said that her backpack looked like it was packed to the hilt."

"Interesting. Can you think of anything else?"

"She disappeared after lunch. She wasn't in her classes after that."

"And nobody saw her in school then?"

Kelly shook her head.

"Do you know if she was talking about going anywhere?"

"She hates it here," Charles said. "I can't really blame her. I've kept so busy after my wife's passing, that...that I haven't had time for her."

"I think she was really hurting inside," added Kelly. "My daughter, Cindy, said some things that might be of help."

"What did she say?" Charles asked quickly.

"She said she wanted to go out west with a friend on spring break," Kelly said.

Charles nodded his head in recognition. "Oh, yeah. Right. We had a talk about it a few weeks ago. But I talked her into going to New York City instead. I was so busy at work, I didn't think about it. Oh my God, it's my fault! I don't even know my own kid!"

Dana patted his shoulder and said, "It's okay. It's not your fault."

Logan looked from Kelly to Charles to Dana and said, "Can you think of anything else?"

"Maybe we could check her Facebook and Twitter posts," Kelly suggested.

Charles slapped his forehead and gasped. "My God, why didn't I think of it in the first place?"

"You were just upset," Dana reassured him. "I'm sure you would've thought of it sooner if you weren't so flustered."

"Show it to me," Logan said.

They quickly followed Kelly upstairs. Charles sat in front of the laptop and logged on. He accessed her Facebook page, and the others stood over his shoulder reading her recent posts.

In the private message center, they saw that she had been having conversations with Anna McWilliams all winter.

Anna: Are you going anywhere on spring break?

Tricia: Not sure.

Anna: In April I'm going out to see a high school friend in California. Wanna come with me?

Charles scrolled down an incredibly long list of Tricia's other friends, until Anna's name popped up again.

Anna: Wanna try out the West Coast with me?

Tricia hadn't responded to Anna's post. Charles scrolled down another long list of conversations Tricia had had between her other friends. About a week later, Anna asked the question again.

Anna: I really could use some company in California.

Tricia: I'll have to see.

Anna: I'm sure your father wouldn't mind. I promise I don't bite.

Tricia: I'll talk to him.

Anna: I know a talent agent out there.

Tricia: You do?

Anna: I could set up an appointment for you to meet with him.

Tricia: I'll let you know soon.

Anna: It'll be a lot of fun.

Charles slapped his forehead again and shouted, "Oh my God! I've been so absent-minded. She wanted to go out there with Anna! She's her friend!"

"Now that I think about it, I didn't see Anna after lunch," Dana said.

"Come on, we don't have much time!" Logan shouted. "We've gotta get to the airport fast!"

CHAPTER 40

"Anna is her mother," Logan explained in the car. "We have to get her before it's too late!"

Dana gave a startled gasp. "I don't understand. How did you know that?"

"I asked Penny to get you girls to let your hair down a few nights ago, and Anna opened up about her past. I put the pieces together."

"I had no idea that she had it so rough."

Charles was not saying anything. He just stared out the window, hoping this ordeal would be over soon. His main concern was making sure Tricia was okay.

Logan sped around a slow poke driver and said, "That's right. Her parents were so strict that she decided to rebel when she got to college. She got pregnant and dropped out after her first year there. She was afraid to tell her parents. She didn't know how her father would react. He served time in jail for hitting Anna's sister. So, you can see how scared she must have been when she found out that she was pregnant. She had the baby and gave her up for adoption." He turned to look at Charles and said, "That's where you two came in."

Charles never thought that their secret would come crashing back to haunt him. "Veronica was so desperate to adopt a baby that she bribed the caseworker," he finally said. "It's surprising what a load of money can accomplish. Sure, we broke the rules, but nobody had to know. We were shoo-ins to adopt Tricia anyway. We had good jobs. It's not like we were struggling for money."

"You didn't have to keep it a secret, Charles," Dana said. "Why didn't you tell Tricia that you adopted her, sooner?"

"Veronica and I were having problems. We figured if Tricia knew, it would make matters worse." He gazed at the lush farmland out the window. "We had just settled in Philly, and met Anna at a diner we frequented in Center City. She was a waitress, and was about six months pregnant. It was really hard for her to be on her feet all day. I felt sorry for her. One night, I dined alone, and had a good long talk with her when she went on break.

"She was desperate and didn't know what to do. She eventually told her mother about her predicament. Her father was out of the loop at that point. Her family didn't want to have anything to do with him."

"That's understandable," Logan said.

"Well, I gave Anna enough money to make a new start, with the understanding that we'd take the baby off her hands. We made arrangements with the adoption agency–"

"Through Veronica's generous donation to the agent," Logan remarked in a sarcastic tone.

Charles's eyes watered. His throat knotted up. "We promised Anna that she'd be able to see her daughter once or twice a year.

I knew it would never happen. I've always felt bad about deceiving her. Adoption agencies don't let the birth mothers ever see their babies again. For good reason, I'm sure."

"If they did, these girls would want their babies back when they've had time to get their act together," Dana put in. "Don't feel bad, Charles. You two gave Tricia a much better life than Anna ever could have. Despite Veronica's temper tantrums and downright bitchiness."

"Well, Anna used the money I gave her to get herself straightened out," Charles continued. "She went back to art school. And a few years later, she got a job at Creative Concepts and saw us there."

"Did she know that you were both there, or was it just a coincidence?"

"I'm not sure," he admitted. "But now I know one thing for sure. When she got there, she probably had one thing in mind–to get Tricia back!" Charles wiped perspiration from his forehead. "I hope we can get to them in time."

* * *

Charles felt like a fool. He dissected every conversation he and Anna had had, whether brief or lengthy, for any clue that she was Tricia's birth mother. Conversations with Anna were usually brief. She was always so quiet. Maybe it was just an act. She obviously knew they worked at Creative Concepts. She did a good job of keeping her identity a secret. A different hair color and glasses made a world of difference. She had been stalking them for years without them knowing it. Was she planning on constantly spying on them, until she lured Tricia away from them like she was doing now? He thought about his conversation with Veronica on the way back from work the day of her confrontation with Anna.

"What are we going to do about Anna?" Veronica had asked him. "She looked me right in the eye and flat out admitted that she ruined my ads!"

"You make her nervous. Maybe–maybe if you would stop breathing down her neck so much, she wouldn't make the mistakes."

"I don't trust her. I can't believe Dobson agreed to keep her on after what she did! I would've fired her a long time ago!"

"She does good work–despite the screw-ups."

"Whose side are you on anyway? There's something really weird about her. I just can't put my finger on it. I don't trust her!"

"You're being paranoid."

"You are too trusting, Charles."

Maybe Veronica was right. Maybe he was too trusting. Did she purposely sabotage Veronica's ads? Was it part of a darker plan? Was it possible that mild-mannered Anna could have poisoned Veronica?

* * *

"She's driving a blue Honda," Logan said into the radio microphone.

"A vehicle matching that description was spotted approaching Philadelphia International Airport an hour ago," a female voice sounded over the radio.

"Don't let them board the plane. Thanks, over." Logan slammed his foot on the accelerator and sped down the highway.

Charles looked on uneasily as I-95 slipped by. "I hope we make it on time," he muttered. "I can't believe this is happening. Why hasn't Tricia tried to text me or something? She just picked up and left without a word. It's not like her."

"We need to make a plan," Logan said quickly.

* * *

A wave of paranoia came over Anna as she watched two burly security guards walk by. Fortunately they had not been looking in her direction. She looked back at the crossword puzzle she had been working on, and tried to remain calm.

Tricia glanced at the clock. They would board in thirty minutes.

There was no need to panic. Her father had probably called the police. Detective Logan probably contacted the airport. Security guards were probably looking for them right now. She watched guards shuffle up and down the long corridor. Some of them talked on their walkie-talkies. Others walked hurriedly to wherever they were going.

Tricia felt her stomach knot the closer it came to boarding time. If security guards hadn't taken Anna away by now, Tricia thought they never would.

She fished in her purse again, and pulled out her cell phone. She started to text, when Anna yanked it out of her hands.

"What are you doing?"

"My dad should know what we're doing. Why are you so insistent on getting me out of here?"

Anna looked around to see if anyone was watching. An old woman studied her intently.

Anna lowered her voice, "You said it yourself, honey. Your dad wouldn't want you to go out there."

Tricia glowered at her and looked at the floor.

* * *

Logan punched the steering wheel and cursed at the gridlock. I-95 just became a parking lot. Charles's stomach knotted, his heart pounding uncontrollably. He was overcome with a feeling of dread. Dana looked frantically at the line of traffic that stretched for miles ahead of them.

"The hell with this!" Logan cried. He turned on his siren and sped down the shoulder.

"Oh thank God," Charles muttered.

Logan grinned and said, "It's one of the fringe benefits of being a cop."

"I don't care what you do, just get there as quick as you can," he ordered. "There's no telling what Anna will do!"

* * *

A flight attendant announced that it was time for passengers to board. Tricia's face blanched. Her skin felt moist.

Anna sprang to her feet. Tricia was reluctant to do so.

"Come on, honey," Anna said brightly. "Why the long face?"

"This isn't a good idea."

"The change of scenery will you do you a world of good! Come on." She nudged Tricia to her feet.

Tricia's eyes darted in many directions as they stood in the long slow line. There were now seven people in front of them. By now, passengers waiting to board eyed them suspiciously. They probably all thought that the teen-age girl was about to jump out of her skin. They probably thought the older woman seemed a little off too.

In the distance, Tricia thought she saw the tall, slender figure of her father rush through the crowd, followed by Detective Logan, Dana, and a security detail.

Tricia screeched, "Dad! Dad!"

People gaped at them in horror as they raced toward them.

"Stop that woman!" Logan shouted.

Anna tore down the corridor and they gave chase.

"Stop that woman!" the guards shouted.

People leaped out of the way, staring in stunned silence.

Anna merged with the crowd, but knew she couldn't go far. Guards were everywhere!

She ducked into a ladies room, thinking of a plan.

* * *

Anna knew that she couldn't stay in the ladies room for long. The moment she stepped outside, the guards would seize her. She was trapped.

About five minutes later, she slipped out the exit behind three women. She walked hurriedly down the corridor, on the lookout for guards.

She merged with the crowd again, and had made it about halfway down the bustling corridor, when guards swooped in on her. They handcuffed her and went to the airport security office. Logan, Charles, Tricia, and Dana were there waiting for them.

"Your father has something he has to tell you, Tricia," Logan said. "Go on."

Charles hugged his daughter and said, "Oh darling. I love you very much."

Dana put her arms around both of them. Charles motioned for her to leave them alone for a moment.

Logan went into the office and said, "It took a while, but I finally put the missing piece together. Penny got you to lower your inhibitions, and you told her everything I needed to know. Did you know Veronica was working at Creative Concepts, or was it just a coincidence?"

"I've been tracking her career for years! Of course I knew she was there!"

"Well, then I was wrong. I thought you didn't know. So you were stalking them?"

"I wasn't stalking them. I was just waiting till the right time to get what was mine!"

"Tricia, you mean?"

Anna nodded and said, "Can you believe that Veronica didn't even recognize me?"

"Well, you don't look anything like you used to. But you purposely concealed your identity. Congratulations for pulling it off!"

Her voice sounded harsh and beaten. "Veronica had no right being a mother. She treated Tricia like dirt! I didn't want her to go through what I did. So I-so I figured out a way to get rid of Veronica so I could have Tricia all to myself. I had earned enough money to provide a good life for her. If it hadn't been for you, we'd be halfway across the country now!"

"And Charles would have never seen her again, right?"

"Tricia was extremely unhappy. I just—I just wanted to help her, is all."

"So you think murdering her mother would solve her problems?"

"It was the only way! The things that Veronica did to people! She was a despicable woman and everybody hated her! Believe me, I did everyone a favor! I was a bundle of nerves when she got the promotion. And then—and then the day before the party, she called me into the office to discuss my future at Creative Concepts. It felt like she was going to lower the gauntlet on me."

* * *

Anna felt like a lamb being led to slaughter upon entering Veronica's office.

Veronica scowled across the glass table at Anna, clipboard in hand.

"I guess you know why you're here," Veronica began.

Anna nodded her head but said nothing.

"As you know, I plan to make changes now that I have taken over Ben's position. The company is leaking money and sinking fast. Some people will have to be let go, do you understand?"

"It's such a shame that it's come to this, but I understand."

"Business is a cutthroat animal. To survive, I must decide who the weakest players are." She scanned several pages of notes, then looked back up at Anna. "You made a careless error that cost Creative Concepts a lot of money."

Anna swallowed hard. "It was a stupid mistake, and I am really sorry about it. I promised Mr. Dobson that it wouldn't happen again."

"But you did it again. You left out pertinent information. The Weavers have been loyal clients for decades. They got so angry that they went to our competitor."

"It was an unfortunate mistake. I told Mr. Dobson how sorry I was."

Veronica sneered at her. "Why should we keep you here? I think you're the reason that we're in this financial hole."

"Well, maybe it's your fault. You have a nasty temper and everybody around here agrees."

"I know that I'm not an easy person to deal with at times," agreed Veronica, "but I make a lot of money for the firm. And clients trust me. I can't say the same thing about you, I'm sorry to say. Now, I have made recommendations to James about who we should get rid of. Your name is on top of the list."

"But he promised he'd give me another chance."

Veronica got up, went over to the counter, and heated a cup of water in the microwave.

"There are things you need to learn if you're going to succeed in business, Anna. Don't be so trusting. I can't dismiss carelessness. You didn't check your copy before it went to print."

"Well, you looked at it and didn't catch the mistake. Nobody else caught it, either."

"It's funny that you never screw up other people's ads. Is it me?"

"Well, to be honest, Veronica, you make me nervous with all your tirades. Wouldn't anybody make mistakes with all the commotion you create?"

"At least I produce. It's your responsibility to triple-check copy before it is sent to the printer."

The microwave oven beeped. Veronica pulled open the door and poured in a tea bag, and stirred it. While her back was turned, Anna reached in her jacket pocket and stuck chopped up Monkshood leaves into Veronica's salad. Veronica sat back in her seat and stared coldly at Anna while she drank her tea.

Anna pursed her lips and scowled at the woman.

"I will let you know in a couple weeks about the status of your job. You may go."

"If you—if you fire me, maybe I—maybe I should take something that's precious to you!"

"What the hell are you talking about?"

Anna looked intently at her and said, "You'll find out very soon."

"You are truly the oddest woman I have ever met."

Anna's legs felt rubbery as she got up and headed for the door.

Veronica lightened her tone. "I'm sorry that it has come to this point, and I hope you realize that this is just a business decision. I don't like being put in this position. Firing people is never an easy thing to do. On a personal note, I hope you can still come to my party."

"I'll see you there," she said flatly.

Anna watched her take a couple bites of the salad and shove it aside. She boxed it up to eat when she got home.

"What are you staring at?" Veronica asked in alarm.

Anna didn't say a word, and slammed the door as she went out. She saw Tom Daniels shuffling toward her and pitied him. She didn't want anyone to be subjected to similar treatment, but she was also fighting for her job. He was retirement age. He had made his mark decades ago. Maybe he should let somebody else have a chance.

Within minutes, shouting emanated from Veronica's office. Tom was not as timid as Anna, and was sticking up for his rights. When the meeting was over, he stormed out and slammed her door. A few minutes later, the Dragon Lady claimed her next victim.

* * *

"We all knew her habits," Anna continued. "She always took salad home with her. I just figured she'd probably eat it before the party. And I guessed right."

"You did your homework," Logan said. "You knew that the poison would take several hours to take effect. That gave you the perfect alibi during the party. I originally thought it was either in the Bloody Mary or in something she ate. You had me baffled, that's for sure. There was a lot of confusion at the party. Nobody remembered where they were or what they were doing. Or what she was doing. They all heard her bawling out the caterers for bad food. All along, you sat there thinking you were going to get away with it. But you were sadly mistaken, Ms. McWilliams. The truth always comes out eventually."

Tears streaked down Anna's face. "Veronica was a horrible witch and didn't care who she hurt! She bribed the caseworker at the adoption agency! Giving up my baby to Veronica was the worst mistake I ever made in my life. I don't regret killing her. I do regret giving up Lily for adoption. It's a shame that Veronica got her clutches on her. She never loved Tricia. She only loved money and her career. It's no kind of life for a child. I'll regret allowing that...that bitch to harm her for the rest of my life. Isn't being haunted about giving up your baby punishment enough?"

"I feel bad for you, Ms. McWilliams, but murder isn't the answer. You could have solved your problems with Veronica in other ways."

The security guards took her away. Dana was waiting for Logan when he came out.

"Will Tricia be okay?" he asked her.

"I don't know. She took the news pretty hard."

"The police station has a list of psychiatrists."

"She'll probably be in analysis for the rest of her life. This isn't something you get over with quickly. She just found out that she was adopted, and then it turns out that her birth mother murdered her adoptive mother!"

"It's too bad. She's a decent kid."

"She's got a good head on her shoulders. It'll take time, but I think she'll be okay."

"I hope so."

* * *

It didn't take long for word to get out around the office that Anna was the one who slayed the Dragon Lady. Everyone's reactions were mixed.

"I didn't know she had it in her," Dana muttered.

"Who knew that such a mild-mannered woman was really that disturbed inside," Michelle said.

"It probably all stems back from her unstable childhood."

"It's such a shame. She's such a nice girl."

"Well, apparently not so much."

"I had no inkling that she was so troubled."

"Well, none of us did."

"And to think that she was really Tricia's mother."

"She must have been planning this for a very long time."

"No, I think she just snapped under the pressure. Veronica's tirades drove poor Anna over the edge."

Dana stared at Michelle incredulously a moment. "I can't believe you're actually defending her."

"No, I just pity her, that's all. I wish she had talked to somebody about it. Maybe we could've helped her deal with the stress better."

Dana shook her head. "I think she planned on taking Tricia from the first time she stepped foot at Creative Concepts. The whole quiet, aloof business was just a rouse."

At that moment, Tom appeared in the break room door and smiled at them.

"It's such a shame about Anna," he said.

Dana and Michelle nodded their agreement.

He looked at Michelle and said, "Maybe if you're free later, we could go out to dinner?"

"I think I can arrange it."

"With Bart and Nicholas gone, I hope James will hire some more people. Poor Craig. He's looking so tired lately."

He went back to his office. Dana and Michelle went back to working on their projects as well.

* * *

"It all boils down to this," Dobson said. "You do excellent work, and we're short a person now that Anna has been arrested."

Nicholas stared at James in astonishment. "You want me back?"

"We were all under stress–what with Veronica's murder, and all. I'm willing to give you a second chance."

"I don't know what to say!"

"It still doesn't give you an excuse to yell at me like you did. But under the circumstances, I would've been upset if had been me."

"It's all on account of my big mouth. I should learn to zip it. But you know me, I get excited when I'm upset about something."

"It's something you need to work on."

Nicholas sprang to his feet and reached out to shake James' hand. "I won't let you down this time."

"Just learn to curb your temper. And don't be such a perfectionist. I know you want everything just right, but there are deadlines, remember?"

"I'll try to do better! Thank you!" He stood and quickly exited the room.

* * *

Penny's face beamed when she saw Nicholas hanging up his fantasy designs on the cubicle walls.

"You're back," she said.

He filled her in on James' decision. "I was a bit of a jerk, I suppose. It was really decent of him to take me back."

"Well, we need somebody to liven the mood around here. It's been so dreadfully quiet since Anna was arrested."

He grimaced and continued getting his office back in order. He shook his head and groaned. "I can't believe it. You work across from somebody for years and you never know what's going on in their mind."

"I think she was a tortured soul."

"And to think that my folks wanted me to go out with her."

"Well, you didn't know. She fooled all of us."

"Who would've ever thought that Anna would be the one to slay the Dragon Lady?"

"It's too bad that she couldn't have handled Veronica in a different way. Maybe if she had talked calmly to her, it wouldn't have happened."

Nicholas disagreed strongly. "Nah. You couldn't handle anything rationally with that woman. Anna did us all a favor."

"It still doesn't dismiss the fact that Veronica was poisoned, Nicholas."

"That's true. It makes me sound as bad as Anna!"

"Well, I'm really glad to see you back. I'll see you around."

He grinned. "Yeah, likewise."

She waved and walked hurriedly toward the conference room at the end of the hall.

She took notes and smiled at Tom as he made his pitch to the new clients.

* * *

"I'm Bart."

"Hi Bart," everyone said.

The usual chatty Bart couldn't think of what to say next. He looked at the warm faces of the people around the room. "I'm dependent on pills to keep me going at work. It's a stressful job, with a lot of deadlines. I take pictures for ads. There's a lot of pressure. There's a high burn out rate.

"The pills help me keep going. But they...but they messed me up real bad. I've screwed up the best relationship I've ever had...my Daryl. We were supposed to get married and I screwed up big time.

"I passed out during the wedding and wound up at the ER. Daryl is so understanding. But my family's pissed off with me. They're so disappointed. Not about...not about the wedding. They're so nice to Daryl. And my dad finally came through about the whole thing."

Everyone clapped.

"I feel like I've let everybody down. I have a great job and I've blown it. My boss is the most understanding man. He's gonna hold the job for me while I get straightened out..."

* * *

Bart was a sweaty mess when he followed everyone out of the meeting room an hour later. He felt like a bundle of nerves. It felt so good to get it off his chest. He was not expecting to see Daryl.

He gave Bart a bear hug. They wept like babies.

Bart led him to his room and Daryl sat at his bedside. "If I had known you were coming, I would've cleaned up better. I look like a slob."

Daryl held his hand and stared intently at his friend. "You look fine."

"No I don't. My hair's a mess. And I need a shave."

"You have more important things to worry about, my love."

"I totally botched everything up. I'm surprised you showed your face here. I wouldn't blame you if you found somebody else. Somebody without all the drama."

"Those are things that I love the most about you."

"It was all my fault that I screwed up the wedding."

"Our friends just had a really nice party. We can get married when you get out. I can't wait till we go to St. Thomas."

"Thank you for being there for me. You don't know how much it means to me."

"I've got your back. And you've got mine."

They sat there holding hands, happily planning their future together.

* * *

Michelle gladly accepted Tom's dinner invitation at the restaurant down the street from the office. She was relieved and nervous at the same time. He would never understand what she had done so many years ago.

Over wine, they discussed the murder case until the subject ran dry. There were no hidden clues to indicate that Anna had done it. They hoped that Tricia would be okay.

"I guess Anna isn't the only one with secrets," she said.

"We all have things we don't want people to know about."

"I've been meaning to tell you what I did then, but I didn't know how."

"I don't agree with what you did. You know I'm totally against abortions."

"I know."

"But I can't fault you for something you did before we met. Hell, I've made my share of mistakes."

"I was terrified. I don't like feeling vulnerable–but's that's the way I felt. Alone and scared. I wasn't even thinking about the consequences of my actions. Maybe if I had given the baby up for adoption, it might have made a young couple happy to raise the baby as their own."

Tom finished off his Merlot and poured another glassful. "Fortunately adoptions don't usually lead to murder."

"It's a shame that Anna didn't get the help she needed. It's too bad that we didn't notice anything. Can you believe it? She was pretending to be this shy, quiet woman, when she was really quite the opposite?"

"I feel like I've been around a bit in the world. And I missed it too."

"She even fooled Frank Logan. But he eventually figured it out."

Conversation drifted to more pleasing subject matters. Then, halfway through dessert, Tom got sentimental.

"I'm so happy I met you," Tom said. "You've made me a happy man."

She patted his hand. "I feel the same way."

"You don't know how miserable I was before you started working at Creative Concepts."

"I know."

"Maybe we should set a wedding date."

Her eyes sparkled with life. "It sounds like a winning idea to me."

* * *

Two days later, a picture of Anna McWilliams being dragged through the airport by security guards was on the front page of the *Times-Sentinel.* The headline read: "WOMAN ARRESTED

FOR TALBOT POISONING; TAKEN INTO CUSTODY FOR ATTEMPTED KIDNAPPING."

By Kim Weston

Townsend–A woman was arrested Thursday afternoon for allegedly poisoning Townsend resident Veronica Talbot last October. Anna McWilliams, 34, of Norristown, worked with the victim at Creative Concepts, an advertising firm in Philadelphia. Williams was a graphic artist at the company. Ms. Talbot had recently been promoted to creative executive for the company. On Saturday, October 26, Ms. Talbot invited her coworkers to a party at her home to celebrate the promotion.

Guests reported witnessing Ms. Talbot displaying erratic behavior during the party.

"She chewed out the caterers for serving bad food," said housekeeper Kelly McDougal. "Everything she ate tasted bad. Everybody else thought the food tasted good."

Most of the guests thought Veronica was acting drunk. Her speech was slurred, and she stumbled when she was walking. She was also feeling chilled and perspiring a lot.

"She was flitting about all afternoon like nothing was wrong," said her husband, Charles Talbot. "And then she got tired all of a sudden and went to take a nap."

About a half an hour later, Talbot went into the study to wake her and found her dead on the loveseat.

"I thought she was asleep and tried to get her up," Talbot said. "She had no pulse. It was just awful."

According to Coroner Stan Green, Ms. Talbot was experiencing side effects of the deadly poison monkshood. "The poison was coursing through her veins during the party."

Lead Detective Frank Logan has been working closely with Green for several months to determine how Veronica Talbot was poisoned.

"We collected samples of everything Ms. Talbot ate and drank prior to the party to determine how and by what means she was poisoned," Logan said.

The samples were taken to the Philadelphia forensics lab for analysis. Detective Logan's investigation reached a dead end last fall, when technicians could not find the answers he was looking for.

In January, there was a break in the case. Monkshood, a lethal household plant, was found in the salad that Ms. Talbot ate the day of the party. The plant was in the lobby at the Creative Concepts office in Philadelphia. Ms. McWilliams confessed to sticking it in Veronica's salad the day before the party.

Ms. McWilliams was allegedly angry that Veronica was going to fire her for making mistakes on an ad that cost the company millions of dollars. Veronica called McWilliams into her office to tell her that she was going to let her go. While Ms. Talbot's back was turned, McWilliams admitted putting chopped up Monkshood leaves in Talbot's salad.

"Veronica did not eat the salad right away," Logan said. "She took it home to eat later."

"I saw her eating it a few hours before the party," McDougal said. "An hour or two later, she started not acting quite right. I just figured she was nervous getting ready for the party. She was always high-strung."

Upon further investigation, Logan discovered there was more to the case than a disgruntled employee seeking revenge on her employer. Fifteen years earlier, Ms. McWilliams had been in her first year at an art college in Philadelphia when she got pregnant. She struggled to keep her nose above water as a waitress at a diner when she crossed paths with the Talbots, who were regular customers.

"I felt sorry for the poor girl," Talbot said. "She was really scared and didn't know what to do. She was afraid to tell her parents. She had to drop out of school and work full time. We gave her enough money to help her out and adopted her baby."

The Talbots spent the next fifteen years raising their adopted daughter, Patricia Jean. Little did they know that Ms. McWilliams had been keeping tabs on their careers. The Norristown police searched Anna's apartment and found newspaper and magazine clippings of the Talbots throughout the years. A book about household plants was also found in her possession, with lists of ones that are poisonous.

McWilliams got a job working with the Talbots at Creative Concepts. She disguised herself so they wouldn't recognize her, so she could keep a closer eye on her biological daughter.

Last Thursday afternoon, Tricia disappeared from William Penn High School in Angola. Students and faculty did not know where she had gone.

"I always pick her up in the afternoon," McDougal said. "I was frantic when she wasn't there."

"Kelly called me at work to tell me what happened, and I got to the school as fast as I could," Talbot said. "I was terrified!"

A short time later, Detective Logan arrived at the Talbots' home to look for clues to where Tricia could have gone. Talbot accessed his daughter's Facebook account and discovered that she had been in contact with Anna McWilliams for several months.

McWilliams allegedly convinced Tricia to go to LA with her to meet with a talent agent. Tricia, who wants to be a movie star, gladly accepted the offer.

Detective Logan went to the airport to stop Anna from getting on the plane. Security guards took McWilliams into custody, and Tricia was rescued.

"I've never been so glad to see her [Tricia] in my life," Talbot said.

"It was really scary," said Tricia Talbot. "I guess it teaches you not to be so trusting. The sad part is, I thought we were friends."

Tricia recently performed in *Grease* at William Penn High School.

"It just goes to show you what lengths people will go when they are really desperate," Logan said. "It's too bad Ms. McWilliams couldn't have figured out another way to channel her anger. If she had done that, Veronica Talbot would be alive now."

* * *

Frank put the newspaper on his coffee table and glanced at the clock on the wall. It was about nine thirty. Penny still hadn't gotten back yet. He couldn't find anything appealing on TV and turned it off. He leaned back in his recliner and read a mystery, which was something he had not had time to do much lately.

He heard footsteps outside the door and looked up to see Penny enter the room. Her face was bright and cheerful. She came over and leaned down to kiss him.

"I got a promotion!" she announced.

"That's great, honey!"

"I'll be working more closely with clients from now on."

He wrapped his arms around her waist and kissed her. "This calls for a celebration. How about if we go to Barney's and pop a cork?"

"That would be great!"

He handed her the newspaper and said, "At least they spelled my name right this time. I'm thankful it's over with."

She sat on the sofa and read the article. When she was finished, she said, "To think that I worked with Anna every day and never knew what was going on inside her head. People really do have secrets, don't they?"

"I know."

They snuggled on the couch and watched TV.

"I'm so glad that Gramps is doing better," she said.

"I am too. It's a relief."

"Now that you're finished with the case, maybe we should go see him."

"That sounds like a wonderful idea. Maybe I should call him up and ask him if he wants to go fishing."

"That's something he hasn't been able to do in a long time. He'll love it."

"It's certainly something to look forward to."

They held hands as they watched TV, neither saying a word.

"Guess what?"

He looked in awe at her and said, "What?"

"Mr. Dobson let Bart go to rehab and is going to hold his job for him."

"That's decent of him."

"And guess what?"

"What?"

"Bart and Daryl decided to reschedule their wedding."

"It's probably good that they're waiting till Bart is up to it."

"And guess what?"

Frank grinned. "What?"

"Tom talked to Michelle about the abortion she had when she was in college. He told her he was upset at first, but said he didn't know her then and can't fault her for something she did when she was younger. They patched things up."

"That's a relief. They make such a happy couple."

"And guess what?"

"You're full of a million questions, you know that? What is it?"

"They finally set a wedding date!"

"You don't say?" He kissed her again.

"And Mr. Dobson gave Nicholas his old job back."

"That was really decent of him."

Her face was glowing, and her eyes sparkled with life. "Everything worked out!"

He rubbed his nose against hers. "You're such an optimist."

"Frank."

"What?"

"How would you like to go to a great party?"

He rolled his eyes and grunted. "You're kidding! The last party we went to didn't work out so great."

He hit her with a pillow, and they chased each other around the room.

ACKNOWLEDGMENTS

I hope you enjoyed *Poisoned at the Party*. I would like to thank the people who helped me get this book published. For several years, my mom and dad have spent many hours proofreading various versions of my books in notebooks. I appreciate their help and suggestions. I also want to thank my family and friends for their constant support.

I would also like to thank the members of the Rehoboth Beach Writers Guild for their encouragement to write outside my comfort zone during our 8:00 a.m. free write sessions.

I also appreciate the fact that John Kelly took the time to discuss crime cases with me. His suggestions were very helpful.

I also want to thank the staff of CreateSpace for all their assistance during the production process for the book.

BIBLIOGRAPHY:

Chapter 5. p. 66 and Chapter 24, pp. 252-253.

Forensics and Fiction, Clever, Intriguing, and Downright Odd Questions from Crime Writers, D.P. Lyle, MD, Thomas Dunne Books, 2007, pp. 129-130.

Deadly Doses, Serita Deborah Stevens and Anne Klarner, Writer's Digest Books, 1990, pp. 47-48.

The Encyclopedia of Forensics Science, Suzanne Bell, PhD, Facts on File Science Library, 2004, pp. 11-12